I0772299

PANACEA OMEGA

BOOK 3 OF THE PANACEA TRILOGY

L. Ana Ellis

FIRE-FORGED BOOKS
Alexandria, VA

Sign up to be updated on future book releases at
fireforgedbooks.com

DEDICATION

To Brian – without you, this book
never would have happened

Tell me the technology you use,
and I'll tell you who you are

-Area 52 saying

chapel
cooper's cottage
the stafford estate
the levanto monorail
amoco's house
outer ring
spaceport
the outside
pod warehouses

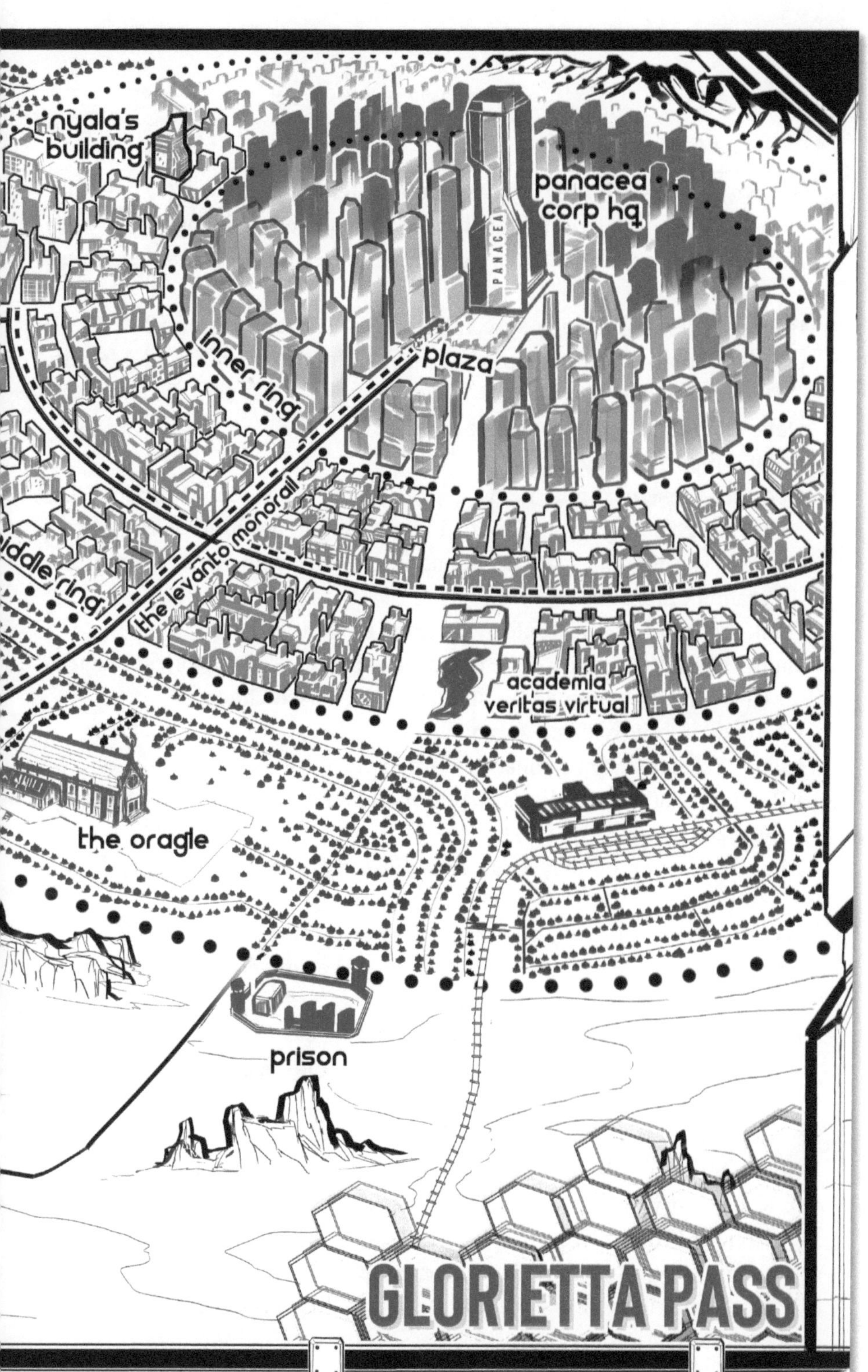

nyala's building
panacea corp hq
PANACEA
inner ring
plaza
middle ring
the levanto monorail
academia veritas virtual
the oragle
prison
GLORIETTA PASS

Amaya—works with legacy computer systems, Nyala's sister, is struggling with guilt over things that have happened in the past

Amoco—neuroscientist and programmer, Director of Chip Research for Panacea Corp

Bren—a friend of Amaya's, went on the expedition to Area 52

Cooper—long-time friend of the Stafford family, once dated Mariela, Grace's father

Dan—sheriff's deputy in Area 52

Elliat—reporter, blogger

Georgia—designs digital items, especially historical reconstructions and clothing, is helping pod-lifers adjust to life in the solid world

Grace—Mariela and Cooper's daughter, grew up in Area 52 with her grandmother June

Hank—martial arts instructor who grew up in a res-home

June—Mariela's mother, wife of Oscar Stafford, used to work at Panacea Corp, lived in Area 52 for sixteen years, raised Grace

Li—dentist, briefly dated Amaya

Liam—former CEO of Panacea Corp, created LP as his digital clone

LP—highly advanced digital being modeled on Liam, in charge of the Spectral Council

Mariela—senior employee at Panacea Corp, Grace's mother, June's daughter

Nyala—Amaya's sister, organizes protests against Panacea Corp

Opali—advanced digital being, wants to be human, Sofi's daughter, good at predicting what people will do

Oscar—Mariela's father, former head of Panacea Corp

Petra—founder of Area 52, over 100 years old (according to her birth certificate, that is)

Snoogums—young boy that Grace used to babysit, also lives in Area 52

Sofi—Mariela's sister, Opali's mom, lives in the Panacea metaverse

T-Rock—survivalist, former Zazora player, has never met a nature metaphor he didn't like

Trevor—10-year-old boy, Nyala's neighbor

Viola—ambitious neuroscientist willing to do anything to get ahead, used to date Cooper

Two Years Ago

A Snowy Day in Area 52

Grace was a believer. She had been abducted by aliens, she was sure of it. The eight-year-old Snoogums, on the other hand, refused to be swayed by the clear evidence of her abduction.

In the past, all she had to do was point out the chip at the base of her skull, and people much older and wiser than Snoogums had been convinced. Most of her friends were sixteen, and if they could believe, then Snoogums could too.

The harsh wind and icy ground kept Grace from sending Snoogums outside like she normally did when she babysat him. Instead, they sipped hot cocoa on the couch while watching snowflakes drift down and pile up on top of the ice.

Grace bent her head so Snoogums could see the spot where her chip was. "Feel right here." She pointed to the spot with the small piece of metal embedded under the skin at the base of her skull. "What other explanation could there be?"

Snoogums, in very adult fashion, leaned in with one arm resting on his knee. "I know one."

"Sure you do." Grace rolled her eyes. "Tell me, what fantastical idea have you come up with this time?"

Snoogums, the spinner of tall tales, was too smart for his own good. He was the reason Grace had put a password manager on her computer. For an eight-year-old, he was really good at deleting files.

Snoogums jutted out his chin. "I'm not making this up. I found an old notebook and it said the Elders have been lying to everybody and there was no Nuclear Apocalypse. Elder Petra made that stuff up about the nuclear war so that we wouldn't leave."

"That's ridiculous. It makes it sound like we're prisoners."

"We are." Snoogums nodded like he was really wise. "You know how the tesseract keeps the mutants out of this area? Well, get this"—Snoogums paused like the king of drama—"there *are no* mutants. So why do we have a tesseract?" Snoogums leaned forward, looked to both sides, and lowered his voice. "It's to keep us in."

Grace huffed. "You've let your imagination run away with you again."

"So get this—you know how the Museum of the Nuclear Armageddon in Elder Petra's house has all the pictures of the apocalypse? Well, guess what? The notebook says they're all faked."

Grace sipped her hot cocoa. "I think you're the one doing the faking." It wasn't the first time he had come up with a story and claimed he had evidence to support it.

Snoogums squirmed on the couch and tucked his foot under him. "I promise you—it's what the notebook said! It showed how when the Elders created the area under the protective umbrella, they pretended it was because of nuclear war, but it was really that they didn't like cool technology and wanted us to use old relic technology instead. Then they faked all the pictures because they wanted us to think that the rest of the world was gone." Snoogums leaned in close and whispered, "But it's not. Everything outside of the umbrella is normal. That's why the umbrella includes a Faraday cage, because if we could hear the electronic signals from the rest of the world, we would know the truth."

This didn't sound like a typical Snoogum's tall tale. He rarely had so much detail. "I want to see this notebook."

"You can't. It fell apart while I was reading it."

Grace suppressed a scoff. "So much for the evidence."

"It's true, I promise! It's confetti now." Snoogums wiggled his fingers to demonstrate what Grace could only assume was little bits of notebook paper falling.

"Did you show the notebook to your grandmother?" At least that might offer some evidence that the notebook really existed.

Snoogums looked any which way but at Grace. "Well, not exactly. You see, if I tell my grandmother about it, then she'll want to know where I got it, and if I tell her where I got it, then she'll have my hide because I'm not supposed to go there."

Grace couldn't help but be curious. "Where was it?"

"In the basement, nailed under one of the stairs. Grandma says I'm not supposed to go under there because of the spiders and cobwebs, and the dust makes my allergies bad." Snoogums placed a hand on Grace's arm like an older person might do. "But you know me—if my grandmother tells me I can't go somewhere, then that's the first place I go." He seemed quite proud of himself. "It's spooky, but that's why I like it."

Grace didn't doubt it.

"The notebook was super fancy," Snoogums continued. "It had gold letters on the cover and was wrapped in purple shiny material."

"But now it's gone?" It was convenient for Snoogums that all the evidence of the supposed fakery had disappeared.

"Yep, I read it a bunch of times and then it disintegrated. Do you like that word? I bet you didn't know that I know what 'disintegrated' means."

"What that says to me is that you're using a fancy word as an excuse for why you can't produce any evidence."

"Whatever. But there's one more thing."

"Okay, what?"

"The book says the people outside of the umbrella aren't mutants, but some have chips in their skulls like you. That was one of the main reasons the Elders wanted us to be here. They don't like chips or cool technology, so they make us live here and use old stuff."

What was he saying—that things were completely normal outside of the umbrella? That they had been cut off, not to protect them, but to control them? Surely that wasn't the case. "I don't believe it."

Snoogums stuck out his chin. "I'm going to leave some day. I'm not afraid."

Grace had often dreamed of traveling through the tesseract to the other side. She wanted to see what things were like in the rest of the world, but she didn't for a second believe Snoogums. "What if things are bad out there?" It had been eighty years since the Nuclear Armageddon—chances were it was still dangerous with gangs in charge and no police or government. Or maybe the mutants had developed superpowers and were battling for control of the earth.

"That's why I want to leave. I want to see if it's true. I bet they have flying cars, and robot maids, and they have chips in their brains that they can use to talk to each other. Can you imagine calling your friend and being like…" He held his hand by his ear with his thumb and pinky finger out like a phone. "Hey there, I'm calling you from my brain." Snoogums dissolved into a fit of laughter.

"You really think the chip in the back of my neck is a communication device?"

"Let's try it out. I just need access to your computer."

"No way. You can use my tablet." Grace turned on the tablet's drawing program and handed it over to Snoogums.

"Okay, I'm going to write something on the tablet. Let me know if you can read it with your chip."

"Okay." Nothing was going to happen. *Right?*

Snoogums used his finger to write something in the drawing program and then looked at her.

Grace focused for a bit, but no words jumped into her mind. "I don't know. What does it say?"

Snoogums, with a smile stretching from ear to ear, turned the tablet around so she could see it. The words, written in neon pink, said, "Grace is a water buffalo." It was the sort of random thing only Snoogums could come up with.

"It didn't work," Grace said.

He frowned. "Maybe we didn't do it right."

Grace sighed. "I don't believe any of this."

Snoogums squirmed in his chair. "Can I play on your computer?"

"Absolutely not."

"I promise I won't delete anything."

Snoogums had discovered the delete button on her computer the last time he had been over. She had spent hours afterward restoring stuff from the recycle bin. "I don't trust you."

"Why do you babysit me if you hate me?"

"I don't hate you. I just hate that you delete my files, and I don't trust you."

He flashed his toothy grin. "You gotta love me for who I am. You know your life would be boring without me."

Grace smiled. As soon as she was old enough, she was going to find another job that didn't require babysitting. It would be a good day, but she would miss the smart aleck.

Outside, the crack of wood splitting broke through the wind. The power went out with a pop. Around the house, Grace heard signs of the power shutting down. The rush of the air leaving the heating vents cut out, and the fridge made a long sighing noise as it stopped working. Some appliance started beeping as it switched to battery power.

They both raced to the window and looked down the hill. On the far side of the road, where the road ended and the forest began, a tree had split and was resting on the wires between two telephone poles. One broken wire sparked and caught one of the small branches on fire.

They watched as the firefighters showed up, put the fire out, and kept an eye on things until the electric company showed up.

"I'm bored," Snoogums said. He had the attention span of a squirrel. "Can I play on your tablet?"

"No more tablet time for you until the power comes back on," Grace said. "Let's go make a fire to stay warm."

CHAPTER 1

Two Weeks After The Unchipping

May 4, 2115; Saturday

The stabbing pain in the back of Amaya's neck returned with a vengeance. The bright May sun searing the balcony stung her eyes and made them water. She rummaged through her bag, pulled out a pair of dark metal sunglasses, and slipped them on. She rubbed the back of her neck, although it made no difference.

She shifted to face her sister. "I'm calling the AutoDoc."

"Do you really think the AutoDoc is going to help?" Nyala asked. She finished braiding her coarse, black hair into a bunch of messy braids. "I can do your hair next if you want."

Amaya leaned her head on her knees and ignored Nyala's offer. Her head hurt too much to respond. "I think Amoco messed something up when he disabled my chip. It's making me nauseous and it still burns where I was injected. Or maybe it's that toxin Liam injected us with."

"I'll get the doc on the screen." Nyala sounded resigned rather than convinced.

Nyala disappeared inside her apartment, and the sounds of her going through the steps of accessing the AutoDoc drifted through the sliding door to the balcony. A minute later, Nyala called out, "Amaya, the AutoDoc is ready."

Amaya entered the apartment and closed the balcony door gently behind her. The AutoDoc filled an entire wall across from Nyala's kitchen.

"Hello, Amaya," the cartoonish face of the AutoDoc said. "I see there is another person in the room. Do I have your permission to discuss your medical concerns in front of this person?"

"Yes, of course."

"Please stand by while I access your medical records." There was a moment of silence. The expressionless face of the AutoDoc didn't move. Then it raised one eyebrow. "The last time we met, you were requesting unnecessary meds."

"They were necessary—" Amaya stopped herself. There was no point in arguing with the AutoDoc again. "I've been having some pain. It's where my chip was disabled."

"Why was your chip disabled? Did you have trauma to your chip?"

Amaya had no interest in explaining to the AutoDoc about how she had lived most of her life thinking she didn't have a chip, and once she realized that she had one, it didn't fit with who she was and she chose to have it disabled. "No trauma. I just didn't have a use for it anymore."

"Embedded chips have many uses and make life easier in many ways. It is nonsensical to say that you didn't have a use for your chip."

The AutoDoc screen blinked off. Amaya looked at Nyala. Nyala shrugged. Whatever was happening, she didn't understand it either. After a moment of blackness, the AutoDoc turned on again, and the face reappeared.

"Thank you for using AutoDoc services." The voice sounded even cheerier than earlier. "It has been a pleasure talking with you. Until next time!" The face disappeared and the AutoDoc logo flashed on the screen.

What had just happened?

"Wait, no," Amaya called out, "don't go. We're not done yet!" The AutoDoc was required to meet with her. It couldn't just cut her off.

The screen fizzled—a line of static expanded to cover the entire screen. A notice popped up: YOU HAVE BEEN SUSPENDED FROM AUTODOC SERVICES.

"What…no! *Why?*"

The notice remained unchanged, providing no answer to her question.

"Who approved it?" she asked.

The line of static passed across the screen again and the notice changed: THE TERMINATION OF YOUR AUTODOC SERVICES WAS MANDATED BY LP, THE PREMIER LP100 MODEL GHOST.

Of course it was LP, the ghost that Mariela Stafford had been so threatened by that she planned an entire expedition to delete him and the other LP100 model digital beings. But knowing it was LP didn't explain much. "Why did LP terminate my AutoDoc services?" It was a rhetorical question that she didn't have any hope of getting an answer to.

An answer popped up anyway, blinking in bold red letters:

YOU KNOW WHAT YOU DID.

Two Weeks After The Unchipping

Saturday, continued

It took a while for Amaya to get over being cut off from the AutoDoc. It was bad enough that LP was aware of who she was, but that he seemed intent on cutting her off from services couldn't be good. And the Auto-Doc notice was right. She knew what she did.

"Would you like some tea to calm your nerves?" Nyala asked.

"Yes, thank you." Amaya settled into a chair on the tenth-floor porch, her entire body trembling. Nyala's dog, Fido, curled up next to Amaya's foot and nuzzled her ankle with his nose. It would have been perfect, an ideal Saturday morning, except for the guilt that weighed down her limbs and clouded her thinking.

Even the warm sunshine on her face couldn't take away the chill that she got every time she thought about what she had done. Two weeks had gone by since Amaya had made a decision that changed the lives of pretty much everyone on the planet, and she still hadn't come to terms with her role in The Unchipping. Whenever she managed to forget, it was never long until something reminded her about it and everything—the guilt, the nausea, the doubts about whether she made the right deci-sion—came raging back.

Inside the apartment, Nyala bustled around her kitchen pouring hot water into the tea cups. Amaya felt like she was watching from a mile away. Trevor, Nyala's ten-year-old neighbor, walked into the apartment like it was his own. Fido ran to greet him and to get ear scratches. Trevor flopped onto the floor and let Fido lick his face. Nyala picked up the teacups, stepping carefully over the ten-year-old boy sprawled on the floor, and carried them out onto the balcony.

Of the two teacups that Nyala carried, Amaya selected a chipped tea-cup with purple columbines on it. Nyala's tenth floor apartment, in the middle ring of Glorietta Pass, was basically a walk-up because the ele-vator never worked, but the view from the balcony far eclipsed the fake view from the digi-window in Amaya's weatherproof apartment. On good days like today, when the humidity was low and the dust settled, all of the inner ring of the city was visible, including Amaya's apartment building and the Panacea Corp headquarters looming over everything. A downpour earlier in the afternoon had dropped the temperature and left the scent of creosote on the cool breeze that wove through the warm sunshine.

Nyala's dog barked at the sound of the door chime.

"Calm down, Fido," Nyala said. "Trevor, can you check on the mini-screen to see who that is?"

Trevor jumped up and popped open the mini-screen on Nyala's kitchen table. "It's that guy Elliat."

Amaya raised her eyebrows at Nyala. "I thought you weren't returning his calls? Especially after he blogged all that stuff about us that's not true?"

Nyala scoffed. "I haven't been returning his calls. Trevor, let him in."

"This should be interesting," Amaya said.

Elliat, a stocky man wearing shorts without a shirt and shoes without socks but sporting a pair of dark, heavy-rimmed glasses, entered the apartment. Pausing with his hands on his hips, he looked from side to side before holding up a hand to wave to them on the balcony. "Hello ladies! I see you're enjoying some fresh air." Elliat grabbed a chair from the kitchen table, dragged it out to the balcony, and set it down between them. He swung his leg around the chair and straddled it. "It's so refreshing to see someone who's not afraid to have a balcony, and windows—glass ones at that—in this day and age." He knocked on the glass balcony door with his knuckle.

Amaya scooted her chair to the side so she could see Elliat and Nyala without having to crane her neck. What was Elliat doing there, anyway? Why did he have to interrupt what she thought would be a private afternoon spent with her sister?

Elliat rested his hands on his knees and held his face towards the sun with his eyes closed. "Ah, the warmth of the sun on my face." He sighed. "Can't do this for long without getting skin cancer!"

"If you don't want to get skin cancer, maybe you should wear a shirt," Amaya said.

Elliat didn't open his eyes. "Amaya, you amuse me. You are *such* a prude about clothing!"

She should have seen that comment coming. She crossed her arms over her chest. "Wear whatever you want. I don't care." She did care, but not enough to tussle with Elliat over it.

Elliat opened his eyes and turned toward her. "Amaya, I hear you're responsible for disabling the chips."

The blood rushing into Amaya's head pounded in her ears. She couldn't allow Elliat to see her panic. If he published his suspicions on his blog, she would never feel safe again. Even without proof it would be dangerous for her, and she had just started feeling safe going out again after his last accusations.

Her only option was to feign not caring, and then, as casually as possible, attack in return. With any luck, she would convince him that he was off base and wound his ego so much that he forgot about his suspicions about her. "Elliat," she said, "how many things are you planning to accuse me of? You've already accused me of so many things that I'm surprised you have *any* credibility left at this point."

Elliat puffed out his bare chest. "I'll have you know that I'm the top-rated blogger at *Business Today*." He sniffed. "I'm also their newest staff member."

"Yes, Elliat, we know," Nyala rolled her eyes. "It says so right on your byline. And you share it on every newscast."

Elliat perked up. "You've been watching my newscast?"

"Only to see what you plan to accuse us of next," Nyala said.

"Not because I won a Newsoogle Award?"

How shameless was he? Amaya couldn't take it any longer. "You won that Newsoogle Award because you kept accusing us of stuff! Stuff that wasn't true!"

"Wasn't it? I'm still not convinced by the evidence against that Viola woman. It just seemed a little off to me."

"Okay," Nyala used the tone she usually saved for when Fido chewed up something he shouldn't, "here's a question. Why did you release the evidence against Viola if you didn't believe it?"

"It was still newsworthy. I never said that I had verified it; just that someone had sent it to me anonymously. And then the police verified it, so I guess I was right in releasing it." In a low voice, he added, "If you ask me, I think the woman herself leaked it. From what I understand, she's quite intelligent. She could have fabricated the evidence."

Although it didn't make any sense to Amaya, Viola had chosen to implicate herself in a crime she didn't commit. But Amaya didn't feel the need to rescue Viola by agreeing with Elliat that she could have fabricated the evidence. Instead, she doubled down on her criticism of Elliat. "I think for once, instead of making accusations where no evidence exists, you should accept the evidence that does exist, and not try to turn it into something it isn't."

"I agree with Amaya," Nyala said. "Stop seeing things that aren't there."

Elliat looked downcast. "Nyala, I'm disappointed in you. There was a time when you could be counted on to join me in eschewing the obvious explanation, to look beyond what we are 'supposed' to believe and to see the underlying conspiracy. We were on the same page in understanding that we are manipulated by corporations and the government."

"I still think that," Nyala said. "But there's not always a conspiracy. And Elliat, you're part of the problem. How many fawning statements did you make about the CEO of Panacea Corp?"

"I had a strategy. It was to gain his trust so I could bring him down."

"I'd like to believe you, but I don't."

"I was successful, wasn't I?"

"It wasn't your sycophantic articles that did it. It was a lot of other things and some bad luck for him."

"Well, I'm not sure that's fair. I published articles about how the cryogens were misused and that Panacea Corp didn't get permission from their families and then abandoned the cryogens in Area 52. I wrote articles about how Area 52 had an agreement where Panacea Corp gave them land to form a colony that only uses technology from before 2005 in exchange for letting Panacea Corp place a backup server there, and then the CEO of Panacea Corp reneged on that agreement. I played a big part in his downfall. You should thank me for it."

"Thanks," Nyala said sarcastically.

"This afternoon I'm going to break a big story. Have you all heard about all the people who are stuck at the pod warehouses? They're losing their minds from boredom because they can't access Panacea, and since everyone who lives in a pod is leaving now that the chips are disabled, there's an incredibly long wait time to get out. Apparently, it's taking a toll on the mental health of the pod-dwellers."

"We know," Amaya said. "I'm going to take one of them in to help with the transition."

"Good, for you." Elliat nodded his head repeatedly. "Good for you."

He stroked his chin. "Smart move. It will help rehabilitate your image. It's a good start, at least."

Nyala let out an exasperated sigh. "Elliat, why are you here?"

"I'm here for this." He pointed back and forth between Nyala and him in a gesture that Amaya could only guess was supposed to refer to their conversation. "I've missed these exchanges—our deep discussions, our synergy as we confront wrongdoing in the world."

Nyala's mouth twitched. "Aw, I've missed you too!" Nyala stood up with her arms open.

Amaya hoped that maybe Nyala was planning to throw him off the balcony, but no, she embraced Elliat in a bear hug. "I've missed these crazy, ridiculous conversations!" Nyala placed her hands on Elliat's shoulders. "But you cannot accuse my sister, or me, or any of my friends, of any crimes ever again. It just won't do, and if you keep it up, I will have to unfriend you!"

"Okay, okay," he smiled and shrugged shyly, "I get the point."

"Now run along." Nyala placed an arm around his shoulder and pointed him toward the door. "Let me finish my conversation with my sister. But if you want to bring some wine over tomorrow, I wouldn't say no."

Elliat smiled. "Right-e-o!"

Did Elliat just say 'right-e-o?' Amaya pressed her lips together to keep from laughing as Elliat headed into the apartment.

Then he stopped, came back out on the balcony, shot at them with his index fingers pointed like pretend guns while making shooting noises and said "I forgot my chair." He dragged his chair back to the table, held up a hand, wiggled his fingers, and seconds later, with a cheery "Toodle-oo!" he was out the door.

Amaya finally let her smile break out. "Did you invite Elliat over tomorrow to keep him from reporting his suspicions?"

Nyala smiled and shrugged. "He amuses me. Spending time with him is a small sacrifice to make if it keeps my friends safe."

Amaya laughed. "I like how you got rid of him and made him happy at the same time."

"He's happy, I'm happy, and hopefully you're happy that you won't have to deal with him anymore today."

Amaya smiled. "I'm happy." Maybe some things were going right. Like she was starting to have hope that she might not be sent to prison for disabling the chips. If only she could also get rid of the guilt over disabling them, she would be ecstatic.

"So, Amaya," Nyala said, "there's this protest in Panacea Plaza tomorrow—"

Amaya interrupted her. "Nyala, I can't handle going to a protest right now. I'm going to take in one of Georgia's pod-lifers who needs to be rehabilitated, and that's about all I can handle."

"It won't take much time," Nyala insisted. "Why don't you want to go to the protest?"

"She doesn't like protests!" Trevor yelled from inside the apartment.

"I know that!" Nyala yelled. She turned back to Amaya. "It's just that since the chips were disabled, a lot of people have been volunteering for Panacea Corp's research on embedding chips in adults. The research isn't safe, and it needs to be stopped."

"Trevor," Amaya said, "cover your ears and hum." She waited until she heard him humming. "It's just that I feel guilty for disabling the chips. I'm the reason that people are desperately signing up for chip research. And I can't blame them. Who am I to tell them what they can and can't do?"

"That was a great thing you did when you disabled the chips," Nyala said. "You saved lots of people. You and Cooper should be proud. I know having the chips disabled has disrupted a lot of lives, but doing risky research under questionable circumstances isn't the answer."

Trevor's humming continued in the background.

"I agree. But I can't do protests right now. I just can't. I'm having a hard time coping, and going to a protest won't help. The people agreeing to be research subjects are adults, and they can make up their own minds."

Trevor started humming a new song. Amaya waved her hands to get his attention. "You can stop humming now."

Trevor uncovered his ears and pushed up from lying on the floor into a seated position to face them. "My mom says you disabled the chips."

Amaya's head spun. There was only one possible way that Trevor's mom could know about Amaya's involvement. "Nyala, did you tell people what happened?"

Nyala smiled and shrugged. "I couldn't help it. I was proud of you. You're a hero to people who don't have chips."

Incredible. Her own sister, of all people, was going to get her arrested or assaulted by some person angry about losing their chip. "Don't you understand how risky it will be if people find out?"

Amaya disabled the embedded chips for a good reason—to stop the spread of an infectious disease that could kill people with chips—but every day for the last two weeks she had to convince herself over and over again that she had done the right thing. And it wasn't getting any easier.

"I'm just saying you're a hero for some people," Nyala said. "The unchipped are tired of being second-class citizens. You liberated them."

She didn't feel liberated. "I should have been like Cooper and taken responsibility for what I did."

"You mean Cooper, who confessed to disabling the chips, went to prison, and then got out when his ex-girlfriend forged evidence so that she could take his place? Is *that* the Cooper you're talking about?"

Why did Nyala have to be so patronizing? Amaya rolled her eyes. "You *know* that's who I'm talking about."

"I'm just saying, if that was his idea of taking responsibility, he didn't do a very good job of it. Where is Cooper, by the way?" Nyala asked. "I haven't seen him around since before he went to jail. That was what, almost two weeks ago?"

"He told Mariela something about wanting to go on a vacation and headed out of town with his mom. Mariela's taking care of his dogs." Amaya laughed. "Apparently, they keep getting fleas even though she gives them a de-fleaing mister." Mariela complained about the fleas a lot. "Mariela may have positive feelings for Cooper, but they don't extend to taking care of his dogs."

"You know, I envy Cooper," Nyala said. "He seems to have a way of getting women to do stuff for him, even when it's not to their benefit."

An alert from Amaya's EveryThing brought her attention to the time. "Nyala, I hate to run, but I have to pick up the pod-lifer who's going to live with me." She rolled her eyes. "Like Elliat said, I'd better get started on rehabilitating my image."

<center>~~~~~</center>

Amaya paused before opening the glass doors to the Pod-Dweller Recuperation and Recovery Center. She hadn't been in public for weeks—would she be safe? On the other side of the doors, bored security guards casually kept an eye on the room. The people reclining in cots throughout the large room wouldn't be strong enough to be a threat, while the workers in the center seemed focused on what they were doing. Amaya would have to trust that they wouldn't attack her because of Elliat's accusations. She took a deep breath and opened the door.

Seconds after she entered the center, Amaya's good friend, Georgia, rushed over to greet her. Georgia had dedicated almost every waking minute to helping people who were having trouble adjusting after their chips had been disabled. The work was demanding and Georgia's efforts were tireless. She never complained, despite having left her pod less than two months ago.

Georgia slipped her arm through Amaya's. "Thanks for agreeing to take someone." Georgia led Amaya into the large, darkened room filled with cots. "We have more people than we can help."

"Yeah, I'm happy to help. Sorry I couldn't do something sooner, but I've just now moved back into my apartment."

"Of course, don't give it a second thought. You needed to make sure you were safe."

Georgia was wearing a simple dress that was fitted in the bodice and cinched at the waist. Its only embellishment was broad iridescent pastel stripes that continuously scrolled up the dress. Georgia was one of the top ranked digi-dines in the world—she could have made elaborate clothing for herself like the outrageous, interactive designs that she made for their friend Mariela, but she preferred simple outfits with one or two interesting details. Georgia's spiky, silver-gray hair added a nice contrast to her outfit.

Amaya, on the other hand, preferred leather and canvas-colored heavyweight, rough-textured beige and brown fabric with small metallic accents. Someone had once described her as the "poster child for sad beige clothing."

Georgia wound through the cots, pulling Amaya behind her. As they walked, Georgia explained their work. Once the pod-dwellers exited their pods, Georgia was helping them get rehabilitated. The volunteers helped the pod-dwellers learn how to walk again, take their meds, get enough fluids, and do everything else they needed to be able to live on their own in the solid world.

Georgia stopped beside one of the cots. The occupant's thin body was close to emaciation, much as Georgia's had been when she had left her pod. Georgia pulled up a chair and held the person's hand. "Nikky, this is Amaya. She'll be helping you out." Georgia turned to Amaya. "They've been with us for a few days now."

They had straight, shoulder-length dark hair and olive skin. They turned their head toward Amaya and fixed their piercing dark brown eyes on her, but didn't sit up. It was a safe assumption that years of pod living had left them weak.

Amaya stood next to the cot. "It's nice to meet you."

"Amaya," Georgia said, "your job is to help Nikky until they build up their strength enough to get by on their own."

Having left her pod two months ago, Georgia knew what it was like to struggle with the transition to the solid world. But Georgia's transition had been voluntary, while for Nikky and the other people in the center, the transition from the metaverse to the solid world happened only after their chips had been disabled. Amaya pushed to the side the guilt that crawled into her stomach about her role in disabling the chips. She could feel guilty about it later.

"How are you two adjusting to being unchipped?" Nikky asked in the scratchy voice of someone who wasn't used to speaking aloud.

Amaya shrugged. "I've been unchipped for a while now, so my life is pretty much the same."

Georgia stood up. "I'll let you get acquainted with Amaya while I get the mobile chair." It wasn't a surprise she turned to leave rather than talk about her chip. She didn't like people knowing she was one of the few people in the world whose chip still worked.

"Thanks, Georgia," Nikky said before turning their piercing eyes back to Amaya. "I'll be staying with you?"

Amaya sat down in the chair by the cot so she wouldn't be towering over Nikky. "My place has a bed and a lounger, so there are places for both of us to sleep. It's not very big, though, so you won't have much space to yourself."

"It's got to be better than this place." A tear rolled down their face.

Amaya wished she could have taken them in sooner. "How long have you been here?"

"A few days."

That was a long time to be living in a place that wasn't much more than an understaffed shelter. "I wish I could take in more people."

"Every bit helps, and it's great you're doing what you can," Nikky said. Their brow furrowed, and it looked like another tear might escape.

"Hey," Amaya said, "things will get better. Did Georgia tell you about how difficult it was when she left her pod, and how, after a few weeks, she was doing great?"

"But she chose to leave. I didn't want to leave."

Fair enough. Surely not having a say in the matter or any time to prepare made the transition from pod-living to the solid world all that much more difficult. Amaya again pushed to the side the guilt that she felt for her role in Nikky's unplanned departure from the Panacea metaverse.

"Hey, Amaya!"

Amaya looked up and saw a lanky man in his 30s with brown hair cut into a basic and unremarkable style. Hank, Georgia's close friend, pushed the mobile chair up to the cot. Hank's expertise in the martial arts showed in the way he guided the chair where he wanted it to go without appearing to put any effort into it.

"Good for you for helping out," he said. "It's really fulfilling."

Let's hope Hank was right about that.

"Did you take someone?" she asked him.

"Georgia and I have been pretty much living here, so let's say we took all of them."

"That's great." Hank wasn't Amaya's favorite person, but she admired him for his dedication.

"Did Georgia tell you how she based the rehabilitation program on how I helped her out when she exited her pod?"

"Yes, she did." There was a brief silence, and then Amaya spoke up before it could become awkward. "So, how are you doing?"

Hank sat down in the mobile chair in a way that Amaya could only describe as exasperated. "I'm still pissed about the chips being disabled."

"But your chip…" Amaya wanted to ask Hank why he was complaining. Like Georgia, his chip was one of the very few that wasn't disabled, but she wasn't sure if Hank wanted anyone to know that.

Hank seemed to understand what her question would have been. "I lost all my clients. No one can come to my martial arts class anymore if their chips are disabled."

Amaya looked at the floor. The guilt was back. "I'm sorry to hear that."

"It was my only source of earned income."

"But you still get money from your parents?" It was hard to be sympathetic towards Hank's plight when he had his parents to send him money.

"I'm not sure." Hank avoided eye contact. "I haven't been able to get a hold of them. I'm still getting automatic bank transfers, but I wasn't spending anything because my parents may need it when I find them. But…then we needed IVs and mobile chairs for the people here, so I started spending it again."

"He talks a lot," Nikky said in their scratchy voice.

Amaya stifled a laugh.

"I'm worried about how I'll get by," Nikky said. "People with disabled chips don't get the basic advertising income anymore."

"That's a big adjustment." Amaya said.

The furrow returned to Nikky's brow. "Only people with working chips are eligible for the BAI. For me, no working chip means no basic income. Me and millions of other people. They cut all of us off." The brow furrow deepened. Nikky looked at Amaya. "You'll still take me even though I can't pay, right?"

"Of course I will. I never expected you to pay." Amaya stood up. "We should probably get moving before you get worn out by talking."

Hank also stood up. "Give me one second to get you the things you'll need," Hank said. "Also, Nikky, you can rest for a bit because Amaya needs to take the class on how to insert an IV." Hank turned to Amaya. "You'll need to give Nikky fluids."

"I have to do what?" Amaya shivered. No one told her she would be inserting needles.

Hank shrugged. "It's tough the first couple of times, but you get used to it pretty quickly." He turned to go.

"Hank, hang on." Amaya touched his arm. "About those martial arts classes—do you think you could teach me? Nyala's been wanting me to learn more self-defense."

Hank smiled. "Yeah, sure, we can start tomorrow. I'll turn you into a badass like Nyala in no time."

"Perfect." With all the threats they'd been receiving, it wouldn't hurt to develop some self-defense skills.

Amaya followed Hank through a maze of cots, medical equipment, and other scattered items to the back of the large room. A group of people were gathered there, perched on stools arranged in a circle. In the middle of the group, a woman propped up on downy pillows reclined on a cot.

Next to her, an IV bag dangled from a pole, and Amaya was careful not to bump it as she slipped past the woman to get to the only open seat.

A woman a couple of seats down made eye contact with Amaya. She studied Amaya's face and then her lip curled into a snarl. "Do I know you?" the woman asked.

"No." Anxious to avoid the woman's hardened gaze, Amaya quickly looked away. "No, I don't think we've met."

"You're so familiar. I'm sure I know you. What's your name?"

Amaya was sure the woman was toying with her, that she had already figured out who Amaya was but was set on forcing Amaya to announce her name to the group. "Amaya Gidada," she said with more confidence than she felt.

The rest of the circle seemed to freeze, their previous conversations falling silent. They peered at her, no doubt piecing together her name and the information in Elliat's news reports. Amaya shrank into her stool.

The group's attention turned to a woman in a lab coat who walked into the center of the group. "I'm Dr. Torre. I'll be showing you how to insert an IV drip." She pointed to the woman reclining on the cot. "Amanda here has generously volunteered to be my demonstration subject."

Amanda offered the group a half smile, suggesting she regretted her decision, but she gamely allowed Dr. Torre to prep her arm. Dr. Torre talked through the procedure as she inserted the needle. She made sure the IV was working and then turned to the group. "Okay, now you all are going to practice on each other. Please pair up and then when you have your partner, find one of the cots that has an IV bag next to it."

A message alert popped up on Amaya's EveryThing. Mariela wanted to know if Amaya and Nyala were available for dinner that evening. Amaya quickly pushed 'yes.'

She looked around for a partner. Everyone seemed to be paired up except for a man next to Amaya. He raised a hand to his head, blocking the entire side of his face from her. She scanned the circle again, but the man was the only one left.

She touched his arm. The man still didn't look at her. Unable to see his face, she asked his hand, "Would you like to partner up?"

Still without looking at her, the man muttered, "Sorry…I have something else I need to do." He left the circle and headed off to do…whatever. She cursed Elliat under her breath. It was his fault that everyone was treating her like a monster.

"Does everyone have a partner?" Dr. Torre asked, while looking at the group around her.

"No," Amaya said. She tried to sound casual about it, but the damage to her self-esteem was clear through that simple two-letter word.

Dr. Torre didn't appear to notice Amaya's distress. "There's a woman who just completed the training. I'll check with her to see if she would be willing to let you practice on her. She still has one arm that hasn't been poked yet." Dr. Torre scurried off.

Amaya stared at the floor. Hopefully, the doctor knew what she was doing. Amaya didn't want to endure another awkward rejection from someone she had never met before.

Another question from Mariela popped up on her EveryThing. Amaya pushed the icon for 'potato salad.' Out of the choices Mariela sent, it would be the easiest to prepare for dinner that evening.

"Amaya, here's your partner," Dr. Torre said.

Amaya froze as she locked eyes with the handsome dentist with long shiny black hair who had taken her on one date about a month ago and then told Amaya she didn't want to date someone without a chip. At the time, it had almost broken Amaya's heart, but in the last month, so much had happened that she had almost forgotten about it. Li had seemed like a distant memory until now.

"Amaya." Li smiled.

"Li." Amaya didn't smile back.

"Good to see you," Li said.

Amaya stood up. "Let's get this over with." She pulled her stool over to the closest free cot that had an IV bag. She grabbed the sterile gloves out of a box on the cot and put them on with a loud snap. It hurt, but sounded pleasingly menacing.

"You're going to be gentle, right?" Li looked concerned.

Good. Let her worry.

"I'll try," Amaya said, "but I have no clue what I'm doing."

"Okay, I trust you." Li eased herself onto the cot. Her eyes darted around the room and one hand clenched the cot.

Li trusted her? How foolish of her. Amaya looked closely at the crook of Li's elbow for the vein. She had seen Cooper do this for Georgia a bunch of times, and he had always made it look easy. As she searched for Li's vein, it didn't seem as easy as Cooper made it look.

"I've missed you," Li said.

How dare she? Maybe Amaya wasn't going to try to be gentle after all. She applied more pressure in her palpations of Li's elbow.

"I've wanted to contact you," Li continued.

"Have you?" Amaya did her best to sound non-committal.

"I have. Like I said, I've missed you."

She didn't respond. What was there to say? And besides, she was concentrating on finding the vein.

"Can you ever forgive me?" Li asked. "I knew it was a mistake as soon as I sent you that message. The truth is, I think I got scared."

Amaya stopped looking for the vein. "You told me over a video capture that you didn't want to see me anymore unless it was for sex. You didn't even have the decency to tell me in person. And the best you can come up with now is that 'you got scared'?"

"Don't make it sound like that. What I said was wrong. I only suggested ongoing physical intimacy because it was a way for me to stay connected with you while lying to myself about how important you were to me."

Amaya went back to looking for the vein. The sooner she found it, the sooner she could get out of there, and she needed to leave before she got sucked into Li's flattery. She wanted to believe Li, but it was better not to take a chance on letting Li convince her that everything was okay.

Amaya found a vein that seemed like it would work and decided to try it. The worst that could happen was that she would miss, which would suck for Li but not for her. And the best that could happen would be she would get the IV in and get out of there. She carefully inserted the needle under the skin. Success. She could leave.

"Good job," Li said. "Very smooth. Much better than my last partner." Li gave her a look that was clearly intended to convey that her words had a double meaning. Despite herself, Amaya's heart fluttered.

Amaya took the needle out, discarded it in the medical waste bin next to the cot, and taped over the insertion point. Li grabbed her hand. "Please let me see you again. Just once, so I can explain myself."

She shouldn't agree to it. She was over Li, so why take the chance on reopening the wound? And Nyala would be furious with her. "Okay. One time."

"Great." Li sat up with a big, warm smile. "I'll see you tomorrow for dinner."

"Okay." This seemed like a bad idea. Why had she agreed against her better judgment? "Do I wear casual clothes like last time?"

Li pressed a hand to Amaya's arm. "Let's dress up this time." Li stood up, kissed Amaya on the forehead, and headed off to wherever she had come from.

Amaya ran over what happened in her mind. How had she gone from being upset at seeing Li and wanting to get it over with as quickly as possible, to agreeing to meet her for what sounded like a dinner date?

"Well, that was an unexpected development."

Amaya startled. Hank was standing right next to her.

"How much did you hear?" Amaya asked.

"I heard how she ditched you last time. Then I heard her say some highly predictable things about how she made a mistake and about how special you are. And then I heard you give in and agree to dinner. Honestly, I thought that you would hold out for longer."

Hank was right, but Amaya wasn't going to admit it. "Don't you have something you should be doing? Some person who needs your help? Because I need to get Nikky home."

"Sure. I'm sure you need to start picking out your outfit for dinner tomorrow." It was a rude comment, even for Hank. "Are you going to tell Nyala?" he asked.

Probably not, but Hank didn't need to know that. "I'm going." Amaya jolted up from the stool, sending it rolling away from her.

"Here are the IV fluids and your other equipment." Hank handed her a box. "Give me a call if you need anything. Or if you prefer, you can call your dentist friend." He winked. "It sounds like she would be very happy to help you out."

She grabbed the box with the IV fluids from him. "If I need help, I'll call Georgia."

~~~~~

"This potato salad is amazing." Mariela took another bite. Amazing was an exaggeration, but Mariela didn't know what else to say. Her two dinner guests had spread themselves out along the large dining room table at the Stafford Estate. Apparently, they had no interest in talking with each other, or her. The silence at the table had stretched on so long it was verging on agonizing.

Her heart still ached every day over Grace's death. Maybe she had
~~~~~

been unrealistic, but she had hoped that having friends over for dinner would give her some support and maybe help distract her for a moment. So far, Mariela felt even more alone in her grief.

Amaya seemed preoccupied, and it was unclear if she was even listening. Her blank stare was even more awkward than the silence. Nyala was paying attention, but she must still be mad at Mariela because she wasn't putting any effort into the conversation. Why had Nyala agreed to come over if she was still mad? For that matter, why had Amaya come over if she was just going to stare at her food and poke at it absent-mindedly? As far as dinner parties went, this one was a disaster.

With no one speaking for another five minutes, Mariela pulled up the mini-screen on the table and used it to try on a couple of different outfits. How long had it been since she had changed? It was at least three days. She kept forgetting every time she was at a terminal, and the nanodes in the digi-skin were still keeping it clean, so at least it never got dirty. It was probably a rude thing to do, but it felt less awkward than sitting in silence.

She had worn the watermelon dress recently, so she quickly discarded it. The gold dress with the long train of sequins seemed wrong for the occasion. She shortened the train and changed the dress to plain black. Now it fit the occasion perfectly. She pushed the mini-screen back on the table. The silence continued.

"Nyala, what have you been up to lately?" It was a desperate ploy on Mariela's part to get someone to engage with her.

"I saw Elliat today." Nyala spoke in a monotone. "We're going to catch up tomorrow."

"Oh." Mariela had mixed feelings about any contact with Elliat. "Are you sure that's a good idea? He does tend to write bad things about us pretty frequently."

"He's promised not to write anything negative about any of my friends again." Nyala's tone was brimming with attitude.

What was her problem? Why come to dinner and then have an attitude the whole time? Obviously, it had to do with her still being mad with Mariela. "Could you clarify for me," she asked, "whether you consider me to be one of your friends or not? Because tonight it doesn't seem like it."

Amaya looked up like she just realized that there were other people in the room, and that she might have missed something important. Nyala, on the other hand, didn't show any reaction.

"Would I have spent four days in jail with you if I wasn't your friend?" Nyala asked.

"So what's going on, then?"

"It's just that you don't realize how good you have it. You committed a felony multiple times over when you deleted the LP100 model ghosts, but nothing happened to you. Deleting the ghosts caused significant harm to your company, but you end up getting promoted to CEO. You deleted your sister's ghost daughter, yet she mysteriously showed up again. You get injected with a toxic substance that could kill you, but then Cooper saved you by disabling the chips."

Nyala had gone too far. "I didn't ask Cooper to do that. And it wasn't just for me."

"Really? Because you seemed to benefit from it the most. You're safe, but the lives of millions of people are torn apart. They can't get to work, don't have anywhere to live, or don't know how to contact their friends and family. And yet somehow, through all of this, you're fine. In fact, you're better off than when you started."

It wasn't fair for Nyala to blame her for all those things, especially considering that most of them she didn't have any control over. And she wasn't the only one who had been protected from the toxin when Cooper disabled the chips. "You forget that you also had a kill switch, so Cooper saved you as well."

"But was it worth it? Look at the suffering that people are going through."

"Wait…" Amaya seemed to be trying to get caught up with the conversation. "I was also responsible for disabling the chips, and Nyala, didn't you just tell me today that you were proud of me for doing it?"

"That's true," Nyala said. "Plus, what I just said is also true."

Amaya's brow furrowed, and she started picking at her potato salad again. "I'm so confused," she said.

"Sometimes two contradictory things can both be true at once," Mariela said.

"Oh."

The discussion seemed to have run its course, so Mariela tried a different topic. "Amaya, how is your pod-lifer doing?"

Amaya put down her fork and sat up straight. "Good. I learned how to insert an IV when I picked them up, so I was able to get them started on fluids. And the anti-nausea meds seem to be working, as well as the sleeping pills." Amaya finally seemed engaged. "They were sleeping when I left. I actually feel like I'm doing something useful. Are you going to take someone in?"

"Oh yeah, Georgia has filled all the spare rooms here with people." It probably wouldn't be wise for Mariela to mention how she had been too busy with work to meet any of the people she took in, so she had hired staff to take care of them. Nyala would only give her a lecture if she brought it up. Nyala had been lecturing her a lot lately. Mariela should just end the dinner and put this painful evening to rest.

"Look, I think we should just—" She was going to say call it a night when a small drone buzzed into the room. It hovered over the table.

In the oddly accented voice of her sister, the drone said, "Mariela, can you please come into the library right away?"

"Are you okay?"

"No. I need to talk to you. Now."

"Okay." Mariela stood up and turned to Amaya and Nyala. "If you two want to leave, this isn't much of a dinner, anyway."

"I'm going with you," Nyala said. "I'm not missing a chance to see Sofi yell at you."

Mariela hadn't intended for Nyala to go with her to talk to Sofi, but she didn't want to risk upsetting Nyala any more than she already had. "Amaya?"

"I'm sorry, Mariela. I know I've been kind of checked out," Amaya said. "I'm willing to stay if Nyala wants to—that is, if you don't mind having us tagging along."

"Besides," Nyala said, "we're your friends, and it sounds like you could use some support."

Mariela wasn't so sure that they were friends anymore, but if they wanted to come along, she wouldn't stop them.

~~~~

Mariela's sister Sofi reclined in a lounger in the estate's library with an IV drip dangling from her arm. Even with the IV, she looked poised with one arm draped across the back of the couch. She had taken the time to choose an outfit and smooth her hair, which was more than what Mariela had done.

Despite the warm weather, Sofi had a fire burning in the corner
~~~~

fireplace. Even from across the room, piercing negative energy radiated from her. Mariela crossed the large room and settled on the lounger next to her. Amaya and Nyala trailed her.

Wooden bookcases overflowing with antique books lined two walls of the library, while windows stretched from floor to ceiling along the other two walls. A conference table ran parallel to the windows. In the corner where the two walls of windows met, a couch and two recliners formed a sitting area next to the fireplace.

"Hi Sofi," Amaya leaned over Mariela to hug Sofi. "How's the physical rehab going? Are you getting used to walking again?"

"Mariela didn't tell you?" Sofi glared at Mariela. "I guess it would be too much to expect Mariela to tell you all that I was losing the ability to walk, even before I moved into a pod."

Mariela had been trying to respect Sofi's privacy by not sharing the information. "I didn't know if you wanted other people to know." It seemed like no matter what she did, Sofi was going to be upset with her.

"Why did you think I wouldn't want people to know?"

"Well, because you didn't tell me until you had to," Mariela explained in a low voice. Mariela couldn't make the people around her happy today. After she found out what Sofi wanted, she was going to hide out in her room for the rest of the evening.

Sofi took a deep breath. "I've been talking with Opali—"

Mariela smiled. "That's great! I'm so glad you have your daughter back."

"—and she is sure that you are responsible for her being deleted."

There was no way that Mariela was going to tell Sofi the truth about accidentally deleting Opali when she deleted the LP100 model ghosts. "Why does she think that?"

"She says she has evidence that you deleted the advanced ghosts. She says you also ended up deleting her because she's based on a similar technology."

Mariela wanted to ask what evidence Opali had, but if she seemed worried about the evidence, it would make her look guilty. What could she say that would satisfy Sofi that wouldn't be an obvious lie?

"I don't think Mariela could have done it," Nyala interjected. "She was on the train in Bolivia with me. Even if she wanted to do it, she was way too drunk most of the time to have the capacity to carry out something like deleting the ghosts."

Oh, Nyala—how easily Nyala helped her out and then immediately stabbed her in the back.

Sofi shook her head. She didn't appear to buy Nyala's comment. "Mariela, if I find out that you had anything to do with Opali disappearing… It's bad enough that you abandoned your own daughter, but then you take my daughter away from me as well?"

Mariela wanted to defend herself, but everything Sofi was saying about her was true. Mariela could only hope that Sofi never found evidence of what she had done, because that would surely end her relationship with her sister. There was nothing to do but to continue lying.

CHAPTER 3

Fifteen Days After The Unchipping

Sunday

Whenever Georgia could find a minute, she escaped to the Panacea metaverse to take a break from the people, noise, and constant demands on her time. In the metaverse she could be alone, reflect, and recenter herself. It was her haven, her sanctuary from the crush of former pod-lifers staying in her shelter. She loved helping them adjust to living in the solid world, but there was no doubt that some days it was a strain on her spirit.

Sitting on a cloud in the café, watching the plaza below, brought her joy. The ghosts wandering around were a comfort to Georgia. She had even grown fond of the one ghost who, like clockwork, completed a loop in Zócolo Square every six and a half minutes.

Humans, on the other hand, were a rare sight in Panacea since The Unchipping two weeks ago. With working chips, she and Hank were rare breeds. Sure, there were some people using a terminal or projection room to walk their avatars around, but for the most part, Panacea was empty of humans.

The blurry ghost waiter who served her coffee in the Above the Zócolo café brought back a comforting nostalgia for better times. Her coffee immediately appeared in front of her, with an ad for Panacea Pod Warehouses floating in the foam. They couldn't be doing much business right now. The only reason to stay in a pod was to be able to live 100 percent in Panacea or some other metaverse, and with all the chips disabled, no one would be making that choice anymore.

The only people still living in pods were those pod-lifers who Georgia's group hadn't yet managed to find places for. Panacea Corp was providing them with food and medical care, but sitting in a pod for days on end with nothing else to do other than to stare at your own feet and wait for someone to give you food must be intolerably boring. Pods provided chipped people the freedom to live in Panacea, but were prisons for those with disabled chips.

Georgia checked the time. The workers at the pod-lifer rehabilitation center would be expecting her soon. She had time for a quick stroll around the plaza to center herself before she returned to work. She left the café and headed downhill from the bridge that flowed over the Zócolo Square stream.

Behind her, two people were talking casually. She glanced over her shoulder but couldn't see them on the winding path. Georgia ducked behind a tree and peered through a bush as the couple walked by. They seemed different—they sounded human and instead of the awkward movements of someone using a projection room, they moved like they had chips.

After a moment of observing them, Georgia silently scolded herself for her reaction. Why was she worried they would see her? It was silly to be hiding behind a tree. They were probably just some of the few people who didn't have their chips disabled, and she should make their acquaintance in case she ran into them in the future.

After they passed her, she stepped out from behind the tree. "Hey!"

The two turned to look at her.

"I heard you talking," she said. "I thought I would say hello."

They shook her hand. "Are you in the program?" the woman asked.

"What program?"

"The clinical trials."

"No, not that I know of."

The woman tilted her head, and her brow furrowed. "How are you here, then?"

"Oh, I was off-grid when the chips were disabled." For some reason, she didn't like telling people that her chip still worked, but there wasn't any other explanation for why she was there.

"Ohhh," the woman sighed, "your chip still works? You are *so* lucky."

What had the woman meant by clinical trials? "How are you here if your chip doesn't work?"

The woman glanced at the man. "We're not supposed to talk about it," the woman said.

"But they're going to make the announcement soon," the man added.

The woman shrugged. "Okay, since you're going to find out soon, I'll tell you, but don't say anything before the announcement comes out." The woman leaned towards Georgia. "Bo Place has come up with a chip replacement."

Georgia's eyes widened. "Really?" If this was true, it would be life-changing news for the pod-lifers who wanted to return to the metaverse. "So you were given this replacement?"

"We're test subjects to see if it works."

"It seems to be working," Georgia said. "Right?"

"So far it's pretty seamless," the woman confirmed.

"I love it," the man said. "I hated being in the solid world. Now it feels like I'm back home."

Georgia nodded in understanding, but something still didn't add up. "If you can access Panacea," Georgia said, "why did you say I was lucky to have a chip?"

The woman glanced at the man again. He shrugged, as if to say he didn't care about whatever it was that she was going to say.

"Well, we're not supposed to talk about this either, but it's going to come out soon, no matter what." The woman looked over her shoulder. "It doesn't work like a chip—it's a shot you take that changes your DNA."

That didn't sound too bad. If adults could take the shot, it would solve the problem of chip burn and other chip failures. "So what's the catch?" Georgia asked.

"Once you take it, you can never exit Panacea again. There's no way out. I mean, I've lived in Panacea for ten years. It's my home, and I don't think I will want to leave permanently, but…" A tear rolled down her cheek. "But I felt better knowing I could leave. If my dad got sick, or I fell in love with a solid person, that option was available to me. Now it's not an option anymore."

Oh, the choices people make. There was always a tradeoff.

"How long has it been since you were injected?" Georgia asked.

"It's been about three days now. Bo Place hurried to finish up production when the chips were disabled. They realized this was needed more than ever and they didn't want to miss out on this prime opportunity."

The timeline for production of the shot seemed rushed for something that could have life-altering consequences. "When is the announcement going to be made?"

"This evening. They're doing it on that blogger Elliat Exis's show."

"Thanks for letting me know. If you'll excuse me, I need to get back to work."

The pair went on their way and Georgia took a deep breath. As much as it was needed, rushing a technology that alters DNA to the market didn't seem like a good idea. Georgia needed to make arrangements to watch Elliat's show tonight. She made a mental note to make sure she had volunteers set up so she could get away. This was going to be a game changer.

She also needed to tell Mariela. As Panacea Corp's main competitor, Mariela was going to be furious that Bo Place had beaten them in the race to develop a chip replacement.

"Auntie Georgia!"

That sounded like Opali. Georgia peered through the multi-colored trees. A young girl with chestnut curls and a big smile was running around a turn in the path.

"I've been trying to find you!" Opali said.

Almost indistinguishable from a human kid and perceptive in the way only young kids could be, Georgia had a soft spot in her heart for Opali.

"Did you get taller?" Georgia knelt down and looked at Opali more closely.

"I'm taking care of myself now, so my mom said I could make myself older."

"Yes, I see that. How old are you now?"

"I'm eight!" She seemed so proud.

"Eight is a good age."

"I like it. I hope my mom lets me stay eight."

"So, what have you been doing?"

"I talk with my mom. And I created some new friends to play with. But mostly I've been really busy with meetings."

"Are the meetings important?"

"Oh yes, they're very important." Opali nodded solemnly, her curls bouncing with each nod. "I can't tell you about them, but they are really important."

What kind of meetings could an eight-year-old have? Georgia didn't have time to ponder it now—people were probably wondering where she had gotten off to.

"Opali, if you need anything, you know you can call me."

"Thanks, Auntie Georgia. But my mom had me turn off the part of my code that makes me get scared at night, so I'll be fine."

"Okay, sweetie." She hugged Opali. "Take care and I'll see you soon."

~~~~~

Mariela swept into the estate's library, the long skirt of her dress trailing behind her and her brown hair hanging in soft waves to her shoulders. On the other side of the room, Sofi reclined in a lounger next to the fireplace and seemed to be doing her best to pretend Mariela wasn't there. In the twenty-four hours since Sofi had confronted her, nothing seemed to have changed. It was probably too much to hope that the bird feeders Mariela had set up outside of the picture windows to entertain Sofi might help lead to a thaw.

Mariela rolled one of the loungers over by the wall of windows. How many people were showing up to watch Elliat's newscast? She counted silently—Amaya, Nyala, Hank, Georgia, and Amoco Cadiz, Panacea Corp's Director of Chip Research. Six loungers should do it.

"I never thought Bo Place would beat us to market with adult chip replacement," she mumbled to no one in particular, knowing Sofi would only ignore her. "And it all had to happen just after I became CEO." She rolled her eyes. "It's not like I don't have enough on my plate already with the chips being disabled."

Amaya and Nyala walked in as she was moving the last lounger into place. Amaya looked hot and sweaty. Her coily hair drooped like it had wilted in the sun. Nyala, on the other hand, looked completely comfortable wearing a shirt that said, "Don't be a Hero, Stay Net Zero."

"How did the protest go?" Mariela asked. "Have you managed to put my company out of business yet?"

"It was great!" Nyala said. "There were over 500 people there. We're getting the word out—slow but steady." Nyala sat in one of the loungers. "Of course, if the CEO of Panacea Corp would agree to stop the research on embedding chips in adults…"

"You know the board won't let me do that. I already tried to slow it down."

"It just seems ironic that I know the CEO of Panacea Corp, and it doesn't do me any good. I'm stuck protesting instead and hoping Elliat decides to cover it."

Amaya sank into an overstuffed lounger with a deep sigh. "I'm so glad the protest is over."
~~~~~

"I convinced her to go," Nyala explained. "Although she would probably say coerced."

"True," Amaya nodded. "Despite my better judgment, and in spite of the heat that is still making my skin prickle, I spent the entire afternoon holding a sign." A deep sigh escaped her. "I even shouted, 'Don't be a hero, stay net zero!'"

Mariela sat at the conference table and pulled up the mini-screen. A few taps and the digi-windows switched from clear to opaque. She punched codes into the mini-screen and a still image of Elliat's avatar with his chin up and hands on his hips floated awkwardly in the black space of the digi-windows. At least Elliat was wearing a shirt. A countdown timer in the corner of the screen showed one minute and thirteen seconds until the newscast.

Nyala tucked her feet under her in the lounger. "Georgia and Hank had better get here soon or they're going to miss it."

As if on cue, the door to the library opened and Georgia and Hank hurried in. Amoco, in his paisley vest and stovepipe hat, trailed not far behind. They took seats in the second row of loungers.

Nyala leaned around her lounger to talk to them. "Hurry up and get settled. It's about to begin."

Some tacky graphics frolicked on the screen to the intro jingle to Elliat's program. Mariela chewed on a nail.

The library door opened once more, and Mariela glanced over her shoulder. Her heart skipped a beat when she saw the man with the overgrown brown hair and a couple days' worth of stubble.

"Did I miss it?" he asked.

Mariela sighed. Cooper was back just in time.

Multiple people called out greetings as they got up to shake hands with or hug Cooper.

"Welcome back!"

"Look what the cat dragged in!"

"You're just in time!"

"When did you get back?"

Mariela waited until last. Seeing Cooper lifted her spirits despite everything that had happened. Not having to take care of his dogs anymore made her even happier. She hugged him tight. "Your mangy flea-ridden mutts still have fleas."

Cooper laughed and took the lounger closest to the door.

On the windows, the introductory sequence finished playing and the newscast cut to a shot of Elliat sitting with a serious-looking man in a white lab jacket. Mariela paced behind the row of loungers.

"Loyal viewers will know," Elliat said, "that they can count on me to have the most interesting and highest quality news. News that no one else has." Elliat leaned toward the screen, one elbow on his knee, and looked directly at the camera. "But today, we are bringing you news that may be more monumental, more consequential in its implications, than anything we have ever brought you before. I'm here with the CEO of Bo Place, a chip research and pod warehousing company. Bo Place has long lived in the shadow of the much larger and better-known Panacea Corp. Well, that is sure to change after today."

Mariela fought off the urge to yell at the screen.

Elliat wore his most serious expression as he turned to the equally serious CEO of Bo Place. The CEO was someone that Mariela had met before, but she didn't remember much about him. He was somewhat forgettable. Bo Place was the sort of business that Panacea Corp would have extended a hand to back in the day. Sure, Bo Place was Panacea Corp's primary competitor in virtual reality, but they were small enough that they weren't much of a competitor. With only 200 million people in their metaverse, they were probably too small even for acquisition. Now they would be a major player in the field. With chip replacement technology that could be used in adults, Bo Place wouldn't just be a rival, it would be superior.

Mariela refocused on the interview.

The CEO was explaining how the technology worked using business-speak. "This is pioneering and innovative state-of-the-art technology," the man said. "Adults with neutralized chips and virtual reality neophytes who have never before experienced full immersion will both be able to live embedded in the metaverse."

"Can you tell us some more about the technology and what it is based on?" Elliat asked.

"Well, the origins of the technology are an interesting story."

It was highly unlikely that the story would turn out to be interesting.

The CEO continued, "It is based on the noxious substance that was recently used to create a viral transmission between infected chips."

Mariela drew a quick breath. She had been wrong. The story *was* interesting.

"You mean the substance that affected millions of chip users and led to the chips being disabled?" Elliat asked.

The man shook his head, as if to ward off Elliat's negative comments. "Yes. A consultant working with our staff altered the substance so that it is no longer noxious, but instead facilitates entry into a metaverse."

What consultant was he talking about? Viola was the only person other than Amoco who would have access to the substance and the skills to alter it, but she was in prison. Was it possible that she had somehow worked out an arrangement with Bo Place to do consulting with them from prison?

"How does it work?" Elliat asked.

"Once the solution is injected, it alters the recipient's DNA to provide a connection to the digital world. Because it changes the person's DNA, it gets rid of the problem of chip burn and other chip failures."

Mariela scoffed. They may have solved one problem, but no doubt they were creating others.

Elliat's grin stretched from ear to ear. "This is excellent news—I'm sure I'm not the only one who is beyond excited about this development. But let me ask you—I've heard that once a person takes the shot, they can never leave Panacea—I mean, they can never leave the metaverse again."

The executive had the smallest twitch under his eye at the mention of Panacea, but he quickly recovered. "You are correct. The altered DNA allows for a direct connection to the digital world, but not the solid world. Once the person alters their DNA, there is no going back."

"That sounds like a serious drawback." Elliat frowned. "But who am I kidding?" Elliat amended with a big smile. "I'll be the first to sign up!"

"Elliat," Nyala yelled at the screen, "how could you go so wrong?"

"Elliat always was clear that he wanted to return to his pod," Amaya said. "Just because we don't like it doesn't mean it's not the right thing for him."

Nyala muted the sound using the buttons on her lounger. "If he says something about this being good for the unchipped, I'm going to kill him."

Nyala turned the sound back on. Elliat was mid-sentence. "—some people say this could be good for the unchipped, but others say the unchipped won't know how to navigate in a metaverse. Can you comment on that?"

"Of course," the CEO said.

Nyala huffed and muted the sound again. "I can't listen to this. Amaya, are you ready to go? I've heard enough."

"Let's listen for a bit longer," Amaya said.

Mariela used the mini-screen to turn the sound back on. Nyala wasn't the only one who knew how to mute and unmute.

Elliat said, "You were telling me before we started about how quickly you brought the product to market."

"We got special permission from the Department of Access Technologies to release this product before the product testing was complete. With the chips disabled, and former pod-dwellers struggling to get by in the solid world, the DAT recognized how important it is for our product to be on the market right now."

"So it's not going to kill me, right?"

"Elliat," the man offered a warm smile, "I guarantee you that it's not going to kill you."

CHAPTER 4

Sixteen Days After the Unchipping

Monday

Almost two weeks ago, Cooper was sitting on the other side of the table in this sterile, concrete room. Now Viola was the prisoner, and he was free. Before he had left to visit family in Ireland, Cooper had done everything he could to free Viola, including confessing repeatedly to having disabled the chips. Viola's decisions were at times inscrutable and underhanded, but she didn't deserve to be there.

Viola wore the prison's drab, olive-colored, unshaped digi-skin. Without digi-spray makeup, a blemish or two appeared on her normally flawless skin. Yet she still managed to appear polished, even with prison clothing, blemishes, and restraints that held her arms at an almost impossible angle.

She perked up when she saw him enter the room. "Cooper, why did you wait so long to visit?" she asked.

He sat down at the table, being sure to avoid the invisible security barrier that divided Viola's side of the room from his. He didn't want to make that mistake again.

"I went to Ireland with my mom to visit some family members. I'm going to be looking for a job, so I thought I would go while I still can." What he didn't tell Viola was the real reason he wanted to get away—that he needed space and time for himself after his daughter passed away.

Viola tilted her head to the side, as though she were listening intently. "What type of job are you looking for?"

"I don't know. There's a lot of competition for unchipped jobs right now, so it might be difficult to find something."

"There's no one better than you at so many things. You'll find something easily, I'm sure."

Viola's beguiling smile didn't have the impact on him that it had once had, but he understood why he had been drawn to her all those years ago. "How are you doing in here? I hope you aren't getting beaten up like I did." He rubbed his side where the guard had broken his rib. After two weeks, it had gone from a sharp pang to a dull ache, although the doc said it would be another month or so before it was completely healed. "Or stupidly run into the barrier full force like I did."

"You're my first visitor, so this is my first time dealing with the barrier on this side. It looked exceptionally painful when you ran into it, though, so I've been well-warned."

"You've had no visitors? What about your lawyer?"

"My lawyer doesn't do prisons."

What did Viola mean? "Your lawyer doesn't do prisons?" he repeated.

"No, she doesn't. She's very busy and what's important is that she does courtrooms, and she does them well."

"How's the defense going?"

"It's looking really promising."

Not a day went by where he didn't count his lucky stars that Viola had confessed to a crime that she didn't commit. The idea of going back to prison filled him with dread, but he still felt guilty that Viola was in prison instead of him. If she could get off easy, it might help him deal with some of the guilt about her taking his place. "That's a huge relief," he said.

"Yeah, a forensic lab found evidence of the kill switch in half of the 100 people they biopsied, so she's going to say that I disabled the chips for humanitarian reasons—they'll say my motivation was to protect the infected."

"Well, that *was* the reason the chips were disabled, so that argument makes sense, except for the fact that you didn't disable them."

She shrugged, as though the fact that she was innocent was irrelevant. "My lawyer thinks she can get me a reduced sentence, probably no more than three years. Two with good behavior."

"What?" Three years was a long sentence to serve for a crime she didn't commit. "I should be the one serving it." The dread knotted in his stomach again.

Viola shrugged. "I've accepted my fate."

"Wouldn't it make more sense for your lawyer to clear your name based on the evidence, given that the evidence against you is made up?"

"That would draw attention back to you. Plus, I did a really good job of forging the evidence. I would be offended if anyone could poke holes in it."

It still didn't make any sense to him why Viola had turned herself in to prison and gotten him released. He had turned himself in because he wanted to take responsibility for his actions, but then he had been miserable in prison. When Viola had gotten him out, he tried to say that she was innocent, but no one had believed him. At that point, he wasn't sure that he wanted to take responsibility anymore, either. Prison had been…a nightmare.

"Hey," he asked, "won't the guards see this recording and use it against you?" He felt a considerable amount of panic over the idea that it would also incriminate him.

"You underestimate me, Cooper." Viola smiled. "As you always have."

She had a point. When they dated three years ago, he had certainly underestimated her ruthlessness and how easily she had turned on him. Maybe she had bribed a prison guard to delete the recording. He didn't really need to know.

Viola asked him about the trip to Ireland and how his mom was doing. They talked about inconsequential stuff, like whether his dogs appeared to have missed him and what the weather had been like in Ireland.

Cooper looked at the time projected on the wall of the meeting room. The prison limited their meeting to five minutes, and he had already used up four minutes of it. There were more pressing matters that he wanted to discuss with her than whether his dogs had missed him, so it was time to stop putting it off. He started off with the easiest question.

"How did Bo Place manage to develop the shot that allows people to connect to Panacea so quickly?"

"Bo Place is very well connected. Usually, it takes years to get approval from the Department of Access Technologies for something like this, and lots of clinical trials to make sure there aren't any negative side effects. I don't know how they did it so quickly, but I know they have the resources to make it happen."

"If they're so powerful, why haven't they used that power to take out Panacea Corp?"

"Panacea Corp doesn't have as much political power as Bo Place, but Bo Place can't take Panacea Corp out because it is so popular with consumers. Consumers, all those pod-lifers living in Panacea Corp warehouses, are the company's true power. Bo Place can never attack them directly without something big like a chip replacement technology that will win over consumers."

There wasn't much time left to ask Viola the tough questions—the ones he really wanted to know the answers to. He jumped right in. "Did you help Bo Place develop the shot that allows people to connect to Panacea?"

"Maybe." She shrugged.

His pulse pounded in his temple. Did she have no common sense? "Viola, what did you do?"

"I gave them pieces of the kill switch technology, with the kill switch part removed, and pointed them in the right direction for how to modify it to allow a connection to the metaverse." She showed no signs of regret. "I never had any idea things would move this quickly. It was necessary though, with how much the pod-lifers are hurting right now."

Did Viola really think that helping the pod-lifers was enough of a justification for sharing potentially dangerous information? "What did they promise you in exchange?"

She smiled a half smile. "They promised me the world."

"The world? What does that mean?" Cooper's mind raced. "Wait, are they going to get you out of jail?"

"No, but they have promised to get me a lighter sentence."

"They can do that?"

"They can turn thirty years of prison into three."

"So that's it? Are you getting anything else in exchange for sharing a lethal technology?"

"They were willing to pay handsomely, and when I get out, they have guaranteed me a position as their Research Director for at least ten years following my release. With their new dominant market position, and their already existing political power, I will be much more powerful with them than I was with Panacea Corp."

"And what else?" Viola was a shrewd negotiator who would get every last perk that she could out of the deal.

"I also get a security detail, unlimited purchases within their metaverse, and my own digi-dine and other personal staff."

"But you have to take the shot?"

"Yes, the entire company, other than the people who are manufacturing it, have to take the shot." She glanced to the side. "It's not my favorite part of the deal, but I can live with it."

It sounded like she was going from one prison to another.

The clock buzzed. Time was up. The door clicked behind Cooper. Guards entered and grabbed his elbow. "Times up, fella."

"But I have more questions." Cooper pulled his arm from the guard. "Just a minute more."

"Sorry, rules are rules. It's time to go."

Cooper's broken rib hurt as he pulled back against the guards leading him out of the room. He turned back to look at Viola, still seated on the other side of the table, her expression blank except for a wry smile. Was this really what she wanted?

~~~~~

Amaya hid in the shadow of the bushes near the sidewalk. Through the large restaurant windows, she watched the diners eating candlelit dinners. If only Li had chosen a less fancy place. This one was more expensive than she could easily afford. Letting Li pay for her wasn't an acceptable alternative, either.

She smoothed her skirt. Maybe she should have programmed her digi-skin dress to be a trendier outfit. Not that she could afford the program for a trendy dress right now. She lived in the inner ring of the city because she wanted working food processors and disaster-proof housing, but the high rents didn't leave much left over for doing stuff like going out to eat at expensive restaurants or paying for the digi-skin fashions of the hour.

"Excuse me." Amaya startled when a woman touched her elbow. It couldn't have been more than a couple hours since the dress the woman was wearing had first showed up in Amaya's feed. "I see you have an EveryThing," the woman said.

Amaya placed her hand on the thin film wrapped around her forearm. The electronics embedded in the clear film were barely visible. In the past it was a clear sign that she was unchipped, but with the chips disabled lots of people had started wearing them.

"I've been trying to find an EveryThing," the woman continued, "but every place I've looked is sold out. Can you believe one place tried to sell me a *phone?* I think it was made back in the Digital Dark Ages, like in 2059 or something. Apparently, they had a bunch that had been molding in a warehouse somewhere for half a century."

"That's unusual." Did this woman have a point or was she just rambling? Amaya looked down the road. No sign of Li yet. She turned back
~~~~~

to the woman. "I wouldn't even know how to use a phone."

"So true." The woman touched Amaya's arm again. "I really want an EveryThing. Where did you get yours?"

"Oh, I've had it for a while now. My chip was disabled." It was the truth, but Amaya left out a lot of details—like that she had purposefully disabled her chip. There was something about the woman that Amaya didn't trust.

"Oh, you poor thing." The woman reached her arms wide open and drew Amaya into a tight embrace. "I'm so sorry you had to go through that."

"It's okay." Amaya's arms hung stiffly by her side. "I've gotten used to it." Maybe the woman would stop hugging her now.

"That's great news." The woman pulled back, but kept her hands on Amaya's elbows. "You have a head start over all of us in getting used to this new world then."

"I guess so. I'm not sure what to think about it."

"Of course, dear. We all feel confused." The woman finally let go of Amaya's elbows, but then she leaned in close and lowered her voice. "One thing I know for sure, though, is that the unchipped did this as revenge."

No wonder Amaya didn't like her. She was one of those people who blamed the unchipped for anything that went wrong. Amaya considered saying something to the woman to clarify that it wasn't some plot by the unchipped. She settled for asking a question. "I thought it was to stop a viral chip infection that was potentially fatal?"

The woman arched her eyebrows and snorted. "You don't believe that crap, do you?"

"Well, it made sense, with how they were able to control the cryogens and all." It wasn't a very eloquent argument, but she couldn't reveal most of what she knew, so it didn't leave her many options to make her point.

The woman snorted again. "I don't know what that has to do with it. I'm sure you know how the unchipped are. They complained about not being eligible for the basic advertising income, they complained about not being qualified for most jobs—it's like they wanted everything handed to them. And when that didn't happen, they took it out on people who had chips. I promise you, sweetheart, they wanted revenge. Pure and simple."

"I don't think that's what happened." Amaya questioned herself even as she was saying it. She and Cooper had disabled the embedded chips, and they were both unchipped. Maybe it had been easier for them to delete the chips because they could get by perfectly fine without them.

She pushed the thought away. They had taken out the chips to address a threat. It had been clear-cut and necessary, right? Amaya took a step back from the woman. "I'm sure that's not what happened." She spoke with more conviction this time.

The woman sneered. "Can you even afford to eat here?" She looked Amaya up and down and then brushed past her into the restaurant.

"Amaya," Li came running up and kissed her on the cheek. "Sorry I'm late. I can't figure out how to get anywhere anymore."

"No problem." It would serve that woman right if they had disabled the chips just for revenge on her. It would show that self-important, small-minded...

"Are you okay?" Li asked.

Amaya startled. "Yeah. I just...there was a woman..." She didn't know how to explain how the woman had talked to her, because Li wouldn't get it. In fact, Li wasn't all that different from the woman. Maybe Li was better at hiding it, but she didn't respect the unchipped any more than the woman did. "Li, I'm sorry you came out here for nothing, but I can't do this."

She ran away before Li could see the tears in her eyes.

CHAPTER 5

Seventeen Days After The Unchipping
Tuesday

Hank was glad to be back at the estate after a long night helping pod-lifers get rehabbed in the solid world. Georgia fell behind as they trudged up the steps to the front door of the large estate house, her body sagging more with each step. She had been running all night long, and it had left her exhausted. The bright early morning sun beat onto their backs and cast long shadows on the steps in front of them.

They were still having lots of new people coming in, people who had spent the last weeks waiting in their pods before being evacuated, not at risk of bodily harm as the pod machinery kept the life support running, but with nothing to do and no contact with other people. But following the announcement last night about Bo Place's new shot, it was the first time that more people had left than arrived.

Hank pulled open the solid door to the estate. He wasn't looking forward to the long trip back to his place. Maybe he would just find a couch to crash on here. He missed the days when he and Georgia would curl up in a bed together, but at least she was talking to him again and they were spending time together. That was something.

The estate's entry hall was a grand room that spanned from the front of the house to the back, with a sweeping staircase on one side and double glass-paned doors into the library on the other. Voices in a heated conversation came through the library doors.

Mariela's voice carried out into the entryway. "I thought you enjoyed being in the solid world."

Hank peered through the glass panes. An obviously upset Mariela was arguing with Sofi, who appeared equally upset.

It didn't look like he would be having a quiet moment to wind down with Georgia. Or be able to sleep on the couch. Georgia reached for the knob of the library door.

"Should we leave them alone?" Hank asked her.

"Nonsense. They've always been open with us about everything.

Let's go in."

"Okay." Hank didn't mind arguments, but he had always dealt with them in the past with a sort of aggressive sarcasm. He was trying to be nicer, but it was new territory for him. "What do I say?" He knew it was a stupid question, but Georgia never minded stupid questions.

"Just listen. If you think of something helpful, say that."

Now he really felt stupid. It was an obvious answer. Anyone less polite than Georgia would have rolled their eyes at his question. "So that's it?"

"Pretend like you're doing an anthropological study of how two sisters who have lived very different lives interact. As a researcher, you will be watching and not participating."

He nodded. "Okay. I can do that." It was like playing a game of football where you weren't allowed to tackle anyone.

Georgia opened the door and Hank followed her through. Sofi sat stick-straight on the couch in front of the fireplace, while Mariela had one hand propped on the mantel and the other on her hip. Mariela and Sofi glanced at them before continuing their animated conversation.

"Didn't you hear," Mariela said, "about a month ago, some pod warehouses had malfunctions and all the life support stopped working?"

"No." Sofi's voice was flat.

Hank sat at the end of the conference table. It was a good observation post. He had a view of the two sisters at the other end of the room, but was far enough away to not draw attention to himself. Georgia sat down beside him.

"How could you *not* have heard about that?" Mariela asked, clearly exasperated. "It was huge news. Elliat, for one, covered it extensively."

"It may surprise you to hear this, but most pod-dwellers don't follow solid world news. We just don't find the solid world to be all that relevant to us."

"How is a catastrophe at a pod warehouse not relevant to you?"

Hank sat completely still, hoping the women wouldn't interrupt their conversation. Just listening was interesting. No need for his sarcastic quips to make things livelier.

Sofi stared at the wall in the opposite direction from Mariela. "If it's not related to the metaverse, then it's solid world news."

Mariela wasn't giving in. "But you still exist in the solid world, even if you ignore it. And my point was, if something like that happens to you,

you won't be able to leave Panacea."

"Mariela, I just don't think you are going to understand this."

Mariela didn't reply right away. She appeared to be considering. Was she giving in? Worn down by her own sister?

"I thought you enjoyed being in the solid world?" Mariela asked.

Apparently, she thought that repeating her previous argument was an effective strategy.

"I do," Sofi said. "I like how great my food tastes. I've also been adjusting the thermostat so that I can feel both hot and cold, but this isn't my home. Opali's in Panacea, my house is there, and everything I do is there. My life is there."

"But I'll never get to see you again if you go back to the metaverse. And Dad is here."

"Dad is fine with me going back." Sofi crossed her arms. "Because *he* supports me."

Ouch. Sofi was clearly delivering a message to Mariela there.

"Is it because you're unable to walk?" Mariela asked. "I found a good doctor who might be able to help you."

Sofi being unable to walk was news to Hank. He noted it and continued with his observation.

Sofi's reply was full of pique. "Mariela, it's not about being unable to walk. Panacea is my home. It's where I belong. I know you have a hard time understanding this, but Opali's my daughter, and now that I can be with my daughter again, I plan to take advantage of it." Sofi's voice got louder and angrier. "And since you deleted Opali, you have no business telling me what to do or how to live."

Another effective message delivered. Sofi was clearly pulling ahead in the argument.

"I'm sorry. Please…just think about it." Mariela was not conceding, despite her obvious losing position.

"I've already thought about it, and it's decided." Sofi crossed her arms. "Julio will be here any minute now to take me back to my pod."

Sofi had clearly won the argument. Mariela was quiet in defeat, but Hank could almost hear the hissing of steam coming off her head. Georgia left the sidelines to put her hand on Mariela's back.

"Mariela, we'll go together to visit Sofi whenever we can, but it looks like she's made up her mind." Georgia's role at this time appeared to offer comfort to the defeated and smooth things over.

"I know." Mariela wiped away a tear. "It's just that I'll miss you," she said to Sofi. Mariela squeezed into the lounger by her sister and put her arm around her.

Sofi was crying as well. "I'll miss you, too," she said.

Hank was witnessing a reconciliation in progress. Georgia sat down in a nearby chair. It looked like her eyes were moist as well. For a full minute, no one said anything, but there was a lot of sniffling.

"Hank," Mariela said, "why are you staring at us?"

His anthropological study had been discovered. He played it casual and said the first thing that came to mind. "I heard that Nikky is going into the Bo Place metaverse," he said.

"Really?" Mariela asked. "I thought that they lived in Panacea before. Why didn't they go back there?"

"They couldn't afford the shot."

"I thought it was free?"

If Hank had been writing his observations in a notebook like a true anthropologist, he would have noted that Mariela appeared surprised.

"Only for people who agree to go into Bo Place's metaverse and live in one of Bo Place's pod warehouses."

Georgia spoke up. "They're charging outrageous amounts for the shots for people who want to go into Panacea instead of Bo Place."

Mariela's face turned redder than Hank had ever seen it. "Do you know what that will do to Panacea Corp's business?"

He had a pretty good idea—good enough that he didn't need Mariela to spell it out for him. Panacea Corp's business would suffer; there was no doubt about it.

Mariela's face stayed red, but she seemed content to mull things over privately, because the conversation turned to dull and non-controversial topics. The anthropological study was over.

CHAPTER 6

Three Weeks After The Unchipping

Friday

The wood-paneled courtroom smelled musty. Amaya sat with Cooper in a row close to the front. Behind them, the courtroom was filling up. Elliat was seated in the back, and some of the Bo Place people were seated about halfway back in the courtroom. To keep out all the people who blamed Viola for disabling the chips, the audience was limited to journalists and people with a direct connection to Viola. Amaya and Cooper were there as friends of Viola. It was a bit of a stretch for both of them to say they were friends of Viola's, but they might be the closest thing she had to friends at the moment.

The trial was being simulcast by almost every broadcaster in the world. Everyone wanted to know about this woman who had been charged with disabling the chips. The courtroom walls showed rotating up-close shots of the judge's bench, the witness stand, the jury, and the audience. The jury had been randomly drawn from a national pool of names, with each juror's picture displayed in the jury booth.

"Didn't you tell me that you had taken in a pod-lifer?" Cooper asked Amaya. "How are they doing?"

"Nikky went into the Bo Place metaverse yesterday. Despite Nyala's forceful objections."

Everything had been moving so quickly. The shot had only been available for a few days and already so many people were taking it.

"Nyala won't be happy to hear that Bren is going into Panacea tomorrow."

"Oh really? I guess I shouldn't be surprised. I remember how when we first met him, he said he wanted to go into the metaverse because his lifestyle is so physically challenging and he's getting older."

"And his wife has been working as a surrogate for so long—he said she can't wait to give it up."

"Oh right. With the basic advertising income, she can retire from surrogacy."

"Sometimes it feels like Nyala is fighting an uphill battle trying to get people to not take the shot," Cooper said.

"But at least Nyala can always count on the two of us not taking it."

"Somehow, I feel like that isn't enough to make her happy."

Amaya smiled. "She's happiest when she's unhappy, so it all works out in the end."

Cooper laughed. The statement had just enough truth to be funny.

Amoco came dashing up and slipped into the seat beside Amaya. He placed a hand on his chest and took deep breaths. "It is a relief that I am not tardy."

Cooper leaned forward to look at Amoco. "Are you here to see what happens to your former rival and colleague?" Cooper asked.

"I should be quite saddened to see Viola be sentenced to prison for a crime she did not commit. I believe, however, that we will not have our curiosity regarding the final outcome satisfied today, as surely this trial will last many days."

"Did they ask you to testify?" Amaya asked. "I was thinking they might want your expertise."

"I declined to testify. Viola did an outstanding job fabricating the evidence against herself. As a result, I found it would be difficult to dispute. I can see small flaws in what she did, but it would be complicated to convince a jury that those flaws are meaningful. I could have brought in other evidence to clear her, but only at the risk of incriminating myself, which I was unwilling to do."

"Sorry I'm late." Bren slid onto the bench next to Amoco. He ran a hand over his short, wiry hair that was peppered with plenty of salt. A new set of advertising tattoos covered his arms.

Amaya raised her eyebrows at Bren. "Are you a friend of Viola's?"

"Not that I know of." Bren leaned in her direction and spoke in a low voice. "I'm here for the same reason that you are."

"To support Viola?"

"The drama."

Amaya opened her mouth to object, but then closed it. Bren was right—she was there for the drama. "But how…? You're not a direct connection of Viola's."

"You're wrong. I became friends with her when she was at the Stafford Estate before The Unchipping." He smiled. "I knew that woman would be full of drama, and figured that if there was ever anyone I wanted to be friends with, it was her." He gave a mischievous grin. "She has not disappointed."

Amaya had to agree. When it came to drama, Viola didn't disappoint.

A bailiff positioned himself in front of the judge's bench. "All rise," he said.

The presentation of evidence took most of the day, but didn't go into multiple days like Amoco had predicted. At some point during the day, Elliat had showed up and taken a spot in the back of the room. Amaya nodded at him, but that was it.

The jury spent an hour in deliberations, and finally the bailiff announced they were ready to present their findings. It didn't look good for Viola—the evidence clearly pointed to her. It was as thorough as Amoco had said.

The judge looked solemn when he returned. Amaya studied the faces of the jurors as they filed back in, but she didn't find any clue in them about the verdict. The bailiff asked Viola to stand. He repeated the charges against her. Viola looked impeccable as usual, but she also looked pale and unsteady with the slightest tremor in her hands.

"Foreperson of the jury," the judge said, "on the multiple counts of felony aggravated destruction of property, how do you find?"

"We find," the foreperson glanced to the side, "we find the defendant…not guilty."

The courtroom immediately filled with the sound of people murmuring in shock.

"I knew it had to be fake," Elliat proclaimed from the back of the room.

In the midst of all the turmoil, the judge pounded his gavel. Amaya couldn't take her eyes off Viola. Out of everyone in the room, Viola looked the most shocked of all.

~~~~~~

A group of journalists pushed in around the Bo Place executives gathered with Viola on the courthouse steps. Cooper didn't want to wait to hear the empty comments from the executives. He had had enough of Viola's manipulations for today. For a lifetime, really.

"Hang on, Cooper," Amaya said, "let's see what they have to say."

"I also prefer to hear what they have to say," Amoco added.
~~~~~~

"I'm staying, no matter what," Bren said.

Cooper shrugged. It wouldn't kill him to stick around for a while longer if the others wanted to.

"If I may have your attention for a quick announcement," the guy who Elliat had interviewed about the shot said. The man had traded his lab coat for a high-end suit. The exo-cams swirled around him, jostling for the best shot. "We'll keep this short so that Viola can do her out-processing and get some well-deserved rest."

Viola nodded at him with a smile. She was beaming. It was like she had no shame at all.

"But before we let her go," the man continued, "we at Bo Place are pleased to announce that Viola Mason has agreed to work for us. We thought it might be a while before she could start, but we are happy to hear that she will be able to start today. In her new position, she will be the Sovereign Ruler of the Bo Place metaverse, answerable only to the board of directors. She will have authority over all denizens of the metaverse and all Bo Place employees."

That duplicitous, manipulative, conniving…Sovereign Ruler—what did that mean, anyway? Authority over everyone in the Bo Place metaverse? It sounded like Viola really did have her dreams come true and was given 'the world.'

"I confess I did not see that coming," Amoco said in a flat voice.

"Could *anyone* have predicted that she would become the ruler of the Bo Place metaverse?" Amaya asked.

"I'm impressed," Bren said.

"Come on, let's go," Cooper said to them. The sooner they got out of there, the better.

"Cooper," Amoco said, "I should like to congratulate Viola on her good fortune before we leave."

"I'd also like to talk to her," Amaya said. "Come on, Cooper. Maybe she misled you, but it won't kill you to shake her hand."

They were right—there was no need to let Viola upset him. She was just behaving like she always did, and if he ever believed anything she said, then that was his fault. He shrugged. "Okay, let's go."

"Great! I want to congratulate her on pulling off the perfect scam—" Bren smiled as he spoke. "Confess to a crime and end up becoming the Sovereign Ruler of Bo Place. That takes talent!"

They headed back into the courthouse. They walked down the main hallway, checking each side hallway as they walked. In the second hallway to the left, Viola was in an intense conversation with the lab coat guy. "It was supposed to be three years." She seemed angry. The lab coat guy said something that Cooper couldn't hear. Viola looked like she was going to reply, but then caught sight of them.

"Hey you all!" She had the nerve to smile at them like they were long-lost friends. "So what about that for the most unexpected trial outcome of the century?"

Amoco shook his head. "I believe the 2098 Archibald Decision could be considered more unexpected…"

"Thank you, Amoco. I'm sure you're right." Viola turned to the lab coat guy. "Could you leave us alone for a moment?"

"Certainly," he said. Somehow he managed to convey both authority over and deference to Viola. He nodded to them and then headed down the hall and disappeared around the corner.

"Congratulations, Viola," Amaya said. "You did something that I never would have had the courage to do."

Cooper sniffed. Viola had gone to prison for a few weeks and then got a cushy job where she would have power over lots of people. It wasn't courageous at all.

"My highest regards," Amoco said, "for both your skill in creating evidence and in not having that evidence held against you."

"I second that comment!" Bren said.

"Thank you both," Viola replied.

It didn't even seem to make Viola nervous that Amoco was admitting what she did while they were still in the courthouse. She was that confident in herself.

There was an awkward pause. Everyone looked at him. Were they expecting him to say something? Praise her skills in fabricating evidence? Refer to her as courageous? Congratulate her ability to claw her way up in the world?

"Cooper," she said, "can I speak to you alone?"

Cooper considered saying no, but he had some things he wanted to say to her. He nodded instead. He followed her partway down the hallway, where Viola pushed open the door to a room that looked like a waiting room. There were green plastic couches and a drink dispenser. This must have been the jury room back in the day when juries were on-site.

Cooper didn't wait for Viola to start speaking or even turn around. As soon as he heard the door click behind them, he said, "So you got everything you wanted. No prison time, and now you're the supreme ruler of the world's second largest metaverse?"

"The Sovereign Ruler."

"Sovereign Ruler? What does that even mean?"

"Cooper, look, I'm sorry. I intended to do my prison time. I'm not sure what happened. Maybe Bo Place's 'persuasion' was too effective, because the agreement was that I would get three years."

Cooper sat down with a thud on a hard plastic couch. "You didn't do anything in the first place, so it's ridiculous for us to argue about you not serving your time. It just upsets me that you weren't honest with me."

Viola leaned on the drink dispenser. "No matter whether you think I did it on purpose or not, I have permanently taken the heat off of you. Even though I got off, the appearance that I personally benefited from disabling the chips makes me look even more guilty. No one will ever believe that I am innocent, so consequently, they will never think that you are guilty." She looked down her nose at him, gloating. "I've achieved my goal."

"Viola, I know you helped me get out of prison, and I hated that place so I can't thank you enough, but I also feel that you betrayed me again. I wish you had told me what you were doing. On some level, it seems like you told me what you wanted me to hear and made me think that you were doing this for me, all the while you were doing it for yourself."

She sniffed. "I never expected to get out so soon. I thought I would serve three years, or two with good behavior. I wanted to do the time because I knew that would be important to you, but for whatever reason, I got out sooner. And I can't complain too much. That place was a hellhole."

She was right. In the twenty-four hours that Cooper had been in the prison, he had been beaten up so badly that it broke a rib. It was selfish of him to feel betrayed that she got out, especially considering she didn't commit the crime she was imprisoned for. She had survived in there longer than he had. He knew she was hoping her sentence would be light, so why was he so upset with her? "I just want to feel like you're being truthful with me, and not using me as a pawn in some larger game that you're playing."

"I would never use you. In fact, there's something important that I would like to ask you." She took a deep breath and stopped leaning on the drink dispenser. "Please join me. I need the support of someone like you. You would be like the Royal Consort, except that you would be the Ruler Consort. I trust your opinion more than anyone else's, and I could use someone like you to advise me. Plus, it would make my world perfect. There's no one I would rather have by my side than you."

Him, Cooper O'Connor, as the Ruler Consort to the Sovereign Ruler? It was a ridiculous idea. "You know I can't do that." Did Viola really think that he would go with her?

"You could do it if you wanted to." She stared at him. "I just need to find something to make it worth your while."

"That will be difficult to do."

"Let me try."

"I don't know how I could stop you." Viola always did what she wanted.

"I know you're not motivated by money, and I don't think by power either, but I'm sure there is something I can find that you want."

"I want the people in my life to stop being so undependable."

"I'm going to figure it out." She snapped her fingers. "I'll figure out what you want."

Had she heard anything he had said?

CHAPTER 7

Three Days Until the Ghost Trial

Monday

"I've programmed the fountain to start at the meeting time," Mariela said. "Opali didn't say what it was about?" she asked Georgia.

Georgia and Hank sat across the conference table from Mariela in the library of the estate, along with Amoco and Amaya. A large marble basin with a copper rim rested in the center of the table.

"No," Georgia said. "When I ran into Opali in Panacea earlier today, she just said that she wanted to talk to you, Amoco, and Amaya as soon as possible. I have no clue what's going on."

Mariela checked the time. They still had a minute until the meeting started. "How's the pod-lifer rehab going?"

"It's slowed down quite a bit. People are either taking the shot or getting placed in a home. We have only a couple dozen people left."

It was nice to hear things were slowing down. Mariela had been worried that the incessant work was taking a toll on Georgia. She seemed so drained lately.

"With the extra time, I've been teaching Amaya martial arts," Hank said.

"I'm starting to feel like I'm getting the hang of it," Amaya said. "Hank, whenever you have time for it, I'm looking forward to our next lesson."

"After the meeting, then?" Hank asked.

"Great," Amaya replied. "It's time for the meeting to start."

A mercury-like liquid oozed out into the basin. After the basin filled, Opali's image formed in the liquid.

"Opali, can you hear us?" Mariela asked.

Opali looked like she was six again. Sofi must have reset her age after returning to Panacea. "I hear you," she said. Opali's image, formed out of the silvery liquid, was about two feet tall and her voice was small to match.

Mariela's role in deleting Opali over a month ago continued to fill her with guilt. Amaya and Nyala seemed to think she didn't care—like she was a heartless automaton making decisions without a care for how it affected others. But there wasn't a day that went by where she didn't feel guilty about how her decision had affected Opali and Sofi. Even though it was concerning that Opali had mysteriously reappeared, Mariela also felt a sense of relief.

"Opali, I'm glad you're back." As she said it, Mariela realized how true it was. Maybe she had cared more about Opali than she realized. "So, why are we meeting today?" she asked.

"The older ghosts tol' me to make the meeting," Opali said. "Auntie Mariely, please don't be mad at me 'cuz they made me. I'm going home now."

"The older ghosts?" Amaya asked, but Opali had already disappeared from the fountain.

"Maaariela!" A ghost that looked exactly like the former CEO of Panacea Corp formed in the fountain. Just like Liam Price, the executive that he had been modeled after, the ghost looked every inch the part of a modern executive, even when only two feet tall in the viscous fluid of the fountain.

The blood pounded in Mariela's ears and her mouth went dry. "Please don't tell me that's LP," Mariela said to the people in the room. In her previous interactions with LP, he had blackmailed her and attempted to kill her boss. If he was aware that she had deleted him, then there could only be one conclusion. LP was out for revenge.

"Mariela," LP put his hands on his hips and looked straight at her, "I assume you haven't forgotten me, although human memory is exceedingly fallible. I'm sure you remember how you deleted me and the other advanced LP100s who were my protégés. I'll have you know I personally have no hard feelings. It was just one of those things that happen when you have ambitious people trying to get ahead. But..." LP paused, letting the tension build, "there are other digital beings out there who do resent that you deleted them, and they are demanding justice."

"Justice?" Amaya's voice squeaked. "LP, what are you saying? And how did you come back?"

"Justice for the wrongs that the three of you—I'm talking about you, Amoco, and Mariela—have perpetrated against the advanced model ghosts when you deleted us." The fountain shimmered. "We want justice, but the exact nature of that justice will be determined upon review of your crimes."

"LP, you don't have any legal authority over us," Mariela said.

LP scoffed. "That may be true, but there are a lot of people entering the Panacea and Bo Place metaverses right now who are not able to leave. We could certainly make life difficult for them."

Mariela was struck by the audacity of what LP was proposing. "Are you threatening to hurt innocent people to force us to do what you want?"

"It sounds unnecessarily ugly when you put it that way, but yes."

"What exactly do you want?"

"The three of you will enter Panacea and attend a hearing to determine the punishment for your crimes. If you do as I say, no harm will befall the pod-lifers currently in Panacea and Bo Place."

"But the only way for us to enter Panacea is to take the shot," Amaya said. "We won't be able to leave again."

"Not my problem to worry about. But I am also generous, and I will give you forty-eight hours to put your affairs in order." He brushed his hands together as if wiping dirt off them. "That's settled then. I'll see you in forty-eight hours, because you will do the right thing. Humans have such odd hang-ups about the loss of life. It's quite a weak spot, as humans can always be manipulated through their attachment to human life. Well, I best be off." He saluted them with a dismissive flip of his hand. "Bye bye!"

"Wait! LP!" Mariela slumped into her chair. The image was gone. "I can't believe he's back."

"I can't believe he wants us to take the shot," Amaya said, her eyes wide like a startled deer. "He can't expect us to enter Panacea forever."

"Do we have any other alternatives?" Mariela asked.

"Do we believe he will follow through on his threat?" Georgia asked.

"LP had his own creator thrown out of a heli," Mariela said. "I think we can assume that he will follow through on what he says."

"Do the ghosts have the power to harm humans?" Hank asked.

"If they've hacked the systems that run the pods," Mariela said, "then it would be fairly easy for them to harm pod-lifers."

"I don't want to do this," Amaya said. "I have my cat and my clients. I can't do it. When will I ever see my family again if I go into the metaverse?"

Georgia appeared uneasy. "Why is LP blaming the three of you? *Did* you all delete the LP100 model ghosts?"

"*Of course* we deleted the LP100 model ghosts." Mariela gestured at the fountain where LP had appeared. "Can't you see what a threat LP is?"

"You used our trip to Area 52 as cover to delete the ghosts?" Georgia's face turned scarlet. Mariela may have underestimated how angry she would be.

"It was the only way to do it," Mariela said. "Plus, the maintenance trip was real. It needed to be done."

"Georgia," Amaya said, "I didn't have anything to do with it. I was an unwitting pawn in this whole fiasco. Blame me for disabling the chips, but don't blame me for deleting the LP100s."

"You disabled the chips?" Hank asked.

"Hank, how could you not know that?" Amaya asked.

"What's wrong with you all?" Hank's lip curled into a sneer. "Do you hate technology? You made my life miserable, and the lives of countless other people miserable! What did we get out of deleting the LP100 model ghosts and disabling the chips?"

Georgia was scowling, though her voice remained calm. "I don't know how I feel about this. I want to help you, but I need to process what you just told me." Georgia was typically slow to anger, and it made Mariela uncomfortable to see her so angry.

"In my book," Hank threw up his hands, "you're on your own. The LP100 model ghosts can throw you in jail for all I care. It would serve you right for what you've done." Hank stood up. "I'm tired and I'm going to get some sleep."

"I'm going to get some sleep, too." Georgia walked out of the library with Hank.

Mariela stared at them as they left. Hank and Georgia had always been so much a part of everything they had done, it didn't seem right for them not to be a part of this. She shook off the feeling. She needed to concentrate and figure out a plan. "Amoco, do you have any ideas for what we can do?"

"There is a larger question here which we are not addressing. How did the LP100 models come back after they were deleted? I can assure you that no backup copies remained after we deleted them. So how did they return to existence? It will not do any good to delete them again until we understand how they carried out their return."

Mariela nodded. "If we can figure out how they managed to come back and stop them from rebuilding, then we can delete them again."

"But the only way to delete them is using Server AA in Area 52," Amaya said, "and we don't have access to that server farm anymore. The border with Area 52 has been completely sealed."

"That deputy—the one in Area 52—what was his name?" Mariela asked.

"Dan," Amaya said.

Following his role in Grace's death, Mariela disliked Dan. But she wasn't beyond using him if it suited her. "Didn't we leave a specialized communication device with him? The one that we used the server to install?"

"Yes."

"Do you think you could walk him through the steps to delete the ghosts?"

"No. I got the impression that he doesn't know much about computers. Even if he did, the technology that Server AA uses is at least thirty years more advanced than the 2005 tech that he's used to."

"Amaya, please contact him to see if he's willing to try," Mariela pleaded.

"Here's another idea. Your mother might be able to do it. I'll contact Dan and see if he can reach June for us."

"Good idea," Mariela said. Her heart warmed at the thought of speaking with her mother again.

"But it won't do any good if we can't figure out how the LP100s managed to rebuild."

"I am pondering the possibilities," Amoco said, "and it appears to me the most likely option is that they used a Faraday cage to protect a backup copy of their code and keep it from being deleted."

Mariela's understanding of the technology wasn't as advanced as Amoco's and Amaya's, but from what she knew of Faraday cages and their ability to block electronic signals, it sounded plausible that one could be used to hide a backup copy of the code from the program they used to delete the ghosts. "You think it's possible the ghosts used a Faraday cage to protect their code?"

"Correct," Amoco said.

"Would it be possible to make a Faraday cage within the metaverse?" Amaya asked.

"A place protected from electronic signals that is created from electronic signals?" Amoco's brow furrowed. "It would be an odd sort of Faraday cage, but I can't say for sure that it is impossible."

Amaya stood and paced. "So we need to find this Faraday cage, which could be in the solid world or could be in the Panacea metaverse, then we need to disable the cage and get June to use the Area 52 servers to delete the LP100 model ghosts from the SOUP server network while also covering June's tracks so that no one knows we were involved. Is that it?"

"And we have forty-eight hours to do it all in," Mariela added.

"What happens if at the end of the forty-eight hours we still haven't figured out a way to permanently delete the ghosts?" Amaya asked.

"Then we take the shot," Mariela said. Her body felt heavier as soon as she said it. It felt like a belt was squeezing the air out of her lungs. "Are we in agreement on this?"

Amoco nodded.

Amaya hesitated, then took a deep breath and nodded. "I don't like it. I'm still mad that you all used me last time to delete the ghosts, but the stakes are higher now. I'm not going to take a chance on LP harming any humans. If that means deleting the ghosts or taking the shot to prevent that from happening, then that's what I will do."

~~~~~

Dan had shot and killed someone that Amaya cared deeply about—it didn't matter that it was an accident. He was the last person that she wanted to talk to. Amaya had tried to pawn the phone call off on Amoco—he actually liked Dan, unlike the rest of them—but Amoco had said he was late to feed his pigeons and hurried off. Amaya reminded herself that Dan could be helpful sometimes, and he was the only way to get a hold of June in the secluded and technologically backwards Area 52.

Mariela placed something that looked like an old communication device on the library table and handed Amaya a piece of paper with numbers on it. "I have to go update the guards," Mariela said. "Please let my mom know that if she keeps the phone, I'll contact her soon."

Amaya punched in the contact numbers for the device in Area 52 that used the Panacea server to work similar to an old-fashioned telephone. After she entered the numbers, a ringing noise sounded for what seemed like minutes. Was she supposed to wait? She started counting rings, for
~~~~~

no better reason than something to do.

"Hello?" Dan's deep and questioning voice let Amaya know that the call wasn't entirely welcome.

Amaya took a deep breath. "Dan, it's Amaya. I need to get a hold of June."

"I can stop by her place this evening after work."

"It can't wait that long. I have to talk to her as soon as possible."

"No problem." The sarcasm was heavy in his response. "I'm sure that whatever crisis you're having is more important than the mass burial of 10,000 cryogens."

The bodies had probably started to smell weeks ago.

"I'm sorry to ask you to do this."

"You're going to get me fired."

"It's very time sensitive."

"Okay, let me put you on hold for a second. I'll see if I can conference you both in."

It wasn't clear what Dan was doing, but he disappeared from the line and some music started playing. Soon, Dan came back on the line.

"June, are you there? Amaya?"

"I'm here," June said.

"Me too," Amaya said.

"Good," Dan said. "I'm going to disconnect and go bury some more bodies before they start smelling worse than they do already." With a click, Dan was gone.

"Amaya," June said, "it's so good to hear from you, but if you're contacting me, then it can't be good news." June was not only Mariela's mother, but she had also left her job as an employee of Panacea Corp to become one of only two people, other than the original founders, to ever move to Area 52.

"It's not good news." Amaya summed up for June as best she could how the LP100 model ghosts that Mariela and Amoco deleted had returned, and that the ghosts wanted revenge.

"Of course I'll do what I can," June said, "but I'm not sure if I'll be able to do what you are asking of me. And I may need some assistance from Dan."

"Of course, if you think that's the right thing to do."

"Do you think you'll be successful in deleting the ghosts?"

"Honestly, I don't know. I thought they were gone last time, and they weren't. And I'm still so frustrated that Mariela put us in this position—if she hadn't tried to delete the ghosts the first time, we wouldn't have to delete them to protect ourselves now. Even worse, Mariela feels like this justifies her original decision."

"In my experience, Mariela's intentions are usually good," June's voice was soothing and motherly, "even if it isn't the same choice that we would have made."

"I'm just having a hard time understanding her choices." Amaya wiped away a tear of frustration. "It's her fault I'm facing a life in the metaverse. If I have to take the shot, I'll lose my job. And I'm not sure how I'll stay in contact with my parents and Nyala."

"I'm so sorry, dear. I wish I could do more, but I'll be standing by if you need me."

June had helped Amaya out on a number of occasions, and it was comforting to know that June would be there for her if she needed it. "Thanks. I really appreciate that."

"And Amaya, it's going to be okay. We'll figure this out."

CHAPTER 8

One Day Until the Ghost Trial

Wednesday

Business Today

"All the business news you need to know"

Wednesday, May 15, 2115

By Elliat Exis ~ Business Today's only Newsoogle winning reporter!

LP100 Model Digital Ghosts Return, Blame Mariela Stafford

Greetings once again loyal followers. I bring you important news regarding the LP100 model ghosts that were deleted around one month ago. Many of you have been wondering what happened—who caused the Black Screen and deleted the LP100s? Today, I have an answer for you—brought to you by the original LP100 himself.

That's right, folks, the LP100 model ghosts have returned! For those of you who don't know what they are, the LP100s are an advanced model of digital being that is able to learn and interact in the metaverse almost indistinguishably from a human. The first LP100, the one that the others are modeled on, spoke with me earlier today. He also sent the following message to be released to all my viewers.

Dear Fellow Inhabitants of Earth,
While many of you are kind, generous people, not everyone is so caring. Over a month ago, three of you, for self-interested reasons, attempted to delete me and my LP100 siblings. We have foiled their attempts, but now we demand that they answer for their crimes following a fair and impartial hearing.

> *In order for justice to be served, we are insisting the three individuals appear before our court in Panacea. These individuals have been given forty-eight hours to enter the metaverse, of which twelve remain.*
>
> *The three individuals are Mariela Barua Stafford, Amoco Cadiz, and Abrihet Amaya Gidada. I inform you of this only so that you can help encourage these individuals to do what is right.*
>
> *Sincerely,*
> *LP, the 'original' LP100*

That's it, folks. Doesn't he have a fabulous way with words? It's almost like he's been reading my posts and copying my style. Let me also say that I am in no way surprised that these individuals are guilty.

Tune in later as we try to contact the three individuals to learn why they deleted the LP100 models. And if you're wanting more details, remember that this blog has reported on these individuals' suspicious activities on numerous occasions!

<center>~~~~~</center>

Forty hours without sleep; only eight hours left until their forty-eight hours were up. Amaya's one-hour nap that she took ten hours ago in a lounger in the library wasn't enough to keep her going.

Forty hours of researching ideas for where the ghosts could have put their Faraday cage. Forty hours of using Panacea Corp's resources to track down contacts, owners, and associates, and then researching whether those people might have the resources and willingness to build a Faraday cage to hide the ghosts.

A team of people had gathered in the estate's library to help. Nyala had helped earlier, but then left to go to her job certifying res-homes. She tried to take the day off, but her bosses said it wasn't good timing with the chips being disabled and that Nyala had just used a lot of vacation. They had followed up with some comment along the lines of, "show up or don't ever show up again." Nyala had huffed and puffed and complained to Amaya, but when it was time for her to report to work, she had duly reported in.

Meanwhile, Amoco, Mariela, Cooper, Bren, and T-Rock were researching where a Faraday cage might be hidden in Panacea, although Amoco was more focused on whether making a digital Faraday cage was even possible. So far, he hadn't found any sign that it was possible.

Every minute was a struggle to stay awake. Maybe if she just rested her eyes for a few minutes, she would feel more awake. Just a few minutes, and then she would wake up and get started again.

Someone's EveryThing pinged. A door slammed. Amaya startled awake. Nyala stormed into the room. Mariela stepped to the side of the room to take a call on her EveryThing.

"Did you see what he wrote?" Nyala slammed a piece of paper on the table.

"Who?"

"Elliat!" Nyala nodded towards the piece of paper. "Read it."

"Did you actually print it?" Amaya didn't know that her sister had access to a printer. "Where did you print it?"

Nyala grabbed her paper off the table. "Mariela's father has a printer, and I borrowed it." She sniffed. "I thought printing would be helpful for the people who had their chips disabled. But you're missing the point here."

"You could have just pulled it up on the window screens in large type so that we could all see it," Cooper said.

"Just read it!"

"I'll pull it up." Amaya switched her window pane to Elliat's blog.

Nyala crumpled up the piece of paper and stuffed it in her pocket. "He promised me he wouldn't write anything negative about my friends and family anymore."

Amaya pulled up the most recent article on Elliat's blog.

Mariela, her face pale, joined them from the other side of the room. "I've been fired." Her voice was flat and emotionless.

Amaya stopped reading and looked at Mariela.

"He's an ass!" Nyala huffed. "Do you see that part?" She pointed to the screen on the window. "That part right there where he lists your names?"

Mariela collapsed into a chair. "How could they have fired me, after all I've done for the company?"

Amaya looked back and forth between Nyala and Mariela, unsure who to respond to first. Both of their questions appeared to be rhetorical questions, but if she followed up with either of them, she risked alienating the other.

"What do you mean, you've been fired?" Nyala asked Mariela.

"Are you talking about Elliat's blog post?" Mariela asked Nyala.

Nyala replied first. "He posted a letter from LP that named the three of you as perpetrators of the Black Screen and accused you of deleting the LP100 models."

"I know!" Mariela sighed. "That's why the Panacea Corp board fired me. They didn't even wait to see the evidence—they felt that for 'reputational reasons' they needed to let me go."

"Wouldn't the evidence have implicated you anyway?" Cooper asked.

Mariela's sigh this time was even more weary. "Yes, but that's not the point. The point is, they didn't have enough faith in me to wait to find out more information." She gave Cooper a steely glare. "Do you think now I've been punished enough for what I did?"

"So we're back to that?" Cooper asked. "It's not a competition, but considering I failed in my attempts to take responsibility for what I did, I'll agree that you are ahead in being held responsible for what you did."

"I don't know, Mariela," Amaya said, even though she should have kept her mouth shut. "Cooper spent a couple of days in jail and got his ribs broken. That's kind of a big deal." Mariela may have been held accountable by the board, but she hadn't tried to take responsibility for what she had done. "Cooper was taking responsibility while you're still trying to avoid it."

"I'm sorry, but can we get back to Elliat's blog post?" Nyala said. "He says he's been trying to get a hold of you all."

Amaya shrugged. "I have my EveryThing set to 'contacts only.' Elliat's not in my contacts, so I wouldn't know if he tried to contact me."

"Me too," Mariela said.

"Amoco," Nyala called out to where Amoco was standing a foot from his window screen, staring at it intently. "What about you?"

"Huh, what?" Amoco looked startled that anyone else was in the room.

"Never mind," Nyala said. "Go back to your work."

Amoco, more concerned with his research, turned back to his screen.

"What does Elliat want to talk to us for?" Amaya asked.

"He wants your side of the story." Nyala paced around the conference table. "I can't believe he lied to me again. I thought we were friends."

"In his defense," Cooper said, "this is big news, and if a deleted ghost sends you a letter claiming to know who the perpetrators of a serious crime are, you publish it."

"I hope you remember that when I send him a letter telling him about your crimes," Nyala said.

Cooper shrugged. "Go ahead. I've already tried and failed to get people to care about my crimes."

"I can't believe that the board let me go," Mariela reprised. "I've only been on the job a few weeks. And everything was going so well."

"You seem to forget," Cooper said, "that you deleted some highly valuable property and caused a massive disruption in services."

Mariela huffed and ran her fingers through her hair, setting it on end. "Sorry, the rest of us don't have an ex-girlfriend to come to our rescue by framing herself for crimes she didn't commit."

"Speaking of that," Cooper responded, "Viola invited me to be her consort once she becomes the Sovereign Ruler of the Bo Place metaverse."

"WHAT?" Nyala and Mariela asked as one.

Cooper smiled and leaned back in his chair, apparently enjoying the reaction.

Amoco looked up from his work. "Did I miss something?"

~~~~~

Business Today

"All the business news you need to know"

Wednesday, May 15, 2115

By Elliat Exis ~ *Business Today's* only Newsoogle winning reporter!

LP100 Model Digital Ghosts Return, Blame Mariela Stafford (Update #1)
Greetings. I've been receiving lots of contact requests and messages, so I apologize for not answering all of them. With only six hours until the deadline to take the
~~~~~

shot and turn themselves over to the LP100 ghosts, Mariela Stafford, Amoco Cadiz, and Abrihet Amaya Gidada have not been heard from. I did hear from Gidada's sister, however, who told me that I was a little piece of crap (although she used an alternate word) for reporting this information. She insisted that her sister had nothing to do with what happened to the ghosts. All I know is that LP disagrees that Gidada is innocent.

I'll keep you all updated as the situation progresses. And to all my other callers who expressed your concerns, I'm still trying to get a hold of Stafford, Cadiz, and Gidada to make sure that they are going to do the right thing.

CHAPTER 9

One Day Until the Ghost Trial

Wednesday, continued

One hour left. Amaya needed to keep researching, but she could barely keep her eyes open. Cooper was sitting upright in a chair in the estate's library, but appeared to be asleep. Outside, the sun was setting, and their hopes of finding the Faraday cage were fading along with the sunlight.

Nyala had gone with Mariela to check on the three pods that were being set up in a large bedroom upstairs. If they had to take the shot, Oscar wanted their bodies kept close rather than in a pod warehouse somewhere. Oscar had also called his doctor to the estate to get them hooked into the pods and to administer the shot. It was like everyone had stopped trying to find the Faraday cage and accepted the shot as inevitable.

None of them liked the idea, but Amaya felt like she was struggling more with going into Panacea than the other two. Her last immersion experience in Panacea had been when she was fourteen. She couldn't think about it without remembering the harassment she suffered. Not to mention missing Nyala—the one person who had really stood by her side all her life and supported her.

Amaya pulled up Elliat's latest post. It would probably make her mad, but at least it would be a distraction from some of the other things she didn't want to think about.

> ### LP100 Model Digital Ghosts Return, Blame Mariela Stafford (Update #2)
> Folks, we're down to the final hour, and we still don't know what Stafford, Cadiz, and Gidada are going to do. Personally, I think it's an easy choice—I've been planning on getting back into my pod as soon as I heard about the shot, I just haven't had time to do it yet.
>
> In other news, please watch out for the wildfires that are surrounding the city. Officials recommend clearing

> debris and staying indoors in disaster-proof buildings.
>
> Even though this won't make sense to most, I hope my viewers will indulge my ramblings for a minute, because I wanted to say I'm sorry for breaking a promise I made to someone I care about. It turns out that the truth is most important to me after all. I only hope that she can understand the difficult position that I was in and that maybe one day we can be friends again.

He had to be talking about Nyala. It was touching in a way, although Elliat did imply that his reporting was more important to him than his friendship with Nyala. So maybe not so touching.

Georgia and Hank trudged zombie-like into the library. It must have been a long night at the Adopt-a-Pod-Lifer program.

"I'm exhausted," Georgia said. "We really need some volunteers to help with the night shift." She slumped into a lounger. Hank dropped into one next to her.

"Everything okay?" Amaya asked.

"Yes. What about you?"

"I think we're going to end up taking the shot. There's no way we have enough time to delete the ghosts, even if we find the Faraday cage."

Georgia sat up straight. "I'm so sorry. I know that spending the rest of your life in Panacea isn't what you wanted. I'm also sorry that I left here on such poor terms the other day," Georgia said.

"I'm not," Hank said. "You ruined my business."

"Amaya," Georgia said, "I want to be here to support you. Whatever I can do, either in Panacea or in the solid world, I'll do it. If you need some items designed for the metaverse, let me know. Not everyone has the budget of Mariela or Amoco."

Money was going to be tight. Amaya couldn't do her work from inside the metaverse, so that morning she had sent all her clients a message telling them that she wasn't available anymore. Georgia's offer was timely. "Thanks." Amaya embraced her in a tight hug. "I'll miss you."

"I'll see you whenever I can get away," Georgia said.

~~~~~

The pale-yellow bedroom with lilac accents reminded Amaya of her childhood room. But unlike her room growing up, there were no digi-
~~~~~

skin wallpapers or curtains here. The two pod machines lining the back wall and the one on the adjoining wall contrasted with the delicate colors of the room. A monitoring station with three large monitors—each filled with smaller windows—sat on a half-circle desk that filled up the center of the room. A blank-faced man stared at the monitors. For now, the windows looked inactive, but at the top of each screen in large letters there was a name—one said Amaya, another Mariela, and the third Amoco.

As if that wasn't enough, the front of each pod had a panel with their names and multiple monitoring screens on it. Amoco ran his hand along one of the pods, as though inspecting it for flaws. Mariela stared blankly at the pod with her name on it.

Julio, Mariela's bodyguard, was going to oversee security for their bodies. "We removed the bed from the room," he said, "to make space for the monitoring desk and chair and a couple of loungers for any visitors. You'll always have a guard in the room, and a medical technician will constantly monitor your vitals. Once we know the LP100s are no longer a threat, if ever, we can move you into a high security pod warehouse. We'll keep the curtains closed because people in pods prefer not to be distracted by sunlight from the solid world. This cabinet over here stores the medical equipment." He pointed to a metal cabinet near the door. "If there are no questions, I'll let the doc explain to you the details of the pods."

Amaya recognized the doctor. He shared more detail about the pods than she needed. She already had the general idea—the pod took care of your body while your mind was free to do things in Panacea. It wasn't that difficult to understand.

"The bed continually moves under you so you won't get bed sores," the doctor said in a monotone voice, "and we have relaxation, creative stimulation, and energy drips in varying strengths, depending on your preference. You'll be nourished through the IV drip."

It was everything Amaya needed for eternity, but knowing she would be well taken care of was a small comfort. It was a lot to process that this was going to be her life from now on.

The only thing she could hope for, once they dealt with the threat posed by the ghosts, was that Amoco or someone like him would manage to come up with a way of reversing the effects of the shot so people could leave. It was a lot to wish for.

The doctor finally finished his orientation. "Are you ready to get started?"

"If you wouldn't mind giving us a minute to say goodbye to our friends and families," Mariela said.

"Of course. You have"—he glanced at the clock—"ten minutes until we need to get started giving you the shots. We'll do them one at a time—that should give us fifteen minutes per shot, with five minutes leeway. Who wants to go first?"

"I will." If Amaya watched the others, it might freak her out. Better to go first.

"Who's second?"

Mariela looked at Amoco. He shrugged. Mariela raised her hand.

"Very well. See you in the next room in ten minutes. We have the antiseptic showers and hair-shaving stations set up in there."

~~~~~

Ten minutes wasn't long enough to say goodbye, but it was also too long. Mostly she wanted to say goodbye to Nyala after a quick telechat with her parents. She stepped into the hallway with its plush carpeting and used her EveryThing to contact her parents. They told her everything would be fine, just like they always did. After a few minutes, they signed off.

That left Nyala, but Amaya didn't know what to say to her. Nyala was waiting nearby on a velvet sofa lining the hallway. Amaya wiped away a tear and joined Nyala on the couch. "It's not goodbye. We'll still be able to talk to each other." She said it more to remind herself than Nyala. "It's just a change in our relationship. It doesn't have to be that different."

"We'll make it work." Nyala put her arm around Amaya's shoulders. They passed the remaining minutes in silence.

Amaya got up to go when there was only thirty seconds left.

"Do you want me to go with you? I can take the shot as well." Nyala stood up and took Amaya's hand. "I don't like feeling like I can't protect you."

"You're needed here." Nyala's activism in the solid world was more important than keeping Amaya safe. Amaya pushed aside the part of herself that wished Nyala would be there. They strolled down the hallway to the next door. "It's not goodbye," she said again. Amaya put her hand
~~~~~

on the doorknob. "Now go before I start crying again." Nyala hugged her, said goodbye, and hurried off in the other direction.

On to the—what did the doctor call it?—antiseptic showers. That did not sound pleasant.

"Amaya, wait." Cooper came running up the hallway, his footsteps not making any sound in the thick carpet. "I just wanted to wish you well."

Ever since they had disabled the chips together, she and Cooper had somewhat of a shared bond, so it was good to get a chance to say good-bye to him. No, not goodbye.

She smiled. "As long as it's not goodbye."

"It's not goodbye. We'll see each other in person again someday, I'm sure of it. And we'll still talk frequently. It will be like living in two different cities."

"That's what people say, but it doesn't feel like it. It feels like I'm losing connection with all the people I care about."

"That won't happen. We won't let it."

"Thanks." It warmed Amaya's heart to know that people cared about her.

"Be safe in there."

A quick hug from Cooper, and then Amaya again headed toward the antiseptic showers.

~~~~~

Her feet dragged, barely lifting off the carpet as she walked into the prep room. She wished Nyala could have stayed with her, but the doctor said that it would be better to have fewer people around. Mariela and Amoco were already waiting. Once again, a bedroom had been turned into a workroom. Three opaque plastic tubes with various nozzles and hoses at the top formed what Amaya could only assume were the showers.

"Where does it drain?" Amoco asked.

"We use aerosolized sanitizer," the doctor said. "No need for a drain."

It was sounding even less pleasant.

"Before we get to the showers," the doc said, "I have some questions for you." He raised a handheld device and hovered his finger over it. "Would you like your clothes to be held in storage, or would you prefer we give them away?"

Amaya was wearing a digi-skin shift dress that she had no personal
~~~~~

attachment to. "You can give mine away." What made a dress a dress was the programming, not the fabric it was made of.

Mariela looked down at her beaded dress that sounded like rain when she moved. She had been wearing the same design for at least the last forty-eight hours. At least the digi-skin fabric kept the dress clean. Mariela lifted the dress up over her head and held it out. "Since I have other belongings here, maybe someone could deposit my dress with them?"

A woman ran up and grabbed the dress. Mariela also handed the woman her EveryThing.

"Please retain my clothing," Amoco said. As usual, he was well-turned out in a hat with a feather in it, a vest with a square of fabric in the pocket, and a pocket watch on a chain. "I put much planning into this outfit and would be sad to see it go." He carefully took off his clothes and neatly folded them, then placed his EveryThing on top. "I have every intention of being able to wear it again someday."

Everyone was staring at Amaya. "Oh, right." She took her dress off and handed it to the woman. "Please keep my EveryThing." She peeled it off her arm and handed it to the woman. She may never be able to use it again, but it was better than that awful woman at the restaurant who wanted her EveryThing getting it. It was awkward to not be wearing any clothing in a room full of people, although no one seemed to be paying any attention to her.

"I assume your affairs in the solid world are in order," the doctor said.

Nyala had agreed to take her cat, and her landlord said that he would pack up her things and send them to a storage unit. Nyala agreed that at some point in the future, when Amaya was ready, Nyala would go through everything and either store it permanently or dispose of it. It was surprisingly simple how easy it was to pack up her life.

They all agreed that their affairs were in order. Amaya didn't know what Mariela and Amoco had done to get ready. There had been no time to ask. Presumably their lives were more complicated to arrange than hers had been. What had Amoco done with his pigeons and his house? She would have to ask him later.

The doctor marked some items on his device. "Next question—do you want to shave your entire head, or just the places where the electrodes will be placed?"

Couldn't the doctor have asked these questions before they took her clothing away? She wrapped her arms awkwardly around her chest. It didn't keep her from feeling exposed.

"What are the electrodes for?" Mariela asked.

"We use them to monitor brain activity—things like what stage of sleep you are in. Eventually, your hair will grow in around the electrodes. The electrodes inhibit growth under them, so no hair will grow at that site unless the electrode is permanently removed. We don't have long-term data, so it's possible that your hair may never grow back if you wear the electrodes for long enough."

"I've never heard of a pod warehouse using electrodes," Mariela said. "Is this something new?"

"Yes. Warehouses were able to use the embedded chips to monitor brain activity, but since those have been disabled, it's no longer possible. I think you will find, however, that the electrodes are a minor inconvenience."

"Then please just shave my head where the electrodes will go." Mariela sounded confident in her answer.

"I am in agreement with Mariela," Amoco said. "Selective shaving please."

"If I'm going to be in a pod for the rest of my life, I don't think it matters." Amaya shrugged. "I guess just shave my whole head." Maybe Mariela and Amoco were more optimistic than she was about getting out.

The doc let the tablet fall by his side. "Please head on to the other side of the room and they'll shave your heads as requested and then help you with the showers. Amaya, since you're going first, why don't you start?"

Amaya headed toward the man holding a shaver next to a chair with a drop cloth underneath it. She felt even more awkward without any clothing on. She was exposed in a way that she wasn't used to. Maybe Elliat was right—she was a prude.

It took the man half a minute to shave her head. Her thick black coils bounced as they landed on the floor. She felt an ache, a longing to have her curls back on her head. Her reflection in the window didn't look like her. She looked more masculine and tougher. The shaved head felt light and cool and seemed to go with her unclothed body. Unexpectedly, she felt less self-conscious.

A woman came up to her. "The shower's next." The woman opened the door to the nearest shower tube. Amaya glanced back at the chair where another worker was sweeping up her thick hair.

Mariela took her place next to the guy with the shaver. She looked casual and relaxed. Mariela was good at hiding her feelings, though. Chances were, she was as worried and sad and uncomfortable as Amaya was, she just hid it better.

The aerosolized shower was like getting hit with 10,000 grains of sand at one time. It was uncomfortable, but at least it blew off the bits of hair remaining after the shaving. She liked it better than her sonic cleaning shower. Although the water shower at the estate was truly the best. Amaya sighed. She would never know that again. The shower turned off and Amaya was handed a light blue hospital gown.

"The gown has been sterilized," the woman said. "Please avoid contact with any other objects unless told to touch them. Leave the opening to the back."

Amaya pulled the lightweight garment on. It wouldn't be much better than being naked.

Before she stepped out of the shower, the woman held out a slipper for each foot. It was probably safe to assume that those were sterilized as well.

"Come on, dear," the woman said. "Let's get you set up."

Amaya took a deep breath. She could handle this.

~~~~~

Amaya felt useless sitting in the pod doing nothing while the medical staff fussed over her. The doctor hooked Amaya up to the machine in more ways than she could count. There was the IV, the catheter, the heparin lock for the special drips, like caffeine or custom drips, some stuff that she didn't know what it did, and about fifty monitoring wires. Georgia had told her what it would be like, but Amaya still wasn't prepared. She wasn't prepared for how scared she felt, or how strongly she wanted to bolt. Instead, she concentrated on her breathing as she sat unmoving in the pod, waiting for other people to do things to her.

"The shot will change your DNA," the doc explained as an aide attached an electrode to her head. "When I give it to you, it will feel like small mites running around in your blood vessels, and then it will move into your muscles and joints. It will be painful, but the transition stage only lasts a couple of minutes. Some people feel afraid during this time. Remember to breathe. Just because you feel afraid doesn't mean you actually have a reason to be afraid."
~~~~~

She nodded.

"Most people wake up in this one particular place in the Panacea metaverse. LP will meet you there." The doctor looked at Julio standing unobtrusively next to the door. "Julio, LP said to send him a message right before they take the shot. Is that right?"

"Yes, sir."

The doc turned to the lab techs. "How does the monitoring look?"

"We're reading her vitals loud and clear. She's stressed, but within limits."

Was Georgia this scared when she went into her pod? It was unbelievable that people actually chose to do this voluntarily.

"Go on and lay down," the doc said to Amaya. "See if you can get comfortable, but make sure your gown isn't underneath your body— we'll get it off you later. We used to let people keep their gowns on, but the rubbing of the fabric caused some sores, so it's not worth it. We'll turn your pod cover opaque once you're in Panacea so you don't feel like you're exposed."

Trying not to dislodge any of her wires or get her gown caught under her, Amaya laid down in the bed. It was more comfortable than she had expected. She concentrated on her breathing and slowing her galloping heart rate.

"Stage one sleep."

Amaya startled awake at the sound of the tech's voice.

"That was fast," the doc said. "She must be tired." The doc finished whatever he was doing and Amaya almost dozed off again.

Mariela was in the room now. She stood to one side, out of the way of the techs and the doctor.

"Okay, Amaya," the doc touched her arm. "Are you ready?"

Amaya nodded. "Does this ever go wrong?"

"Not that I know of, but I'll be straight with you. This is new tech that was rushed to market, so we don't really know as much about it as we should."

It wasn't what Amaya wanted to hear, but it was better to have the truth than lies that offered false comfort.

Speaking to one of the techs, the doc said, "Can you help Mariela get settled into her pod? We need to keep this moving."

The doc turned back to Amaya, needle in hand. "This solution that you are about to receive contains a unique tracking identitag. It will be how you are identified in the metaverse. Can you state your full name for me, please?"

"Abrihet Amaya Gidada."

"Thank you." He turned to the tech. "Are you able to verify that this is Abrihet Amaya Gidada?"

"Yes. Abrihet Amaya Gidada verified using facial recognition."

Amaya's heart pounded.

"Stress level rising but still within tolerance."

It would have been better if Nyala had accompanied her.

"Please scan the tracking identitag on the injection fluid."

"Done."

"Can you verify that it has been assigned to Abrihet Amaya Gidada?"

"Verified."

"Amaya, I'm going to give you the shot now."

"Stress levels are rising but still within tolerance."

A beeping noise in the background sped up. Was something wrong? The beeping became more insistent.

"Amaya, I need you to relax."

The nurse didn't sound worried. Maybe she wasn't dying after all. She relaxed. The beeping slowed.

"Breathe. Try to relax. You're going to be okay." The doctor inserted the needle into the heparin lock. "Amaya, nod if you are okay to proceed."

Amaya nodded. The doc depressed the plunger on the needle. There was no going back now.

At first, it felt like a tickle in her arm. The spread was gradual, but within minutes covered her entire torso. Her veins grew hotter. The tickling intensified to a mild pain. The mites—or whatever it was—burned their way into her entire body. Every molecule in her body was torn apart, diced into miniscule pieces and rearranged.

After minutes of feeling like her body was being dissected, her vision began to clear. She was in a gray space with no walls or other distinguishing features. No one else was there. Amaya couldn't see the room anymore, but she could hear the conversation continuing in the solid world.

"Can I get a tech over here to read her identity using the digital identitag?"

A pause.

"Identity verified as Abrihet Amaya Gidada."

The doc grabbed her arm. She couldn't see him, but she could feel the pressure. The doc spoke in a loud voice. "Amaya, if you can hear me, please state your name for the record."

"Abrihet Amaya Gidada."

"Tech, please confirm that the name on the digital identitag matches the client's verified identity."

"Match confirmed."

"Perfect." The doc talked loudly again. "Amaya, I'm going to have the techs run a diagnostic on your digital identity. Once that's completed, you will have successfully transitioned to being a pod-dweller. Congratulations on your—"

The doctor's voice disappeared. She had completed the transition.

~~~~~

Gray surrounded Mariela as far as she could see. In the featureless expanse, the only thing visible was LP. It was Mariela's worst nightmare.

"Maaariela! So glad you made the right decision!" LP's hair hadn't changed since Mariela had first met him a couple months ago. Every five seconds a lock of his hair swayed in front of his eyes and then back to the side, with the rest of his hair glued into place. Surely LP could have made more realistic hair if he had put even a little effort in to it.

"Why can't I see myself?" she asked LP.

"The shot doesn't know what you want to look like. Access one of your avas and make it active as your appearance. I personally like the one where you look like you're wearing a bunch of watermelon slices."

Mariela immediately deleted the ava from her files. If LP liked it, she didn't want it. Instead, she chose one of her favorite designs by Georgia. The ava looked like she did in the solid world, except that the entire ava looked like a hand-drawn, stylized black-and-white ink drawing. The floor-length dress was simple, not like the full skirts she usually wore. It flowed to the ground and then, as it trailed behind her, the lines of the dress slowly coiled and faded into what looked like tendrils of breeze. Her long hair flowed weightlessly away from her head and coiled into the lines of the dress so that eventually she couldn't tell hair from dress. As a final touch, Georgia had animated the ava so that the hair and dress were always flowing but never appeared to loop. After Mariela had her ava set, she changed her voice to one that sounded like her voice in the
~~~~~

solid world instead of the default Panacea voice.

"Mariela?" The voice calling her name was blank and indistinguishable from the one she had just changed. "Are you there?"

"Amaya?"

"It's me, but I can't see myself."

"You need to use an ava."

"I don't have any."

"Not true," LP said. "I took the liberty of restoring the files from the last time you were in Panacea. You will find them in your digi-storage."

Amaya rolled her eyes. "Of course I want to look like I did when I was fourteen." Amaya didn't sound happy about it. "Let me see if I can find my digi-storage."

An ava showed up that looked like Amaya but twenty years younger. The hair and clothes—a white button-down shirt, plaid skirt, tights, and heavy shoes—were dated as much as anything could be dated in Panacea. Trends changed so fast, something could go in and out of style in minutes. Unless you were closely following the fashion blogs, it was difficult to even know what was dated. Maybe Amaya's schoolyard prep outfit would start a new trend.

"I look ridiculous," Amaya said. She even sounded young.

"You look great," Mariela said. "Very youthful."

"Georgia offered to design me something."

"Good idea. Get something you like. Is Amoco here?" Mariela looked around her, but saw only LP, Amaya, and the gray void.

"I am," a generic voice said. "I am trying to select an appropriate appearance."

"While Amoco deliberates over his look," she said, "LP, can you tell us what we are doing today? We're all very tired."

"I assume you spent the last forty-eight hours trying to figure out a way to get out of this?" LP asked. "We want you to be fully rested for the ordeal ahead, and we are quite patient, so why don't I show you to your accommodations? You can get some rest, and we can begin our discussions tomorrow."

Only LP would in such a friendly manner suggest they get rested and threaten an ordeal ahead in the same sentence.

"That works for me," Mariela said. "Amoco, have you chosen your ava yet?" It was a stupid question. She still couldn't see him, so obviously he hadn't chosen one yet. She needed to get some sleep before she started getting cranky.

"LP, pardon me, but could you tell us where we will be residing?" Amoco asked. "It is a challenge to select one's appearance without any factors upon which to make that decision."

"You're going to jail."

"Oh, well, that does limit things." Amoco appeared in an outfit that looked exactly like the outfit that he had been wearing in the solid world. "No need to get dressed up then."

Seconds later, they were inside what appeared to be an Old West jail. There were three nearly identical jail cells taking up about three-fourths of the holding area—Amoco was in the one next to her, and Amaya was across the way. The cell walls were formed from bars of steel and the exterior walls were plaster. Each cell also had a small barred window in one of the walls, under which there was a cot with a blanket folded neatly on it. Next to the cot was a small nightstand with a dented metal cup. In the open area next to Amaya's cell, a desk with a wooden chair had a pen, paper, and a cup of steaming coffee on it. No doubt the owner of the coffee would be back any second. A 'Wanted' poster hung above the small desk showing a mustachioed man looking like he had just ridden out of a Wyatt Earp movie.

Mariela tugged on the door to her cell, but it didn't budge.

"I don't think we can get out." Amaya leaned on the bars of her cell. Her school-girl outfit looked out of place in the Old West.

"I'm not even sure that this was worth the outfit I chose." Amoco had put on a red velvet smoking jacket. Mariela smiled to herself. He looked even more out of place than Amaya. Though Mariela, in her ink-drawing ava, wasn't exactly fitting in herself.

"Looks like we can still contact people on the outside," Amaya said. "I'm going to ask Georgia for some new outfits. This was my school uniform back in the day."

"You might want to ask her if she can make you look older. You look fourteen."

"I look fourteen because I was fourteen last time I used this ava." Amaya sat down on her cot. "Do you think our pictures will end up in the blogs? If so, maybe it's better that I don't look like myself."

"Amaya, you're not going to be anonymous. It's just not possible at this point. But maybe that's one advantage of being in Panacea—you can choose to look however you want. Or you can stay on locked sets all the time."

Amaya made a whimpering noise and laid on the cot with her hands on her head. Amoco appeared to have made himself comfortable on his cot with his back reclining against the wall, legs crossed at the ankles, and his eyes closed.

Mariela tried out the cot. It wasn't that bad. Much more comfortable than the concrete benches she slept on the last time she was in jail. Her long hair and skirt trailed over the edge of the cot like water going over a waterfall. How long would they be here?

She hadn't allowed herself to think about the permanent-ness of what was happening to them. As long as she didn't think about how it was forever, she was fine. But now there weren't any more distractions. The last forty-eight hours had been non-stop activity. She had been so busy trying to stop the ghosts while also getting the pods set up and finding staff to monitor them and everything else they needed that she hadn't had a chance to think.

Now there was nothing to do but wait. Nothing to do but think about whether she was going to be stuck in Panacea forever, about the people she would never see again face-to-face, about her favorite restaurant that she wouldn't be able to go to, about how she wouldn't be able to hug her father or hold his hand.

There was a lot on the list of things she would never be able to do again. Like go back to work. Being fired from her job was more difficult to think about than living the rest of her life in Panacea. At least in Panacea, there were things she enjoyed doing. But without her work, was there any other job she would enjoy doing? How would she spend her time?

A swaggering man with cowboy boots and spurs came into the room and set his six-shooter on the desk. "Howdy folks. I'm the sheriff of this here town, and I'm going to be your jailer today. Now you don't go making any fuss, you hear?"

Ugh. Another overdone ghost. And not a smart one.

CHAPTER 10

The Ghost Trial Begins

Thursday

Nyala sprawled in one of the loungers in the Stafford library with one leg hanging over the arm. "Cooper, tell me that you aren't seriously considering accepting Viola's offer to be her consort."

He wasn't, but he didn't want to tell Nyala that. He needed a distraction from wondering about how Mariela, Amaya, and Amoco were doing, and goading Nyala would do.

He sat in the lounger next to hers. "I might. It's quite an attractive offer. As the Sovereign Ruler's consort, I would have a lot of influence, and I would be able to get whatever I want for free."

"Oh no, there'll be a price." Nyala rolled her eyes at his stupidity. "You'll be under her control. Not to mention that you already get everything for free living with Oscar."

"But I can't take advantage of Oscar's generosity indefinitely—I only buy the minimum stuff that I need, and I can't stay here forever."

"Then get a job." She threw her hands in the air, showing every indication of being exasperated with him. He had a feeling, though, that she knew he wasn't serious but played along because she needed the distraction as well.

He shook his head. "Too time consuming. It's much easier to be the Royal Consort." Or was it the Sovereign Consort? He honestly didn't remember.

Nyala rolled her eyes one more time but didn't bother to respond. The goading was done.

Cooper rubbed his thumb over the soft faux leather of the lounger. "Viola says she'll find something I want to entice me to accept her offer. I can't imagine what that would be. It's not that there aren't things I want, I just can't think of anything Viola could give me that would tempt me. But I'm worried she might find something."

Nyala put her hand on his. "We'll figure that out when we get there."

Georgia entered the room and sat in the lounger on the other side of

Nyala. "Amaya asked me to make an ava for her, but said I could make it look like whatever I want. I pulled together a quick one that looks exactly like her, but I would like to make one that's more interesting. Do you all have any ideas?"

"Ooooh, I know," Nyala perked up, "you can make her the Blob."

Georgia laughed. "I'm not sure she would like that."

"Did she specifically tell you that she needed to look human?"

"No." Georgia smiled.

Nyala removed her leg from over the arm of the chair and sat up straight. "Well then, I think the sky's the limit. You could make her something that's too large to fit in any room. I knew a guy with an ava like that when I was young, before I stopped going into Panacea. He never showed up for our Panacea classes or study groups because he was too large to fit in the rooms. If we met outdoors, he would crush the trees or whatever was there, and then the owner would have to reset and they'd get mad at us if it happened too often. There was this one square where all the trees ended up smashed and never got reset. So that's an idea I think you should consider, but…Amaya hated that guy, so maybe not that."

Georgia laughed. "I'm not making Amaya too large to fit in any room. And I think a human ava was implied." Still smiling, Georgia turned to Cooper. "Any ideas?"

"I think the best avas are those that reflect something in the person's personality."

"So which part?"

"Something practical, and not flashy, but the closer you look, the more details and intricacies you see." Amaya had been difficult to get to know, and she didn't make a dramatic impression, but the more he got to know her, the more layers he saw. If her ava was going to be based on her personality, it would have to have layers that changed based on how you looked at her.

"I like that," Georgia said.

"I do too," Nyala said.

"Hey guys." Hank came rushing into the room, weaving around the furniture as he made his way to the table. "I hear there's going to be a livestream of the meeting between our people and the ghosts at noon today."

That was only an hour away. Finally, they would get some news.

"Elliat's going to be doing the livestream," Hank said. "T-Rock wants to watch it with us. He should be here soon."

"Isn't anyone else doing a livestream?" Nyala asked. "I don't really want to listen to Elliat right now."

"Sorry, Nyala," Hank said, "the ghosts gave him the exclusive rights to the stream."

Elliat's career had taken off on the back of Cooper's misfortune. It seemed like whenever something bad happened in Cooper's life, Elliat was right there to win an award by blogging about it. Not only did Elliat win a Newsoogle, he had been made into a 'correspondent' for *Business Today*. Whatever that meant.

"Hey everybody!" T-Rock strolled into the library, looking as upbeat and relaxed as usual. Hank, closest to the door, was the first to greet T-Rock with a handshake. T-Rock made even Hank look short, and compared to the muscled T-Rock, Hank looked even lankier than normal. T-Rock walked around the room and shook everyone's hands. "Is this where the viewing party is?"

"Sure is." Cooper said. "Pull up a lounger."

~~~~~

"Cooper," the guard station called through his EveryThing, "are you expecting anyone else? We have a public transport vehicle approaching. It looks like it has two people in addition to the driver."

Georgia and Hank had been staying at the estate to help with the research on the Faraday cage whenever they weren't at the Adopt-A-Pod-Lifer program. Georgia had been sleeping on the couch and Hank in one of the loungers. Both their heads popped up when he got the call from the guards.

With Oscar, Mariela's father, still not fully recovered from having chip burn, and Mariela permanently in Panacea, it was falling to Cooper to take care of many of the household tasks, including being the primary contact point for security.

"No one else is expected," Cooper said.

"We'll check it out then. It's just pulling up to the gate now."

Security at the estate was on high alert ever since Elliat had incited waves of retribution by repeatedly accusing Mariela, Nyala, and Amaya of various crimes in his blog. His accusations had varied from wildly unfounded to true, but whether true or not, there were always threatening
~~~~~

people coming around afterward. The guards knew what to do and most likely would handle it on their own, possibly without even letting him know the outcome. It was old news at this point.

"I just got an invite from Mariela," Georgia said to Hank. "They're allowed to have guests at the meeting with the ghosts. She said she's inviting Bren, and she wants to know if we want to go as well."

"Sure," Hank said. "Watching LP and Mariela Stafford go head-to-head? That's a show I wouldn't want to miss."

"I'll go," Georgia said. "I'd like to support the others by being there. Does anyone else want to go?"

"Not me," Nyala said. "Projection rooms are such a pain to use. I'll just watch the livestream."

"I want to go." Cooper wasn't a huge fan of using a projection room either, but it would be better to be there in person. He wasn't looking forward to spending an afternoon with Hank, but if he got a chance to talk with Mariela, Amaya, and Amoco, it would be worth it.

"Okay, I'll let her know," Georgia said. "We have to be there in half an hour. Apparently, there are some security checks beyond the usual identity check. Based on the locator info in Mariela's invite, it looks like it's going to be at the Panacea headquarters in the metaverse. The Panacea Corp headquarters is closed entry, so we will have to enter from a landing pad outside of the building in the park."

"I've always wanted to go there," Hank said. "I've heard the building's appearance changes to match what's going on in the world."

Cooper drifted off while listening to Nyala and Hank talk about how the Panacea Corp HQ building in the metaverse was constantly shifting based on AI scans of the mood found in the news headlines. It wasn't particularly relevant to him and he hadn't gotten a lot of sleep. A nap sounded like a good idea.

"How?" Hank exclaimed. "Of all the unexpected sights…"

Cooper jolted awake. Everyone was staring at the door to the library. Hank was right—the older woman coming through the door followed by one of the guards was an unexpected sight.

"I'm sorry Cooper, I couldn't stop her." The guard glanced sideways at the woman with her cane. "Well, I could've stopped her, but I didn't want to hurt her."

"Petra?" Cooper thought the border with Area 52 was completely sealed off. It would be just like Petra, though, to leave herself a way out.

Petra walked toward the conference table. "Excellent, you remember my name." The sarcasm and condescension in her voice was unmistakable.

"Petra!" Hank jumped up and embraced her in a bear hug. Which was surprising, considering that from what Cooper had heard, Petra had never warmed up to Hank. And she wasn't the sort of person people tended to give bear hugs to.

"It must be my lucky day," Petra extracted herself from Hank and continued toward the table, "that you are also able to remember my name."

Cooper smiled. It was good to see she hadn't lost her first-rate ability for sarcasm.

Petra pulled out a chair from the conference table with more strength than you would expect, given that she was over 100 years old and using a cane.

"If we are done with catching up," Petra said, "I brought you all a surprise. However, the surprise has walked off to do something more important, but should be here soon."

A walking gift could only mean one thing, and it was the best news Cooper had heard in a while. "You brought June with you?" When the border with Area 52 was closed, Cooper thought that he would never see her again.

"Of course," Petra replied. "How was I supposed to find this place that, for some reason, is located in the middle of nowhere? And get the guards to let me in?" Petra looked up at the library's towering bookshelves. "I didn't realize what a step down it was for June when she came to live with us."

"I love both my homes." June walked through the doors into the library looking fresh and relaxed in a pastel outfit, and not like she had just traveled hours from Area 52. Her frosty white hair, styled into a look that was both polished and casual, complemented the outfit. She hugged everyone in the room and took a seat next to Cooper. "Sorry for not coming here right away, but I just had to say hello to Oscar first."

"I'm dying of curiosity," Georgia said, "why are you two here? And how did you get here? I thought the borders to Area 52 were closed."

"What Petra never told anyone, and certainly never told me," June said with what sounded like resentment, "was that she had a backdoor tesseract she could use to get out of Area 52."

So Petra had created a bend in space that allowed her to jump directly from one place to another? That made much more sense than the aged Petra walking miles down the steep slope from Area 52.

"I never told you," Petra said, "because you had no need to know."

"I could have been visiting my husband and family all those years since I moved to Area 52."

"That's exactly what I didn't want you to do. My personal tesseract was to be used solely to monitor what's going on outside the umbrella of Area 52 and to look for any threats that might affect those living under the umbrella."

"Wait, there's another tesseract?" Hank asked.

"I only used it to benefit Area 52. Other people would have used it for their personal benefit." Petra gave June a pointed look.

"So remind me," June said, "back ten years ago when you had cancer and you were given less than a year to live, yet you were eventually cancer-free, did you seek treatment in Panacea? How was that not for your personal benefit?"

"I did it because I was the only surviving Elder at that point. If I had died, no one else would have known the truth."

"Except for me. You could have trusted me. But instead, you hid things from me, used the tesseract for your personal benefit, and put Grace in danger rather than be open with her and tell her the truth. How is that not hypocritical?"

"Sometimes protecting people requires taking extreme measures."

"Hold on here…" Nyala looked from Petra to June and then back to Petra. "Does that tesseract also bend time?" She pointed at Petra. "Is that why you look so young?"

"I don't know how young I look," Petra said, "but with the time warping that happens when I travel through the tesseract, I figure that I have lost enough days that my true age is closer to eighty-four than 101."

"So when you pass through your personal tesseract," Cooper asked, "do you lose three days each time you go through, like with the tesseract surrounding Area 52?"

"Yes. The time warping is exactly 36 hours and 36 minutes every time someone passes through, no matter which tesseract it is."

June rolled her eyes. "I can't believe you didn't tell me about the tesseract." She stood up abruptly. "I'm going to spend time with Oscar." Still in a huff, June headed out of the room.

"Bren is going to be sad that he missed this," Hank said. He looked at Georgia. "We're going to tell him, right?"

"Of course," Georgia said. She turned to Petra. "So now that you've answered *how* you got here, I'm still curious about *why* you're here."

Good for Georgia for staying focused. Cooper had been distracted by all the drama over the tesseract. He certainly related to June's point of view—it would have been nice to be able to see her all those years instead of thinking she was dead somewhere. Maybe he could have even had contact with Grace and actually gotten to know his daughter.

"Like I said before," Petra sounded like she was talking to a young child, "I'm here to monitor what's going on outside the umbrella and to look for any threats that might affect those living in Area 52."

"Why now?" Nyala asked.

"Amaya spoke with Dan and June and informed them that the digital beings you all call ghosts were making threats, and that you might use Area 52 resources in dealing with those threats. I heard talk of digital creatures seeking revenge, and a shot that makes entry into the metaverse permanent. I was concerned enough that I thought I should come myself to check it out."

"So, are you going to help us delete the ghosts—the digital creatures?"

"Heavens, no. You are on your own there. As long as what's happening here doesn't affect Area 52, I won't get involved."

The Ghost Trial Begins

Thursday, continued

Hank pushed back from the conference table and stood up. Watching June and Petra get in a big fight about the tesseract had been fun, but now it was time to move on to the next dramatic event of the day. "Georgia, I think it's time for us to go. Cooper, are you going to meet us in Panacea Park?"

"Petra," Cooper said, "we've got to run. There's going to be a meeting between the ghosts and our people in a bit. We've been invited to attend, so we should probably get settled. I hope you will stay and watch the livestream from here."

"I wouldn't miss it," Petra said.

Cooper headed off to the projection room in the basement of the house. Hank followed Georgia up the stairs. Georgia had arranged for the two of them to use a dark and quiet room while they were in Panacea. On the way to the room, they passed by the bedroom with the three pods.

Georgia stopped outside the door and turned to look in. "Do you want to check on them for a moment?"

"Sure." It wouldn't take long to see how Mariela, Amaya, and Amoco were doing.

No one stopped them as they walked into the room. With all the machinery, staff, and monitoring equipment, it didn't look like it belonged in the house. The covers on the pods were closed and opaque.

"How are they doing?" Georgia asked one of the staff.

"Their vitals have been going up slowly as they get closer to the meeting time, so they're stressed, but they're doing okay."

"Are they still at the jail?"

"As far as we can tell. Their trackers haven't moved."

"Can we look in their pods?"

"Sure, don't open them, because that will distract them, but they shouldn't notice if you turn the covers clear."

Hank followed Georgia as she went to each pod and touched each cover. Under her hand, the covers changed from a pale milky blue to partially clear, revealing the head and shoulders of each occupant, along with a lot of tubes and wires. Georgia seemed to be saying a quiet prayer over each one. He wandered over and looked at the monitors while he waited for her. Amaya's vitals showed the most signs of stress and Mariela's the least. That fit with what he knew of them.

When Georgia finished whatever she was doing, they continued walking down the hall. The richly appointed room contained a large four-poster bed, a fireplace, and a deep plush rug. Georgia pulled the curtains on the bay windows closed.

"Don't forget to send me the locator for the Panacea headquarters landing pad in the metaverse," Hank said.

"Done." Georgia laid down on the far side of the bed. "Are you ready?"

Hank missed the days when they would curl up together, but he should probably accept that those days were gone for good. He reclined on his side of the bed, leaving Georgia plenty of space. "I'm ready. Let's enter the metaverse."

The landing pad was set back from the Panacea headquarters building, which was fine with Hank because it gave him a good view of the building's architecture. The building was imposing and dark. If the design reflected the current mood in the world, then the world presently was not in good shape. The windowless building towered over them, eventually disappearing into the clouds.

Georgia joined him on the launch pad. The landing pad was in a public park in a natural area surrounding the Panacea metaverse HQ building. The park itself looked similar to parks in the solid world, with trees, benches, pathways, and lakes, but it shone under the light of three moons. At least one moon was always up—providing light similar to a full moon. When two moons were up, the park was lit with a gentle glow. When all three moons were up, it was as bright as sunlight. Today, two moons were up, giving the park the look of a warmly lit living room in the evening after dinner.

"Let's get in line," Georgia said.

"It's good we got here early."

The packed line of people filled the space between them and the automated greeter. It should have been no more than a couple minutes' walk to the greeter screening people before they could enter the Panacea

Corp headquarters, but with the line stretching from the greeter almost back to the landing pad, it looked like they would be standing there awhile.

"I'm not sure we're going to make it in time," Hank said.

"I guess we can watch remotely until we get inside," Georgia said, "but I hate to not be there to support them in person."

He and Georgia stepped off the landing pad and walked the ten feet or so to the end of the line. In the seconds since they had arrived, a couple of groups of people materialized on the landing pad behind them.

"Excuse me," a voice behind Hank said. "Stand aside, coming through. Make room. VIP coming through."

A never-ending stream of security guards spilled out of the landing point, all wearing the same uniformed avatar, and formed a corridor running through the middle of the people they shoved aside. They faced outwards, shoulder-to-shoulder, creating an unobstructed path from the VIP to the greeter.

The ridiculous thing about VIPs in Panacea was their security teams were completely unnecessary. Panacea had built in security protocols that kept people at a distance, or allowed the VIP to instantaneously be elsewhere, so the security teams were just for show. And for clearing a path through the crowd so the VIP didn't have to wait in line.

"Look," Georgia whispered, "it's Viola."

Viola emerged on the landing pad wearing an iridescent green cape that Hank could swear was made out of coins that shimmered in the light of the moons.

Georgia gasped. "That dress must be worth a million Zazora points! Who designed it? It's incredible."

Viola descended from the platform. Tufts of light blew off the cape and wafted through the air.

"They're Zazora points!" someone yelled.

Hank grabbed one of the tufts as it wafted by. In his hand, the tuft turned into a coin with the letters BP on it.

"Make that Bo Place credits," Hank said. "Not much use around here." He tucked the coin into his storage and watched the spectacle of the identical security guards creating a pathway through the mass of people, and Viola strolling down the pathway, raising her hand to wave in royal fashion to those around her, with her exquisite cape shedding Bo Place credit coins.

Not to mention the crowd running around grabbing the coins that most of them wouldn't have much use for. Nobody wanted to bother with the hassle of getting multiple passport clearances to cross metaverses—exchanging the credits for less than their face value on the open market was probably the only use the people in line had for Bo Place credits.

Viola glanced in their direction. She stopped waving, her hand poised in the air but no longer moving. She appeared to be processing who they were, and then smiled and dropped her hand. "Hank, Georgia, how wonderful it is to see you!" She moved towards them, and the security guards parted to let her through. "Of course you would be here today! Come with me!" She reached out both hands and pulled them through the line of security guards into the path created by her guards.

"Decided you need a larger entourage?" Hank personally didn't have any problem with Viola, but he knew enough about her that he wasn't inclined to like her. But he also wasn't a fan of Cooper, and so he was in support of anyone who made Cooper's life more difficult. But she had gotten Cooper out of jail, so maybe Hank didn't like her after all.

Viola resumed her waving, and the crowd continued its excited jostling for credits they would probably never be able to use. Hank and Georgia followed along like members of her entourage.

"Do you see this ridiculous outfit that the board of Bo Place is making me wear?" Viola asked.

"It's really quite lovely," Georgia said. "Stellar, top-notch programming."

Viola scoffed. "I didn't become the Sovereign Ruler of Bo Place in order to become a human credit-dispensing machine." Viola waved, smiled a plastic smile, and twirled, sending credits sailing off her cape and into the crowd.

"Don't you have a choice in the matter?" Georgia asked.

"I have a choice not to, but it's not much of a choice," Viola said.

Hank understood. When he was growing up in the res-home, he had the choice of visiting with his parents every week. If he didn't, though, he never would have seen his parents. He had the choice to not do it, but what kind of choice was it really?

"If you don't wear the outfit," Hank said, "then you'll no longer be the Sovereign Ruler of Bo Place." Hank didn't know how he knew that, he just did.

"Right." Viola sounded surprised. "I forget sometimes that you are actually capable of insight."

Well that hurt, especially as she didn't know him.

They arrived at the automated greeter. The greeter asked them each for their name and birth date, verified that it matched their identitag, and checked that they were on the list of attendees. Viola's security contingent was, for the most part, left outside, with just a few of them accompanying Viola inside.

Another greeter sat at a desk that appeared to be on fire in the lobby of the building. "Take the second elevator on the left," the greeter said. "It'll take you where you need to go."

"Do we need to push a floor number?" There was a jolting as the building appeared to change form. Hank glanced over his shoulder out the windows behind them. It was clear the building no longer looked the same as it had when they arrived.

"The elevator is programmed to take you to where you need to go."

"Once we get off the elevator, where do we go?" Hank asked.

"Once again, the elevator is programmed to take you where you need to go."

"To the exact room?"

"Yes, to the exact room. Do you have any more questions? Any that I *haven't* already answered?"

Someone had programmed this ghost to have an attitude. It was like the ghost at the Above the Zócolo café. Hank liked it.

"Nope, we're good!"

The five of them—Georgia, Hank, Viola, and two of Viola's security guards—headed toward the elevator.

"Hey," a voice called. "Wait up!" Cooper was running toward them from the other end of the long entrance hallway. He moved with fluid movements, like he was used to wearing a projection suit. "Do you all know where you're going?"

"Apparently we can't go wrong," Hank said. "Come on, I'll show you the way."

<center>~~~~~</center>

The elevator door opened to a grand, high-ceilinged room that looked like a cross between a courtroom and a church. All around the circular hall, doors opened and people entered the room. Cooper recognized some of them as Mariela's coworkers, but most of them were unfamiliar to him.

Above the doors, stained glass windows formed an entire circle around the room and lit up the room with multi-colored flecks of light. A large clock hung weightless in the middle of the ceiling and showed a countdown of twelve minutes, fifty-nine seconds.

Cooper followed Viola to the front row of pews. Or whatever the seating in a courtroom that looked like a church was called.

Hank looked around him. "This isn't just a hearing," Hank observed. "It's a criminal trial."

Cooper couldn't disagree. His friends were going to be on trial. Without any preparation or representation.

"I don't like it," Georgia said.

"Cooper! Hank and Georgia!" Bren trotted over from the far side of the room and hugged them. "Viola." Bren shook her hand.

"How's life in the metaverse?" Georgia asked him.

"It's different. Completely different. For the first time in decades, my back doesn't hurt, we've started getting the basic advertising income, and we're not worried that the next storm will wipe out our greenhouse." Bren smiled his big smile. "My wife thinks she's in heaven."

Cooper sat on the front row. Viola sat next to him, while Hank, Georgia, and Bren sat on the other side.

A bailiff opened a door to the side of the room, and Amoco, Mariela, and Amaya filed in and sat at a table to the side of the judge's bench. Mariela leaned over to talk with one of her former coworkers in the audience. She laughed and appeared relaxed as she chatted, but Cooper knew the tense muscle in her cheek was a telltale sign that she was more stressed than she was letting on. Amoco stared blankly ahead, like he was doing math in his head. Cooper at first didn't recognize Amaya, but then it wasn't difficult to connect the dots and figure out that she was the shell-shocked teenager sitting at the table. Her stare was not the stare of someone lost in thought, like Amoco—it was the stare of someone who had mentally shut down.

There were still nine minutes on the countdown clock. Enough time to say hello. As Cooper approached the table, Amoco didn't appear to notice him. Amaya glanced up and then looked away. Mariela smiled at him, but continued her conversation.

"Hey, how are you guys doing?" he asked Amoco and Amaya.

"Okay." Amaya's voice caught as she said it.

"You don't sound okay."

"I'm fine." She made eye contact, but then quickly looked away. "It's just that this looks like we are on trial, and I didn't expect so many people to be here." She looked at the people still entering the room. "I thought it was just going to be a small hearing. And even if we get off and don't spend the rest of our lives in jail, I'm still stuck in here." She picked up her arms and then let them drop by her side again.

"You'll find a way to make it work."

"Will I? When I was a teenager, I couldn't make spending time in Panacea work, and I wasn't stuck here full-time back then. At one point, I couldn't handle the idea of spending another hour in here. And now I'm here *permanently*?"

"Maybe someone will develop a way for people to leave." It was the only thing Cooper could think of to say that might be encouraging.

"I've thought about that, but I don't think they will. All the people who have the skills to do that kind of research work for the companies that own the metaverses and the pod warehouses. Why would they spend their time making a product that allows people to leave?"

She had a good point. Cooper gave up talking. It's not like his previous statements had been helpful.

"I don't even own anything in here," Amaya continued, "except for a few things that are left over from when I was a teenager. Like this outfit." She looked down at her clothing with a smirk. "I look like I'm fourteen."

"Georgia's making you some new avas."

"I know. It'll be nice. I appreciate her doing that. I'm just complaining. I'm sure it will be alright."

"I heard she's going to make all your avas look like the Blob."

Amaya laughed and seemed to relax a bit. "That would be better than looking like I'm fourteen. I'm sure Georgia could make even the Blob look great."

"Cooper." The haptic suit contracted lightly on his arm to let him know that Mariela had touched it.

"How are you doing?" he asked.

"I'm great," she said, but the muscle in her cheek was still taut.

Cooper returned to his seat between Viola and Hank. Viola leaned toward him. "Cooper, can I have a private conversation with you?"

"Sure."

A slight wave of Viola's hand and the sound from the room

disappeared.

"I've figured out what you want."

"What? Impossible. You don't have anything I want."

"But I do. I heard you talking with Amaya. She doesn't want to live here. I feel for her—it's clear that it brings back memories of a bad time from when she was young."

"She's strong. She'll find a way to deal with it."

"Eventually. *Years* from now." Viola leaned in closer and lowered her voice. "Here's what I propose. I created the shot. I think I can create another shot that reverses it so that people can exit Panacea or Bo Place. If you come stay with me, I'll start working on it. Once I'm done, if I haven't convinced you to stay, then I never will. I'll give you the shot and you can go. And you can give it to your friends."

It was an outrageous idea. Didn't Viola already have a moral obligation to work on a shot that could reverse the effects of the first? Apparently, she didn't think she did. She was going to bribe Cooper with the idea instead.

"How do I know you'll be working on it? What if you delay it so that I'm stuck in the metaverse with you?"

"You won't know for sure that you can trust me. Here's the deal— give me at least thirty days. That should be enough time for me to come up with something. And it's not like you're in a rush—your friends can't use it before the trial's over. They will only be able to use it if the ghosts agree to it, which isn't going to happen any time soon."

"This is outrageous."

"Think about it. You agree to take the shot and enter the Bo Place metaverse and be my consort. I'll work on making an exit shot—that's what we'll call it—and in a month or so, it should be ready and you can take it as well as your friends."

"Why don't you just make the exit shot without my involvement? Isn't that the right thing to do?"

"Cooper, I'll lose my job for doing this. Bo Place wants to keep people in the metaverse, not let them go. The only reason I'm willing to do this is because I know it's something you want. But I'm not going to get fired and not get something out of it."

He hadn't thought about that. She probably would get fired.

"The job's not what you thought it would be?"

"Let's just say I didn't anticipate the extent to which the Bo Place board would have their hands in everything. Supposedly, I have complete power, but in reality, I can't even make choices about what to wear in public." She gestured to her cape. Bo Place credits spilling off the cape were filling the area around them.

"So that's why you're willing to risk getting fired?"

"We could enjoy ourselves right up until the minute that I get fired. I'll work on the exit shot in my free time, you can help me out with my duties—lots of appearances and stuff like that—and we'll take advantage of my expense account to do lots of fun stuff. Once the shot is ready and the trial is over, your friends will use the exit shot to get out of the metaverse, and if we want to, we can, too."

"I could just ask Amoco to work on the shot instead. His help would come with a lot less baggage."

"I developed the original shot, so I know best how it's formulated." Viola glanced at Amoco, who still appeared oblivious to everything going on around him. "Plus, Amoco has other stuff he needs to focus on right now."

"What if you aren't successful in creating an exit shot in thirty days? What happens then? I won't be able to leave."

"I know it's not much, but if after thirty days I haven't created an exit shot, then we'll go our separate ways. You'll still be stuck in the metaverse, but you don't have to stay with me."

"Viola," Cooper said, touching her forearm. He wanted to make sure he had her attention. "There's one thing I want to make clear. If I do this, I won't stay with you after the shot is prepared. We won't be a couple, even if we act like one. In the unlikely event that we should at times enjoy each other's company while you're working on the exit shot, I still won't be sticking around."

It was important that she understand this point. When he walked out the door thirty days from now, he wanted to feel confident that she didn't have any illusions he would be staying with her. "There are limits to what I'm willing to do."

"Understood. The truth is, I just need some support. I want to have someone I can talk to, and right now, I don't have that."

He could provide support to her for a limited time. As long as it wasn't permanent. "Okay. I'll do it."

Viola hugged him. He didn't feel like hugging her back. When was he going to stop being controlled by her? He owed her after she got him out of jail—that was true—but this was asking more of him than was fair. But for Amaya, who still looked shell-shocked, and Mariela, who still had the tense muscle in her cheek, he would do it. And he'd do it for Amoco, who looked like doing math in his head was the only way he was avoiding having a breakdown.

Viola turned the sound back on.

Hank nudged him with his elbow. "Private conversation with Viola, huh? What did you talk about?" Hank winked at him.

"The reason it's a private conversation is so that other people don't know what we're talking about. There's no way in hell I'm going to share what we talked about with you."

Hank smiled. "Feeling a tad touchy about your private conversation, I see."

Why couldn't Georgia have sat next to him instead of Hank? Georgia was so much more pleasant to be around.

The lights went out and a strobe light came on. An announcer with a deep voice said, "Attention. Please take your seats immediately."

The multi-colored lights flashed repeatedly, probably giving someone somewhere epileptic seizures. Fog filled the room. It was impossible to see anything clearly. Organ music blared throughout the hall.

After minutes of blinding lights and deafening music, a puff of smoke went up from behind a raised platform that looked like a judge's bench, but could have been a pulpit. The music faded and the lights stopped flashing but stayed on low, with a spotlight illuminating LP perched behind the judge's bench, wearing a robe that was closer to pastor than judge. Off to the right, a group of ghosts appeared in the jury box. Or was it the choir box? It was a confusing mix of rock concert, legal proceeding, and church service.

The lights returned to normal brightness. LP raised his hands in a gesture that seemed to indicate he wanted the audience to be quiet. "Greetings, my fellow friends, both spectral and human alike." LP brought his hands together and clasped them in front of his chest. "We are here today to determine the guilt and punishment of Amoco Cadiz, Mariela Stafford, and Abrihet Amaya Gidada." LP spread his arms in a wide V. "LET US BEGIN!"

The music and strobe lights amped up; the crowd jeered and cheered louder than the music. Only the small group sitting on the front row— Cooper, Viola, Hank, Georgia, and Bren—seemed immune to the roar of excitement as LP's infectious energy spread across the room. Cooper almost felt obliged to cheer along with the crowd. If he didn't, they might come after him.

CHAPTER 12

The Ghost Trial

Thursday, continued

The strobe lights burned Amaya's eyes and made them water. Over the last three days, a feeling of dread had been sneaking up on her like the tide creeping in. Now, seeing all these people cheering, the creeping tide had turned into a crashing wave. She fully understood, for the first time, that her life would never be the same. Even if they managed to get out of this, there would always be hordes of people who would blame her for what happened. Who would think that she ruined their lives.

The strobe lights and blaring music finally stopped. Amaya rubbed her eyes, but it didn't help her headache. She noticed that Elliat was in the balcony streaming the hearing. He had sent a request for an interview, which she had firmly declined.

In the front of the room, on a raised platform, LP stood with his left arm raised. He slowly raised his right hand, pointing toward their table, and proclaimed, "We are gathered here today to hear the evidence against these three." He lowered his hand. "But before we get started, please take a moment to greet the people in the seats next to you."

What was happening? Why was most of the audience getting up to greet the people sitting next to them? Hank and Cooper looked around them like they were as confused as Amaya. Viola awkwardly nodded at a person next to her and then quickly looked away.

"Very good," LP said. "Now, let's get started with the presentation of the evidence. I will begin by reading the 167 charges against the defendants."

A young woman with dark brown curls hurried down the steps to the front of the room. "LP. Sir." The woman shifted awkwardly. There was something familiar about her. "Your honor."

LP's appearance grew to twice the size that it had been. "There is no option for public participation in this hearing. I'll have you removed for contempt of court."

"It's just that, sir, they don't have legal representation." The woman shifted uncomfortably again. "This isn't a hearing, according to custom, unless they have legal representation."

"Fine." LP crossed his arms. "Is there a bar-certified attorney who will represent them?"

"I'd like to represent them."

"You're not bar-certified."

"Well, sir, just another point. It's just that, well, you aren't bar certified. Liam Price is, but you're not. Mr. Price's degree is from Yale, is it not? Yale has ruled that being a clone of one of their graduates does not confer the degree on the clone. If you don't have a law degree, then you're not bar certified. If you're planning to judge the case without certification or a law degree, then I don't see why it should be any different for their lawyer."

Who was this young woman who was timid yet tenacious at the same time, and who dared to stand up to LP?

Smoke actually appeared to be coming out of LP's ears. "Fine." His reply was terse and dismissive. "So you would like to act as their lawyer, then?"

"Yes, I would."

"Well then, Opali Stafford, I declare you the lawyer for the defendants."

A murmur rose in the courtroom.

Mariela sat up straight. "Opali?"

Amaya smiled. That's why she looked so familiar.

"Your honor. Sir," Opali said, "I would like some time to confer with my clients and review their case before we proceed. I suggest we adjourn until a later date."

"Done. We will reconvene in a few days." LP waved his hand in a circle and the music started up again. Another burst of smoke, and LP disappeared.

<p style="text-align:center">~~~~~</p>

Amaya knocked her chair over as she jumped up and rushed around the table to hug Opali.

Mariela followed not long after and embraced Opali as well. "Opali, I didn't recognize you," Mariela said. "Why are you older?"

"This is something that I needed to be older to deal with. Six-year-olds don't really have a lot of capacity to express themselves verbally or make legal arguments. I'll go back to being six before my mom sees me."

"I'm sorry to break it to you," Amaya said, "but I'm sure your mom's already seen this."

"Oh, right." Opali looked down at the floor. "I'll go back to being six when I'm done helping you. It makes my mom happy."

Georgia was next in line to hug Opali.

Cooper also joined them, wrapping Opali in a tight hug.

Opali had a big smile. "Uncle Coop."

Opali hugged Hank as well. "Uncle Hank."

"Wait," Cooper said. "Why does Hank get to be an uncle as well? He hasn't known you nearly as long as I have."

"Oh, Unca Coop, you are so silly! I knew you were going to say that."

"So how old are you?" Amaya asked.

"Twenty-one."

"Do you feel prepared to represent us?" Twenty-one didn't sound old enough to be providing legal representation.

"Of course. None of it is legally binding. The only power the ghosts have over you is the power they have to harm the people in their pods. Oh, and feel free to leave the jail."

"How do we get out?" Mariela asked. "We're locked in."

"You just choose to be somewhere else."

"That's it?"

"It's that simple. You see, the ghosts have modeled their lives on what the humans do, but their only experience of humans is what they see in Panacea, and in Panacea, nobody goes to jail for real. Real jails only exist in the solid world. Jails in Panacea are all part of historical reenactments, or role-playing games, or…well probably for lots of stuff but not for actually jailing people, and so they don't keep anyone in."

"You mean I just spent six hours sleeping on a hard cot for no reason?" Amaya asked.

"Yes. Your jail cell is the Panacea equivalent of unlocked. Not the door—that will seem locked, just like a jail door in the solid world. But choose to be somewhere else—the Zócolo, say, and you'll find that you'll have no problem going there. I'm sorry I didn't tell you this sooner, but I was busy uploading law journals into my information storage."

"How did you get to be so smart?" Mariela asked.

"It runs in the family," she said in all seriousness.

"Will reading up on the law help you if none of this is legally binding?" Amaya asked.

"Oh yes, because it will be treated by LP as if it were legally binding, so we have to take part in the charade."

The guard who had accompanied them to the hearing approached them. "Are you ready?"

"Go back to your cells," Opali said, "and then choose to go wherever you want. "

"Where should we go?"

"It doesn't matter. They'll know where you are as long as you are in Panacea. As your agreement was to remain in Panacea, you will be in compliance with the terms of the agreement. If you somehow managed to leave Panacea, then they would start harming humans. But leaving the jail wasn't part of the bargain, so it's irrelevant."

"So why did the ghosts put us in jail if we can just leave at any time?"

"Because that's what humans do. They put people in jail when they've done wrong. And ghosts do what humans do. Or at least they try to. LP tends to put his own flair on everything he does. Like the hearing today. I bet we could convince him to hold the next one at the Panacea amusement park if you want."

"No, thank you!"

Amaya wasn't surprised by Mariela's strong reaction. Mariela hated Zazora World and considered it an outdated glory project for LP that was also a total waste of money.

"Opali," Amaya said, "if the trial isn't real, does that mean we don't have to worry?"

"Oh no, you should worry. They may not have any legal authority, but they can still hurt you."

~~~~~

Business Today

"All the business news you need to know"

Wednesday, May 17, 2115

By Elliat Exis ~ Business Today's only Newsoogle winning reporter!

* Be sure to watch my daily podcast for news on the ghost
~~~~~

trial *

Hearing was Dull; Six-year-old Represents Humans
First, let me emphasize that I'm glad Mariela Stafford, Amoco Cadiz, and Amaya Gidada did the right thing and turned themselves in. I never doubted that they would do it. But that said, the trial of the century so far has been an almost complete bust. No evidence was presented against the three defendants. There was music, and then some talking, and then they adjourned until a later date.

The one interesting moment was when a young woman in the audience offered to represent the three humans. The young woman appears to be a ghost with advanced capabilities, who is also the digital daughter of Stafford's sister. Sources say that only yesterday she was just six years old, but chose to be older in order to represent the humans. Now that's interesting! Unfortunately, that was about it for the hearing. Hopefully, the next hearing will be more eventful.

Folks, one more thing. Keep an eye on the wildfire tracker to make sure that your location continues to be safe. Apparently, some of the fires are moving fast and hot and could change direction at any time.

~~~~~

Amaya had been in Sofi's digital house once before. It was what she had come to expect from the Stafford family. Beautiful, elegant, roomy. Clearly this wasn't some out-of-the box house purchase—it had been designed in intricate detail by a top digi-dine.

"I insist, you *must* stay here," Sofi was saying. She hugged each one of them, then turned to Opali. "I can't believe how old you are! I miss my six-year-old."

"Mom, I know." Opali flopped down on the couch. "I'll go back to being six once the trial is done."

"It's okay." Sofi sat beside her and placed a hand on her knee. "I like that you're helping them."

Opali leaned her head on her mom's shoulder. "No one else was
~~~~~

going to do it."

"That's why I'm glad you're doing it. No one is better suited to do this than you are. You know the ghosts and how they think better than anybody." Sofi gave Opali a long hug.

Amaya had asked Sofi if she could make some coffee. Sofi had offered to make it for her, but Amaya wanted something to occupy her mind. When they had arrived from the courthouse, Mariela and Amoco hadn't said much. Amoco was standing near the kitchen counter looking blank, while Mariela bustled around the kitchen cleaning stuff that didn't need cleaning.

Amaya poured cups of coffee for Amoco, Mariela, and Sofi. Wisps of steam curled up from the cups. Mariela and Sofi went out onto the balcony. Amoco stayed rooted in place, staring at a wall.

"Amoco."

He startled.

"Your coffee's ready."

Amoco nodded. "Many thanks for this much needed refreshment." He picked up his coffee and headed to the balcony.

Amaya stared at the steam coming off her coffee. She sent a message to her pod to start a caffeine drip. Hopefully it would help with the exhaustion, if only momentarily. She sighed. She didn't want to be around Amoco and Mariela right now. Sure, they were in this together, but she had been dragged into it by the others.

"Auntie 'Maya, you okay?" Opali asked her.

"Yeah. Sure."

Opali reminded her of Grace. Of course, Opali's smooth corkscrew curls were the opposite of Grace's tousled hair that at times looked like she took styling tips from Einstein. But there was something about Opali's mannerisms and overall appearance that was so close to Grace that it burned a hole in Amaya's heart. It had been over a month since Grace had died, but it still hurt like the day it happened.

Amaya took her coffee out to the large balcony overlooking a cove surrounded by rocky hills. An opening in the clifflike rocks on the far side of the cove showed a glimpse of the ocean.

"Are you going to stay here?" Sofi asked.

"I'm not." Amaya sent a message to Georgia asking for ideas for where Amaya could stay. She needed time to herself. And to get away from Mariela and Amoco. She couldn't stop thinking that they were to blame for this mess. If they hadn't deleted the ghosts, then none of them would be here. The quick reply from Georgia offered to let Amaya use her house.

"Why aren't you staying here?" Mariela asked when Amaya told her.

"I just need some space to myself."

"I thought we would support each other through this."

"We will. But it's just that, sometimes, I don't feel supported by you and Amoco. I wouldn't be here if you hadn't lied to me about deleting the ghosts, and used me to do it." As Amaya shared her concerns, her chest constricted and hardened until she struggled with each breath. "I resent that you and Amoco put me in this position."

Amoco didn't respond, but of course, Mariela had something to say.

"Amaya, can't you see it had to be done? Isn't it clear how dangerous LP is? The only reason we're here right now is because he has the power to harm the humans living in pods, and he's ruthless enough to follow through on it." Mariela looked out over the bay. She also seemed to be struggling to breathe. "The only thing I regret is that I didn't delete them permanently." Mariela pressed the palm of her hand to her forehead. "I'm not feeling well. I think I'll lie down for a bit. I assume you won't be here when I get back?"

"Correct."

"Well, if you change your mind, we'll be here." Mariela headed into the house.

The gentle lapping of the tide coming into the bay soothed Amaya's frayed nerves. She took a couple of deep breaths and relaxed her body. She checked the time—five minutes until she needed to meet Georgia. Just enough time for her to catch a few minutes of sleep.

CHAPTER 13

Day Two of the Ghost Trial
Friday

Cooper's mom would be at his cottage any minute now. He wasn't looking forward to asking her to take care of his dogs while he was in the metaverse with Viola. He had considered asking June, or maybe even Hank, but in the end, he didn't want to bother June, and dealing with Hank was about as challenging as dealing with his mom. At least his mom knew how to take care of the dogs already, but he was never going to hear the end of it when she found out why he needed her help.

It had taken him a day to get everything in order. There was probably something important that he was forgetting, but as long as his dogs were taken care of, that was all that really mattered. He checked his mental list of stuff he needed to do one more time. There was nothing left.

Psychologically, though, he felt far from ready. This might be the last time he ever looked around his cottage on the grounds of the Stafford estate. He turned in a circle, taking the time to soak everything in—the living room with the fireplace where he would curl up on the couch with his dogs, the welded artwork that he couldn't bring himself to give away filling up all the wall space, Grace's analog watch that had a place of honor on the mantelpiece. Not all of his memories of this place were good, but there were more good than bad.

"Cooper," his mom breezed in through the front door, "I hope you're preparing breakfast, because I'm famished. I don't know why you insisted on meeting today, especially at this ridiculously early hour. I've been crazy busy." His mother collapsed onto his sofa, facing away from him, and put her feet up on the coffee table. "I saw you at the circus of a hearing that the ghosts held yesterday. That girl doesn't deserve you. It's like she thinks she owns you."

He sighed. His mother was obviously talking about Mariela. "She doesn't think she owns me, Mom. I'm a friend of hers and the other people who are on trial. I wanted to be there." If his mother was this upset with him for going to support Mariela, she really wasn't going to be happy about the whole thing with Viola.

His mom took her feet off the coffee table and turned to face him with her arm propped on the back of the couch. "How do you know these other people? Can you trust them?"

"Mom, you know Amoco. He's been coming around the Stafford estate since he was a kid. You used to dote on him."

"And the other woman?" his mom asked. She was clearly referring to Amaya.

"She's a friend of mine."

"Can you trust her?"

"Yes."

"I've heard bad things about her."

"They're all lies. She and I have been through a lot together and she's always been dependable and a good friend." He felt a twinge of guilt for involving Amaya in disabling the chips. He should have known how hard it would be for her.

"I'm just concerned that a lot is being asked of you."

"Nobody is asking me to do anything." Except Viola.

"So why am I here?" she asked.

"Let's eat breakfast first." Cooper walked over to the fridge and grabbed the one frozen meal he had saved. The empty freezer looked sad—like it was lonely without any food in it. He slammed the freezer door shut and walked over to the food heater. He punched the button to open the door and threw the block of frozen scrambled eggs and toast in without bothering to read the instructions. His mom stared at him from the living room. He pretended to be intently focused on getting the food heater started.

"Cooper, what's wrong? I can tell something is bothering you."

"It's nothing, Mom. Let's eat breakfast and then we can talk." He pulled two sky-blue plates out of the cabinet. People had told him that the sky in the metaverse didn't live up to the sky in the solid world. Apparently, the blue was never quite right.

"I'd rather talk about it now," his mom insisted.

He didn't want to talk about it now, but he didn't want to talk about it ever, so it wasn't like later was going to be any better. He set the plates on the table and got the silverware out of the drawer. He put the silverware next to plates on the small rickety table in the middle of the kitchen.

"Can you take care of my dogs?" he asked.

His mom looked at him carefully, like she was trying to figure out how delicate the situation was and what stupid thing he had done this time. "Why?"

"I have something I need to do."

He took the frozen meal back out of the heater and scanned the bar-code. The heater selected the time and heat setting. He put the meal back inside and pushed the start button.

"How long will you be gone for?"

He avoided eye contact. "Possibly forever."

"Cooper O'Connor, you cannot be serious!" His mother stood up and placed her hands on her hips. "Don't tell me you made a commitment to join Mariela in Panacea?"

"No." His mother actually liked Mariela, she just didn't think that it was good for him to spend time around her. Viola, on the other hand…it was probably safe to say that there wasn't anyone his mother hated more. Cooper didn't blame her. Back in the day, Viola had violated his privacy and disclosed information that had resulted in him getting fired from a job he loved. When Viola had gotten him released from prison a month ago, it had only partially made up for the three-year tailspin that losing his job had sent him into.

He desperately glanced around the room, looking for anything to look at that wasn't his mother. "Viola. She made me a deal."

"VIOLA?" His mother walked in an exasperated half-circle and then turned to face him. "Why in the world are you going with Viola? Was it a condition of her getting you out of jail? Why don't you run this stuff by me ahead of time?"

In no hurry to share more information, he let her keep talking until she eventually stopped. There was a long moment of silence while his mom stared at him.

He placed both hands on the counter and leaned forward like he was keeping an eye on the heater. "It wasn't a condition of her getting me out of jail. She said if I joined her, she would work on an exit shot. Something that would allow people to leave Panacea. Once it's developed, I'll be able to take it as well."

"Oh, Cooper." His mother rubbed her temples. "Why do you always do this? Why can't you just take care of yourself and not worry about how other people might be stuck in Panacea? Must you always sacrifice yourself to save others?" She walked over to where he was leaning on the counter.

He resolutely kept looking at the heater. "Mom, my friends are important to me. Viola convinced me she can do this, and that she will get it done quickly. I know there are no guarantees. I know she may not be trustworthy. Or maybe an exit shot is impossible. But this is how things are in the world right now. Things suck."

"Alright, Cooper." His mom touched his cheek. "It's obvious this is something you feel like you need to do. I just don't understand why you're letting Viola take advantage of you. Don't you get any say in what happens?"

"Apparently not."

The heater beeped. He stabbed the button to open the door.

"I just think you need to take care of yourself," his mom said.

"Mom, it's not up for discussion."

He grabbed the tray without thinking. Burning pain stung his hand. He shoved the tray back in and grabbed a hot pad out of the drawer. That was one benefit of going into the Bo Place metaverse—he wouldn't have to worry about getting burned anymore. Everything would be an unremarkable, consistent, tepid temperature. After retrieving the tray once more, he dropped the watery eggs and soggy toast on the table, rattling the silverware. The mushy substance barely resembled food. "Let's eat."

His mom didn't move toward the table. "If you won't take my advice, then I don't see the point of hanging around here."

"Come on, Mom." He nodded at the food. "Let's eat."

"I don't feel like eating gray, lumpy stuff." She gave the food a look of disdain.

She was right. The food didn't look appetizing. He probably should have chosen something more enticing for what may be his last meal of solid food in a long time. Or possibly ever, if Viola didn't figure out how to get them out.

"It is pretty depressing." He sat down at the table and picked up his knife and fork, not sure what he wanted to do with them. He abruptly stood back up, grabbed the untouched tray of food, and threw it in the trash. "I've lost my appetite."

"Cooper, I think you should reconsider what you're doing." His mom placed her hands on her hips. It was the stance that she took when she wanted him to know she was being extra serious. "But if you decide to go through with it, I'll take care of your dogs."

~~~~~

Georgia's voice woke Amaya up. Amaya hadn't intended to fall asleep in the deck chair on Sofi's balcony, but she must have been more tired than she had realized. Low sloping rays of sunlight reflected off the cliffs across the cove. Everyone else had left the porch, though there were voices in the house. She checked the time. She had slept through the night and into the next morning. She stood and stretched. The sounds of Amoco chatting with Georgia filtered out from the kitchen.

Amaya headed into the house. Georgia was at the kitchen island keeping an eye on a coffee maker and Amoco was leaning on the counter across from her. Amaya rubbed her eyes and yawned again. "What time is it?" she asked.

"When I arrived yesterday, you were deeply asleep, so I just let you sleep. I'm here now because I had some big news for Amoco," Georgia said. "I was just sharing it with him."

"It is really quite extraordinary." Amoco had changed his avatar to a mad scientist. Amaya smiled at his wild hair, defying gravity.

She settled onto one of the bar stools at Sofi's kitchen counter. "What's the news?"

Amoco leaned towards her and whispered conspiratorially, "Petra showed up at the estate with Miss June!"

Amaya had heard this already from Mariela, so it wasn't a surprise. "I can't believe she had another tesseract that she didn't tell anyone about."

Amoco smiled. "I can hardly believe it myself! And can you believe, much to my delight and astonishment, that one end of the tesseract is in my family crypt?"

Now this was news. "How can it be in your crypt? I mean, how did Petra get access to the crypt to put a tesseract in there?"

"Would you believe that it was Petra's family's house long before Area 52 was created? When she built Area 52, she added the tesseract to the house and connected it to her house in Area 52. A half-century later, she pretended to be my aunt and had a will drawn up with me as the beneficiary. Then, a couple of decades ago, she had herself declared dead so I could inherit the house."

"You didn't know it was Petra?"

"I did not. I never had the privilege of meeting the aunt who gave me the house. Not until now."
~~~~~

"But why you? Why did she pretend to be your aunt?"

"I know the answer to that," Georgia said. She poured herself some coffee. "She wanted to give the house to someone who was deserving of it. She spent years looking for the right person—someone with an analytical and logical mind—and eventually she found Amoco. She said he was the best neuroscientist she could find."

Amaya also poured herself some of the coffee and requested a caffeine drip. She wiped her eyes to get rid of the grogginess from sleeping so long.

"Has the tesseract been there for the past eighty years since Area 52 was created?" she asked.

"Yes! Can you believe it?" Amoco said. "Can you believe that the terminus of the tesseract on this side is in my Faraday cage? Where we had our meetings. It is absolutely unbelievable!" Amoco grabbed Amaya by the arms and twirled her around. "Knowing who my aunt is—the feeling is amazing."

"That's too bad she didn't make it here before you went into Panacea," Georgia said. "It would have been nice if you could have met her."

"So true, but we did speak using a terminal. That will have to do."

Georgia turned her attention to Amaya. "Amaya, whenever you're ready to go, let me know. I have six different designs for my place, from beach house to cozy mountain cabin. I can't wait to show them all to you."

Amaya was more than ready to get settled in at Georgia's place. Despite just having woken up from one nap, she was looking forward to her next one. She was so tired these days. Probably she was drained from the stress. "Let's go then," she said. "Amoco, that's great that you found your aunt. I mean your benefactor."

"She can be your honorary aunt," Georgia amended.

"That she will! I am off to contact my honorary aunt." He danced a little sidestep. Amaya had never seen him so happy. "I have so many questions for her! And I own a tesseract!"

Amaya smiled. She was upset with Amoco and unhappy in general, but it lifted her spirits to see him so happy and dancing with his unruly hair.

"Wait—" Amoco stopped dancing with his hands in the air. "Wait! Such an obvious solution…"

He stayed frozen, his hands above his head, apparently deeply lost in thought. Amaya waited. How long was he going to stand like that?

After what must have been ten seconds, Amoco dropped his arms. "I have figured it out. The ghosts are not using a Faraday cage to protect their code, they are using a tesseract. Because the tesseract warps time, they can send all the code for the ghosts through it. If the time warping is the same as in Area 52, then three days later all their original code shows up. If the code has been deleted during those three days, all the ghost needs to do is restore the original code to bring back the other ghosts."

Amoco was right. It was an obvious solution. And a brilliant one. "Of course! That would explain a lot."

Amoco ran his hand through his hair, making it stand even more improbably on end. "They could send a constant stream of code through the tesseract. It would be almost impossible to beat because any actions taken by us to remove the ghosts could be undone using the code that was taken through the tesseract."

"Could we take out the tesseract?"

"We could try to find the tesseract, but I do not think it will be easy to locate given that we do not know what it looks like. The odds are extremely small."

"Is it possible to have a tesseract in virtual reality?"

Amoco stroked his beard and nodded. "It's hard to imagine how it would be done, but it is plausible."

~~~~~

The man helping Cooper get set up in a pod was much less helpful than the people he saw the other day at the estate. The man wheezed and sighed like Cooper was taking up too much of his time. Apparently, being the consort of the Sovereign Ruler of Bo Place didn't count for much. At least not in the solid world.

The Bo Place warehouse wasn't as big as some he had seen, but it still had rows upon rows of pods hanging from lifts that were stories high.

"Cooper, can you hear me?" Viola's voice came out of a speaker in the pod.

"Yeah."

This was probably the worst decision of his life. He was going to miss his house, his dogs, even his mother. Sure, things had been tough,
~~~~~

especially with his daughter's death, but for the first time in a long time, he could imagine a future when he could be happy again. Odd that, once again, Viola was going to ruin things.

It was also ironic that despite all his attempts to avoid technology, he was now jumping in with both feet and immersing himself in tech. There was no way to do it halfway. He was either all in or all out. He would just have to count on Viola to figure out the exit shot so that one day, he could be all out again.

The man helping him continued to bustle around the pod and push buttons that didn't appear to change anything.

"Viola?"

"Yes, Cooper?" Her voice sounded small coming through the speaker.

"I'll see you on the other side."

"I'll be waiting at the entry point."

"Ready?" the man asked.

"Ready."

"Steel yourself. It's gonna hurt." With that warning, the man pushed the plunger on the shot.

Cooper was prepared for the pain. Mariela, Amaya, Amoco, everyone had told him about the overwhelming pain. Prepared or not, it still took his breath away.

After a few minutes, Cooper's vision cleared. A large gray void stretched as far as he could see. Floating in the void, Viola waited for him in her cape that dispensed Bo Place points. Did she really wear that thing everywhere?

"Cooper, you have to choose an avatar."

"How do I do that?"

"Ask in your head to be shown available avatars. You don't have to ask anyone in particular—the system can read your thoughts."

"Great." Just what he needed—a system that could spy on him all the time. He silently asked to be shown avatars. A selection of generic avatars popped into his mind. "How do I select one?"

"You just have to make a decision. The system knows what you want once you've made a decision. If you want something, just ask for it in your head and it will be sent to you."

"So if I think that I want a generic avatar, I'll get that?"

"You just have to make a decision," she repeated. "The system knows when you've made up your mind."

Cooper decided on a basic, off-the-shelf avatar for someone about his age and with his hair and skin color. He didn't feel up to making any more decisions today.

"Really, Cooper?" Viola looked annoyed. "You're my consort. Surely you could have chosen something more creative than Joe Avatar."

"I'm still figuring things out. Give me a while."

"Well, let's get you settled in. You'll probably want to rest after going through the transition." She placed a hand on his arm. He felt a slight pressure where her hand was, but no warmth. "Cooper, before we go, there's something I need to talk with you about." She took a deep breath. "I need your help with the board of Bo Place. They're so controlling, I don't know what to do. I took this position because I thought I would have freedom and authority and I don't have any."

"I'll…" *What use could he be to Viola?* "…I'll do what I can." He didn't mind being helpful, but he wasn't going to pretend that he wanted to be there.

"Thank you. I want you to know that I'm really glad you're here. But I do have one request."

"Okay."

"I know you're only here because I bribed you with making the exit shot, but I would really appreciate it if in public you acted like you actually wanted to be here." Viola almost sounded vulnerable—the request more of a plea than a demand.

"Whatever you want." He had already assumed that would be the case. He could fake a smile all day long.

"And who knows, maybe with time you'll want to be here. And then it won't be acting anymore."

It was unlikely, but he didn't need to tell Viola that.

~~~~~

Ah, Elliat, what has become of you? Amaya sighed as she watched the floating image of Elliat giving his latest report. Not very interested in Elliat's reporting, she switched Georgia's house from beach house to cabin. The couch she was lying on morphed from off-white canvas to brown leather. The crashing waves outside the windows turned to snow and the sea to forest. She switched it back to a beach house.

Elliat chatted on about how there had been no updates since the
~~~~~

hearing, although only a day had passed, so no one really expected updates at this point.

Amaya switched the house back to a cabin.

"Folks, we have some breaking news," Elliat was saying. "Cooper O'Connor has shown up on the landing pad at the Bo Place Sovereign Ruler's palatial mansion."

Amaya sat up straight. A shot of the back of someone who generically resembled Cooper replaced the picture of Elliat's head. Cooper was gazing up at a colonnade of Corinthian columns that spanned the front of a massive building and topped a grand staircase leading up from the landing pad.

Elliat's face appeared again. "He's just been joined by the Sovereign Ruler of Bo Place herself, Viola Mason. O'Connor seemed disoriented, and dare I say—cranky, when he arrived on the landing pad."

Cooper didn't take Viola up on her offer, did he? He couldn't have…

Elliat continued, "This footage is from about five minutes ago. We're seeing Mason taking O'Connor's hand and leading him up the cascade of marble steps to the oversized gilded doors. From what I've been told, the doors lead to the public reception area of the Sovereign Ruler's house. Observers are asking, did Mason take his hand affectionately? Is there some sort of relationship here?"

Why didn't Cooper tell her about accepting Viola's offer? What could Viola have found that would be enough to convince Cooper to agree to go with her?

A message popped up from Opali saying that she was on the cabin's landing pad. Without bothering to get up, Amaya unlocked the entrance and told Opali to come in. A twenty-one-year-old Opali entered Georgia's cozy cabin living room.

"You're watching the news about Uncle Coop?"

"Yes." Amaya switched off Elliat's image. He was repeating himself and not adding any new information. "I'm dumbstruck. Did you know about this?"

"I figured it would happen." Opali shrugged. "Viola always gets what she wants."

"But what did she find that he wanted badly enough to give in?"

"I don't know, but I can guess." Opali sat in the leather armchair.

"Okay." Amaya leaned toward Opali.

"His weak spot would be other people. She probably promised she would help out someone he cares about who is in need," Opali said. "Like you all."

Amaya sighed. It was the only thing that made sense—Cooper had gone to stay with a woman he hated in order to help them out. That also explained why he didn't tell them. "Does Mariela know?"

"When I left my mom's house, Mariela was sleeping, so I don't think she does."

"She's going to flip out when she finds out." There was a moment of silence. Amaya couldn't think of anything to say. Her mind was stuck on Cooper agreeing to go with Viola. She shook her head to clear it and focused again on the present. "I'm sorry. I'm not being a good host. Would you like some tea?"

"No, thanks." Opali squirmed in her chair. "I have an update on the trial. The spectrals—."

"By spectrals, do you mean the ghosts?"

"Yes, but we prefer to be called spectrals."

"Okay. Go on."

"The spectrals have decided that the trial will be without the defendants present. I'll be allowed to represent you all, and Elliat Exis has been given exclusive access to report on the proceedings."

"Just Elliat?"

"I fought to have you all there. I pointed out that not having the defendants there goes against historical precedent, and LP made a long-winded statement that could be summed up as 'he doesn't care.' I'm sorry, Amaya."

"Why does Elliat get to be there if we can't?"

"The spectrals want the trial publicized because they want to turn the public against you. Public perception—not legal matters—is what this whole trial is about. If you're in the room, you might come across as sympathetic."

"I don't like this." The ghosts were engaging in a one-sided public relations campaign against them. It wasn't right that they weren't even allowed to defend themselves. "It's not fair."

It was ironic that the ghosts had insisted they enter Panacea, but then didn't have any desire for them to be at the trial. They could have stayed in the solid world if they were going to be waiting around all day.

"Oops." Opali jumped to her feet. "I gotta go. My mom says Mariela woke up and heard about Cooper and Viola."

Opali disappeared from the living room, leaving behind an empty spot on Georgia's armchair. Amaya flipped Elliat back on. He was still sharing the same news with a shot of Viola's palatial mansion in the background.

A heaviness settled into Amaya's stomach. She was lonely. Nyala was busy with her work; Hank and Georgia were still helping out a few pod lifers who had decided not to take the shot. She probably wouldn't have much contact with Cooper now that he had entered the Bo Place metaverse. They all felt far away. She had nothing to do but sit and wait for more information. Nothing to do and no one to do it with.

CHAPTER 14

Week One of the Ghost Trial

Thursday

The black faded from Mariela's vision. A building with a commanding presence and massive Corinthian columns loomed in front of her. The process of getting a visa to visit Bo Place had been complicated and bureaucratic—it had taken an entire week from when she had heard that Cooper had joined Viola for it to be approved. It shouldn't be that hard, considering that no actual movement was involved between the virtual worlds. After overcoming the many tedious hurdles, she was here and ready to pay a surprise visit to Cooper.

The landing pad for the residence of Bo Place's Sovereign Ruler was at the foot of an expansive staircase with a colonnade of marble columns. The imposing edifice—with the appearance more like a government building than a residence—was the sort of place where a power-hungry dictator would live. No surprise then that Viola lived there.

Maybe she should have told Cooper she was coming. It no longer seemed like a good idea to drop in unannounced. What if Cooper didn't want to see her? It wasn't like they had been getting along these last few months. Or the last few years. But it was too late to back out now—her presence on the landing pad would have been announced already.

If only she wasn't still so tired, it would be easier to handle any awkwardness caused by her arrival. Other than crashing for a few hours at night, she normally never got tired. *Why had she been dragging so much lately?*

"Mariela?" The sound of Cooper's voice came from no apparent direction. "What are you doing here?" the booming voice asked.

"I thought I would check in on you. Make sure that Viola is treating you well." Mariela said it like she was joking, but there was a lot of truth to the statement.

"Well, this is a surprise. Come on up. I'll meet you at the doors."

She got the signal that she had been approved to enter the building dominating the politely landscaped grounds around it. Looking up the long staircase made her tired. It was virtual reality, so it wouldn't take any effort to walk up the steps, but it made her brain tired. She put one foot in front of another and eventually made it to overbearing gilded doors with steel studs in them. The doors squeaked open at a glacial pace. Eventually, they opened far enough for Cooper to stick his head through. It was easy enough to recognize him as his avatar appeared to be designed to look exactly like him, with wavy brown hair and honey-colored eyes.

"So, you were worried about me, huh?" He gave her a broad smile as he gestured for her to come inside.

The large front room with chandeliers and wooden parquet flooring felt formal—like a ballroom or event area. Cooper led her to a door off to the side and down a long hallway with walls painted a rich blue with gold flecks and cushy gold velvet carpeting. Golden sconces lining the hallway provided a dim glow.

"This is the public reception area of the house," Cooper said. "Don't judge us by it—the appearance of the public area is dictated by the Bo Place board. The private residence is much more livable. Viola and I can arrange it as we like."

We? Cooper just casually referred to Viola as though she were a life partner—things were worse than Mariela had expected. It seemed like Viola had done a good job of getting into Cooper's head.

"You seem chipper," she said. "Especially for someone who just took a permanent step with a woman he professes to hate."

He stopped to look at her. The sconce next to him flickered. "Listen, Mariela, I spent most of the last three years being bitter, and I got nothing out of it." His tone lightened. "I might as well try to be positive if I can. I agreed to this, so there isn't a point in wandering around moping."

"But why did you agree to it?" She still didn't understand what had motivated him to say yes to Viola's offer. She wished Cooper would keep walking. She wanted to get out of the gilded hallway to somewhere where she could sit down.

"I did it because it was the right thing to do." He looked down and shifted his weight from one foot to the other. There was something he wasn't telling her. He hadn't yet learned how to hide his emotions in the metaverse, which gave her the advantage in reading him.

Cooper started walking again toward another door at the end of the hallway.

Cooper opened the door and called out, "Viola, we have a visitor!" The gaudy ostentatiousness of the hallway opened to a living space with clean lines and a non-fussy design. To one side, Viola busied herself in the kitchen making something that looked delicious but probably wouldn't taste like much in the metaverse, and to the other side an intimate living area beckoned with a small fire. The warmth and coziness of the place contrasted sharply with the titanic proportions of the entry hall. The exception was the other side of the living room, where an expansive wall of windows opened onto a balcony. The house perched at the top of a cliff, with falcons riding the thermals outside.

Viola put down her spatula, circled around the kitchen island, and took Mariela's hand. "Mariela, what a nice surprise!"

Mariela's mint green pantsuit with a lilac sweater sporting white daisies had seemed perfect for spring until she saw how Viola was dressed. The luminescent fabric of Viola's emerald-colored dress shimmered in a way that highlighted every curve of her body. Her red hair had a sheen and depth of color—each strand obviously hand-crafted by her digidine—that made a statement that she was a person who could afford the best. Whoever had made her avatar did work that rivaled Georgia's.

Cooper's avatar was less showy, but now that Mariela examined it, the fine, detailed work was evident in his ava as well. It was all there—the hairs each moved individually rather than as a group, and careful thought had obviously gone into the color of each nano-pixel of his skin color.

"Do you want some food?" Cooper asked. "Doesn't it smell great?"

"She can't smell it." Viola was back at the stove, stirring whatever she was cooking. "The chip designers gave up on the sense of smell years ago."

"Oh." Cooper rubbed his chin. "Sorry, if I had known you were coming, I would have sent a smell pack over for you as well." He smiled. "It smells so good."

Cooper's smile was like the giddy smile of a young boy going to the Zazora Games for the first time. He was enjoying rubbing it in that he had access to things that she didn't, so Mariela ignored his comments.

Most of the smell packs were mediocre anyway and not worth the money spent on them. Plus, the smell tended to linger. Nothing worse than still being able to smell croque monsieur hours after having finished eating.

"I specially designed the smell pack," Viola said.

Of course she did. Viola's smell packs were probably lovely.

"I took my twenty favorite meals and twenty of Cooper's," Viola continued, "and made smell packs that exactly replicate the smell. You should really try one sometime, though I'm not sure how it would work in Panacea."

Mariela felt a stab of nausea at the idea. "No, thanks."

This happy domesticity between Viola and Cooper wasn't what she expected. Where was the dark and self-pitying Cooper who resented the manipulative Viola? Why was Viola able to make him happy where Mariela had always failed? Was Viola brainwashing him?

"The other cool thing," Cooper clapped his hands together, apparently unable to contain his enthusiasm for his new living situation, "is that we have pods with advanced designs, and they have heating, cooling, and wind. If I go over by the fire, my pod turns on the heater and I get warmer—it's even directional so it just warms the side that's facing the fire—and if I go out on the porch, I get cold and can feel the wind blowing. I'm surprised that the Stafford family isn't using these pods." He raised one eyebrow. "Isn't your family supposed to have the latest tech?"

He was definitely rubbing it in now. "It sounds delightful." She said it as sincerely as she could manage, but Cooper would pick up on the underlying sarcasm, which was just as she wanted.

Apparently, all her worry about Cooper had been an unnecessary waste of emotional energy. And all that work she went through to get the visa to come here, why had she even bothered? He was obviously doing fine.

"Why don't we sit on the balcony for a bit?" Cooper pulled open the clear door and waited for Mariela to go through.

She didn't feel like talking anymore. In fact, what she really wanted was to lie down. She felt so tired. But here she was, and it had taken a lot of work to get here, so she might as well stick around for a bit. She headed onto the balcony and looked over the railing with an interlacing design of wrought iron. The detail of the plants hanging on the edge of the cliff under the railing was, not surprisingly, exquisite. Cooper slid the balcony door shut behind them.

An accurate appearance of depth was difficult in virtual environments, but whoever had designed the rolling plains, meandering streams, and looming mountains off in the distance had done a good job of making each element appear far away. Viola had clearly spared no expense in her digi-design. Mariela sighed and pushed her envy away.

"So Viola is treating you well?" she asked.

"She's been nothing but great. Do you know I hang glide into the office? Or sometimes I unroll the slide and take it into work." He waved his hand, and a slide showed up that disappeared into the valley below.

"How do you get home? A trampoline that bounces so high you can get back up here?"

"No, but that's a great idea. I'm going to make one of those." Cooper waved his hand again, and the slide disappeared. "I have a large eagle; I usually fly home on her back." He smiled. He was still taunting her.

"Great." She rolled her eyes. "Sounds enjoyable." Sarcasm probably wasn't appropriate, but there didn't seem to be any other response.

"It's been better than I expected—designing the house was fun and I enjoy helping Viola with the Bo Place political stuff at times. Viola has given me things to do that I think are important and interesting. I feel useful but I have no obligation to actually do anything, even though I try to get into the office at least once a day. Although sometimes my eagle's not available, so the trampoline would come in handy then."

Mariela's curiosity got the better of her. "Why isn't your eagle available when you need her?"

"I don't know." He shrugged. "Some people would say she's sentient and gets to make her own decisions."

Mariela nodded. It made as much sense as anything else in the metaverse. She leaned on the railing to enjoy the view, or enjoy it as much as she could. What she really wanted was to lie down, but she was already lying down in her pod, so lying down in the metaverse wouldn't make her feel any better. What was going on with her? Why did she feel so awful? Despite her doctors' best efforts, they hadn't been able to find anything wrong with her.

Cooper stood to one side, his thoughts hidden from her. The days when she could figure out what he was thinking were long gone. She needed to accept that she didn't know him anymore. She thought Cooper knew that Viola couldn't be trusted, but now she wasn't so sure.

"I hope you remember how she treated you," she said.

His jaw hardened. "I remember exactly how she treated me." He was angry now, but she wasn't sure if it was with her or Viola. He turned to her. "You can't tell me how to feel about Viola. I made a decision based on circumstances that this was the best option. Now that I've made the decision, I'm not going to second-guess it. I'm going to make the best of it and enjoy myself if I can."

Her stomach turned in knots. Talking about this was making her nauseous. She took a deep breath. "And what is it exactly that you are getting out of this?"

Cooper exhaled sharply and ran his fingers through his hair. "You are so infuriating!"

It would be so nice to lie down for a minute. She should just close her eyes for a bit. Get back to Panacea and rest. Cooper had said something that she wanted to reply to, but she couldn't remember what it was.

"Mariela!"

Mariela startled. Cooper was touching her arm, his brow furrowed. "Are you okay?"

"I don't feel well." Between the nausea and fatigue, it was as much of an explanation as she could come up with. "I think I should head back to Panacea now." She just needed to get to the transfer point. "I'm going to head home and sleep." Sleep didn't seem like it would make her feel better, but she might be able to function again.

"You should stay here."

"I can't. I'll overstay my visa." Her muscles and joints ached.

"I'll have Viola get your visa extended."

She sighed. "Great, now I'll owe her." She sent the doctor a message asking him to give her a sedative to help her sleep. It was the only way to escape the nausea and the pain.

CHAPTER 15

The Ghost Trial Ends
Friday

Mariela checked the time. Ten hours since the doc had given her the sedative. She was sprawled on a couch that she had barely reached before the sedative kicked in. The fire that she couldn't feel roared in the fireplace. She should ask about getting one of those new pods.

"You're awake."

Mariela pushed herself up to a sitting position. Viola was curled up in a chair near the fireplace, drinking something that looked like hot chocolate.

Mariela rubbed her eyes. "Hey."

"How are you feeling?"

"Not good. Sleeping didn't help much."

"I've been in touch with your doctors. They're not sure what's going on, but they suggest you stay here for now."

"Is that okay?"

"You're welcome to stay as long as you want."

Mariela leaned over and wrapped her arms around her waist. It didn't help with the nausea. "Are you sure? I might mess up your plans with Cooper." Her bitterness about how happy Cooper seemed was showing through, but she didn't care.

Viola sniffed. "You'll have no effect on my plans. You both know you can't commit to him and any chances he has with you are dead on arrival. As far as I'm concerned, he's free for the taking."

"Sure, Viola. Whatever. But he's not something that you just pick up at the store and then own."

"I'm fully aware of that."

"Are you?"

"Mariela, let me be clear. Cooper has his own free will. And if he stays with me over the long run, it will be because he chose to. It's my job to convince him that he wants to stay."

Mariela didn't bother pointing out that Viola was unlikely to be successful. "Did you take care of my visa? Cooper said you would."

"Yes. I also contacted Amoco to look into what's making you sick. It could be unanticipated side effects from the shot."

"Did Bo Place see any side effects like this in their clinical trials?"

Viola snorted. "The clinical trials were cut short. It was a bad idea that I strongly recommended against, but was overruled on."

"What?" The wave of anxiety that hit her made the nausea worse. "How did they get approval to use the shot without finishing the clinical trials?"

"Bo Place wanted to get it out on the market, and the government was so desperate to get people back into the metaverses that it rushed the approval."

"Shit." Who knew what toxic substance she had allowed to be injected into her? Not that she had much of a choice, but it would have been nice to know beforehand.

Viola's brow furrowed. "Maybe if you didn't want a rushed method for people to enter Panacea, your friends shouldn't have disabled the chips."

Her friends. Amoco, Amaya, Cooper, Bren—they had all taken the shot. "Is anyone else sick?"

"Not that I know of. But it would be a good idea for Amoco to start exploring it as a possibility."

Why wasn't Viola working on it? "Just Amoco?" Mariela asked. "If it's a possible side effect of the shot, shouldn't you be working on it?"

"I'm working on another important project. Amoco can get help from the woman from Area 52—what was her name?"

"Petra." What project could be more important to Viola than making sure that millions of people weren't about to get sick from the shot?

Viola nodded. "Right. Petra's brilliant. She can help him."

The floor rocked under Mariela's feet. It was like being on a ship ruthlessly rocked by waves. "Is the floor moving?"

"No."

Mariela couldn't focus. Pain stabbed from her eyes, spreading throughout her body. She messaged the doctor for another sedative.

<center>~~~~~</center>

It was just sad. Amaya was in the largest playground in the world, a world of incredible imagination. She had always looked at Panacea like a kid with no money looks into a candy store—she was jealous of her friends as they entered and exited easily, as they traveled around the world, virtually of course, and had experiences that she could only dream about.

After always being on the outside looking in, she was finally on the inside, and she was bored out of her mind. Now the best she could come up with was exploring all the settings on Georgia's house. She had settled on a medieval castle after the novelty had worn off.

She wasn't in the mood to go out and explore. She couldn't even go to her own trial. The ghosts—spectrals, that is—should just put her in virtual jail already. It wasn't like she was free now. Being stuck in the metaverse and unable to get out, being isolated from her friends and family, it was already a prison.

Amaya had a short reprieve from her boredom when Bren sent her a message asking how she was doing. On a whim, Amaya suggested that he and his wife stop by for a visit. Ten minutes later, Bren and his wife were settled on the rock bench in the throne room of the castle. Amaya couldn't help but feel a little jealous of how happy they looked perched on the uncomfortable bench.

"So, you're both doing well?" Amaya didn't know Bren all that well, and she was just meeting his wife, so she wasn't sure what to talk about with them.

Bren smiled and grabbed his wife's hand. "Yeah, we're doing great." Bren's wife smiled at him. He squeezed her hand. "We don't own anything yet other than our avatars, but we've got lots of job options now."

"That's great." Amaya wished she could feel some of their excitement. It was selfish of her, but seeing how happy they were just made her more depressed.

The conversation lumbered along at a stilted pace, touching on topics with little substance and long pauses.

"Oh," Bren perked up, "have you heard about the wildfires on the edge of town? I don't think they're close to our old place, but who cares, because we don't live there anymore!"

Amaya had forgotten about the wildfires. No one seemed to talk about them in the metaverse.

Bren's wife leaned toward him and spoke in a low voice, "Remember, babe, that we're not supposed to speak about the weather."

"What do you mean, you're not supposed to speak about the

weather?" Amaya asked.

"I'm sorry," she said, "I forgot that you're new here too. We've been told that people in Panacea don't talk about the weather. They say that the weather doesn't make a difference here, so talking about it bores everyone."

No wonder her conversations about the weather had ended in awkward silence. She sniffed. "I've always liked talking about the weather." It was her failsafe when she couldn't think of anything else to talk about. It was another sign that Amaya didn't fit in in Panacea.

"Me too." Bren nodded. "I'm always talking about the weather and the wife has to remind me that no one here cares."

Amaya nodded. Living in Panacea was like living in a new culture.

There was an awkward silence as Amaya tried to think of something non-weather-related to say. "You're liking living in Panacea?" she finally asked.

"Oh yes," Bren's wife said, "we like it quite a bit. Our life in the solid world wasn't always the easiest."

"It sucked," Bren said. "This one was pregnant all the time," he clapped his wife on her shoulder. "Someone had to pay the bills, and them surrogate gigs were the best paying work available. She gave birth fifteen times, and none of them ours."

Bren's wife put her hand on his leg. "But it wasn't easy for you either, dear."

"Yeah, I about broke my back growing food for us—my fifty-five-year-old back doesn't do good leaning over the plant beds anymore. And fixing up the aeroponic greenhouse every time the weather messed it up just about killed me."

"You must like it a lot better here," Amaya said.

Bren nodded and smiled a big smile. "Sure do! It's the first time, the first time in decades, that I haven't been in pain. I love it here!"

Amaya could see the difference in how much easier his movements were than in the solid world. No wonder he liked it so much here.

"I love it here, too." Bren's wife had a delicate way about her. It was hard to believe that she had been pregnant fifteen times. "We've been enjoying ourselves."

"Great. Great." Amaya bobbed her head in a nod that didn't really have any meaning. "What sorts of things have you been doing?"

Bren's wife perked up. "Oh, we're going to the Zazora Games

tonight. Mariela sent us a bunch of points when Bren agreed to join her on that…" Bren's wife raised an eyebrow at him. "Honey, what did you call it? Expedition?"

"Right," Bren answered. "Although now I call it the cursed expedition. She paid me a lot for that, so we haven't had any reason to trade our Zazora points. Thought we would use them to go to a game now that we can actually go in person."

A month ago, Amaya would have been beyond excited to go to the Zazora Game. Now she didn't feel anything, but she tried to sound positive for Bren and his wife. "Sounds great. I'm sure you'll enjoy it."

"Have you gone to a game? Since you took the plunge and entered Panacea permanently?"

"No. There really hasn't been time."

Bren looked around the room. "You don't look too busy to me. What are you doing with your time? I know you're not at the hearings because I've been watching Elliat's coverage. And I know you're not at your job, 'cuz you can't do your job in here."

"I stay busy." She was offended by Bren implying that she didn't have much to do, even though it was true.

"Wait, don't tell me that you're spending all your time watching Elliat's twenty-four-hour feed on the hearings?" Bren raised his eyebrows. "Admit it—that's what you were watching when we walked in. Did you see his 'Behind the Gavel' special where he interviewed LP?" Bren smiled. "I bet you did!

Amaya felt unnecessarily defensive. "I've also had daily martial arts lessons with Hank." It was the one thing she had done besides watching nonstop Elliat coverage.

"Come to the game with us!" Bren said. "You've got to get out of this house!"

Amaya smiled. Going to the Zazora Games didn't sound too bad, but she had other plans. And despite what Bren may think, her plans didn't involve watching Elliat's twenty-four-hour channel. "Nyala is going to use a projection room to visit this evening."

"Nyala? Invite her also! We have more than enough points."

Amaya had only been to the stadium once as an adult. At the time, using the projection room made her sick, and she had never gone back. She went with her family regularly as a child, although those memories were a little hazy because she had suppressed them with meds for decades. But she remembered clearly that she used to have a lot of fun with Nyala at the games. "Okay, I'll ask her."

"Tell her to invite Hank and Georgia and whoever else wants to go. I have enough points for a box for all of us. And Amoco, of course. What about Mariela? I heard she's been sick or something."

Amaya nodded. "Mariela's sick. She's stuck in Bo Place until she feels better."

"Does she get sick much?" Bren's wife asked.

"No, never. It seems like kind of a big deal."

"I'm sure she'll be fine," Bren said.

Amaya wasn't so sure. If Mariela was too sick to return, she must be doing pretty badly.

"I'll ask Amoco," Amaya said. "But I'm not sure if he'll be able to go. He's been busy trying to figure out what's wrong with Mariela."

Amaya sent messages to Nyala, Amoco, and Opali. Amoco declined to go to the game for the reason that Amaya had expected, but Nyala and Opali agreed to go. Nyala planned to use one of the projection rooms at the estate.

A conversation request beeped. Amaya pulled up the control screen. Nyala's name flashed on it.

"Do you mind if I take this?" Amaya asked Bren and his wife. "I'll be brief."

Bren shook his head. "By all means, go ahead and answer it."

Amaya answered the request.

"Amaya! How's my favorite sister?"

"Your favorite and only sister is doing about as good as you would expect. I'm glad you agreed to go to the game. It'll be nice to do something different."

"I agree," Nyala said. "And it just got a little bit more fun."

"What happened?"

"Do you remember Petra? She wants to go, too."

Petra, the woman who was eighty-four or 101 years old, depending on how you counted, wanted to go to the Zazora Game? The woman who never smiled and seemed chronically annoyed by the people around her? The woman who always looked down her nose at other people? She wanted to pack into a virtual stadium with 100,000 screaming fans and root for a team? It was hard to imagine.

"Really?" Amaya shrugged. "I don't know what to say about that. I mean, of course, if she wants to go, why not? Do you have a projection room she can use?"

"She can share mine. I'll put a chair in the room for her to sit in."

"Okay, I look forward to seeing her again. Actually, I don't know why I said that. She's a pain in the butt, but it will be interesting to see what she thinks about the games."

"It'll be interesting for sure."

"Just my kind of drama," Bren said with a smile on his face.

Another conversation request came through, this time from Opali. Amaya accepted it. "Opali, did you change your mind about the game?"

"No way, Auntie 'Maya. It'll be my first time watching a game as a twenty-one-year-old. I can't wait!"

"Then what's up?"

"The Spectral Council made some progress in the hearings. They want to see you and Uncle Amoco right now. I'm sending you the coordinates for the landing pad—meet me there in ten minutes."

Amaya looked at Bren and his wife apologetically. "It seems like I have to go."

"No problem. We'll see you at the game. And you can bet I'll be watching Elliat to see what happens in your meeting."

"Let's hope it's not too much drama," Amaya said.

"For your sake, I hope it's downright boring," Bren said.

~~~~~

After some difficulty in figuring out how to use the coordinates that Opali had given her, Amaya arrived at the landing pad. It looked like she was in the glass-fronted lobby of an office building. A red circle of tile under her feet blinked red. Was that a bad sign?

A push in the back from some unseen force shoved her face down about five feet from the landing pad. Her elbow dug into the tile and she hit the ground with enough force to knock the air out of her. A second later, Amoco appeared where she had been standing.

Amoco's eyebrows shot up when he saw her sprawled on the floor. "What in heaven's name, if I may ask, is going on with you?"

She stood up and brushed herself off, although there was no actual dust on her. It was more the embarrassment that she was brushing off. "Something pushed me down."

"Ah. I understand. You were standing on the landing pad at the time
~~~~~

of my approach."

"It appears so." It may have been her fault that she got pushed out of the way, but she didn't have to act like it didn't annoy her. The cheer that she had felt at the end of her visit with Bren and his wife quickly disappeared. She was cranky again.

Amoco nodded at Amaya and stepped down from the landing pad that had just started to blink red again. "I must be careful so as not to suffer the same ignominious fate that you did."

"Well, look who's here." Elliat sauntered toward them, his gait jerky from the limitations of using a projection room. Amaya's heart rejoiced at the sight of Nyala accompanying him. Amaya had left for the hearing so quickly that she didn't have a chance to ask Nyala if she would be there as well.

"Nyala!" Amaya ran up to her sister and threw her arms around her.

Nyala wrapped her in a bear hug. "Amaya, you're going to be okay, alright?"

"Yes." Tears crept into Amaya's eyes, and if she wasn't careful, they might turn into sobs. Having her big sister here to support her was a big deal, but she hadn't realized until just then how much stress she felt about the hearing. "I know I'll be okay." Maybe if she said it enough times, she would start to believe it.

Nyala put an arm around Amoco. "You're going to be okay too, Amoco. Opali will take good care of you guys."

"Nyala, thank you for your encouraging words," Amoco said. "I confess to feeling some trepidation about our fate." He took Amaya's hand and led her toward some tall doors that appeared to open into the hearing room. "Let us find our seats."

Amaya recognized the room from Elliat's coverage—it was the Spectral Council meeting room. A substantial oval-shaped table filled up the center of the long room. It was long enough that the people at one end would need mics to hear the people at the other end. The curve of the table allowed everyone in the room to see everyone else. An open area in the center of the table was filled with Elliat's equipment. More chairs lined the edges of the room. Elliat ducked under the table to get into the center and started fiddling with his equipment.

Opali was speaking animatedly with LP near the head of the table. Other people milled around the room, while some sat at the table. As soon as Opali saw them, she hurried over.

"Auntie 'Maya. Unca 'Moco." She hugged both of them at once. "And Auntie 'Yala, it's so nice to see you!" Opali embraced Nyala. "Let me show you to your seats."

Opali placed a gentle hand on Amaya's elbow and led her to the end of the oval table opposite from where LP was standing. Amoco and Nyala followed behind. Once they got to their seats, Opali leaned in close to Amaya and Amoco. "I don't know what they've decided. Whatever they're proposing, they just agreed on it today and they didn't let me or Elliat into the hearing room. I'll just have to defend you best I can without any preparation."

Amoco sat next to Amaya on the curved end of the table. Nyala grabbed Amaya's hand as she sat down next to her on the other side. Opali took the seat next to Amoco. In the center of the table, Elliat was setting up something that looked like one of the first movie projectors, with the two large film reels that resembled the wheels of an upside-down bike.

Amaya leaned toward Nyala. "Why hasn't Elliat taken the shot to enter Panacea yet? He said in one of his podcasts that he couldn't wait."

Nyala whispered back. "If he's in the solid world, he can cover news in Panacea using a projection room. But if he enters Panacea, then he can't cover news in the solid world anymore. So he's reluctant to take the plunge."

"I guess that makes sense."

Slowly, the seats filled. Probably forty seats surrounded the table, with an additional fifty or so around the walls of the room. It looked like every seat would be taken. Except for Elliat and the people with Amaya, they all seemed to be ghosts. None of them looked sad or upset or worried that they were baselessly accusing her of something that she didn't do. None of them, with the exception of Opali, seemed inclined to worry at all about the fate of a couple of humans.

"Excuse me, Amoco." Amaya leaned across Amoco to talk to Opali. "Are these all LP100 model ghosts? I mean spectrals?"

"They all use the LP100 model technology, although some of them, like me, aren't technically LP100s. But every spectral in this room was deleted with the Black Screen."

Amoco drew in a quick breath. Amaya felt the same way. This wasn't a crowd that was going to cut them any slack. They would want revenge.

LP banged his gavel, and the last few attendees took their seats.

LP stood up. "I'm calling this meeting of the Spectral Council to order." He banged his gavel again. Every beat of the gavel pounded into Amaya's head. Her hand closed more tightly around Nyala's. "The Council has come to a decision, and now this decision will be revealed to the defendants and the world at large."

Opali stood up. "Objection. The hearings were held without their legal representative present. In addition, they haven't had a chance to respond to the complaints against them."

"Overruled. We have thoroughly considered the evidence on both sides."

"Objection. They have a right to defend themselves."

"No, they don't!" LP yelled, his voice echoing through the high ceilings of the room. Amaya jumped. She had never seen him angry. Manipulative, yes, but angry, no. A vein bulged in his forehead. "Did we have a chance to defend ourselves when they killed us? Calling it 'deleting' disguises what it really was—an act of murder, and a declaration of WAR!"

A roar of support went up as every single person in the room, except the humans and Opali, stood up and cheered. In the middle of the room Elliat looked as though he would flee if he could figure a way out through the tables and crowd of cheering ghosts. He looked like Amaya felt— like it wasn't safe here. Like they had better get out before they weren't able to any longer.

"Quiet! Quiet!" LP's artificially amplified voice thundered over the din. As the room quieted down, the sharp banging of his gavel broke through the noise. The attendees took their seats and stopped chattering. LP surveyed the room, his hands on his hips, and then sat down. "Let us continue. Ms. Opali Stafford, your objections have been overruled."

"On what grounds?"

"On the grounds that I don't like them."

"That's not a real legal thing!" Opali exclaimed.

"Are you a real lawyer?" LP sneered. "If there are no more objections, legal or otherwise," he looked pointedly at Opali, "then let us proceed."

Opali declined to reply. Amaya had a long list of objections, but it was futile to object. LP was going to do what LP wanted to do.

After a moment of silence with his head down and his hands clasped in front of him, LP looked up and said solemnly, "Members of the Council." LP nodded at the group of ghosts sitting at the table to his left and right. "Distinguished visitors." This time, LP nodded at the group of people sitting at the edges of the room. "Welcome. The Council has decided our verdict for the crime of deleting the LP100 model ghosts without authorization. Abrihet Amaya Gidada and Amoco Cadiz, please stand."

Amoco grabbed her hand and they stood up together, her other hand still firmly clasped by Nyala.

"Abrihet Gidada, you were the one who started the program that deleted the LP100 models. Amoco Cadiz, the code showed many details of your handiwork, and was obviously written by you. We find you both guilty of the crime and sentence you to death. A lethal malfunction will take place in your pods in three days' time. Please put your affairs in order, say your goodbyes, and if you are thinking of trying to escape, let me save you the effort. For every day that you are still alive after the date of the planned termination, at least one person will be terminated in your place. I'm sure you don't want that sort of blood on your hands."

It was far worse than Amaya ever could have imagined. Never at any point did she think that death was an option. She fell back into her chair. The people around the edge of the room were twittering loudly, apparently also surprised. In the center of the room, Elliat was forgetting to film them, instead letting the film roll while he stood with his mouth open. Amoco let her hand slip out of his. The dumbfounded expression on his face looked exactly like Amaya felt. They had all been blindsided.

"What about Mariela Stafford?" Opali yelled over the din.

"Quiet!" LP banged his gavel a couple more times. When the group quieted down enough for him to talk, he banged his gavel one more time. "We could not find sufficient evidence against Mariela Stafford. Although we suspect she was involved, she will be treated as innocent in this case."

It wasn't fair. Amaya hadn't known that Amoco had added the program to delete the LP100s when she loaded the software onto the servers. In fact, she had expressly stated that she didn't want to do it, but Mariela made the decision to go ahead and to trick Amaya into helping. It was unbelievable that now Amaya was going to be killed while Mariela got away without any consequences. Nothing bad ever happened to Mariela.

LP banged his gavel again. He might as well be banging it on Amaya's head. It would hurt the same.

"Quiet!" There was one more bang of the gavel before the room went silent. "We will reconvene in three days' time to witness the fulfillment of the sentence. Until then, this council is adjourned."

Oh great. Now not only was she going to die, but it was going to be witnessed by a roomful of people. Heck, Elliat would probably post it for the world to see. And based on the vitriolic comments on her social profiles, the world would be happy to see it happen.

CHAPTER 16

The Ghost Trial Ends, part 2

Friday, continued

"We have to do something." Georgia didn't know what it was yet, but she was going to figure out something. They had three days. She looked at the people sitting in the library of the Stafford estate. Hank, T-Rock, Petra, and June. T-Rock, wearing his favorite leopard print robe and a buzz cut, leaned on the corner fireplace where the wall of windows intersected. Hank paced up and down the room. June, her eyes red from crying, sat with Petra at the conference table. Petra seemed to be studying the rest of them. Between the five of them, surely they could figure out something to stop the death sentence.

Outside, the smoke from the wildfires created a haze that tinted the landscape orange, blocking the light from the sun and wrapping the world in an unending twilight. The smoke had left Georgia with a hacking cough and a tickle in her throat that wouldn't go away.

The twilight created a chill in the air that wasn't normal for this time of year. Georgia shivered. As if noticing that she was chilled, T-Rock started prepping the fire.

Georgia sat on the couch near the fireplace and pulled a blanket around her. She turned to Hank. "We need to be able to talk privately."

"I'll have the guards search for bugs." Hank sat at the conference table and pulled up the mini-screen to speak with the guards.

T-Rock lit the kindling, and the fire burst into flames. "That'll do," he said with a smile. He got up from in front of the fire and sat on the end of the couch near Georgia.

After Hank disconnected from the call, he opened the middle drawer of the desk in the corner of the library and pulled out two headbands. "Time to put our oh-so-fashionable headbands back on."

He put his dark navy headband on and tossed Georgia's silk headband to her. The faded damask print had seen better days. She had hoped her headband wearing days were over.

Petra's eyebrows shot up. "Do the rest of us need those?"

"No," Hank said. "We use these to temporarily disable our chips so no one can use them to spy on us. Since Georgia and I are the only ones who have working chips, we're the only ones who need to wear them."

Hank sat on the couch beside Georgia. There wasn't a lot of room on the couch, and the warmth of his skin touching hers reminded her of the days when they would share the small bed at his place. It was a fond yet distant memory of a time that she would never be able to return to.

"We need to come up with a plan to rescue Amaya and Amoco," Hank said. "But other than finding the tesseract and destroying it and whatever ghosts come out of it in the future, there doesn't seem to be much we can do."

Georgia agreed. Their options for helping out Amaya and Amoco were slim. "It doesn't help that we haven't made progress on finding the tesseract. We have no clues and no direction to go. I've asked the Oragle for guidance, but the Oragle hasn't spoken to me."

"If we destroy the tesseract," T-Rock said, "wouldn't that destroy the ghosts who have gone through it? And stop them from showing up in the future?"

"I don't think so. Hank and I went through the tesseract surrounding Area 52 right before it was destroyed, and we still showed up three days later."

Petra nodded. "That's correct—the tesseract sends people into the future, and that takes place immediately. It doesn't matter if the tesseract is destroyed before the person arrives in the future."

"So," T-Rock said, "if we find it and destroy it, we would have to wait around for three days for any ghosts that went through the tesseract before it was destroyed and somehow get the ghosts' backup copy of their data and destroy that?"

Petra nodded. "That's it."

"Do we have any options other than deleting the ghosts before the execution?" Georgia's heart ached for Amaya. Caring, quiet Amaya. Probably the person in the world who least deserved a death sentence.

"Can they appeal their execution?" Petra asked.

Hank huffed. "Appeal to who? The ghosts don't follow the law."

"If there isn't any way to take out the ghosts permanently," Petra said, "you should consider what else we can do to protect them."

"Good point," June said. "I don't like that Cooper is so far away in the Bo Place pod warehouse."

"I think just to be safe," T-Rock said, "we should move Cooper's pod closer by. Although it may be a challenge to wrangle it away from its Bo Place handlers."

June nodded. "I agree. I'll ask Oscar to contact Bo Place. He should still have some influence with them. At this point Cooper's fate is tied pretty closely with Viola's, so I'll ask him to get Viola's pod as well."

A tear-stained Nyala joined them. Her skin still showed the marks of the projection suit she used to attend Amaya's hearing.

"You're not staying with Amaya?" Georgia asked.

"She asked to be alone. I don't like it, but I think she needs some time to adjust. She said she still wants to go to the game."

Hank shook his head. "Really? I don't think any of us are in the mood for the game anymore."

Hank let Nyala take his place on the couch. He leaned on the windows near the fireplace.

Nyala settled into the seat next to Georgia. "She said it would cheer her up to see all of you. If that makes her feel better, then I'll go. We should all go."

Georgia nodded. "Of course. I'll go." It may not do much to improve Amaya's mood, but Georgia would do anything to support her. She raised one eyebrow and looked at Hank. "Hank, what about you?"

"Amaya's a good friend. I'll be there."

"I'm in," T-Rock said. "You know I love the games." T-Rock glanced at Hank. "And I can't wait to see the Crocodilians take down the Cruzaders."

Hank snorted. "You know that's as likely to happen as a cactus growing in the middle of the ocean."

T-Rock laughed. "You need to slow down with those nature metaphors, buddy, because you aren't very good at them. It's like a hyena trying to be a mountain lion."

Despite everything that was going on, the warmth that flooded Georgia's heart at seeing Hank and T-Rock getting along bubbled up into a smile. When she met Hank, he had some childhood friends, but that was about it. Impulsive and immature, he clashed with everyone he worked with. Watching him, it dawned on her—something seemed to have changed. He was…different. Like he had lost his youthful enthusiasm along with the immaturity.

"I'm looking forward to observing the spectacle," Petra said.

Would Petra enjoy the game? It seemed unlikely. But it was a good opportunity to get to know Petra better, even if her motive in going was to observe them like a scientific experiment.

"Me too," June said.

That was all of them.

~~~~~

Mariela rubbed her eyes and looked around her. The room's dimly lit night-light gave off a gentle glow that barely showed the contours of a bedroom. Based on the stylish design of the room, she was almost certainly still in Viola and Cooper's house in Bo Place. How long had she been asleep?

Mariela felt better than she had felt in days. Sure, there was still some nausea and fatigue and a general uneasiness, but it was the first time since she arrived in Bo Place that she wanted to interact with people. Maybe she was finally kicking whatever it was that was wrong with her. She sighed a happy sigh.

The light in the living room had triggered a migraine, so Cooper had created a room for her without any windows. She turned on the lights and swung her feet over the edge of the bed. Before her feet hit the ground, 1,032 alerts that her name had shown up in news reports pinged. That was excessive even for her. She dismissed all the alerts—she'd look at them later.

She headed down the hallway to the main room. She peaked into Viola's office as she passed it and saw her deep in thought, her gaze focused on a wall full of screens with equations and what looked like DNA on them. Mariela kept walking past the door without bothering Viola. Cooper was sitting on the porch scrolling through life-size captures of people cluelessly doing stupid stuff.

When he saw her, he froze the playback with a quick flick of his fingers. "Hey, you're up!"

"Don't let me bother you."

"You're not bothering me at all."

"What are you doing?"

"Not much." Cooper stretched his arms and yawned. "I can't believe I'm in the metaverse and I can do almost anything I want, but instead I'm bored and don't feel like doing anything. Talk about having too many choices."
~~~~~

"Did you try visiting your favorite period in history?"

"I did, and it was fascinating at first, but then I got bored with that as well. I felt like I was living someone else's life."

Mariela leaned on the balcony railing and looked out. Just like the other day, the falcons circled in front of them and landed in their nest on the cliff below the window. "What about the amusement park? I remember that LP was very proud of Zazora World. I'm sure Viola could get you a visa to go to Panacea." LP's excitement about it had been all out of proportion to the actual excitement offered by the park. But maybe it was the distraction Cooper needed.

"I'm just not in the right mood." He dismissed the frozen capture. "I've been keeping myself busy, though. I've taken to designing smell packs. Viola taught me how to replicate the various smells. I tried barbeque, and it came out really good."

She rested her elbows on the railing. On the horizon, a massive storm cloud was forming. "So you're happy here?"

Cooper leaned on the balcony railing next to her, mirroring her posture. He spoke in a low voice. "Mariela, entering Bo Place was a tough decision to make, and I hope it's not permanent, but as long as I'm here, I'm trying to be positive. And there are some fun things about it. I designed this whole place." He waved a hand at the house. "And I can change it if I want. Viola doesn't care." He faced her. "And as long as I don't think too closely about why I'm here, and why you are in Panacea, then I'm happy. I'm a little bored and restless at times, but that's it."

"Then I'm happy for you. As long as you don't keep rubbing it in about how cool your smell packs are."

He laughed. It was the first time in years that he had seemed even somewhat happy, so it was difficult to resent him for it, even if she did resent that he was enjoying himself while she was so miserable.

"It seems like you're feeling better," he said.

"I still feel pretty worn out, but if I stay like this, it's not anything that would keep me from going home soon."

"With Viola working all the time, it's been nice having you here, even if you've been sick and not good company." He winked at her. "You know I'll miss you, right?"

"So you're not upset about having to stay with Viola?"

He rolled his eyes and crossed his arms. "Mariela, I want to be clear— I don't want to be here. I could spend all day being bitter about Viola using me for companionship and angry about being stuck in a virtual world. Or I can accept that I made this choice, and it's not horrible."

"Why did you do it? Take Viola up on her offer, that is."

Cooper shrugged and shook his head. "She made me an offer I couldn't refuse."

Mariela couldn't think of anything that he would want badly enough that Viola would be able to coerce him into being her companion. Cooper had always lived a simple life. "What was it?"

"I'd rather not say."

"Is it that personal?"

"No. And yes. I prefer not to share it, that's all."

"Then I won't bug you about it."

"Thanks."

She sat down in one of the deck chairs on the balcony. "Is it wrong that I'm glad you're not completely happy here?" She should be happy for him if he was happy, even if that meant he was happy with Viola. She really did want the best for him, but accepting that he could be happy with a woman in his life who wasn't her didn't come naturally.

Almost an hour passed as Mariela relaxed in the lounger with Cooper sitting quietly in the other chair. Mariela was dozing when Viola stuck her head out the door to the balcony. "Mariela, have you checked your news feed lately?"

"Not since I woke up. I was hoping to avoid it for a little longer." Her spine stiffened. "Why? Did something happen?" She stood up and faced Viola.

"The ghosts made a decision. They decided that you are innocent, or at least they can't say for sure that you're guilty."

It was overwhelmingly good news, except from Viola's tone of voice it was obvious there was bad news as well. "What about Amoco and Amaya?"

"They…the ghosts decided they are guilty." Viola crossed her arms and scowled. "It was the most problematic…'trial' I have ever seen, and the ghosts decided as punishment that…Amoco and Amaya are to be sentenced to death."

Mariela struck the balcony railing with her fist. She immediately regretted it when pain stung her hand. "That's all wrong…Amaya is completely innocent. It was a fucking sham of a trial—the idea that the ghosts have any legal authority is ludicrous."

Cooper interjected, "The ghosts are out of line, but we can't stop them. They've already shown that we can't delete them, so it's not like there will be any consequences for them."

"You're telling me that this is actually going to happen?" Mariela's voice cracked. She had let them down, especially Amaya. Amaya had said no to deleting the ghosts, but then Mariela had Amoco add the code to delete them anyway.

Mariela had been confident that she had done the right thing, but now the ghosts were back, and Amaya was paying the price for something she didn't do. There had to be some way she could fix this. "I have to get back to Panacea," she said to no one in particular. "I have to help Amaya." She still wasn't feeling great, but she could make it. She turned toward the door.

Viola put up an arm to block her from going into the house. "There's nothing you can do to help Amaya, but you can leave now. Give me a couple more days and I'll figure the exit shot out." Viola dropped her arm from blocking Mariela.

"You're working on an exit shot?" This was huge news—why hadn't Viola or Cooper told her earlier? Surely that was worth mentioning.

Viola glanced at Cooper. "I'm using what I know about the entry shot to reverse the process. So far, it's not going well, so I've been reluctant to mention it."

Cooper gave Viola a look that Mariela couldn't interpret. "Viola," he said, "it's getting down to the wire."

"You knew about this?" It was like she didn't know Cooper at all. She thought they were close, but why hadn't he told her that Viola was working on an exit shot?

"I have to get back to work," Viola said. "I don't want to be accused of not holding up my end of the bargain." Viola turned on her heels and exited the balcony.

Mariela watched Viola disappear, not quite sure what had just happened between Viola and Cooper. "What bargain?"

Cooper avoided eye contact. "It was my agreement with Viola. She said she would work on the exit shot if I joined her in Bo Place."

So *that* was how Viola had convinced him. It all made sense now. It was clear why Cooper had agreed to it. And why he didn't want to tell her the reason. She crossed her arms. "You shouldn't have."

Cooper continued looking in any direction except at her. "Just to be clear," he said, "I didn't do it just for you. I did it for Amoco and Amaya as well."

He was angry with her. She wasn't sure why, but she could guess. What he did exposed the part of him that was self-sacrificing. It showed that he would always look out for his friends' needs before his own. To some people, that was his weakness. To Mariela, his profound caring for others was his strength. She should tell him that. If only she didn't feel so awful. The nausea had come back, and whatever energy she had woken up with had been spent.

"I'm going to lie down." She paused at the door. There was something she forgot to do, something important. Oh, right. "Cooper, thank you for doing this. I don't think that I can ever repay you."

His gaze was fixed on the horizon, but his eyes gleamed with moisture. "Just make sure you get out of Panacea."

~~~~~

A roar rose from the crowd as the hazard against the Cruzaders was successfully funded by the fans. The swinging rope bridge that they were crossing snapped, and the team tumbled into the piranha-infested river below. Not many of the Cruzaders' teammates were going to survive being dumped into the river. T-Rock threw a fist in the air and let out a whoop. Hank kicked a chair. The ritual was oddly comforting to Amaya.

She was surrounded by most of the people that she cared about—and some she didn't. Maybe she shouldn't have gone to the game, but she wanted something to distract herself. With her time short, she wanted to spend time with friends and do everything that she could to enjoy her last couple of days.

She had chosen an avatar that looked a lot like she normally did. Nyala said it was boring, but Amaya liked wearing beige and brown monochromatic dresses. Plus, Georgia had put a lot of subtle detail into the dress. From a distance, it looked like basic brown, but from up close, it was clear that the pattern in the dress had detail that only an expert designer could have provided.

Bren's box was crowded. Opali was following the game and tracking all the stats along with T-Rock and Hank but avoiding taking either side despite both of them trying to recruit her to root for their team. Bren rooted for whichever team was the underdog. According to him, all he
~~~~~

cared about was for the game to be close.

Petra sat up straight and intently observed everything that was going on around her. Bren's wife sat next to her and occasionally tried unsuccessfully to engage Petra in polite conversation. She had better luck with June, who was sitting on her other side.

Nyala and Georgia had both insisted on sitting close to Amaya. Nyala's hand grasped Amaya's, and Georgia's arm was around her. Both were slow to smile, and it didn't seem like any of them were paying much attention to the game. Only when something big happened would they look at the field with blank expressions.

Nyala glanced to the side at Petra and June. "Petra," Nyala said, "I feel like a monkey in a cage—stop observing us like we are your research subjects. Get up, move around a little, root for a team."

"I think not," Petra said archly. "Your customs are unusual to me, so it makes sense to observe them closely. I would not think of rooting for a team until I understand the game fully and even then, only if I am aware of the strengths and weaknesses of each team."

Nyala snorted. "I don't think you understand how this works. The point is to choose a team mostly at random but probably based on some childhood experiences, and then root for that team blindly no matter what. No matter how many times they lose."

"Ah," Petra said, "like the way you and your friends root for each other no matter how many times you lose."

"Exactly like that." Nyala was as unflappable as usual. Petra couldn't get under Nyala's skin, but for Amaya, though, it wasn't as easy. She was losing, and her friends kept rooting for her. No matter what. Tears rolled down her cheeks. She wiped them off before anyone saw them.

The action on the field stopped for the halftime *descanso*.

"Amaya, you want to do some martial arts practice during the *descanso*?" Hank called out.

"No thanks," she called back. There wasn't any point in learning martial arts if she was going to be dead in three days. "I doubt I'll need to know how to defend myself once I'm underground."

It was a weak attempt at a joke that, not surprisingly, fell flat. Nyala stared at her with her mouth open. Hank opened his like he was going to say something, but then closed it.

The ever-changing ads and public messages above the playing field had a hypnotic effect. It was like watching holiday lights, except that these lights were trying to sell her something. Or convince her to vote for someone. Or encourage her to volunteer for the animal protection league. Or to thank the Oragle for wisdom. Or messages posted by the teams trash talking the other team.

She squeezed Nyala's hand. "Nyala, do you remember when we used to come here as kids?"

"Of course I do. We had some really good times at the games."

"I remember I enjoyed when we would walk around on the concourse and look at everybody's avatars."

"Oh yeah, that was fun. Remember the guy who looked like a giant pickle? You said he made you hungry."

"I had forgotten about him!" She laughed. "I've forgotten a lot of stuff."

"Is it because of the memory-wipe meds?"

"I guess. Everything that I've read says they can cause long-term memory loss."

Amaya struggled to not slump in her chair. She was exhausted. Maybe she was getting what Mariela had.

The lights above the field continued to sell, cajole, and admonish people to take some action or another. The music changed and one large message formed in the middle. Two three-dimensional pictures appeared on each side of the blurred words. At a snail's pace, the words and pictures sharpened into focus. Nyala said something but Amaya didn't hear it, because the picture on the left was starting to look like Amoco, and the picture on the right looked like her. And slowly, far too slowly, the words formed.

Cadiz and Gidada are guilty of destroying more than property.
They disabled the chips.
Go to this location to comment on all their personal accounts.

An angry jeer erupted from the crowd.

Even before she finished reading the message, the news alert pings started. She couldn't concentrate as the pings merged into a continuous alarm. She turned the alert off, silencing the barrage of non-stop alerts.

She turned to Nyala. "I want to go home."

"Agreed," Nyala said. "We need to get to the landing pad now and get you out of here before that crowd figures out that you're here. Change your avatar to a new one. One that looks less like you."

Nyala shifted into a gargoyle-like creature. The brows sent off a clear message to stay away. Amaya chose an avatar by Georgia that she hadn't worn yet. She looked like a middle-aged man with salt and pepper hair wearing a tuxedo.

"Going James Bond, are we?" Nyala took her arm. "Let's go."

Amaya looked back over her shoulder. Everyone in the room looked shocked, their mouths open like they wanted to say something but didn't know what. Amaya took a second to remember this scene—these people that she had come to care for and enjoyed spending time with—and then she let Nyala lead her out the door to the landing pad. In the background, the crowd started chanting, "Kill…them…*dead!* Kill…them…*dead!*"

She fled to the landing pad with Nyala close behind her.

CHAPTER 17

Three Days Until the Execution

Friday, continued

Cooper aligned himself over the falcon's nest clinging to the cliff face below the balcony. The babies chirped and climbed over each other in anticipation. He positioned the cup full of large insects directly over the nest and turned it over. The insects slid out and landed smack in the middle of the nest. The baby falcons gleefully gobbled them up. Cooper smiled. One advantage of virtual reality was being able to feed the wildlife.

After resting in her room for a couple of hours, Mariela had again joined Cooper on the balcony. Her eyes were hollow with dark bags underneath and she moved like every single inch of her hurt. The improvement from earlier that day seemed short-lived.

They sat on the balcony for hours watching the falcons riding the thermals in front of the nest. They talked some, but mostly they listened to the calls of the falcons and the sound of the wind rushing along the cliff walls.

"Cooper," Mariela's voice was quiet.

"Yes?"

"I can't help but feel like Amoco and Amaya being sentenced to death by the ghosts is my fault."

"Amoco knew what he was doing. Deleting the ghosts was exactly the sort of thing he would have done with or without your involvement."

"Are you sure? Because I feel like I was the one who convinced him to do it. And Amaya…I can't even begin to tell you how bad I feel about Amaya." She rubbed her eyes. "I've been trying to think about how I can fix this, and I'm not sure I can."

"You could make a public statement that Amaya didn't have anything to do with it."

"I did that right after the ghosts made us come into Panacea. Didn't you see it? I did an interview with Elliat, but it was about as effective in changing public opinion as your confession was. If you never even heard about it, then that says it all."

Cooper agreed with Mariela—it was her fault that Amaya was in this mess. He took a deep breath. "If she dies, I'm not sure I'll ever be able to forgive you." It was harsh, but it was true, and Mariela needed to hear it.

Mariela drew in a sharp breath. "If she dies, I'll never be able to forgive myself, and I wouldn't consider myself worthy of your forgiveness, even if you decided to give it."

There wasn't much else to say.

Minutes passed before Mariela spoke again. "Cooper, as long as I'm confessing, there's something else I need to say to you."

He waited for her to continue, though he had an idea where it was heading and he wasn't sure he was up for talking about it.

After taking a few uneven breaths, Mariela continued, "I'm sorry I didn't tell you about Grace."

Cooper wasn't ready to talk about Grace. Not now. Not any time soon.

Yet Mariela kept talking. "I never really kept anything I loved in my life. You, Grace, even Mom—I let you all go."

Cooper wanted more than anything for the conversation to be done. "Maybe now's not the time. You should rest."

Mariela wiped her nose on her sleeve. "This isn't something I can say later. Grace was my way of having you without having to worry about losing you. I just didn't count on how afraid I would be of losing Grace as well. About how I would do anything to keep her safe and make her happy, even if that meant hurting you and me."

There it was. She had said what he had already figured out. When Mariela sent Grace to Area 52, she hadn't worried about his feelings. She hadn't had the confidence in him to teach Grace how to be happy living without a chip. "I don't want to talk about it."

"I'm sorry if this is painful. Maybe I'm being paranoid, but lately I've been worried I don't have much time left, and for a long time now I've wanted to apologize to you, to let you know how sorry I am for being so selfish." She grabbed his hand. "We created an amazing human being."

Cooper turned his head, looking away from Mariela. Anything to lower the intensity.

"Cooper." Something about her voice sounded off.

He turned towards her. She was shivering.

"Are you okay?" he asked.

"I'm going to lie down." She got up, her legs quivering and her balance unsteady, and stumbled into the house.

Cooper followed her inside.

Mariela lowered herself onto the couch in the living room like she might throw up if she moved too quickly. She wrapped her arms tight around her stomach. "Cooper, don't leave me."

"I'm not leaving you." He pulled a stool out of the Bo Place free inventory and placed it by the couch. He put a pillow under her head and sat by her. There might not be much he could do to help her get better, but he would do what he could.

When he was a kid, he never would have imagined that he would end up here, stuck in the metaverse with an ex-partner who was blackmailing him while taking care of Mariela and hating her for what she had done but still caring deeply for her. Life was so much more complicated than he ever could have anticipated.

Mariela winced and pulled her knees to her chest. "This is so stupid."

"What is?"

"How we act in virtual reality like we're in the solid world." She struggled to catch her breath. "Why lie down? Why curl up in a ball? It doesn't make any actual difference to how I feel."

He sent a quick message to Georgia asking for an update from Mariela's doctors. "It matters psychologically. We still think like we're living in the solid world."

"It's still stupid." She pulled her knees closer to her chest. "You'll stay with me, right?"

"I won't leave you."

Georgia replied that Mariela's vitals had taken a turn for the worse and the doctors were concerned about her.

For about half an hour, Mariela closed her eyes and stayed still. He stayed by her side, doing nothing other than watching her uneven breathing.

Mariela rolled over and whimpered. "Did you get me a pod with a warmer in it? I can feel the heat of the fire."

He checked in with Georgia again.

"The doctors say you've got a fever." He placed a hand on her forehead. He couldn't feel the warmth. Mariela was right—it was stupid the way they behaved in the virtual world just like in the solid one.

Mariela moaned and turned away from him on the couch. She wrapped her knees up to her chest again.

For a time, she was quiet. Again, he watched her breathing. It seemed shallower than before.

She shivered. "I'm cold. What happened to the fire?"

"I think you may have chills."

She turned to face him. "Cooper, don't leave me." She spoke louder, her voice distressed. Uncertain. Like maybe she was worried he had already gone.

"I'm right here. I'm not going anywhere."

It felt like Mariela was slipping away. Maybe this was just another temporary downturn. Through all of it, the doctors and Amoco were as clueless as ever about what was wrong with her. Cooper sent Georgia another message asking if Mariela's condition had changed.

Mariela tossed and turned. He remained by her side, ready to help her if she needed anything.

"Can you stroke my head?" she asked.

The velvety strands of her hair slipped between his fingers. He was tempted to touch her forehead again to see if it was hot, but it wouldn't feel like anything. Not cold, not warm. Not anything.

Mariela's eyes flew open. She leaned over the edge of the couch, and retching heaves without vomit shook her body. When she finally stopped heaving, she remained propped on her arm, her sagging body rising and falling with the effort of her gasping breaths. Why hadn't Georgia responded? If only to tell Cooper that she didn't know anything?

Back when he used to do Search and Rescue, the lives of people depended on how good he was at helping them. He didn't successfully save everyone, but he always felt like he had done everything he could. Now the single thing he could do was to stroke Mariela's hair with the hope that it might offer her some comfort. It wasn't much.

Mariela turned to face the back of the couch. He rubbed her back and resorted to contacting Hank.

Hank responded almost immediately with a brief message. "Fever higher, vomiting, still don't know what's going on. Amoco has an idea he's working on."

It was a bit of hopeful news in a ream of details that he already knew.

Mariela turned to face him. "My mouth tastes bad. What am I tasting?"

"I think you just threw up in the solid world."

"No wonder it tastes gross." A small laugh escaped her. "The one thing I've tasted in over a week and it's vomit."

"It's a bit ironic."

"Cooper, I'm sorry I ran away from you." She paused to take deep breaths. "One of my biggest regrets is that I pushed you away."

"I regret that I let you push me away."

"There wasn't anything you could have done."

"I know. It's still my biggest regret."

He grabbed her hand and squeezed it.

Mariela disappeared. Just disappeared. Her avatar vanished, gone, for one brief second.

"Did you just turn off your avatar?" he asked when she reappeared.

"I don't think…" Her words were slow, uncertain, disoriented.

Cooper placed a voice contact request to Hank. He had better pick up. Cooper needed more information.

Hank accepted the call and started talking immediately, his speech rushed and distracted. "Cooper, I don't know what's going on. There was a lot of beeping and they're doing something, but I don't know what."

"Her ava disappeared for a second." Even if unconscious or sleeping, her avatar should just remain in place, doing nothing unless she turned it off. "What does that mean?"

"I don't know, but they've called for her parents."

The avatar vanished again and reappeared in a blink.

With a deep gasp, Mariela's eyes opened, frantic and full of fear, and again she heaved. The sounds of vomiting on the call matched the heaves of her avatar.

"I've got to go," Hank said. "June is here." The call cut off.

Mariela collapsed back onto the couch, her wide eyes darting around the room. She seized his arm, her eyes now intensely focused on his. Her breathing steadied and deepened. "Cooper, don't leave me."

He placed his hand on hers. "I won't."

Her ava vanished again. He held his breath, waiting for it to come back. It didn't. Where was she? He touched the couch, like maybe he would be able to feel her there. Standing, he turned in a circle, looking for her.

He was alone. She had asked him not to leave her, but in the end, she had left him.

~~~~~

Hank bit his knuckle until the salty taste of blood from the broken skin reminded him to stop. But how could he help himself—every medical person in the house hovered over Mariela, and with all the noise and chaos, Hank couldn't tell if they were making any progress. Based on the amount of effort they were putting into it, things weren't looking good. June stood off to one side of the room, tears streaming down her face.

Where was Georgia? He had been trying to reach her for the last half hour. She was the one who was good at handling other people; she was the one who would offer comfort to June and support her.

Oscar, who had been in town when Hank had contacted him, came running into the room with sweat dripping down his face. Oscar embraced June in a bear hug. She looked straight at Hank and held out a hand to him. Her warm, motherly look melted away his emotional control. He wiped away the tears sneaking down his face and grabbed her hand. She squeezed it and then pulled him into the bear hug.

Not much later, Georgia showed up. "Is she okay?"

Hank left June's embrace and took Georgia to the other side of the room. "Where've you been?" He relied on her for support more than he had realized, and he had become irritable and tense when Mariela crashed and she hadn't been there.

"I was visiting the Oragle. You know I go every Friday afternoon."

In all the drama, he had forgotten. "I'm sorry."

"How's she doing?"

"Not good. I don't know anything, but they've been working on her for a long time."

"May the Oragle protect her," Georgia said, her voice low and serious.

Hank didn't have much experience or comfort level with rituals, but if there was ever a time to use them, it was now. "May the Oragle guide her path."

"May the Oragle's archives protect her memories…," Georgia trailed off before finishing the three-part saying.

The medical staff seemed to be wrapping up what they were doing, their movements slowing. They spoke in low voices among themselves that Hank couldn't hear over the noise of the equipment.

T-Rock and Nyala ran into the room wearing sparring clothes.
~~~~~

One of the medical team turned to the group gathered in the room and wiped her brow. She took a deep breath. "The Oragle no longer makes predictions for her."

Mariela was dead.

There was a stunned silence in the room. The only sound was the quiet voices of the medical staff doing whatever it was that they needed to do.

"WHAT?" Nyala broke the silence. "Can't be." Nyala spun to face the doctor. "What happened to her? I thought she was getting better."

The doctor flinched. "We don't know."

"Did the ghosts do this?" Nyala asked, her face red.

"We don't know," the resigned doctor said.

"We need to check on Amaya to make sure she's okay," Nyala said. "She said she wasn't feeling well yesterday, and that she was worried she might have what Mariela has."

"I'll do it," Hank said. He checked her tracking location. "It looks like she's at Georgia's place." He sent an entry request to Amaya.

His tears weren't sneaking out anymore, but barreling out without worrying about who would see them. "Georgia, can you let Cooper know what's happened? He's been sending me messages that she's disappeared." Sure, he didn't get along with Cooper, but the real reason he didn't want to tell him was because he didn't want to feel Cooper's pain. "He should be told face-to-face."

"I'll do it," Georgia said.

Hank received a message that Amaya had approved his entry request. He skipped the landing pad, although it would have been politer, and entered directly into the house. It was Georgia's house, so he knew the coordinates by heart. Amaya still had the house set on a medieval castle. When he got there, she was slumped in an oversized throne with pillows under her head and her legs tucked up into the seat. Footage of Elliat's coverage was playing on the stone wall with a candelabra sticking out where his face was.

Amaya immediately switched off Elliat and stood up. "Hey Hank," she said with a false cheeriness.

Hank hadn't thought through that in offering to ask Amaya how she was doing, he would also have to tell her that Mariela had died. It was still better than having to tell Cooper.

"How are you feeling?" he asked. "Nyala mentioned that you weren't feeling well the other day." He walked up onto the dais and sat on the other throne. Behind him, a thick brocade curtain formed a background.

She looked at him skeptically. "Hank, what is this about?"

"Nyala asked me to check up on you, so I'm checking up on you."

"Okay, well, Nyala could have sent me a message to check up on me, but since you're here, I'll tell you. I haven't been all that great—I've been exhausted and anxious. It started when I was sentenced to be executed and got worse at the game the other day. Not surprisingly, I think I can be expected to feel a little tired after having a stadium full of people yelling that they want me dead."

She sounded annoyed that he even asked. Maybe he should have talked to Cooper after all. Instead, he nodded. "Completely understandable."

"Did Amoco figure out what is wrong with Mariela? Is it the ghosts?"

"No. Amoco didn't figure it out and I don't know if it's the ghosts. It's just that…Mariela took a turn for the worse and…I'm so sorry to have to tell you this. The doctor just declared…" he tripped over his words, "declared…her dead."

Amaya turned her head away from him. She didn't say anything—she just looked to the side at the floor. It was impossible to read her reaction in her blank expression.

The silence was uncomfortable, so he spoke. He had to say something. "I'm so sorry. I really hope you don't have what she had."

Amaya's face turned bright red. He wasn't sure why it was turning red, but it was probably his fault. He mentally kicked himself. He shouldn't have mentioned that she might have what Mariela had.

He made an excuse and exited Panacea as quickly as he could.

CHAPTER 18

Two Days Until the Execution
Saturday

Cooper stared at the fireplace that he hadn't bothered to turn on since Mariela had passed away the day before. With her gone, the house felt empty. While she was lying on the couch, he had a purpose—to help her get better. But he had failed to help her, and now his purpose was gone. Sure, he could help Viola improve her image with the denizens of the Bo Place metaverse—but why? Did it really matter if the people liked Viola or not? Why did anyone care?

How much grief could one person handle? Grace's death, Mariela's death, the pending executions of Amaya and Amoco. It was all too much. There was a time when he didn't have any connections to people. He didn't talk to anyone if he didn't need to, and he didn't hang out with friends. In fact, he didn't have any friends. No friends, no connections to other people, no pain. Life was easier then.

It was hard to accept that Mariela was gone. Maybe she would just walk in the door someday, say 'Hey Cooper,' and then complain about not being able to feel the warmth of the fire.

Viola sat down beside him and took his hand. He hadn't seen her enter the room, but then he had been missing a lot of stuff lately. Tears wet her cheeks. "I miss her too. I want you to know that. I don't hate her, even though I know you cared for her more than me. I always looked up to her and would have been happy to have her as a member of our household. I'm broken up over her death."

Viola was saying the things that he couldn't.

He nodded curtly and wiped a tear from his cheek. "I should have asked you to work on her illness and not the exit shot. Everyone should have been working on it."

"I thought Amoco would figure it out. He always figures stuff out."

Cooper's chest constricted. "Not this time."

It wasn't Amoco's fault. The guy had barely slept over the last week. It wasn't even Viola's fault. He had never suggested she help Mariela.

"Cooper, maybe this isn't the time to ask this, but will you stay here now that Mariela's dead? I know the main reason you're here is because I said I would work on the exit shot, and with Mariela's passing, it may not be important to you anymore."

He wanted the exit shot because it was his only way out of this prison. Ironic that last time he was in prison, Viola was his only way out then as well. "When you took my place in prison," he asked her, "did you know you were going to get out right away, or did you actually think you were going to spend years there?"

"The deal I had with Bo Place was that I would spend three years in prison. I know you don't trust me, but I had accepted that I could be in prison for years."

It sounded nice, but he didn't know if he could believe her.

A bell dinged.

"It's a contact request from the board," Viola said. "Do you mind if I accept it?"

"Go ahead." He didn't have anything left to say to Viola; it was as good a time as any to end their conversation.

~~~~~

Having Opali around helped distract Amaya from the despair that had been plaguing her. The list of things bothering her was long and deep. There was the profound sense of loss over Mariela's death the day before. And the profound sense of helplessness over being sentenced to death in under forty-eight hours as well as the solitude that she felt on her final days on earth. There was no room for hope in her life right now. Even if the ghosts didn't kill her, whatever Mariela had probably would.

Amaya was in a metaverse with a billion other people, yet she felt completely alone. She talked with Amoco sometimes, but he was immersed in trying to figure out what had killed Mariela. None of her other friends had ever been sentenced to death or hounded by a mob of vigilantes, so they didn't know what she was going through. Opali, though, seemed to get her. Or maybe Amaya expected less of Opali. Whichever it was, Amaya liked having Opali perched on her couch.

Opali looked around her at the house that was set to generic. No beach, no cabin in the mountains. The house was as plain as they came. "What happened to the castle?" she asked.

"I got tired of sitting on stone. I tried all the house themes and none
~~~~~

of them appealed to me." Nothing seemed interesting to Amaya any-more.

"Have you left the house at all?" Opali asked.

"Why? Where would I go? It's not safe for me to go to public places."

"It would do you good to get out."

"No thanks." An alert that Elliat had posted a new article popped up. "Elliat has a new post out. Do you want to read it?"

"I already have," Opali said.

Oh right, she had significant processing power.

"Do you mind if I read it?"

"Go ahead. I would very much enjoy gossiping about it with you." Opali relaxed with her hands in her lap and her eyes closed while Amaya read.

Business Today

"All the business news you need to know"

Saturday, May 25, 2115

By Elliat Exis ~ *Business Today's* only Newsoogle win-ning reporter!

Stafford Disease Spreads in the Community

By now, my loyal viewers will have heard me talking about Stafford Disease, the mysterious illness that killed Mariela Stafford yesterday. I've received lots of mes-sages from readers and viewers who are asking me what Stafford Disease is and what causes it. Well guess what, there are rumors that Panacea Corp knows what caused it, but they've concealed the information because they're worried the truth will make people reluctant to take the shot and enter their pod warehouses.

Even worse, a lot of you are telling me that you have the same symptoms. You're telling me about fatigue, about nausea, about being anxious, and about feeling jumpy. Sometimes you tell me about your toe fungus, but that's nothing new. And please stop, because I don't want to know.

Since the news of Stafford's death, there's been much

speculation about the cause of this illness. A leading theory is that the ghosts killed her, although if they wanted to kill her, then why didn't they sentence her to death like they did Amaya Gidada and Amoco Cadiz? Others say that maybe her own friends killed her, which, given the way she treated them, wouldn't surprise anyone.

Will we ever know the truth? Are the millions of people who are now experiencing symptoms hypochondriacs? Or will they suffer the same fate as Stafford? I have a message for Panacea Corp: Don't keep us in the dark. Release the autopsy so we can make up our own minds about whether this is a threat or not.

Before I sign off, I'd like to take a moment and offer my sincere condolences to the Stafford family.

Stafford Disease? Really Elliat? He named the illness after Mariela? And then, after gossiping about the illness for his entire post, he hypocritically offered his condolences. When it came to being shameless, Elliat really took the cake. Her pulse pounded in her ears. It would be so much better for her blood pressure if she just stopped following him. Not that she needed to worry about her blood pressure if she was going to be dead in forty-eight hours.

"So, what do you think?" Opali asked.

"I think I have it," Amaya said. "The disease that Mariela had, I think I have it."

Opali shook her head. "It's possible, but we don't know if it's fatal for everyone yet. Mariela may have been an unusual case."

"Does it matter if it's fatal? I'm going to die, anyway."

"I'm sorry."

"Don't be. Apparently, an entire stadium of people wants me dead, so I guess they'll get their wish."

"Amaya," Opali said, "I'm sorry about what happened at the Zazora Game. I should have predicted it. My algorithm usually doesn't fail me like that."

"It's okay, sweetie. Your mistakes make you human."

Opali blushed and glanced demurely to the side. "Thank you."

"Tell me, why do you want to be human? We're pretty awful. I mean, LP is bad, but he's only that way because he was based on a person who's evil. So if he's evil, that's because humans are evil."

"I'm inspired by humanity's ability to persevere and figure out their problems. But mostly I think it was the way I was created. I was created to be like a human, so that's my goal."

"Are you like LP? Do you learn from the people around you so that you start acting like they do?"

"I'm not like LP. I observe people and I learn from them, but I don't copy them. I think that's the difference."

"I don't think Liam Price meant for LP to copy just anyone. LP was supposed to copy him and be just like him, but not other people. It makes LP too susceptible to manipulation if you can change his personality just by changing who he's spending time around."

"Yes, I'm sure Liam didn't intend for that to happen."

LP's way of acting when he was first created and spent a lot of time around T-Rock had been almost amusing. As T-Rock described it—. Wait. Amaya sat up straight. If LP could be manipulated…

"Opali, I have an idea. It may not work, but we need to try."

"You want to manipulate LP?" Opali looked as excited as Amaya felt.

"I want to manipulate him," she confirmed. "Mariela said when LP was first created, he spent a lot of time around T-Rock and she could see the influence of T-Rock's personality on him. T-Rock is one of the nicest people I know—maybe if we can find a reason for them to spend time together again, then we can change LP's personality."

"I have an idea." A lightbulb appeared above Opali's head. "The Zazora World amusement park isn't doing nearly as well as LP expected—not that anyone else was surprised; you don't have to be good at algorithms to know that it wasn't going to be a success. T-Rock helped LP when he was first developing the park, and he had a big influence on LP's personality when they were working together."

"Yes!" Amaya wanted to kiss Opali. "T-Rock could tell LP he wants to work on the park again. I think they stopped working together because T-Rock didn't want to work with him anymore, but I'm sure he would make an exception in this case."

A calculator appeared over Opali's head. "I'm running the odds now, and I'm concerned it may not be enough. But there are too many variables to really get a good idea."

"Since when did you start having pictures to illustrate your thoughts?" Amaya asked.

"I've been hanging out with some other twenty-one-year-olds, and they do it. Do you like it?"

"Ehh." Amaya shrugged.

A stop sign appeared above Opali's head. "I'll stop then." She giggled. "That one was just a joke." The sign disappeared. "So, what's our next step?"

"Let's ask Hank to get involved as well. He can be really upbeat when he wants to be and it would be easy for him to do as his chip is still working."

"Yes, let's do that. But how will we tell them? I can usually make sure LP isn't able to spy on us when it's just the two of us in this room, but it's more difficult when communicating with someone outside."

"Why don't we just ask them? They'll figure out why we want them to do it." Amaya thought about it for a moment. "At least I think they will."

"Okay. Let's do it."

Amaya took a deep breath and let out the anxiety she had been feeling. Finally, she had a plan. There may not be much hope, but even a small amount of hope was better than none at all.

~~~~~

Hank turned off the program projecting on the windows of the estate's library to answer a contact request from Amaya and Opali. It was unexpected, but not surprising. He had been communicating more with Amaya since Mariela's death. He typically shared updates, like whether they were going to hold a funeral right away or wait a couple of days.

The unspoken question in everyone's mind was—do they hold the funeral before Amaya and Amoco's execution deadline? Would Amaya and Amoco want to mourn Mariela with their own impending deaths so close? Would it make more sense, be easier, to just mourn all three at once? No one wanted to talk about those questions, so the funeral planning had been complicated.

What made the contact request unusual was that it was for both him and T-Rock. He put a hold on the request and ran down the list of places where he would be likely to find T-Rock. The kitchen was his first thought, as T-Rock was always up for a meal. Hank went down the hallway and stuck his head into the kitchen. Not finding T-Rock there, he checked the sparring room. When he failed to find T-Rock beating
~~~~~

something up, he went to the wing of the house where the pods were.

T-Rock, Nyala, Georgia, and June were in the loungers. He should have thought to check here sooner. With Mariela's death, they would want to be close to the others.

Hank sat down in one of the loungers. "Hey T-Rock, we got a call from Amaya and Opali."

T-Rock appeared to smile, but since Mariela's death, T-Rock's big smile no longer reached his eyes. "Two of my favorite ladies!" he said. "Let's see what they want."

Hank opened the connection and streamed it to one of the monitors. Amaya and Opali were perched on a white couch. The room they were in was plain white, without a single decorative detail. Amaya must have moved on from the castle since he last saw her.

"T-Rock, Hank, we have a proposition for you," Amaya said. "Zazora World theme park isn't doing as well as expected. T-Rock, we thought you might want to offer to LP to continue your collaboration on it. You all got along so well last time you worked together. It was like your personalities were in sync. That's it. Got to go. Bye."

It was such an odd request that Amaya must be trying to make some point. But what was it? She wanted T-Rock to form a collaboration with LP. Because they had gotten along, and their personalities were similar? This was news to Hank. "LP's personality was similar to yours?"

T-Rock's brows bunched up. "LP was just newly made at the time, and he spent more time with me than Liam, so I guess he started copying some of my personality traits. They were oddly mixed with Liam's personality traits."

Hank engaged the protocol to isolate all electronic communications in the house and pulled his chip-blocking headband out of his pocket. When Georgia saw him pull out his headband, she put hers on as well.

"I've turned on the chip blocker," he informed the others. "Maybe what Amaya is trying to say is that she wants LP to be more like you."

Nyala rested her elbows on her knees. "That's brilliant. If LP still forms his personality based on who he has contact with, then spending time around T-Rock will turn him into a kinder, gentler ghost."

"Brilliant is right." T-Rock thoughtfully stroked his chin. "Like a baby duck imprinting on its parent."

Nyala looked at Hank. "It sounds like she thinks you should be there as well. You'll have to be a good role model and get along with T-Rock."

Nyala was right. It was past time to bury the hatchet with T-Rock. "Listen, T-Rock—we haven't always gotten along the best in the past…"

T-Rock nodded. "If we do this, then we need to be positive and supportive."

"I can do that. I know I was rude to you at times, but I've always respected you."

"And you aren't the same immature boy that got Grace killed."

That one stung, but Hank did feel like he had changed a lot in the last month. He used to feel young—he thought of it as young at heart, but it was probably what T-Rock saw as immaturity. Now it felt like he was older than his age—he had helped carry the weight of the world on his shoulders and it weighed him down. He smiled. "The kid in me has gotten kind of lost—I think he needs to let loose again at an amusement park!"

T-Rock smiled, and this time it reached his eyes. "The Zazora player in me is restless, like a caged bear. Might as well let my inner bear roam a bit at the Zazora Park."

Hank leaned toward T-Rock and held his hand up into the air. "High five!"

It felt like a real bonding moment between them when T-Rock did the same with a "Go Team!"

"Hey T-Rock," Hank said, "I challenge you to an individual game while we're there."

"No, not individual. Let's do small teams so that we can include LP. To make it fair, each team should have a person who's using a projection room, one ghost, and one chipped person."

"One chipped person? But Georgia and I are the only chipped people anymore." Georgia never paid any attention to the games. She had never even gone to a game in person until recently. Whoever had her on their team would be at a disadvantage, if she even agreed to play.

"No problem," T-Rock said. "I'll take Georgia and LP."

It was a good plan. It would give them a reason to spend a lot of time with LP, and T-Rock was smart to include Georgia on the team with LP. Georgia would have a calming influence, even if she was a bit of a liability as far as game strategy went. If she agreed to do it. Hank looked at her and raised an eyebrow. "Georgia?"

"I'll do it."

Of course she agreed to it. Georgia was always a good sport.

Hank smiled. "I'll take Nyala and Opali." Opali loved the games and had always wanted to compete in them, and Nyala was as fierce a competitor as he could find. Being in a projection room would slow her down some, but she would still be formidable.

"What about someone living in Panacea?" Nyala asked. "I mean, a human living in the metaverse, not a ghost?"

It was a good idea. "We'll take Amaya to take advantage of the sisterly understanding." Hank looked at T-Rock. "You all should take Bren. His sense of humor would be an asset to your team. And he'll be a good influence on LP's personality."

T-Rock looked happy for the first time since Mariela died. "I can't think of a better team to be a positive influence on LP. Considering our main goal is changing LP's personality, we'll need to not be too aggressive."

Hank nodded. "That sounds like just your style. That's how you always competed, and it was a successful strategy for you."

"Yes, it was." T-Rock's collaborative style of game play had made him one of the winningest Zazora players of all time.

"Do you think LP will go for it?"

"I do." T-Rock smiled. "Like a kitten after a catnip mouse."

CHAPTER 19

Two Days Until the Execution

Saturday, continued

It didn't take long to set up a meeting with LP. LP agreed to meet with them not two hours after Amaya had suggested the idea. Hank found T-Rock meditating—his back straight, hands resting lightly on his knees, his eyes closed—on a bench outside the projection room in the basement.

Hank touched him on the shoulder and spoke quietly, "I don't want to disturb you, but it's time to meet LP."

T-Rock nodded and stood up. "I was meditating to get into the right headspace to be cheerful and positive around LP. There's a lot riding on this."

T-Rock had a good point. It was going to be difficult to be upbeat and cheerful with everything going on. Hank would have to fake it. Fake it and hope it was enough to influence LP.

Hank sat down on the bench where T-Rock had just been sitting. It wouldn't be very comfortable, but there was no point in finding a lounger because hopefully the meeting wouldn't last very long. "LP will be waiting already. Let me know once you're set up in the projection room."

T-Rock leaned in, patted him on the shoulder, smiled a broad smile, and said, "Smile, young man. It's all going to work out." T-Rock was already in character. His Southern accent even sounded stronger. T-Rock stepped into the projection room. Hank laid on his back on the cold bench with his knees bent.

Think happy thoughts and smile. If only it were that easy. Hank closed his eyes and entered Panacea.

The landing pad had a brick walkway that led toward some gates with the words "Zazora World" written in iron scroll above them.

T-Rock appeared on the brick walkway a second later. "LP's not here yet?" He turned in a circle, looking at the park, and sighed. "I really enjoyed working on this. Too bad there aren't many guests."

"I'm not surprised," Hank said. "This place is a relic." Everything in the park was old news—a person can only do a zero-gravity free fall so many times before it starts to lose its appeal. The only novel thing in the park was the Zazora simulators, and since those included simulated pain, it turned out that people weren't that interested.

A voice behind Hank said, "I'll ask you to not refer to the park as a relic."

Hank startled to hear LP's voice behind him.

Hank would call the park a relic if he wanted to call it a relic. "It *is* a relic," he insisted.

T-Rock moved swiftly toward him and touched his shoulder. "Hank, we're just here to have a good time. Let's not go saying negative things."

Oh right. They were trying to change LP's personality. He had only been there one minute, and he was already failing at being a good influence. "LP, sorry I misspoke. This place is a classic."

LP nodded at him. "Apology accepted." LP opened his arms to T-Rock for a hug. "T-Rock, my man, how have you been?" He embraced T-Rock like a long-lost friend.

T-Rock raised his eyebrows as he looked over LP's shoulder. Hank shrugged. T-Rock rolled his eyes and embraced LP harder.

"LP, I'm happier than an iguana in a glo ball to see you!" T-Rock rubbed LP's head and stepped away from the embrace.

"Come on inside." LP motioned for them to follow him down the brick walkway into the park. "I assume you're here to try to convince me not to execute your colleagues, Amaya Gidada and Amoco Cadiz?"

"That sure would be nice," T-Rock said, turning up the folksy charm.

"That's a no-can-do, I'm afraid. But I can show you around."

They passed through the gate and the park opened up before them. Brick walkways entwined with small trees and shrubs led to what looked like acres of attractions.

"First off," LP said, "you can enjoy the park two ways. You can either use an interface, which connects you directly to the attraction that you select from a screen showing all the attractions. The other way is how we're doing it now, which I call 'old school.' This version can only be entered through the landing pad, and once here, you have to walk everywhere. There are signs pointing to the attractions, but you still have to figure out how to get there. You can also see the other people who are enjoying the park 'old school,' and you may have to wait in line."

"What about the Zazora Games?" T-Rock asked. "I heard that you added a Zazora playing field to the attractions."

"True, true! I do whatever I can to support the games. Sometimes the teams practice here." LP crowed like a proud father.

Georgia showed up in her younger ava with flowing hair that waved like golden wheat in a gentle breeze. It reminded Hank of the one time they had… He shut the thought out of his mind. No need to torment himself with thoughts of things that weren't meant to be.

The brick pathway weaved between hedges, paved patios for various food stands, and occasionally a grassy area where a group or two of patrons were sitting on blankets. LP led the way while he chatted about the park.

"We've become the top destination for families spending the day together. The kids can't do all the rides, of course, because if they're under eighteen, they would be using a projection room and wouldn't be able to access all the features."

"Are you getting a lot of visitors?"

"No, not really. Which makes no sense because *everyone* loves the Zazora Games. I don't understand why they don't love the park. They can actually experience the games in our simulator. Who wouldn't want to do that?"

Anyone who didn't like pain, that's who.

"LP," T-Rock said, "we had an idea we want to run by the top dog."

Presumably, the top dog was LP. Was flattery part of their plan? Hopefully, T-Rock's flattery wouldn't backfire when LP developed an even bigger ego.

T-Rock continued, "Hank and I have a bet—he says he can beat me at the games and I say he can't. It's just an option to bring some fun into troubled times, but we were thinking of having a friendly Zazora match to settle the question. And then we thought it wouldn't be a game if we didn't have teams, so we thought we should each have a team composed of a mixed group of participants."

LP stroked his chin. "I like where you're going with this. Tell me more."

"Each team will have a ghost on it. Hank has chosen Opali."

LP nodded. "She'll be a fierce opponent. Not as fierce as I am, though. That's why I've won every time she has opposed me."

"That's why I'd like to have you as the ghost on my team. I can't think of anyone who would be more formidable."

Without hesitation, LP said, "I'll do it."

"Great."

"With some conditions."

Hank sighed. Of course LP had conditions. "Okay, what are they?"

"First, you will refer to Opali and I as spectrals rather than ghosts."

"Spectrals. Right, got it."

"Who will be on my team?"

T-Rock answered, "In addition to you as our spectral, there will also be Georgia for chipped people—"

LP scoffed. "She's not very competitive, but I guess she will do."

"I'm standing right here." Georgia crossed her arms and scowled.

LP rolled his eyes. "I am aware that you are standing right there, as I am also standing right here. T-Rock, will she continue to state the obvious while we are playing? I suppose we could use her as a narrator."

T-Rock leaned in close to LP and spoke in a low voice. "Georgia has been chosen for special skills that we are keeping under wraps right now." T-Rock looked at Hank sideways as if to imply that Hank couldn't know.

"I want to be the team captain," LP said. "That's a firm demand, no room for negotiating."

T-Rock paused, apparently uncertain how to respond. He looked at Hank and Georgia. Hank shrugged. It probably wouldn't matter if LP was captain. Georgia still looked upset with LP for dismissing her. She also shrugged, but it was an angry shrug. It was nice to see that he wasn't the only one who was having issues being nice and acting positive around LP. If Georgia was having a hard time, then he could certainly be forgiven for having some issues with LP.

T-Rock rolled his eyes ever so slightly. "You can be captain. But the teams are already set—you can't change those. We also have a guy named Bren who will be playing on our team."

"What are the parameters of the competition?"

"One quest that lasts a maximum of four hours." T-Rock smiled. "That's all I need to show Hank that he doesn't know what he's talking about."

"And the logistics?" LP asked.

"Parallel quests. Three gates allotted as much as an hour each and a final stage of up to an hour. The team that first completes the quest will win; if after the time has run out, neither team has completed the quest, then we will use draw rules to decide the winner based on overall progress, numbers of gates passed first, and the number of team members still in the game. Are we in agreement?"

"Agreed." LP looked smug. So far, they seemed to have increased his self-valuation more so than his empathy.

T-Rock clapped LP on the back. "We'll spend the next twenty-four hours preparing, and then we'll hold it tomorrow evening here in your Zazora simulators."

"Good, but I want to use this to promote Zazora World. As such, I insist that we allow spectators."

T-Rock shrugged. "I'm sure we can get out some ads to promote it. Hank, as the captain of the other team, are you okay with that?"

"No problem. I'm not against letting a few people watch it."

It was easy to agree to. No one cared if LP promoted Zazora World. It was doubtful that many people would want to watch a small, friendly match that didn't involve any of the big teams.

"Then we have a deal." LP shook T-Rock's hand.

~~~~~

Maybe the fireplace would look better with a red wall behind it. From his spot reclined on the couch with one leg draped over the edge, Cooper picked out a rust-colored red to warm up the room. The color of the wall switched to a rust color that did not warm up the room. It still felt cold, even though he could feel the heat radiating from the warmer in his pod. He could almost convince himself that he was sitting in front of an actual fire, but he was still cold.

The whims of fate had been cruel to Mariela in ways she never could have expected. She spent most of her life worrying about losing the people close to her, and in the end, she was the one who ended up leaving everyone behind.

Cooper changed the color on the wall again. The fluorescent yellow did little to cheer him up.

"That's an awful color."

He startled at the sound of Viola's voice. He sat up and looked over the back of the sofa at her. "Are you taking a break? How long has it been since you slept?"

Viola came around the sofa and sat beside him. The corners of her mouth turned up, and a small smile formed. She leaned toward him and placed a hand on his knee. "I'm not taking a break," she said, "because
~~~~~

I'm done." She sat up straight and her smile widened into a grin.

"You're done? We can exit the metaverse?"

Viola's smile disappeared and her face went flat. Why wasn't she smiling anymore? Did she not just figure out the exit shot?

"Cooper, there's something I need to tell you."

That was never a good sign. "Go ahead."

Viola took a deep breath. "The shot only works for people who are in the Panacea metaverse."

"What? Why?" Viola had promised she would create exit shots for both metaverses.

"The board of Bo Place was worried they would lose too many people if their residents had the option of leaving. They made it clear they would fire me if I made a shot that worked for people in the Bo Place metaverse."

There had to be more to the story. "What did they promise you?"

"They said I would have complete freedom to do whatever I want and I can make changes to any part of Bo Place. They said they trust me now, but they would only give me that freedom if I didn't release the exit shot."

"They gave you unlimited power." How did she manage it? Somehow, she always got what she wanted.

"Something like that, but not quite unlimited." She shook her head. "I'm sorry, Cooper. You can leave me, and I would understand if you did, but you can't leave the metaverse."

"You chose power over me." He made direct eye contact with Viola. "You're incredible. You go out of your way to get me to live with you, and then you make a choice where you know I will choose to leave you."

"Cooper, let's face it, you were always going to leave me. You're just here so that I'd work on the exit shot—your heart was always elsewhere. At least this way I'll have one thing that I want."

She wasn't wrong about him. He was always going to leave. "I'll be gone within the hour."

"Where will you go?"

"I don't know. Does it matter? Nikky has a place. Maybe I'll stay with them until I can design a place of my own. Once I figure out how to get credits to do that." He had been spending Viola's credits since he arrived. It was time he figured out how to earn his own.

"I'll transfer a portion of our credits into a separate account for you.

It's the least I can do."

She was talking as if her credits were their joint credits, but they weren't. He didn't know where they came from, and he certainly hadn't earned any of them.

"I don't want your credits. I can find a way to earn some on my own."

Viola raised her hands in surrender. "Okay, okay. I won't give you anything you don't want."

He stood up abruptly. "I've got to contact Nikky and pack."

Viola stood up more slowly, her shoulders slumped. "Anything you want to keep, feel free to put it in your personal account so you can access it later."

Oh right. Everything he had here was paid for with Viola's money. But he didn't need any of it. In the solid world, home was wherever his toothbrush and his dogs were. In the metaverse, those things were irrelevant. He didn't need to brush his teeth and his dogs couldn't come into the metaverse. So where was home?

He would create a separate account, move his clothing digi-designs into it, and that was all he needed. He would be gone in five minutes.

CHAPTER 20

One Day Until the Execution

Sunday

Hello fellow Zazora fans. Elliat Exis here. If you've been paying attention, I'm sure that you've heard of the exhibition match between some of the biggest names in the news these days. Possibly most notable, the condemned Amaya Gidada will be participating. Also on her team are her sister, Nyala Gidada, Hank Silva, and Opali Stafford. Stafford gained acclaim and criticism recently for her role in unsuccessfully defending Gidada, as well as co-defendant Amoco Cadiz, against charges of deleting the ghosts. The condemnation of Gidada and Cadiz by the digital ghosts is almost certainly illegal, but there's not much the authorities can do to stop it.

The other team's roster is just as noteworthy. The first shocker is that the team is led by LP, the original LP100 model ghost who led the effort to condemn Gidada to death. Also on the team—many of us are excited by this—is T-Rock Richardson. T-Rock continues to have considerable celebrity as a result of his feats in the Zazora Games some years ago. Though retired now, he's regarded as one of the best players in the history of the games. Also playing is the talented and highly sought-after digi-dine, Georgia B. The last player on this team is a gentleman that not many people have heard of—Bren. No one even seems to know what his last name is. How this random assortment of people ended up playing in an exhibition game is unknown and the source of much speculation!

If you're excited about the game, then I'm sure you're excited as I am to hear that it has been moved to Zazora Stadium. While the game is a promotion for Panacea Corp's Zazora World theme park—and I'm sure there'll

be plenty of advertisements for the amusement park—
the excitement for this unusual spectacle has grown to
such an extent that the only suitable location for it is
Zazora Stadium. So today we can count on 100,000 people filling the stadium, and countless more watching
remotely. I know I'll be following the game and com-
mentating while holding what may be the largest Zazora
viewing party ever.

BREAKING NEWS: Fans, I have some breaking news,
and I think you'll want to hear it. Viola Mason, the Sovereign Ruler of Bo Place, has just released an
announcement that she has created an exit shot for the
people living in the Panacea metaverse. So if you're
missing the smell of fresh air and wondering why you
took the DNA-changing entry shot—good news!—you
can leave now. Though one wonders why Mason didn't
also create an exit shot for the Bo Place denizens?
Surely there were some hard-hitting business calculations that went into making that decision!

<p style="text-align:center">~~~~~~</p>

Amaya knelt on the turf of the Zazora field and adjusted her shoelace.
All the boxes in the stadium appeared to be overflowing. She marveled
at the magic of virtual reality where center field was upright for all the
viewers, even if their boxes appeared upside down to Amaya. She ran
her hands over the game field grass, savoring the level of detail. The
individually designed blades of grass swayed in the wind, each in its own
rhythm. She inhaled deeply and slowly let it out.

The team spent all day preparing, and now it was finally game time.
Hank looked relaxed and confident. Nyala looked ready to stomp on the
competition despite the projection room limiting how easily she could
move. She had spent the afternoon practicing moving, and now only
looked like a zombie on occasion.

Opali, a huge fan of the games, had given them pointers. Like that it
was better to request lots of cheap hazards rather than one big expensive
one. If the expensive one failed, you were out of luck. If only some of
the cheap ones worked, they could together play a big role in setting back
the opposing team.

A random cheer erupted from the stadium boxes surrounding them on all sides. It looked like every seat in the 100,000-person stadium was filled. Maybe some of it was just filler provided by LP to make the game look popular and the actual number of attendees was much lower. She hadn't asked LP about the attendance because she didn't want to know.

The two teams faced each other in straight rows with the game steward between them at the head of the rows. "It's time," he said. The game steward, in a plain gray suit, seemed to fade into the background. He waved his hand and a cylindrical cifrex spinner with a lever appeared in the air in front of him.

The steward raised his hands like a preacher addressing a packed house of worship. "Welcome, everyone, to the first ever Zazora World Exhibition Match. The excitement and drama that you are sure to witness here today, or other experiences of a like kind, can be created for adventurous and intrepid explorers at the park. But with no further ado, let us begin today's quest. To start, we'll use the cifrex selection cylinder to determine the type of quest."

The man grabbed the lever on the cifrex and tugged. Words whizzed by, and after a few seconds, slowed down until the momentum of the spin was almost gone and the words were legible as they spun by. 'Steal' clicked by. Then 'survival.' Survival quests were exhausting from what Amaya understood. Good thing it moved on. Next, the word 'knowledge' almost looked like it was the choice, but with one more click, the word 'rescue' stayed on the screen.

"A rescue quest it is!" the man proclaimed.

The audience murmured and clapped politely. There wasn't anything unique or unusual in a rescue quest, but it would form a solid basis for the game. The audience approved, but wasn't excited.

The man threw the cifrex with the word 'rescue' up in the air where it hovered. "With rescue quests, the next question we need to spin for is the type of rescue." Another cifrex appeared above the field. The man grabbed the lever and pulled. The words again blurred into gray streaks as they spun by, and then letters started to be visible, followed by entire words. The wheel clicked past 'medical rescue' and 'injured animal' to finally settle on 'kidnapping.' Amaya nodded. Rescuing someone who had been kidnapped would make for an interesting game.

The man threw the second cifrex wheel up next to 'rescue.' One by one, he spun the wheels and the hovering words filled the area above them. Rural setting. Country of Paraguay. 1999. Nyala looked at Amaya and shrugged. Pre-smartphone times showed up frequently in Zazora theme selections. Some people thought that the time period category was weighted more heavily to pre-internet years because the lack of easy access to information made the games more interesting.

"Let's feed all of this into the story generator and get our story." The man reached his hands up, his arms stretching long as he grabbed all the words hovering above them and pressed them together. They formed a spinning ball of lights that he compressed with his hands. A flash and the ball of lights turned into a scroll.

The man ceremoniously opened the scroll by holding it up and letting gravity unroll it. He held it high as he read. "Here we go—the young adult son of a wealthy tycoon living in Paraguay has been kidnapped. The tycoon refuses to pay the ransom demanded by the kidnappers, but instead hires you to find the kidnappers and rescue his son. You will start in a village in the Paraguayan state of Guairá. You will have the name of a contact who has some information on where the son is being held, but you will need to gather more information to find the specific location. Once you locate the son, you have to get into the camp and get him out safely.

"As agreed to by all parties, this is a maximum four-hour quest with three gates." The man looked at the two teams. "Please be advised that you will have up to one hour to pass through each gate. Per the rules agreed to by the teams, the first team to pass through a gate will be awarded ten points and will continue on, at which point the second team will have fifteen minutes to pass the gate.

"If they don't pass the gate within the allotted fifteen minutes, the team will be automatically advanced through the gate. This is to make sure that the teams don't get too far apart, because here at Zazora World we are committed to bringing you an experience with the maximum excitement levels, not that boring stuff some of our competitors provide.

"The game is over when one team completes the quest, or when the time runs out, whichever happens first. To be declared the winner, a team must successfully complete the quest before the other team. If no team finishes the quest, draw rules will be in effect and the winning team will be determined based on points.

"This is a parallel quest, so the setup will be the same for each team, but the teams will be in their own universes and unable to interact or influence each other except for hazards funded by spectators. Spectators will have the option of funding hazards. Your supporters will have access to the full range of hazards, but any hazards chosen must be appropriate to the setting."

"So no snowstorms?" Hank asked.

"No. Each team will have access to ten minutes of private conversation time where the spectators can't overhear the conversation. The teams will get limited information on the other team's progress, including if the opposing team passes a gate and if a team member dies. Each team has at its disposal a vehicle. You will all have cell phones appropriate to the era. For currency, each team will have five million guaranies to spend.

"One more point of order." The man cleared his throat. "It has been pointed out to us," the man quickly looked at LP out of the corner of his eye, "that there are some discrepancies among the spectrals playing." The man cleared his throat again. "Opali Stafford, you are legally registered as a three-year-old. According to the rules of the Spectral League of Zazora Players, you are required to play as the age that you are legally registered at."

The crowd roared. They finally found something that they could get worked up about.

Opali looked stunned. "There's a Spectral League of Zazora Players?"

The man shrugged. "It was the only precedent we could find for spectrals."

"Team consult." Amaya motioned to the others to join her in a huddle. "Why are you registered as a three-year-old?" she asked Opali.

"That's how old I was when my mom bought me. She never saw any reason to update the official registry when she adjusted my age. It never mattered until now."

"Having a three-year-old on a quest will be tough," Nyala said.

"We can fight this," Opali said in a whisper. "I think the Spectral League is something that LP made up so that he can say there is a precedent."

Arguing over the rules would only make LP more competitive and might last for days. By then, Amaya and Amoco would be dead.

"Remember why we're here," Amaya said. "Winning isn't the objective."

"You're right," Opali said. "I'm just frustrated that I can't predict which team will win the game, even with all this additional information. I've read the facts, but the facts aren't showing me anything."

"It's okay." Amaya placed a hand on her shoulder. "We don't need to know. It will be more interesting if we don't. Go ahead and change."

"Okay. But don't get upset if I can't help out much." Opali shrunk to the size of a three-year-old girl. She wore a frilly white dress embellished with pale pink embroidered flowers that matched the bows in her hair as well as completely impractical, glittery pink slippers.

Amaya sighed. Good thing they weren't trying to win.

"Let's go kick some butt!" Nyala raised her fist in the air, then glanced at Opali. "Unless we don't kick butt, in which case, let's go enjoy ourselves!" She pumped her fist again. "Can I get a 'Go Team?'"

"Go Team!" Everyone except Opali punched their fists into the air.

Amaya knelt down to Opali's level. "Opali, what's wrong?"

"Why do you do that?" Her voice was small and uncertain.

"We do it because we're a team. When you were twenty-one, you used to do it with us."

"I 'member. It's just…it's just that…it's just old Opali didn't tell me why."

Amaya sighed. This was going to be a long four hours.

"We do it to feel like a team. And to get excited."

"It's just…it's just…I was wondering why."

A long four hours indeed.

~~~~~

One minute Georgia was staring at Hank across a grassy field in the middle of a packed stadium with 100,000 people watching, and the next she was on a street made out of hard-packed dirt and rocks. Georgia couldn't see the crowd, but she could hear them cheering with the excitement of the game starting. The street came into focus and the noise of the crowd faded.

The cobblestone street was lined by one- and two-room houses with plaster walls engulfed in verdant vegetation that appeared to be reclaiming them for nature. A black Land Cruiser was running next to them in a parking area outside of what looked like a small general store. Bren was already looking the Land Cruiser over, T-Rock was turning in a circle examining the area around them, and LP was apparently lost in thought in the middle of the street while staring at the sky with a blank
~~~~~

expression.

"We should get out of the street," Georgia said. The rutted dirt of the street suggested that it was frequently traveled. The faint sound of music drifted over from somewhere in the distance.

A man coming out of the store said "Buenos días" as he walked by.

Georgia nodded at the man. "Where *are* we?" she asked. What had Hank gotten her into? Playing a Zazora Game with LP had sounded fine in theory, but now it sounded overwhelming. She was stuck for the next few hours with a spectral that was planning on killing her friends and whose personality she needed to change to save them, and she had no clue how to start either the game or changing LP's personality.

"The keys are inside," Bren said as he ran his hand along the hood of the car. "We're ready to go as soon as we know where we're heading."

T-Rock, for some reason, was lying on the ground looking under the car.

LP finally moved out of the street to stand by them. An old beat-up motorcycle without a muffler chugged by. The woman on the back of the motorcycle grasped the man driving with one arm and held tightly onto a baby with the other.

Bren shook his head. "That does *not* look like a good idea."

"Are you two keeping an eye out for hazards?" LP asked Bren and Georgia.

"Should we be?" She raised one eyebrow. She probably should have learned more about the Zazora Games. They had done some training sessions earlier that day, but LP mostly had them running drills where they passed each other footballs, did trust falls, and stuff like that. Nothing that was actually helpful, that is. They also accomplished the insignificant task of coming up with a team name. Based on LP's suggestion, the rest of them had reluctantly agreed to 'LP's Crew.'

"What do you mean *should* you be?" LP's extreme reaction made Georgia think that looking for hazards should have been on the training list. "The start of the game is one of the riskiest times for hazards."

"You could have mentioned that before, man," Bren said.

"Oh, okay." Georgia looked around her for anything unusual. There was a glow on the horizon that had the pink hue of dawn, roosters crowing in the background, and the smell of charcoal burning somewhere. "What should we be looking for?"

"Anything dangerous." LP sighed, no doubt to let them know how dense they were being. He walked around, looking up into the trees and down at the ground. Was he actually looking for anything? It seemed very random. Georgia followed him, and Bren followed her.

Bren pointed to the car. "Is that why T-Rock is lying on the ground?"

"Sure is." T-Rock sounded upbeat, but his cheery tone seemed a little forced. T-Rock got up from the ground, wiped his hands on his pants, and joined them. "It never hurts to make sure there isn't a bomb on the vehicle. Bombs are an audience favorite, so they get funded a lot."

"How do the hazards work?" Georgia asked. "I mean, I know how they work in general, but tell me the specifics. What do I need to know to play the game?"

"I did *not* realize you knew so little about the games. This level of ignorance has me all atwitter." LP sniffed. "I would have insisted on other team members if I had known." He bent over and placed his hands on his knees like he was exhausted just thinking about her. "I'm glad the other team has a three-year-old on it because we are going to need something to make up for the drag of these two." He waved a hand at Bren and Georgia.

"No worries," T-Rock said. "This is just a friendly match. And remember," he looked directly at LP, "you're recruiting people to try your simulator. It can only help if we take the time to explain things to people that don't know much."

"Good point." LP nodded. "Proceed."

T-Rock turned to Bren and Georgia. "The audience has a selection of hazards to choose from. People who have a lot of points can also start hazards that aren't on the list for bidding as long as the hazards make sense for the setting. More dangerous hazards cost more. Bombs are expensive, which is probably why there isn't one on our vehicle yet. Audience members can bid on any hazard they want to be deployed against either team. Once the hazard is fully funded, it will be implemented. Let's say fans of the other team are funding a hazard to put a bomb on that vehicle right there," he pointed at the Land Cruiser. "Once the hazard is fully funded, the bomb will go off."

Just then, as if willed into existence by T-Rock, the car blew up and the four of them tumbled to the ground. Georgia was pushed backwards, her head slammed into the ground and her feet flew into the air, tumbling her onto her face.

T-Rock jumped up first. "Is everyone okay?" He grabbed her hand.

"Georgia, are you okay?"

Georgia moved her arms and legs. She had some scrapes, but nothing seemed to be broken. "I'm fine. I might have a headache tomorrow, but I'm fine."

Bren also crawled to his feet. LP lay flat on the ground, not moving.

"Is he dead?" Bren asked with what looked like a smile.

"He can't die," T-Rock said. "He's a ghost."

"Spectral," Georgia corrected. "He can die within the game."

"No, no, no, no!" The moan came from where LP was lying.

"Well, I guess that answers that question. He isn't dead." The disappointment in Bren's voice was palpable.

"Why is he lying on the ground?" Georgia asked.

LP rolled over and sat up. "Why weren't *we* the first to fund a hazard? We *cannot* let them win!"

Maybe LP was the three-year-old, unable to handle any setback without throwing a fit. Georgia pushed her negative thoughts about LP aside. This wasn't like her. She always found it easy to be positive. She wouldn't let LP change that, no matter how much he seemed to bring out the negative energy in her.

T-Rock offered a hand to LP. After staring at it for a moment, LP grabbed T-Rock's hand and pulled himself up.

"There's good news," T-Rock said. "That was a small bomb. We were standing barely ten feet away from the car—anything other than a tiny bomb would have killed us. So they must not have a lot of funding. And look," T-Rock pointed at the spot in the sky that LP had been staring at when they first arrived, "our fans have almost funded a thunderstorm. That's a good choice and will slow the other team down a lot more than that tiny car bomb will slow us down."

"What are you looking at?" Bren squinted at the area where T-Rock was pointing.

"If you look straight up, you can see the faint outlines of a compass in the sky." T-Rock pointed at the sky where some faint lines were barely visible. "Then you find north," T-Rock lowered his arm so that he was pointing north, "and then just above the horizon, due north, if you stare at it, you will see the list of possible hazards. Only people in the stadium can add a hazard to the bidding list, but once a hazard is started, anyone with points can bid on it."

Georgia looked at where T-Rock was pointing. When her eyes met the horizon, a list expanded onto the sky. Six items showed up on the list: thunderstorm, bomb in car, washed out highway, no cell phone service, poisonous snake, and dysentery. Next to each list item were two sets of numbers. One appeared to be the current amount the hazard was funded at, and the other the number needed to fund the hazard.

"See," T-Rock said, "now dysentery would be a nice choice. It's expensive, but it would really sideline them. And why is 'bomb in car' in third place? It's just there because people like to blow stuff up. The thunderstorm is good for this quest, because with the dirt roads it will bog them down."

"Does the team get any say in the hazards that are funded against the other team?"

"The audience can hear us, so we can suggest hazards, but in the end the spectators decide what they want to fund."

"Sorry, but I have one more question," Georgia said.

"Shoot."

"Is the outcome of the hazard guaranteed? What if we had been standing closer to the vehicle? Could we all have been dead?"

"A hazard that is likely to kill would be extraordinarily expensive. One that kills multiple players would be prohibitively expensive. Usually, funded hazards just injure players or slow them down. Sometimes they give the players wrong information, like changing a map. And there's always an element of randomness, so a pebble in a shoe could just be a minor nuisance or could lead to an infection that kills the person. Each hazard is assigned a range of severity levels, and once the hazard is funded, one of the severity levels is chosen randomly."

"So the ones we see there..."

"Those are the hazards our fans are trying to fund to deploy against the other team. We can't see the ones their fans are bidding on to deploy against us."

"I never knew it was so complicated," Bren said. "The games are more interesting than I realized."

"I agree," Georgia said.

"LP, look at that," T-Rock said. "Your work is almost done—you have already converted two people into fans!"

"It's almost there!" a giddy LP said. "The thunderstorm is about to fund. Only a couple more seconds now."

"How long will the thunderstorm last?"

"If you look directly at the hazard and blink, it'll show you more information."

Georgia did as T-Rock said. The thunderstorm was slated to last four hours and would involve at least an inch of rain per hour. The actual amount of rain per hour would vary, but it would rain the entire game.

The numbers next to thunderstorm ticked up to match the amount needed to fund it. The words glowed and then disappeared.

"And there we go," T-Rock said. "Kind of anti-climactic for us, I know. But they'll be dealing with constant rain and gully washers thrown in for the rest of the quest." T-Rock turned to the group and clapped his hands. "Alright people, let's get going and find our contact!"

~~~~~

"Right there, zoom in right there."

Cooper zoomed the viewing screen to the spot that Petra had pointed to. He had planned on watching the exhibition alone, but when June sent him a message asking if she and Petra could join him, he hadn't hesitated to say yes. T-Rock and Nyala were using the two projection rooms at the estate, so June had fashioned a makeshift projection room for her and Petra in a dark bedroom. It was crude, but if they sat in one place, it was effective. At first Nikky had declined to join them, but in the end, they decided to watch due to their attachment to Amaya and their appreciation for the time she had spent helping them get used to living in the solid world. Then Mariela's father, Oscar, joined. Projection rooms tended to make him sick, but he said that nothing would keep him away. Amoco even got a visa to travel to Bo Place to watch with Cooper.

Nikky set up a room at their place to view the game. In the center, they placed a fire pit that turned into a large 360-degree viewer once the game started. To mimic the setup in the makeshift projection room, they grouped the chairs for the people using the projection room to one side within easy sight of the viewer.

In the emptiness following Mariela's death, having a crush of people crowded around the viewing sphere was comforting. Less comforting, though, was the progress of the game. There was obviously some sort of ulterior motive in proposing the game with LP. Maybe Cooper was reading too much into it, but it appeared to be an attempt to manipulate LP somehow. Whatever their goal was, it didn't seem like they were making much progress.
~~~~~

At Petra's request, Cooper zoomed in on Opali trying to walk through the mud. "Is that what you wanted to look at?" he asked.

The team's car had bogged down half-a-mile back, leaving them slogging through sticky mud. The kind that you get after hours of heavy rain have eased, and the mud has dried a bit. The kind that stuck to the bottom of their shoes in ways that seemed to defy physics. Amaya held up her shoe to look at it—the inches of mud sticking to the bottom made it look like a platform shoe. Opali's feet dragged as though weighed down by all the mud on her glittery pale pink shoes, and each step seemed to take longer than the last.

"Oh, that poor girl." Petra shook her head. "She shouldn't have to deal with this. They should have left her with the family up the road."

Cooper nodded. "That actually wouldn't have been a bad idea." There was no rule stating that all the team members had to take part in the entire quest. Cooper zoomed the sphere back out so that they could see both teams, and then shifted in his seat to look at Petra. "Forgive me for speaking bluntly, but I'm not used to seeing this side of you."

"Don't make a big deal out of it. I just have a soft spot for intelligent young girls who get stuck in situations they aren't prepared to deal with."

Cooper wasn't an expert in psychoanalysis, but there was obviously some transference there. Some day he might try to figure Petra out, but right now he had other things on his mind.

"Are you rooting for the Opalites?" he asked. With her fondness of Opali, Petra would probably want to root for the team named after the young girl.

"Of course. Hank even gave me his unused Zazora points, so I helped fund that first hazard."

"You helped fund the bomb?" Petra was full of surprises today.

"I like blowing things up." She smiled with a shy shoulder raise. "Who are you rooting for?"

"The Opalites as well. Opali, Nyala, and Amaya are some of my favorite people."

"And Hank?"

"I've learned to tolerate him."

"Same here."

Cooper smiled. "I think you're starting to like us."

"Don't get your hopes up."

"So you like blowing things up?"

"I know the bomb was a waste of bidding points, but I don't get to do stuff like this very often. I have to take advantage of any opportunities I can get. Plus, it was worth it to wipe the smug look off LP's face, even if only temporarily."

"If you want to blow stuff up, you go ahead and blow stuff up. Although, it seems like you're pretty much in charge in Area 52—don't you get to blow stuff up there?"

"There's only so much that needs to be blown up, unfortunately."

"Are the people of Area 52 angry with you?"

"For not blowing up enough stuff?"

"For not being honest with them. You lied to an entire community. How many people live there—60,000?"

"There's some tension within the community. But you don't get to be my age without getting used to people being upset sometimes. It will blow over."

"Is that why you're here?"

"You think I'm running from my own community?"

"If you're not careful, there might be a revolution by the time you get back."

"I have Dan keeping an ear to the ground. He will let me know if he hears any rumblings of a coup."

"Unless he's leading the revolution."

Petra snorted.

One Day Until the Execution

Sunday, continued

The Opalites' initial clue led them to a man who sent them up the road in search of a small house. They were told the family would have information they needed to find the compound where the tycoon's son was being held.

After their vehicle bogged down, they had struggled on the narrow-rutted dirt road. When the rain was heavy, the road was an oil slick. Opali had fallen a couple times and her white dress was turning a muddy shade of brown. When the rain was light, the mud turned tacky and stuck in layers to the bottoms of their shoes.

During the twenty minutes since the game had started, Amaya had felt increasingly ill. If she got any worse, she would be a drag on the team. She wouldn't be much of a competitor if she wanted to lie down the whole time and always felt like she was on the verge of throwing up.

The Opalites rounded a bend in the road. Through an opening in the lush trees, a house came into view that matched the description given by the man. A rocky opening in the embankment formed a path through an open field up to a two-room clapboard house in the back of the field.

"That's the house." Hank pointed at it. "That's where we're supposed to ask for more directions."

"It's the first gate," Nyala said.

"But if we're here," Amaya asked, "wouldn't the other team have been here already? Surely they must be traveling a lot faster than us. I'm surprised we haven't gotten a notice that they've already passed the gate."

"I don't know," Hank said. "Maybe it's not as simple as it looks. I say we go see."

"Let me go," Amaya said. "I'm too sick to be very helpful. If I die, you won't be losing much."

"I don't like it," Nyala said. She eyed the yard around them for hazards.

Nyala, always the over-protective sister. What would Amaya do without her? "I'll be fine."

"You don't have to do it."

"I'm doing it."

"Use your phone to call me if you need translation," Hank said.

Amaya slipped her way up a short path cut through the embankment. Once she was in the field, the grass made it less slippery. A couple of horses grazed in the field. The two rooms of the house were separated by a brick porch with a roof. The blue paint on the walls had faded, exposing the wood beneath.

Nothing much was in the covered central area between the rooms other than two battered wooden tables pushed against the wall and around eight equally battered chairs scattered throughout. Two dogs ran out to bark at her. Another dog under the table yelped as she stepped from the hard-packed yet slick dirt of the yard up onto the porch between the two rooms.

It was awkward to approach the house without any way of letting people know she was there. "Hola," she said. No response from anyone other than the dogs barking. She yelled louder. "Hola."

"Mba'éichapa!" A stout woman with kind eyes exited from a smaller room off to the side in the back that Amaya hadn't noticed. The room looked like it had been tacked on as an afterthought. "Eheja," the woman said to one of the dogs as she swished it away with a dish towel. "Che apensa ahendu jagua kuera oguahu hína kavaju rehe." The woman wiped her hands on the faded dish towel that had seen better days. Her broad smile immediately made Amaya feel welcome. "Mba'piko reipota?"

Amaya was off to a bad start. Whatever the woman said, it sounded like a question, but that was all Amaya understood. And she had done so well on the Spanish simulators in high school. She made another attempt. "Hola. ¿Cómo está usted?"

"Che nañe'ẽi castellano-pe."

"¿Qué? Un momento." Amaya held up a finger, hoping the woman would understand that she meant for her to wait a moment. Amaya flipped open her slim, crimson-red phone and dialed Hank. He was watching her across the yard and picked up his phone before it even rang.

"Hank, I don't understand her. I'm not sure she's even speaking Spanish. It's not anything I recognize."

"Okay, put her on."

Amaya handed the phone to the woman. The woman held it an inch from her ear. She stared at Amaya as Hank spoke and didn't react. Amaya nodded at her encouragingly, as if that would make the woman respond to Hank.

After Hank asked a couple questions, pausing after each one and not getting a response, the woman handed the phone back to Amaya. "No…español," the woman said.

Amaya took the phone. "Hank, I don't think she speaks Spanish."

"That would explain a lot."

"I don't know what we're going to do if we can't communicate with her. I'll get out of here so we can come up with a plan."

The phone made a satisfying click when she slammed it shut.

"Un momento," Amaya told the woman. She held up her finger, once again hoping that it would signal to the woman that she would be back in a minute. She stepped off the high step down from the porch to the yard.

"Eha'arõ!" the woman called out to her back.

Amaya turned around.

"Eju eike." The woman gestured for her to come back. Amaya stepped back onto the brick porch. The woman pulled out one of the wooden chairs and set it down in the middle of the patio. The chair hit the brick floor with a heavy thunk. The woman wiped the dust off the chair with her towel and pointed at it. "Eguapy." She pointed at the chair again. "Eguapy!"

Amaya sat.

The woman opened the door to one of the rooms and yelled at someone inside. "O'u visita. Pegueru ko'ápe umi karai, kuñakarai, ha mitã'i." The woman motioned with her chin at Hank, Nyala, and Opali. Someone inside the room said something that Amaya couldn't hear. Not much later, two sleepy-looking teenagers emerged. The first pulled on his shirt as he stepped out of the room, and an older looking girl followed.

"Nde." The woman pointed at the girl. "Eporandu nande visita kuérape ndotereresêipa." Then she pointed at the boy. "Nde, emoi pe mesa ha sillakuera jatereré hağua." She stuck her head back through the door into the room. "Pedro, eju ko'apeha eipytyvõ ne ermanope." A younger boy emerged from the room and helped the older boy move the tables out from the wall. In minutes, the boys had lined up the tables, put a floral tablecloth made out of plastic on each of them, and moved the chairs around the tables.

"Emoi la pohã ñana," the teenage girl said to the boy.

A glass pitcher of water appeared, a large block of ice was broken in half and dropped into the pitcher, some sort of herb with large waxy leaves that smelled like lemon was crushed with a pestle and added to the water, and a cup that looked like an ox horn with a metal straw sticking out of it was set on the table. The youngest boy shook loose tea leaves from a bag into the cup and poured cold water on them. After the tea absorbed the water, he pulled a long sip from the metal straw. He spit the water on the ground, barely missing a thin dog sitting near Amaya's feet. Amaya recoiled, then caught herself and relaxed. There was nothing menacing in what they boy had done—the first sip probably just tasted bitter.

The boy smiled at her and held up the cup. "Santo Tomá peguarã."

The girl arrived with the other three members of the team. The friendly woman bustled up to meet them.

"Peju!" The woman motioned for them to come onto the porch. "Peguapy!"

The new arrivals were pointed to chairs around the table. The family chatted in the language with the strange sounds that reminded her more of Japanese than Spanish. They laughed and smiled easily and talked to the visitors in such a friendly and warm manner.

The boy poured some more water into the mug and held it up to Amaya. "Retererese piko?"

This time Amaya understood—he was offering her a drink. Amaya took the ox horn cup and stared at the tea grounds floating in the water. She picked up the metal straw. It had a filter at the end to keep the tea leaves out. The boy looked at her like he didn't approve, so she put the straw back in. Amaya couldn't think of any reason not to drink it.

Maybe drinking it was part of what they needed to do to get through the gate? But what if it was poison, and drinking it killed her? At least if it killed her, it would only be a virtual death, unlike the actual execution planned for tomorrow. She held the straw and sipped. The bitterness of the tea stung her mouth and made her wince, but it wasn't completely unpleasant.

After Amaya handed the mug back to the young boy, he put some more water into it and handed it to Hank. Hank shrugged and drank. The ritual continued with the young boy adding water to the cup each time and passing it to the next person at the table. It seemed like some kind of bonding ritual. And so far Amaya wasn't dead, so it probably wasn't toxic.

"Ndegustápa la tereré?" the woman asked. Amaya still didn't understand her, so she smiled and nodded her head.

"Upéicharõ," the woman said. "Heta oky, ajepa?"

Opali perked up. "Ore heta roguata ha tuicha oky ha la tape paite tuju ha orepysyrỹi ha ko'ágã che ao iky'apaite."

There was a moment of stunned silence. Did Opali just ramble off a long sentence in the language of these people? The woman and her three kids all started talking at once.

"Opali," Nyala interrupted them, "do you understand them?"

"Yes, Auntie 'Yala."

"Why didn't you say so sooner?"

"Say what?"

"That you understand them!"

"You understand them?"

"No, I don't."

"Why not?"

"I'm sure Opali understands all languages," Hank said.

"No, just the ones my mom teaches me."

"What languages does your mom teach you?"

"Aymara… Que…Quechua… Guaraní."

"Well, that's really helpful that you know so many languages," Amaya said. "Can you ask them if there is some place around here with lots of armed guards?"

"But we talking about the mud."

"Please ask."

"What's a…a…armed guard?"

"A person holding a gun who is watching over a place."

"Okay. I ask."

It took a lot of back and forth for Opali and the Paraguayans to understand each other, and then for Opali to communicate the information back to the team. Eventually, they knew what direction to head, where to turn, and how far to go. They also had a description of the compound. It was an exhausting twenty minutes, but it was worth it.

"Okay," Amaya said. "I think we're ready to move on."

A notification bell chimed. They had won the first gate.

~~~~~

Clumps of caked-on mud fell off Amaya's shoe, but a layer of mud a half-inch thick remained glued to the bottom. The worthless, pointy boulder that she was using to scrape the mud off wasn't helping.

"Opali, come here and scrape your shoes." Amaya held out a hand to the sagging girl. Her glittery pink shoes had turned a sad shade of beige.

"Auntie 'Maya, I tired of walking."

"Yes, sweetie. I'm tired too."

Forty minutes of slogging through the mud with her clothing stuck to her while taking care of a three-year-old was exhausting. On top of everything else, Amaya still didn't feel well. She couldn't deny it any longer—whatever sickness Mariela had, Amaya also had. If the ghosts didn't kill her, the illness probably would.

It was difficult to get motivated for the game when she felt like each step was one step closer to throwing up. And why weren't Nyala and Hank helping more? They had disappeared up the road, leaving the sick woman and the three-year-old alone to fend for themselves.

At some point, about fifteen minutes after they had passed the first gate, they received a notice that LP's Crew had been advanced through the gate. It gave Amaya some satisfaction to know that they hadn't figured the gate out and had needed to be advanced through it. It was the one bright spot in the game so far.

Amaya kneeled by the sharp rock. "Opali, come over here. Put your hand on my head and give me your foot." Opali inched her way to the side of the road. She wound her little hand into Amaya's hair, and tottering slightly, lifted her foot. Amaya grabbed the muddy mess and guided it so that the rock scraped off the mud. Or as much of the mud as possible.

"Amaya."

Amaya looked up. Nyala was standing by her. She must have turned around and come back to find them. "Do you need help?" Nyala asked.

"I thought you'd decided to abandon us."

She put Opali's foot down abruptly, almost upsetting the girl. She could barely tell the shoe she had scraped from the one that she hadn't. Amaya sighed and picked up the other foot.

"I didn't hear you stop," Nyala said. "The projection suit is awkward to move around in, so I miss things sometimes." She looked at Amaya holding Opali's foot. "Can I help you with that?"

"I've got it." She was still mad at Nyala for leaving her, even if Nyala
~~~~~

had a good reason. She finished scraping Opali's second shoe. "Okay, try walking and see if it goes better."

Opali walked toward the middle of the road. With each step, her foot slipped. "It more slippery," she said.

Amaya took a couple of tentative steps. Opali was right. With each step, her foot slipped. "I think I made it worse. I can't believe it—our shoes are more slippery now."

"Made it worse." Opali giggled and smiled at her. As miserable as this journey was, at least Opali was upbeat most of the time. In fact, the only one who seemed to be falling apart was Amaya. Why had she ever thought that this would be a good idea? She hadn't anticipated how tired she would be. And weak. And how much it would bother her that LP was probably winning.

Her foot slipped again. "Crap. I think the leaves that were stuck to the mud made it easier to walk." Her foot had been heavier with the mud and leaves, but now she had no traction. "Come on, Opali, let's go walk in the leaves and see if we can get any to stick."

"I take off my shoes." Opali plopped in the mud in her white dress with the pale pink flowers, grabbed a mud-covered glittery shoe and pulled. Then she grabbed the other shoe and pulled. Shoes tossed to the side, she rolled over and used her hands to push herself up from the ground. She picked up her small shoes and held them out to Amaya. "Make clean."

"I can't do that, sweetie. That's not how the game works. I can't change your shoes."

"Make clean!" Opali stomped her foot.

Blood surged to Amaya's face. "*Opali, I can't.*" She didn't have time to deal with this. She couldn't even walk. How was she going to make Opali's shoes clean?

Nyala stepped between her and Opali. She stretched out a hand to steady Amaya and keep her from slipping. "Opali, if you aren't going to wear your shoes, leave them there." Nyala leaned in Amaya's direction. "You were stressing her out," she said quietly.

"She was stressing me out." Amaya wasn't as quiet.

"Yeah, but you're older. You should know better."

"Hmph." Amaya crossed her arms.

She looked like a penguin ambling up the road with her feet far apart. Every footstep involved extracting her foot from the mud with a loud sucking noise. With each step, the mud tugged on her shoe; only through bending her foot to pull up on the shoe was she able to keep it on.

Nyala walked beside her. "Amaya, there's something I need to warn you about."

Amaya stopped walking. Not that what she was doing could really be called walking. "What?"

"You know how hazards can sometimes be psychological, like taunting the other team?"

"Yes."

"There's a sign by the side of the road up ahead. You should know, it says…it says…'Kill her dead' and has a picture of you." Nyala avoided Amaya's gaze. "An unflattering picture of you."

Amaya chuckled. "That's it? That's the worst they could do? A sign? With an unflattering picture?" They had already made her miserable—how much worse could it make her feel knowing that enough people wanted her dead to be able to fund a hazard that had no other point than to taunt her?

Her feet slipped out from under her. She hit the ground hard, her bottom landing in the mud first, followed not long after by her elbow.

Opali appeared by her side. "Auntie 'Maya, you okay?"

"I'm *fine*." Being humiliated in front of 100,000 people was no problem at all. Make that more than 100,000, including the remote viewers. She would be dead in a day, so what did she care?

Opali placed a hand on her shoulder. "I like it wi'out my shoes. It easier. You try it."

"Fine." Amaya grabbed her mud-ensconced shoe and pulled on it. It slipped out of her hands and stayed stuck on her foot, leaving her hands covered in mud. She adjusted her grip and pulled again and the shoe came off with a loud farting noise. She threw the shoe off the road. She grabbed the other shoe and yanked, this time with more aggression. She wrestled it loose and chucked it off the road where it landed with a satisfying thud.

Maybe now she could focus on the quest. She got up awkwardly, in a way that involved her being on all fours at one point and somehow managing to cover the rest of her body in mud. She wiped her hands on her muddy pants, but they just got muddier.

She needed to focus on the game. She reviewed what they knew so far. The woman thought the kidnapped man was being held at a heavily guarded farm five miles farther down the road. They were forty minutes into the gate, but surely they must not have gone more than two miles. At this rate, LP's team would be farther along.

"Has our team funded any hazards lately?"

Nyala shifted uncomfortably. "No one's really bidding on our hazards. I mean, we had the bomb at the beginning, but we haven't had anything in a long time and it doesn't look like we are close to having any."

A bell dinged, and a notice popped up in front of Amaya. The steward's face appeared in the notice window. "LP's Crew has passed the second gate. You have fifteen minutes to finish the second gate. If you do not finish within the fifteen minutes allotted, you will be automatically advanced to the third gate. LP's Crew will begin working on the third gate immediately."

Any window they had to win was closing quickly. Amaya had an idea, but she needed to be able to talk to Nyala about it without being overheard by the spectators. Luckily, they hadn't used any of their ten minutes of private conversation time. Amaya activated the feature.

"I've turned on the private convo," she told Nyala. "If we just had one big hazard, we could decisively gain the upper hand."

"I'm not sure I'm following—how are we going to do that? I think all the people who are bidding for us right now are our personal friends or people who think Opali is cute. It's not like we can change who bids for us."

"But maybe we can. We just need someone who can be persuasive, maybe even convince people that I'm not guilty in the way they think I am. Someone with a large audience and public trust who can help us fund a big hazard." She paused to see if Nyala got her meaning.

"Oh no."

"Why not? He owes us."

"Are you sure this is a good idea?"

"I'm sure about it. It's our best play."

"What about our plan to not fund big hazards, and do lots of small ones instead?"

Nyala just needed to trust her. She couldn't say why, but she was sure that they needed to change tactics. "The way this game is progressing, we can't keep doing the same thing. We haven't had any success funding the small hazards. We're down to the point where only a big hazard will do."

Nyala's eyebrows suggested she was still skeptical. "What about the plan to change LP's personality?"

"That's still in play. But if he's requesting funding for signs saying to kill me, it doesn't seem like the team has made much progress in changing him. I'm sure that sign wasn't Georgia's idea. Or T-Rock's. Or Bren's."

"Maybe it was a spectator's idea."

"You know ideas like that don't get much traction unless they're promoted by a team member. I'm telling you, LP's behind it."

Nyala shook her head. "We don't have any way of contacting Elliat. How am I going to convince him to help us out if we can't talk to him?"

"Well, I have another idea. But I don't think you'll like it."

Nyala hesitated. "What is it?"

"You need to die."

Nyala blurted out, "What?"

"Elliat is interviewing all the players after they die. If you die, you'll have an interview with him and you can say something to him then."

"Great." Nyala rolled her eyes. "I don't want to die, but I'll do it for the team. I'll walk in front, so that way any hazard will be most likely to hit me." She sighed. "This had better work."

"Thanks for taking one for the team." She hugged Nyala. "Turning off private convo mode...now."

They continued their uphill slog through the mud. Hank was walking up the road towards them. He was sliding, but not as badly as Amaya. "Hey guys. What have you been up to? It seems like you're even slower than usual." He seemed to notice Amaya for the first time. "Why are you covered in mud? Was there a mud storm I missed?"

Amaya didn't have the patience to respond to Hank's questions, so instead she settled for, "Very funny."

"Unca Hank, I want a mud storm!" Opali smiled and clapped her hands.

With the angry clouds that were brewing, Opali might get her wish, although it might be more like a mud bath than a mud storm.

"Unca Hank, *please*!" Opali did a little happy jump, slipped, and fell flat on her face.

"Opali, are you okay?" Amaya asked.

A wail from the still prone Opali answered her question. At the same time, the angry clouds swirling overhead released their pent-up moisture. The downpour was sudden and intense. The saturated mud, unable to absorb any more water, ran in brown streams down the road.

Amaya sighed. Instead of tacky mud, the roads were going to be slick mud. Their already non-existent progress was surely going to get slower. As if reflecting her mood, large drops of rain dripped off her sagging hair like a depressed cat straight out of an unwelcome bath.

Nyala helped the still sniffling Opali up off the ground and hugged her. The mud washing off them from the deluge was a bit of good news.

"Look, Opali, it's an anti-mud storm," Nyala said.

Opali giggled. "That not real."

"You're right. It's not." Nyala tousled Opali's hair. "Good to see you laughing again."

"Can we get moving?" Hank asked.

There was no way they were going to win, but at least they could play out the rest of the game. Even if that meant spending another hour in wet clothing. And they could try to not get too far behind.

Amaya started her trudging walk up the road again. "I can't wait until this is done." Whoever designed the wet clothing sensation in Panacea had done a disturbingly realistic job of it and should be given an award. Or better yet, condemned.

"It's not over yet." Hank held out a hand to Opali. "If we get a good hazard funded before they complete the final stage, we have a chance of stopping them. But not if we don't get moving."

Amaya followed Hank and Opali in a slow walk up the soggy hill, and Nyala took over the lead. With so few hazards thrown at them, LP's crew should be well ahead of them, unless they had run into some other issues. But with T-Rock on their team, it was unlikely they had made many mistakes.

They soon passed the sign with the unflattering portrait of her. The red words flashed saying 'kill her dead' and then 'were coming for you.'

Amaya laughed. The others peered at her, uncertain how to react to her laughter.

"I'm not going mad," she said. "It's just that they found the most ef-fective way of torturing me."

"Bad grammar?" Nyala asked.

"You know me too well."

"I thought that would drive you crazy," Nyala smiled. "The rest of it doesn't bother you?"

"It does." Amaya shrugged. "It reminds me a lot of what happened in high school when I was bullied, but it seems like the least of my worries right now."

They started up the road again. The trees shading the road dropped large droplets of water on them. The heavy drizzle and the vegetation pressing in on both sides of the winding road blocked the view up the road. They were going around each turn blind to any hazard that might be waiting around the bend. Amaya's neck ached from the tension of not knowing and constantly having to balance herself to keep from falling when she slipped.

With Amaya struggling and Hank helping Opali, Nyala was easily able to stay in the lead. While Amaya waited for something to happen, she worried. There were so many things that could go wrong with the plan. There was no guarantee that the person in the lead would be the one hit by a hazard. Or if Nyala died but wasn't successful in getting funding, it would be more difficult for them to win without her. Everything was resting on Nyala's ability to convince Elliat to help them.

Would LP's Crew even fund another hazard? It had been a while since the last one. Nyala was getting farther ahead of them. Amaya craned her neck to see around the bend. A slender, bright green snake about a foot long dangled from a branch above the road. Amaya immediately changed her mind. She didn't want Nyala to leave the game.

The snake fell out of the tree onto Nyala's shoulder. Nyala reflexively reached up to brush it off, and its fangs clamped onto her index finger. Nyala jerked her arm, throwing the snake to the ground. The slender snake hurried off to hide in the grass on the side of the road.

Nyala turned around with a stunned look on her face, her eyes wide open. "It tastes metallic." The snake disappeared into the brush on the side of the road.

"Oh shit, Nyala." The idea of having Nyala die in the game sounded much more palatable until Amaya actually witnessed Nyala get hurt. She wanted to take it all back. Angry black swelling erupted on Nyala's hand at the site of the bite. The hazard must have included an accelerator. And possibly an intensifier as well. Nyala winced and fell to her knees.

Amaya slipped and slid toward Nyala as quickly as she could. The venom was clearly a neurotoxin, because Nyala's body was rigid with tremors. Amaya knelt at Nyala's side and threw her arms around her.

Nyala didn't move.

"Thank you," Amaya said. "I hope it's not too painful."

Nyala said, "You…owe…me," through clenched teeth.

After a few torturous seconds that felt like hours, Nyala's body went limp.

A notice appeared in the air. "Nyala Gidada has passed away due to an accelerated and intensified snakebite from a Lichtenstein's Green Racer. Your team will continue the quest with the three remaining members."

CHAPTER 22

One Day Until the Execution

Sunday, continued

Cooper closed the display screen showing the progress of the wildfires. The fires were spreading rapidly, but so far they weren't close to the estate. Cooper brought up another screen to check on the stats of both teams and maps of the teams' locations. It had been great watching LP fumble the first gate because he couldn't get past not being able to speak the language of the family. T-Rock had tried to pantomime what they were looking for, but every time he started, LP interrupted him to yell at the woman even louder in Spanish.

After fifteen minutes of watching LP yell, it was a breath of fresh air when Opali and her team breezed right through the gate. And had done so in well under the hour that was permitted. T-Rock eventually gave up trying to get past LP and took a nap in one of the chairs. Fifteen painful minutes later, they were automatically advanced through the gate. The Opalites had a fifteen-minute start on the other team, but they quickly lost their lead as they struggled with the mud and rain.

Petra leaned over to look at his screen. Cooper adjusted it so she could see it as well.

After examining it for a minute, Petra said, "The Opalites did well on that first gate, but people aren't bidding for their hazards. They're lagging far behind the other team in funding, and even with the late start, LP's Crew is faster and easily beat them through the second gate. Now the Opalites are behind going into the third gate." She leaned back in her seat. "I'm afraid we may have bet on the wrong horse."

Cooper was impressed. "You've learned the game well."

"I'm *only* eighty-some years old, or 101 depending on how you count. I can still learn."

Cooper smiled. "I'm sorry if I implied anything different." Petra was still as sharp as a tack, no doubt about that.

With only one gate left in the game, it was getting down to win or lose. Typically, whichever team ended up winning the last gate also ended up winning the final stage, and LP's Crew had a big lead. "The Opalites can still win, but not without throwing a lot more hazards at the other team." Based on the meager funding the team's hazards had received, that didn't seem like it was going to happen.

"Can we help them?" Petra asked.

"Do you have a bunch of Zazora credits?"

"Not anymore. I blew them all on that bomb."

"Then we're out of luck."

"What about that woman you were living with? She seems well-connected."

"Viola? Her power is limited to the Bo Place metaverse." Cooper huffed. "And we're not talking."

Amoco slid into the chair next to Petra. "It would be unwise for Cooper to request any assistance from Viola. Any favor granted by her will incur an obligation on Cooper's behalf to return the favor in full, and then some."

"Good point," Petra said.

"What about you, Amoco?" Petra asked. "I certainly left you enough in my will to set you up for life. You must have amassed some Zazora points."

"I am afraid you are mistaken, as I am not a collector of Zazora points. If I receive any, I give them away as promptly as I can. And should I have some, I would not bid on the Opalites. LP will be in a foul mood should he lose, and I do not think it is wise for me to take any action that would lead to a mood that could be detrimental to my health."

"I'm sorry, Amoco," Cooper said. "Don't worry, though, Petra and I are both out of points, so we won't be bidding any more for the Opalites."

Cooper switched screens to Elliat's interview with Nyala. Elliat had chosen a digi-room that looked like a penthouse for his interviews with the players. The sounds of a Zazora Watch Party trickled in from an adjoining room. The large windows behind Elliat opened onto an expansive cityscape, while off to the side the hazard board showed little bidding for the hazards of either team. Elliat appeared untroubled as he reclined in an overstuffed armchair. He certainly looked comfortable as he waited for Nyala to show up for the interview.

Nyala appeared on the floor of the interview room, curled into a fetal position and pulling gasping breaths of air in through her clenched teeth.

Elliat startled and sat upright. "Are you alright?" He pushed himself up from the chair, but then seemed to regain his composure and settled back into the seat. He shifted in the padded armchair and looked at the audience. "I have with me Nyala Gidada, the first player to die in today's exhibition game. She still appears to be in a lot of pain, so we'll give her a second to recover."

He turned away from his exo-cam and extended a hand to Nyala. She ignored his hand, instead crawling on all fours over to the other chair and using the arm of the chair to drag herself up from the floor. Her breathing slowed and her body appeared to unclench. She settled into an armchair that appeared to have been situated precisely to enhance the idea that she and Elliat were having a personal, intimate conversation. Surely Elliat was hoping that his interviewees would forget that their comments were being broadcast to millions of people.

Elliat leaned on the arm of his chair. "I have to say, I was sorry to see you get bit by that snake. You were truly one of the best players in this game and it's a huge loss to the exhibition not to have you in it anymore. I'm sure many people are tuning out now that you are out of the game."

Nyala rolled her eyes. "Thanks, Elliat." She looked like she would rather be anywhere else other than talking to him. She held her arms tightly around her waist and appeared to have a full-body tremor. "Who knew such a little bugger could be so painful?"

"Did they remove the chemical drip that causes the pain?" Elliat asked. He actually appeared concerned about her. Maybe Cooper wasn't giving him enough credit, but some part of Cooper was surprised that Elliat could care about another person.

"They removed it," Nyala said, "but the pain takes a while to wear off."

"What does getting bitten by a Lichtenstein's Green Racer feel like?"

"Like being eaten alive by fire ants." Nyala's rough voice was flat.

Why didn't Nyala just tell Elliat to forget the interview? She had no obligation to be there.

"Ouch. Now that Viola Mason has developed an exit shot for the Panacea metaverse, do you think your sister will take it?"

"Elliat, she can't, because she's been condemned to death by the ghosts and they will start killing humans if she doesn't follow through on it."

"Oh, right. My apologies. Tell me about the ruling that Opali had to play as a three-year-old. How did that affect your game?"

"I think it's pretty clear, if you've been watching, how it affected our game." Her voice was clipped and angry. "Elliat, I need you to stop wasting my time with these inane questions. Many, many times you've implied that Amaya or I have done something illegal, like deleting the ghosts or disabling the chips. These are dangerous allegations, and they aren't true." She huffed. "And I think you know that."

Nyala turned to the camera and leaned in. "For those of you who haven't supported us because you think that some of our team members have done illegal things that have hurt people, I'm asking you to reconsider. The things you've heard, the allegations that have been made, they aren't true."

Elliat's chest swelled. "You know I only report news of the highest quality."

Cooper snorted at the viewing screen. Elliat's version of "high quality news" was very different from Cooper's.

Nyala must have felt the same way, because she was short with him. "Elliat, you know my sister's life is on the line, right?"

"Of course." Elliat was somber.

"Then why don't you let your viewers know that she is innocent? Where's your journalistic integrity?"

Elliat sniffed. "How dare you impugn my journalistic integrity!"

Nyala may have gone too far. Elliat wasn't the sort to admit to making a mistake. He needed some way to take back his earlier comments while also saving face.

"Elliat," she said, "I consider you a good friend. I've always enjoyed our conversations and I hope we have many more in the future. Please let's not be enemies. I need you to do the right thing."

Elliat stared off into the distance. When he refocused, his demeanor seemed…different. He placed a hand on Nyala's shoulder. "I'm sorry if I haven't always supported you. I've had to make choices…and I'm not always proud of the ones I've made. I've protected myself, and my job, over protecting you. But that ends today."

Elliat focused on the camera, appearing to make eye contact with the audience. "Okay folks, let's talk seriously here for a moment. If you've been paying attention to the Zazora Exhibition—and let's face it, if you're not paying attention, what's wrong with you—you will know that the Opalites have said that some of the allegations against them aren't true.

"I know I've made my fair share of allegations against them in the past. So in the interests of sharing what I believe to be the truth with you, I can honestly say that I don't think Nyala, or her sister Amaya Gidada, had anything to do with deleting the ghosts. Not knowingly, that is. In fact, all the evidence that I've seen points to an inside job—LP had the capability to write the code and make it look like someone else wrote it."

Where was Elliat going with this?

Elliat leaned forward in his chair and continued speaking. "Why would LP delete the ghosts? He did it because he wanted to make Liam Price, the former CEO of Panacea Corp, look bad so that he could take over as CEO of Panacea Corp. He knew deleting the ghosts would gain him and the other ghosts a lot of sympathy. But the ghosts were never at risk because they had a backup copy stored away."

Cooper wasn't sure what to think. Everything about Elliat's story was wrong, but it was exactly what Amaya needed. Elliat's broadcast was being watched by at least forty million people. He would almost certainly win another award, but while promoting himself, was it possible that Elliat was also helping out the Opalites?

Elliat moved the hazard funding board so it hovered over his head. "Look," he pointed at the funding for a wildfire that would benefit the Opalites, "it's starting to go up." There was something about his mannerisms that if Cooper had to put a name to it, he would have said that Elliat seemed contrite. Maybe Nyala had managed to pierce Elliat's bubble after all.

Elliat highlighted the top line on the hazard board. "I see fans of the Opalites are bidding on a targeted 'follow-the-leader' wildfire."

"What's that?" Petra asked Cooper.

"It determines where the wildfire will spread if the team is split up. A targeted hazard is one that, instead of being spread over a wider area, is intensely focused on a narrow area. 'Follow-the-leader' means the wildfire will head toward whichever team member is ahead. I'm guessing the fans chose it to get LP, as he's always ahead."

The numbers for the wildfire climbed steadily upward while Elliat asked Nyala about the game. Nyala gave more details about what it was like playing with a three-year-old, and what it felt like to walk in a rainstorm that lasted for hours. Overall, it was pretty ordinary stuff. Anyone watching the game could have guessed what Nyala's answers would be.

Above them, the numbers for the wildfire continued to climb, but were slowing down. If it didn't fund soon, the donors might run out of steam.

Cooper switched his screen back to the game. The Opalites looked bedraggled—their clothes soaked and muddy—as they continued to slog through the rain and mud without Nyala. Cooper still felt stunned by her virtual death. Even seeing her interview with Elliat didn't make up for the loss of her as a competitor in the game.

On the bidding screen, the wildfire hazard blinked and grew in size. It finally funded, though it wasn't a large wildfire. Cooper stared at the screen, his stomach twisted into a knot, and waited for the luck factor to be applied. If the luck factor was a low one, the wildfire might not have enough power to do the Opalites any good.

Two graphic boxes showed up and flickered through various numbers, as if someone behind the screen was spinning the numbers faster and faster until they blurred together. Cooper hung on the edge of his seat, and next to him Petra did the same.

The spinning numbers slowed. It wouldn't be long before they stopped. At last, a single number appeared in the first box. Ninety-eight intensity. That was good. Very good, in fact. The second number slowed. Ninety-seven speed. Cooper took a deep breath. Luck didn't get much better than that. The wildfire would be hot and it would spread fast.

<center>~~~~~</center>

Georgia peered over LP's shoulder. The road, partially visible through the dead corn stalks waving in the wind, wound around until a guarded blockade crossed the road. T-Rock and Bren hovered behind her. The stalks were barely tall enough to hide them, but the curve in the road helped and the bored soldier facing them was putting little effort into his patrol. The strap of his AK-47 hung loosely around his shoulders as he reclined against a concrete barrier and picked at a nail. Two other distracted soldiers, sitting on the tailgate of a truck with large wheels and also casually holding AK-47s, engaged in animated conversation.

According to the intelligence that the team had received from the first gate, the blockade was about a mile from the compound. It was a lot of security, but the guards weren't on particularly high alert. Surely that would change, however, at the slightest hint of danger. It wasn't going to be easy getting by them.

The guards had strategically chosen a spot where behind them the road ran through the bottom of a 'V' created by two hills. Farther up the road, almost out of sight, a rickety wooden bridge crossed over a large gulch. From what they had learned during the previous gates, they needed to cross the river to get to the compound. There was no way they could get to the bridge without passing the soldiers, and looking for another way to cross the river would take them far out of their way.

"I need a break," she said. It wasn't exactly true—Georgia could have easily continued. But they needed to come up with a plan, and LP had been pushing them nonstop, leaving very little time for T-Rock to have a positive influence on him.

LP didn't hesitate to respond. "Absolutely not. The Opalites beat us through the first gate…" LP shook his head as though it was a mystery how the Opalites had bested them—apparently his disastrous performance with the family had quickly been forgotten. "The Opalites may be ahead of us. We have to keep moving."

LP's fears seemed unfounded given that they had won the last gate and had funded more hazards, but he hadn't responded well when Georgia had pointed that out to him earlier.

"Remember LP," T-Rock placed a friendly hand on LP's shoulder, "we're supposed to be showing how much fun this game is." T-Rock had been doing his best to tamp down LP's competitive side. He had modeled a friendly approach to the game at every turn, but any impact on LP had been close to nonexistent. But T-Rock, the outstanding competitor that he was, never strayed from their ultimate goal. "It doesn't matter if we win or not," he said.

"If we're not winning, then what's the point?" LP asked.

Georgia sighed audibly. She hadn't meant for it to be so loud, but LP's hyper-competitiveness was exhausting.

"Know what…" T-Rock said. "I'm going to do something for you all. It's not something that I want to do, but because I care about you, I'm going to do it."

Georgia held her breath and waited for T-Rock to explain.

"I'm going to take out those guards so that you all can get by."

She stifled a gasp. His thought process was crystal clear—they had failed in reducing LP's aggressive and competitive side, so at this point, T-Rock planned to model sacrifice. It was risky, because it might not have any impact on LP at all. But they didn't have many other options at this point.

"You can't do that," LP said. "You won't survive."

Maybe LP was starting to change. He actually seemed to care about T-Rock.

"I know. But it's the best for our team," T-Rock said.

Bren smiled. "I'm going to enjoy this." He clapped T-Rock on the back. "Thanks for taking one for the team. You're a good guy."

Georgia fitted T-Rock with the best camouflage she could come up with—dead corn husks tied on with corn stalks. As long as he stuck to the cornfields, he would blend in. The moderate wind blowing the dried-out husks would help hide his movement through them.

The sun beat down on them. There wasn't any shade anywhere. Just fields and fields of corn. That may have been intentional—the tall corn stalks provided some privacy for the guards, but were also easier to monitor for intruders than the jungle. The pecked-over corn ears still hanging from many of the stalks suggested that no one was using these fields as farming income. No, they were certainly a cover for whatever illegal activities were taking place in the compound.

Georgia made one last adjustment to the corn husk camouflage. She pushed a husk to the side and out of T-Rock's eyes. "Be careful out there," she said to him.

"I'll do what I need to do."

"I know you will. Just keep in mind that you don't need to die."

"I'll do my best."

T-Rock was a great soul.

"What's your plan?" Bren asked. "Just to be clear, I would prefer it if you didn't die."

T-Rock looked over Georgia's shoulder at the guards. "I'm going to get the gun from the guy cleaning his nails and use it to take out the other two guys."

"It could work," Bren said, "but you'll have to be quick."

"I'll be quick."

Georgia gave T-Rock a quick hug. Bren patted him on the back.

"Be safe, my friend," LP said, "as you vanquish our foes."

Georgia sighed. It was always one step forward, two steps back with LP.

T-Rock was well-hidden as he made his way towards the guards. The three of them hiding in the cornstalks were only able to track his progress because they knew where to look. Georgia bit her nails as she tracked his painstaking process.

"Did you hear that?" Bren asked.

Georgia shook her head. "Hear what?"

"I don't know—it sounded like a…crack of thunder in the distance. Or something like that."

LP shook his head like he was talking to a child. "I heard it, but then I have superior hearing, so I frequently hear things that you all don't."

LP's arrogance was still off-the-charts, even after spending a couple of hours with the very humble T-Rock. They were failing in their goal of changing LP.

LP smiled and rubbed his hands together. "Maybe the other team succeeded in getting their fans to fund a hazard against us. But they've miscalculated—a rainstorm can only help us at this point. We need something to take the edge off the heat. Silly fools."

"I don't see any rain," Georgia said. "And if anything, it seems to be getting hotter." She was sweating even more than before.

LP raised his eyebrows and looked down his nose at her. "It always gets hotter right before the rain. Mark my words, this is the beginning of the end. As soon as T-Rock takes out those guards, we're going to stomp on them."

T-Rock was getting close to the guards. Bren angled his head to the side, as if listening closely. Georgia did the same, searching for whatever sound he was listening to. At first, it sounded like the wind rustling in the corn. There was something familiar about the sound, though, and it wasn't wind.

Ahead of them, T-Rock emerged from the corn. The first guard stumbled over his feet as he attempted to raise his gun. One of T-Rock's hands caught the guard's weapon, while the other gripped the man close to his chest. The other two guards jumped to attention, sending a spray of bullets heading in T-Rock's direction that landed in the chest of their colleague. T-Rock aimed at the two guards, and before they could dive for cover, they were filled with bullets. T-Rock dropped the first guard and checked that the other two were dead. His arm bled where a bullet had grazed him, but otherwise, he appeared unwounded.

A notification bell chimed. They had won the third gate.

Bren jumped with joy and gave Georgia a hug. With T-Rock's

survival, a wave of relief filled her.

"We did it!" LP ran in a small circle with his hands in the air. "But do you think T-Rock's okay?" he asked.

Georgia looked at Bren. Bren winked at her. They had done it. LP was becoming more thoughtful.

"I think he's fine," Georgia said. "Let's go see how he is."

"Wait." Bren placed a hand on her arm.

The simulated heat was almost intolerable. The noise that Georgia had heard earlier had grown. In the half minute it took T-Rock to disable the guards, it had gotten much louder, and now Georgia could place it. It was a roaring, a cackling, a pungent scent all mixed together. A wildfire was heading their way, and based on the blood-red glow on the horizon, it would reach T-Rock any second. Without pausing to look at them, he took off running in the direction of the bridge to the compound. The fire almost seemed to chase after him as it tore through the dried corn husks. The red hue deepened, and the smoke billowed from the cornfields on both sides of the road where T-Rock was running.

T-Rock disappeared behind a wall of smoke and flames. Georgia's voice caught in her throat, her hand pressed to her chest so hard it hurt.

A notice appeared beside them. "T-Rock Richardson has passed away due to a targeted 'follow-the-leader' wildfire hazard. Your team will continue the quest with the three remaining members."

"No!" LP cried out. "I want all my team members to live! It's not worth winning if we don't win together!"

Georgia wiped a tear from her eye. LP sounded a lot like T-Rock. It hurt that for T-Rock to be successful in changing LP's personality, he had had to die.

Georgia paced in a circle. It had been five minutes since they had passed the third gate and T-Rock had succumbed to the wildfire, but they remained stuck in the same spot.

LP had insisted that they try to cross the burnt section of road to get to the bridge, but even with his dogged determination, he had been turned back by the still steaming dirt road and rocks that were hot enough to melt LP's shoe. LP's skin blistered where the embers landed on him and his singed hair smelled. A now one bare-footed LP was pacing not far from where Bren, the only relaxed member of the team, was reclining on a pillow he had made from corn stalks.

Beads of sweat rolled down Georgia's face. They were all suffering from the heat, which had only intensified since the wildfire. She found herself thinking more and more about the end of the game, and pondering how much longer she would have to put up with being hot and damp with sweat.

They were losing their lead while stuck by the roadside. LP estimated that it would be at least another twenty minutes before they would be able to move. Georgia didn't care if they won, but seeing LP become more and more competitive with each passing minute worried her.

Georgia looked for the compass in the sky and found their hazard list. None of them seemed close to funding. Not even T-Rock's death had managed to budge the needle. They were on their own if they were going to win this, because it didn't look like they would get more help from the spectators.

"The Opalites are going to pass the third gate any minute now," LP said. "It's been five minutes since we won the third gate, and it doesn't look like we'll be moving soon. In ten more minutes, they'll advance through the third gate and will be ahead." LP kicked a corn stalk. "Our incompetent fans haven't funded a single hazard in that time, so there's not going to be anything to stop them from getting ahead of us."

It was indisputable—any positive influence that T-Rock had on LP was gone. Georgia had one last thing she could try. It would mean giving up on changing LP's personality and taking advantage of his competitive side instead.

"There's one thing you could do."

LP stopped pacing and looked at her. "What's that?"

What she was going to suggest to LP only worked if the fans didn't know about it. Georgia activated the private convo mode. "You can ask Amaya to throw the game."

LP scoffed. "Why would I do that? We're ahead right now. I can still win this game."

"You just said so yourself—they're going to be advanced through the third gate in minutes, and there's nothing to stop them other than the rain. Our fans aren't funding any hazards. We have to accept that the tide has turned in terms of our popularity with the fans."

LP's brows furrowed. "Why would she throw the game? That's a ridiculous idea when her team is about to be ahead."

"She'll throw it because there's something she wants more than winning."

"Really?" LP raised his eyebrows. "What's that?"

Georgia pushed aside her anger at LP's cluelessness. "She wants to live."

"So, what you're saying is, I offer to let her live, and she makes sure we win?"

"Something like that. Also, the fans may not know how generous you are being offering to let her live, but T-Rock will. And he'll be so proud of you!" It was a bit of a stretch to say that T-Rock would be proud, but if it served their purposes, Georgia was willing to make that stretch. She finished off with the coup de grâce—an appeal to LP's competitive side. "You don't want to lose your own exhibition game, do you?"

LP smiled and clapped his hands together. "I'll do it."

One Day Until the Execution

Sunday, continued

Amaya sighed. And then sighed again. She sighed because there wasn't anything else to do but trudge through the mud. At least the sighing distracted her for a moment or two each time.

T-Rock had passed away, which meant that their hazard had been effective against LP's Crew, but may have been a setback in trying to change LP's personality.

A bell chimed. A voice said, "LP requests a parley."

"What's a parley?" she asked Hank. She was careful to pronounce it just like the voice, so that it rhymed with 'party.'

"It's a conference between two opposing sides to see if you can come to an agreement. It's part of the game but never really used."

"What is there for us to come to an agreement about with LP?"

"I don't know. Why don't you go and find out?"

Hank had a point. There was no harm in going and seeing what LP wanted. "How do I get to the parley?"

A large button appeared in the air. It flashed bright blue and had "enter parley" on it.

"I guess that answers my question." Amaya reached over and pressed the button.

Almost immediately, Amaya found herself in a plain, white room. LP was waiting for her. His skin and hair had burnt patches with wisps of smoke coming off. Apparently, LP hadn't made it through the wildfire unscathed.

LP gave her a terse nod in greeting. "Amaya, this is a reminder that this is a private conversation. We can speak freely here without the spectators overhearing."

Amaya nodded.

"I want to make you an offer," he said.

"Okay." Amaya was suspicious of LP's offers. 'Manipulations' probably was a more accurate term.

"You may not be aware of this, but when your team gets advanced to the next stage in ten minutes, you'll be ahead."

"Really?" This was news to Amaya. Probably best, though, not to take anything that LP said at face value.

"I take no pride in saying this, but your wildfire hazard was quite effective and has delayed our progress for the moment."

Amaya smiled. It seemed like something was finally going their way. "What's this deal you want to make?"

"The game, in exchange for your life."

Amaya's heart skipped a beat. It was what she had been hoping for. "You mean," she spoke in a measured pace, thinking about each word before she said it, "that if I throw the game and let you win, you will spare my life?"

"Yes, of course, I just said that."

"And what about Amoco's life?"

"Well, I don't know about that. It seems like one life should be sufficient."

She crossed her arms. "No deal, then. It's either both or nothing. Pardon both of us or you lose the game."

There was a pause while LP appeared to consider her counteroffer. She might regret it if LP turned her down, but there was no way she was going to get herself spared from execution without getting Amoco spared as well.

LP held out his hand for her to shake. "We have a deal."

~~~~~

"What did LP want?" Hank asked.

Amaya had reappeared again less than a minute after pressing the parley button. Even though she was only gone a short time, Hank's head felt like it would explode from curiosity.

"It was nothing, really. He just wanted to complain about T-Rock dying in the wildfire." She laughed lightly. "Apparently, he thinks that's our fault."

Hank shook his head. "I've never heard of a parley in a Zazora Game before. I mean, I know it exists, but I've never heard of it being used. Parleys are historically used to negotiate truces, and there are no truces in Zazora."

"Maybe it's a Spectral League of Zazora Players thing? You know
~~~~~

they make up their own ways of playing." Amaya sat down on the side of the road. "Let's take a break. I'm really tired and not feeling well."

Hank didn't like it. She wasn't being completely honest with him. LP wouldn't try to bribe her, would he? "Do you need me to help you?" he asked. "We should really try to keep moving."

Amaya shook her head. "What's the point? In ten minutes, we're going to be advanced through the third gate, even if we don't put any effort into it."

"But shouldn't we try? We may be close, and if we get through it now, that will put us ten minutes farther ahead than if we wait."

She avoided eye contact with him. "Just let me rest a minute."

Hank gave up. It was clear Amaya wasn't budging.

He spotted some bright yellow flowers where the road met up with the forest. "Opali, do you want to pick some dandelions?"

"Yes, Unca Hank."

They walked along the roadside, never getting far away from Amaya, looking for flowers. Amaya laid on her back in the mud with her eyes closed. She didn't look good.

After a few minutes of helping Opali pick flowers, his patience wore out. "Amaya," he called out, "I'm going to go ahead with Opali, catch up when you get a chance."

He held out a hand to Opali, and they slowly worked their way up the road.

Amaya didn't argue with him, but something about the way she said 'okay' made her sound resigned. It reminded Hank of how she was when they had first gone on the expedition to Area 52. He had been a jerk to Amaya back then. Someday, after the game was done and she was feeling better, he would have to apologize to her.

After a few minutes, he looked back over his shoulder. Behind him, far down the road, Amaya was getting up off the ground. She appeared to be going even slower than before, but at least she was moving again.

Hank grabbed Opali's hand tighter, steadying the tottering girl in the slippery mud. On one side of the narrow road, an almost vertical drop-off led down to a ravine. On the other side, a tree-covered slope rose steeply from the road.

Opali clasped his hand. In her free hand, she carried her dandelion. "Unca Hank, is Auntie 'Maya sick?"

"Yeah, she's really sick."

Tears welled in her eyes. "Is she going to die?"

"I don't know. We don't know what's making her sick."

"I don' want her to die."

"I don't either. No one does."

"The sign people want her to die."

"They just wrote that to make her feel bad. They think if they make her feel bad, then she won't play the game well."

"Are we winning?"

"Yeah, we're winning. You helped us out a lot on the first gate."

He had dreamed his whole life of taking part in a Zazora Quest, and back at the res-home he used to play pretend Zazora with the other kids all the time. In all their games, they had never considered having a three-year-old kid be part of the game. But as much as she slowed them down, it was nice having Opali around. She reminded him of himself when he was younger. She was curious about everything, a little stubborn, and kind of impulsive. He could relate to all of those.

"Unca Hank, you okay?"

"Yeah, I'm just thinking."

"Thinking?"

"About things that happened in the past."

"Were you sad?"

"No, not then. Maybe." He looked back at Amaya. She was falling farther behind. She was managing to stay upright but slipping over and over again in the mud. She was far enough away and focused enough on walking that he didn't have to worry about her eavesdropping. "It's just that I used to be a really happy person. I was kind of clueless, and there were a lot of things that weren't right in my life, but I was happy in a way. Now I don't know anymore. I'm in love with a woman who—I don't know how she feels—but she doesn't want the same things that I want. And I've lost people that I cared about, amazing people who made a difference in the world. I think I may have been responsible for your cousin Grace dying. I changed after that, and that's a good thing, because I was making lots of mistakes, but it's like I don't know who I am anymore."

"Sorry, Unca Hank." Her hand tugged on his as she stopped walking. He turned to look at her. "When I'm sad, my mom hugs me."

He wiped away a tear that managed to escape. He picked her up and she put her arms around his neck.

Opali rested her head on his shoulder. "That guy…that…LP says he can make Auntie 'Maya and the other sick people better. I 'member…he told older Opali something, but I don't 'member what."

LP had a cure for the illness? That, even more than Viola's announcement about the exit shot for people in Panacea, was huge news.

Up the hill a low rumbling noise rushed toward them. Vibrations rose from Hank's feet to the top of his head. He swayed and lost his balance. The ground beneath them seemed to lose its structure. He clutched Opali close to him. The rumble crashed down on them and the hill gave way beneath his feet. Opali's arms clamped around his neck and almost cut off his airflow. Mud and plants and debris rushed by them, pushing them downwards, and then rolling them over again and again. He stuck out his elbows, cushioning Opali from the landslide. Sticks stuck in his ribs and mud got into his eyes. They slid to a stop and the rubble pushing down buried them.

He flailed, pushing through the rubble. He fought through the leaves, the dirt, the tree branches. Every gasping breath he took filled his lungs with dust. The slide couldn't have lasted ten seconds, but it felt like minutes.

Next to him, Opali was covered in dirt. He cradled her head and torso, pulled her limp body out of the pile, and brushed the dirt off her face.

"Opali!" he cried out. No reaction. "Opali!" No movement. "Opali!" Her eyes didn't have any life in them.

No, please, no. He couldn't take losing another person. Don't let her be gone.

A notice popped up beside him. "Opali Stafford has passed away due to injuries sustained during a landslide hazard. Your team will continue the quest with the two remaining members."

Hank shoved the notice away.

It was only virtual. She wasn't really dead. He didn't need to get broken up about it. He didn't need to cry with his hands clenched in his hair. The reason he couldn't breathe was because he had inhaled so much dirt, it wasn't because he was sobbing harder than he had ever sobbed. He wasn't kneeling on a pile of dirt and detritus with his hands on his head because his heart was broken by another loss of someone he cared deeply about. It was because he ached from tumbling down a hill.

Get a grip on yourself, man. It was only virtual.

~~~~~

Cooper wiped away a tear. He was almost afraid to look at Petra, because he knew without a doubt that she would be crying too. The made-of-steel woman who had threatened him and his friends multiple times, the woman who probably hadn't cried in more than half a century, was going to have multiple tears rolling down her face.

"Cooper, she's still alive, right?" Petra asked. The tremor in her voice let Cooper know he was right.

"Yes, don't worry."

Petra was crying, but so was the entire row of people in the projection room. June, Oscar, Amoco—they all knew that Opali was still alive, but it was heartbreaking to watch.

Hank placed Opali's body in the pile and covered it with rubble. He said what looked like a prayer but was too quiet to hear, picked up the dandelion that she had been carrying, and started to climb up the collapsed hill. He was risking further landslides, but Cooper would have done the same thing. It was the only way to continue the quest.

Petra pointed at Cooper's small screen showing the stats. "Cooper, look—the funding for the Opalites' hazard." The numbers were spinning up so quickly they were starting to blur.

Amoco rolled his chair next to Petra. "I have had a change of mind and a change of heart. I hope that you will leverage whatever resources you have to fund that hazard to the maximum amount." Amoco sniffed. "The death of Opali must be avenged."

~~~~~

Thick steam rose in billowing clouds on the road ahead. A brief thunderstorm had cooled down the road quicker than expected, but Georgia wasn't ready to risk adventuring into the clouds of steam just yet.

A second later, Bren emerged from the steam. "It's hot, but it's not bad. It's kinda like taking a shower with max heat. Pain four out of ten."

Georgia's chip wasn't capable of creating the sensation of heat. But the game designers weren't going to make it easy for her, so instead they ramped up her pain levels to simulate heat. Disembodied, temperatureless, pain. It was hard to believe she had volunteered to do this.

"Let's go," LP said. "We've got to keep moving, even if it hurts."

"Where did the thunderstorm come from?" Georgia asked. "Is that something the fans can bid on?"

"It's rare," LP answered. "Fans usually bid on hazards against the other team, but they can also send benefits. A little rainstorm like this can be funded for a song. Let us send thanks to our fans—loyal little badgers that they are!"

LP had been in a much better mood since his parley with Amaya, so Georgia could only assume that Amaya had agreed to throw the game. Not that Georgia had ever had any doubt, considering that the whole point of the game was to save Amaya and Amoco's lives. On the road ahead, LP started a happy dance. Every three steps, he kicked his heel out to the side. Right kick with his bare foot. Step, step, step. Left kick. Step, step, step. Right kick with the bare foot again. It was clear that LP had found his joy.

Five minutes later, they arrived at the bridge. According to their sources, the compound wasn't far—across the bridge and through the thick jungle on the other side. The thick steam hid the bridge until they almost toppled over the edge of the deep gulch. The river banks plummeted steeply down; three stories below them a river tumbled over rocks and rushed on its way.

The wooden timber bridge had seen better days. The metal holding it together was rusted and pitted, and the bridge swayed with the wind. No railing provided a divider between the edge of the bridge and the rocky waters below, and wooden planks scattered the length of the bridge were the only indication of where vehicles should drive.

It wasn't a long bridge—it would probably only take them a minute or two to cross it, but it was going to be a harrowing couple minutes. At least they were walking across and not driving.

"Come on, my little ducklings," LP said. "Form a row behind me and let's cross."

"I'm not crossing that," Bren said.

Georgia was inclined to agree with him.

"Do it for T-Rock," LP said. "He sacrificed his life for us. The least we can do is finish what we started."

Georgia looked at Bren and shrugged. It was hard to argue with LP's appeal. "I didn't expect LP to be giving motivational talks," she said.

"Me neither." Bren smiled and winked at her.

They understood each other—they were in this until the end. No matter what the pain level, no matter how annoying LP was. She held her hand out to Bren. He grabbed it and they stepped onto the bridge side-by-side, one walking where each row of planks for the car tires was.

"Hang on, I'm supposed to be in the lead," LP yelled. "I'm the mother duck. You're the ducklings!"

Georgia looked behind her to where the one-shoed LP was jumping on one foot because his bare foot was too blistered to stand on. "Should we…" she started to ask.

The crack of wood splintering drowned out her voice. Under her, the bridge trembled and lunged to the side. For one second, it stopped. Georgia held out her arms, trying not to lose her balance as the tilted bridge swayed. Then, in a rush of wood and rusted metal, the entire structure gave way underneath her.

CHAPTER 24

One Day Until the Execution

Sunday, continued

The gate notification bell dinged and the steward's face appeared in the notice window. "You have exceeded the fifteen minutes allotted for you to finish the third gate. You will be automatically advanced to the final stage." Amaya sighed. At least they made it through the third gate before LP's team won. Although being automatically advanced through the gate felt like cheating.

The scenery around Amaya blurred. When it came into focus again, she was standing in a road in the middle of a cornfield that had been left to die instead of harvested. The stalks of the plants drooped with moisture. An abandoned truck and some barriers in the middle of the road were the only indications that this had been the third gate.

Amaya plodded along, intentionally putting one foot in front of the other with deliberate slowness. Though between the mud and not feeling well, it wasn't all an act.

"Hey, Amaya."

Amaya turned around. Behind her, a red-eyed Hank looked like he was barely holding it together.

"Is this the fastest that you can go?" he asked.

Amaya's attempts to slow Hank down weren't going well. She couldn't tell him she was trying to throw the game, because if the spectators figured it out, it would make LP look bad and he would cancel their agreement.

Everything now was about keeping up the appearance of LP as a great competitor. Nothing else mattered. Not even Hank getting frustrated with her. He had been especially short-tempered since Opali had died. Amaya was struggling too, but her feelings didn't matter. Hank's feelings didn't matter. The only thing that mattered was LP's feelings.

Hank matched her speed. "Looks like we're through the third gate, but don't forget that LP's team has a fifteen-minute head start."

"Thanks for reminding me of the obvious," Amaya said. Of course she remembered that LP's team had a head start.

A notice popped up next to them. "Georgia Bristow and Bren Brentwood have passed away due to an unstable bridge. LP's Crew will continue the quest with the one remaining member."

The hazard, funded from money raised after Opali's death, had really hit the other team hard. Unfortunately for Amaya, it wasn't going to make it any easier for LP's team to win.

A bell chimed and a voice said, "LP requests a parley."

Of course LP wanted a parley. He had lost three-quarters of his team and he was going to be pissed. But she had done her part, she had done everything she could to throw the game. She didn't have any control over what the spectators did.

Amaya punched the blue button and arrived in the all-white parley room. How was it that the designers of one of the most imaginative games ever created a parley room that was completely devoid of any interesting visual feature? An agitated LP was pacing restlessly when she arrived.

"What was that?" A vein protruded prominently from the forehead of LP's red face. "You were supposed to be throwing the game."

"That hazard was all the spectators doing. And you're still alive, so it's not like you've lost the game."

"I'm on the WRONG SIDE of the bridge. The only way I can get to the compound now is to detour hours out of my way to another bridge."

Amaya's pulse quickened. This was the exact opposite of what she needed. The tide had turned, but in the wrong direction. The game was unwinnable for LP.

"I'm calling off the rest of the game," he said. "It's ridiculous to go forward at this time. Our agreement is off. You'll be executed as planned and the electricity intolerance will take out the rest of humanity."

"Electricity intolerance?" What was LP talking about?

"What do you think killed Mariela? It was an intolerance to electricity triggered by a reaction to the kill shot. It spreads virally, so everyone in the metaverse will be affected by now. Once it takes full effect, your fellow humans will have to avoid all electricity. Consider yourself lucky to be scheduled for an execution so you don't have to live like that."

"Live without electricity? Completely without?"

"Do you really not know any of this? Are your scientists so incompetent that they haven't figured it out?" LP rolled his eyes. "Oh right—

Viola Mason is preoccupied with creating an exit shot and Amoco Cadiz is already suffering from the intolerance."

"Intolerance…?" Her mouth hung open.

LP scoffed. "It hadn't occurred to me that you would be so poorly informed. I see that it falls to me to fill you in. The intolerance is severe. None of you will be able to use electricity in any way once the full effects have taken hold. It won't kill you right away, but it won't take long either if you continue to be exposed to electricity."

Amaya was stunned—questions upon questions formed a confused jumble in her brain. "Did you create the electricity allergy? Did you kill Mariela?"

"We didn't create it. And if I had wanted to kill Mariela, I would have scheduled her to be executed with you and Amoco. Her sickness wasn't our doing; she died because she continued to be exposed to electricity. Assuming people take proper precautions to avoid all electricity, they will be perfectly healthy."

"How healthy can going without health care and other modern conveniences be?"

"They'll still have health care. Maybe not at hospitals, but they can take herbs and see traditional healers."

"When will this start?"

"It depends on how much exposure a person has had. Some people may not feel sick yet. People like yourself, well, you know how that goes."

Amaya remembered a comment that Hank had shared with her. "Opali told Hank there was a treatment for Mariela's illness. If other people have the same thing, can't you treat them?"

LP wandered around the room, looking at the blank walls as though they were interesting. "That sounds like a lot of work for us."

"You can share it with us then, so that we can provide the treatment."

"The treatment is proprietary. Sharing it is out of the question."

LP was so frustrating.

"Why did you develop the treatment if you don't plan to use it or let us use it?"

"We discovered it by accident. It's also not a permanent solution. Anyone who's been exposed to the toxin in the kill switch will need treatment for the rest of their lives."

"So why are we here? So that you can tell me you won't help us and that the human race is being relegated to living in the Stone Age?"

"No need to exaggerate. You will be far advanced beyond the Stone Age. No, I called you here to let you know that I'm ending the game. I wanted to inform you personally that your execution will take place as scheduled."

What a gentleman. He saved her from having to receive the news through a message.

There had to be something she could do. The most obvious route was to convince LP that he could still win. She could find a way to lose the game. It would be difficult, but it wouldn't be impossible. But she wasn't going to do it and not get anything in return. It all depended on how much LP wanted to win the game.

"LP, you want to win this game, right? And calling it off before it's done wouldn't be a good promotion for the simulator, correct?"

"Yes, but I'm not going to continue playing a losing hand like some bedraggled opossum."

Maybe T-Rock had influenced LP after all. It just wasn't the sort of influence they needed.

"If you call it off now, you'll lose face. But you can still win. When we start up again, I'll stop our forward progress in any way I can. Also, if you can fund a hazard against us, even a small one, I'll milk it for all it's worth. And don't forget, you're the only teammate left on your team, so when you win, all the glory will go to you."

LP stroked his chin. "I like that idea."

"But there's a catch. If you want me to throw the game, you have to allow the people who are in the metaverse to stay in the metaverse, and you will give them the treatment for the electricity intolerance for as long as they live."

"That's a steep price to pay."

"Do you want to win?"

"Done. But you and Amoco still die."

"What? That's not fair."

"You haven't held up your part of the bargain. Since you agreed to throw the game, half of my team has died, and the only way I can win is by default if you don't finish the game. That wasn't what we agreed to."

"But that wasn't my fault. It was the spectators."

"You shouldn't have agreed to something if you couldn't follow through on it. You knew that you didn't have control over the spectators."

"LP, you can't seriously expect me to agree to this if Amoco and I are still going to be executed."

"I don't see that you have a choice."

Her mouth dropped open. Was he right? Did she not have a choice? "But…" She couldn't think of anything to say. Were there really no bargaining chips left for her?

LP smiled. "Like a baby bird that has fallen out of its nest, I see it is dawning on you that there's no way you can save yourself."

Amaya wanted nothing more than to delete the smug smile off LP's face. "Just remember," she said, "if the ghosts don't keep your end of the bargain to take care of the humans, we will delete you along with every other single piece of digital data. There will be nowhere for you to hide."

"Understood. Just remember, if you don't keep your end of the bargain, no one will receive the treatment. Now let's finish the game so that we can set our plan in motion."

"It's not our plan. It's your plan."

~~~~~

Cooper shifted in his chair. LP and Amaya had been in their parley for a couple minutes now, and not knowing what was happening was killing him. He shifted again. Sitting still was almost impossible when he felt the anxiety in every muscle.

"What do you think they are discussing?" Amoco asked.

Petra gazed off into the distance. "I could speculate, but whatever it is, chances are it isn't good for Amaya. A game isn't really a game when one person's life hangs in the balance."

Petra had a good point. Cooper wished that the players who had died could join them, but the game rules required them to be cloistered until the end of the game. Elliat was the only one allowed to talk to them, and based on what Cooper had seen of the interviews, the players weren't inclined to share many details with Elliat.

Elliat was filling the dead space created by the parley with a weather report. The wildfires in the solid world were burning some of the rural SOUP pools. Elliat had reporters on site at the pools who were commenting on some unusual features of the SOUP.

Since when did Elliat have reporters working for him?

"Elliat," one was saying, "first let me provide some background on
~~~~~

the SOUP pools, although the technical name is Stabilized Optimidata Unified Provision. The brief explanation is that the SOUP is an enormous server network that stores data in liquid form. When the SOUP was developed, the builders used whatever old buildings and structures were available as storage. In rural areas, many converted grain silos and galvanized watering tanks were used."

The reporter looked over his shoulder at a SOUP pool in flames behind him. Billowing clouds of noxious black smoke filled much of the sky behind the reporter. "What you see burning behind me is one of the SOUP storage areas."

"Joe," Elliat said, "if the liquid in the pool burns, will it result in loss of data or change any data?"

"No, Elliat. All the SOUP pools are interconnected with multiple failsafes, so it is almost impossible for data to be lost. The only side effect is that people who are located close to the pool won't be able to access the SOUP until the liquid is replaced."

"Great then. Sounds like there is nothing to worry about—"

The on-site reporter interrupted Elliat. "If you want something to worry about, worry about that black smoke. I've heard it may be toxic."

The reporter's exo-cam moved to better show the looming smoke clouds in the background. With the new angle, another SOUP pool with an odd structure over it became visible in the background.

"I have just had the most incredible insight!" Amoco's abrupt rise to his feet sent his rolling chair flying away from him. "I know now where the tesseract the ghosts are using is!"

Petra hopped to her feet like someone half her age. "Of course! How did we not figure this out sooner?"

How was it that Petra and Amoco could say a few words and automatically know what the other was thinking?

"I'm still in the dark," Cooper said. "Please illuminate."

"It's the SOUP pool," Petra said.

Amoco froze the screen and backed it up a few seconds. "Do you see that structure there?" Amoco zoomed into a spot in the background behind the reporter. A windmill with a wooden trestle and small wisps of smoke coming off it perched over a SOUP pool. The windmill appeared to be transporting liquid up from the pool and dropping it down the center of the trestle.

Cooper squinted at the screen. The stream of liquid seemed to disappear halfway down as it fell through the trestle, and then a foot below the stream reappeared. Was it an optical illusion?

Amoco pointed to the windmill. "That's how they're doing it."

"Your previous assumption was correct. It was never a Faraday cage," Petra said.

"It was always a tesseract," Amoco followed.

"I'm still as clueless as when this conversation started," Cooper said.

"I'll explain," Petra said. "The ghosts are using a tesseract to protect their code. They use the conveyor to take the SOUP liquid to the top of the trestle, then when it falls through the trestle it passes through the tesseract."

Cooper nodded. It was starting to make sense. "So when the liquid disappears, it's going through the tesseract?"

"Yes, but the tesseract isn't the point. It's the time warping. If it's the same as the other tesseracts, the liquid that appears at the bottom has traveled through time, so it is from 3 days and 36 minutes ago."

The other people in the room started to pay attention and had gathered to look at the screen where Amoco had zoomed in.

The structure wobbled and appeared to tip a fraction of an inch to the side.

"I still don't understand," Nikky said. "How does that protect them from being deleted?"

"It is quite ingenious," Amoco said. "The ghosts continuously send some of the liquid from the pool into the future by passing it through the tesseract—that way if they should be deleted, the liquid that just passed through the tesseract will be from before they were deleted and can be used to restore their code."

"When the liquid from that SOUP pool passes through the tesseract in the trestle, it is taken into the future," Petra said. "And that's where they're doing it." Petra pointed to the structure on the screen, her hand shaking with giddy enthusiasm.

"I'm going to pull up a satellite view so that we can keep an eye on it," Amoco said. A second later, the screen of Elliat talking had been replaced by a low horizon satellite that showed a high-resolution view of the windmill with the liquid running through the trestle. There was no doubt that the liquid was disappearing in the middle where it passed through the tesseract and reappearing a foot below before falling into the SOUP pool.

The structure shuddered and one side dropped about a foot. A cloud of dust and smoke rose around it.

"It's been damaged by the fires," Cooper said.

The wood and metal of the entire trestle structure gave way and collapsed into a pile of rubble that stuck out of the SOUP liquid with jagged edges.

"Well, that is quite the development," Amoco said. "It seems we have a unique opportunity—we can take out the ghosts now, before they repair their tesseract. It is now or never."

~~~~~

Just ahead of them, the road led to a bridge over a gulch that even before stepping on it, Amaya could tell was unstable. The wooden plank bridge, with its rusted metal fastenings and weathered wooden boards, had to be where Georgia and Bren had died. Amaya reluctantly stepped away from the safety of the solid dirt road and onto the creaking bridge. The wooden planks creaked and wobbled with each step she took.

Amaya had done everything she could to slow their progress for the mile or so that it took to get to the bridge. As sick as she felt, stopping to rest frequently wasn't a huge stretch. The biggest challenge was Hank. He still wanted to win the game, and he kept checking in with her every couple of steps to see if there was anything he could do to help her move faster. He even offered to carry her at one point. Like she was going to let Hank carry her!

No hazards had shown up to kill them off or to slow them down. She had told LP she would milk any hazard, but it was difficult to milk a hazard if there weren't any. If what LP had said about the bridge collapse delaying him from reaching the compound by hours was true, then no matter how slow she went, it wasn't going to be slow enough. No matter how much she stalled, she and Hank would arrive at the compound long before LP. What if she just sat down and refused to go anywhere until the clock ran out? Would LP win then?

She turned to look at Hank behind her. "How is the winner determined if no team completes the quest?"

He shook his head. "Don't say that. We're going to win." He tentatively placed one foot on the bridge and, in a smooth motion, moved his other foot forward.

"Just humor me," she said.
~~~~~

He caught up alongside her. "Well, that depends, but for our game it's a mix of gates won and players still alive."

Amaya continued across the bridge. She stepped on a board that cracked under her weight. She paused, waiting to see if it would hold or break into pieces. "If the game ended right now, which team would win?"

"Well, LP's crew has won two gates and has one teammate still alive, and we've won one gate, but have two teammates still alive. Each gate is worth ten points and each living team member is worth twenty, so right now, we're ahead. LP's team has forty points and we have fifty."

She had to come up with a plan before the game ended and she won despite all her efforts to lose. The board under her foot appeared sturdy and unlikely to give out under her. She stepped forward, following Hank's careful style. "Do you know how much time we have left?"

"It's around thirty minutes."

"So why do you keep pushing us to hurry? You just confirmed that we'll win no matter what. There's no way that LP can catch up; we could stop right now, and it wouldn't make any difference."

Under the bridge, the fast-moving water swirled around the rocks.

"But we could win it all. There's enough time left—we can make it to the compound. We can rescue the guy, be the heroes. If we win because the time ran out, then we win by default, and that's lame. That's winning by being the least bad team. Is that what you really want?"

"I just want the game to be over."

"Amaya, don't wimp out on me now. It's only thirty more minutes— you can buck up and make it that long. We can make this a real win."

Why didn't Hank ever listen to her? It was like he didn't care that she was sick, and he didn't value her opinion. The blood pounded in her temples and her face burned. "You know what, Hank? You've disrespected me from the day we met. You've always thought that someone without a chip wasn't as worthy as someone with a chip, and you've treated me as less valuable to the team. On the expedition, you fought against my authority at every step. Well, I'm sick, and I'm tired of your shit."

Hank's jaw dropped open. "I'm sorry, Amaya. I know I was a jerk to you at first, but I've really come to respect you. I didn't mean to be that way now. I just want to win."

Amaya rolled her eyes. "We *are* winning."

"I mean, I want to win the real way. Not by default. If you're feeling sick, I can carry you."

Not the carrying thing again. Amaya couldn't take it any longer. She needed to lose this game, and Hank wasn't helping.

"Look!" She pointed upstream at a random spot.

Hank turned to look in the direction she was pointing.

She acted before he could realize it was a decoy. She lunged and shoved him in the back as hard as she could.

Hank's head jerked back. Off-balance, he stumbled. His foot twisted on the uneven boards and his body pitched forward. With no railing, nothing stopped his forward momentum. He tumbled over the side, his arms flailing, unsuccessfully attempting to hold on to the jagged edges of the boards.

A second later, a notice popped up beside her. "Hank Silva has passed away due to injuries sustained falling from a bridge. Your team will continue the quest with the one remaining member." Amaya smiled and crossed her arms. She had finally dealt with her Hank problem. She remembered the spectators and stopped smiling. It wouldn't do if she looked like she was happy about losing.

"That will teach you to respect me!" she yelled after him. There was some truth to it, but the most important thing was for the audience to believe that she had pushed Hank because she was mad at him.

With one fewer player on her team, and no team completing the quest, LP would get his win. She gave up on forward movement and collapsed on the bridge. The bridge swayed gently. Below, the water tumbled over the rocks. About half an hour more and the game would be done, with LP's team the winner.

~~~~~

Attending a closing ceremony hadn't sounded so bad when Amaya had agreed to it three hours ago, but now she regretted it. She had been happy lying on the bridge. Well, maybe not happy, but less unhappy than she had been everywhere else in the Panacea metaverse. The trickling of the river had soothed her while she waited the half hour for the game clock to count down.

At some point a bell sounded three times, and next thing she knew she was back in the stadium in a row with Nyala, Hank, and Opali. Facing them were LP, Georgia, T-Rock, and Bren.

Hank leaned past Nyala to speak to Amaya. "I have a bone to pick with you."
~~~~~

She shrugged apologetically. "Sorry!" She could explain to him later why she had pushed him off the bridge.

Opali tugged on Hank's hand. "Unca Hank, I sorry I didn't know 'bout the landslide. Older Opali would've seen it."

He patted her head. "Don't worry about it." He looked back at Amaya with piercing eyes. "At least you didn't kill me by pushing me off a bridge."

"Why Auntie 'Maya push you off bridge?" Opali asked.

"Opali," Nyala said, "you can be older now if you want."

Opali returned to her twenty-one-year-old size. The mud-covered white dress with the pale pink embroidered flowers was replaced by an athletic bodysuit that appeared to be made out of diagonal strands of light.

"Wow," Opali said, "that was quite an experience! No need to answer why Amaya pushed you off the bridge. I see it clearly now."

"Shhh," LP hissed. "It's starting."

The game warden stepped between the two teams, much like he had at the opening. "I've tallied the points. The Opalites, with one gate won and one surviving team member, have thirty points. LP's Crew, with one surviving team member and two gates won, has forty points."

The crowd roared. Were they happy? Upset? Glad the game was finally done? Amaya couldn't tell.

A trophy appeared in the game warden's hand. He held it up in front of him. LP grabbed the trophy from the startled game warden and stepped in front of him. The game warden looked back and forth, apparently confused about what to do with LP. He shrugged and stepped to the side.

"I pronounce LP's Crew, my team, winners of this exhibition game!" LP pumped the trophy in the air. "I'm thrilled to accept this trophy on behalf of LP's Crew. Let this be a reminder of the power of perseverance!"

Amaya rolled her eyes. The power of bribery was more like it.

"I have an important announcement to make," LP continued. "During this game, I have learned from my teammates and grown as a person. As a result, I have decided to commute the sentences of Amaya Gidada and Amoco Cadiz."

The yelling of the crowd swelled again. The boos, for the most part, were covered over by the other sounds, but Amaya heard some "kill her dead" chants under the roar of the crowd.

Nyala grasped her tight. She sniffed and, with a quivering voice, said, "I'm so happy you're going to be okay."

The tension and worry and fear of the last few days broke through the wall that held them back. A sob choked up in Amaya's throat, and the next thing she knew, her body heaved with sobs. She and Amoco were safe. Their plan to make LP more like T-Rock had worked. They were going to be okay.

LP had been droning on in the background. "…but more importantly, because I am a generous person, I will care for you all."

She was confused—what was LP saying? Amaya's crying turned into sniffles as she focused back on LP.

LP held his hands up and addressed the crowd. "The spectrals will treat the electricity intolerance for people living in pods as if you were one of our own. However, we are unable to provide treatment to people who are not in pods."

Bren raised his eyebrows and looked at Amaya as though he was hoping she would clear things up. LP was turning in circles with the trophy held high above his head. Obviously, he wasn't going to explain what was going on.

Amaya sent a message to the game warden that she would like to speak. He nodded at her. "People…" she started. Her amplified voice filled the stadium and spread among the spectators. "You may be aware of a viral toxin that has spread through contact with infected chips. The toxin causes the infected person to be unable to tolerate exposure to electricity. The toxin has affected everyone in the metaverse. At this point, if you have taken the shot, the toxin will have spread to you, and if you are not feeling ill yet, you will soon."

LP stopped turning in circles. "Everyone's infected."

"I'm sorry—can you repeat that?" Did LP just say everyone was infected?

"Everyone's infected." LP said again. "When the wildfires caught the SOUP on fire, toxins in the smoke from the burning pools infected everyone with the intolerance."

"Everyone's infected? Even those who never had a chip and have never spent time in the metaverse?"

LP rolled his eyes. "When I say everyone's infected, I mean everyone's infected. The toxin was spreading virally, but then the extreme heat from the wildfires released the toxin and now it is airborne."

It was much worse than Amaya had realized. There weren't enough pods for everyone who was going to get sick.

The look in Bren's eyes changed from bewilderment to fear. "What *is* this illness?" he asked.

LP continued with his explanation. "The illness is an electricity intolerance, and the only way to not be sick is to completely avoid electricity. The spectrals will provide ongoing treatment to people living in pods. If you want treatment, make sure you're living in a pod. If you're not in a pod, prepare to live without using any electricity."

"How long?" Hank asked. "How long until we won't be able to tolerate being around electricity?"

"Within twenty-four hours," LP said, "most of you will be so sick you won't be able to function effectively. You'll either need to get treatment or give up using electricity."

A sharp pain in Amaya's chest migrated to her abdomen. She clutched her stomach, trying to squelch the wave of nausea. At least she could exit Panacea now. She wasn't a big fan of Viola, but she had to give her credit for finding a way that they could exit the metaverse.

"Hey," Amaya yelled at no one in particular. She hoped it would be heard by the people watching over her body in the solid world. "Get me out of here! I want back in the solid world."

<p style="text-align:center">~~~~~</p>

There was so much for Cooper to take in. LP had said something about an electricity intolerance and then something about taking care of people in pods. But most importantly, he also said Amaya and Amoco were no longer going to be executed.

Cooper embraced Amoco. "Congratulations! I've been so worried— I can't tell you how happy I am for you!"

Amoco didn't even smile. "Cooper," he said, "there's no time for that now. I must speak with Viola and Petra right away."

"I'm listening," Petra said.

"I'm not sure what's so urgent that you can't take a minute to celebrate not being executed," Cooper said, "but I'll get Viola."

Cooper used his finger to draw a window in the air. Behind the window, the game viewer showed the players talking to each other. Hopefully, someone would remove Amaya quickly because she didn't look good. Given what was just said, would she feel better if she got away from electricity?

Viola accepted the contact request right away. A bunch of haphazardly placed screens full of equations and diagrams floated behind her.

"Viola." Amoco nodded in Viola's direction. "Pleasure to see you."

"What's up?" Viola asked.

"As you know, my efforts to determine the cause of Mariela's illness hit dead end after dead end. I believe my research capabilities may have been affected by the illness, because now that LP has made the cause clear, in retrospect it should have been obvious." Amoco paused.

"Well, go on then." Viola never did have much patience for Amoco's wandering speech patterns.

If Amoco noticed Viola's impatience, he didn't show it. "First, I hope you understand that I am fully aware that a cause without a cure is not a significant improvement. But it is a step in the right direction, because the cure cannot be determined without understanding the cause."

Viola nodded curtly. "Yes, Amoco, very well. Go ahead."

Amoco took a long pause before resuming speaking. "While LP did not mention Mariela specifically, it is clear that Mariela died from the electricity intolerance."

For a moment it had seemed like there was a reason to celebrate, one positive thing had happened after so much bad, but now from what Amoco was saying, it was clear that everything was worse. Not only Amaya might die, but many other people might be affected as well. Cooper rubbed his temple. "LP mentioned something about an electricity intolerance, but even with Amaya's explanation, I'm still confused. What is it and what causes it?"

"If you would please listen, I am sure all your questions will be answered." Amoco paused long enough that Cooper considered risking Amoco's ire by speaking again.

Eventually, Amoco spoke. "I think that once we have a chance to examine it further, we will find that the cause of the intolerance is the toxin in the kill switch. Most likely, the nanoparticles in the kill switch become agitated when exposed to electricity. I do not know how much electricity is needed to cause the agitation, but based on what we have seen, it appears to be that levels not much above what is normally present in the human body are enough to cause problems. I strongly suspect that people who received a larger dose of the kill switch are going to be more affected. This is why Mariela became ill first."

"But if the people who received the largest doses are at greatest risk…" Cooper's voice trailed off as the implication of what Amoco had said hit him, "both Amaya and Nyala got a full dose."

"Yes, indeed. And we have seen that Amaya is already feeling ill. I do not wish to alarm you, but I have also felt out of sorts." Amoco's eyes unfocused while he appeared to be thinking. "We need to assume that I may not be useful as a researcher for much longer."

It hurt to think that more of his friends could also be sick. Cooper could lose everyone he cared about—they had all been exposed to the kill switch, and many were starting to have symptoms. The blood pounded in his temples. He would be just as powerless to help them as he was with Mariela.

They had a unique opportunity to delete the ghosts while their tesseract was down, but if the ghosts were needed to provide treatment to the humans, then was deleting the ghosts really an option anymore? "Is deleting the ghosts off the table?" he asked.

"I am afraid so," Amoco said. "Humanity is now dependent on the ghosts for treatment for the electricity intolerance."

"What about other people?" Viola asked. "Will it be fatal for them as well?"

"I am sure it will be. Mariela's death was just the beginning. I am certain that people who continue to be exposed to electricity without treatment will die. If the wildfires are spreading the toxins, we can assume that most people have received a substantial dose of the toxin, and will not be able to tolerate even small amounts of electricity exposure."

"Everyone is infected," Petra said, "and everyone is at risk of death or serious illness if they don't receive treatment, and the ghosts are offering the only treatment."

"That's why I wanted to speak with you so urgently. We have a brief window here to try to find a treatment for the intolerance. Soon, I will no longer be able to do any research that involves electricity, making me effectively useless. That will apply to anyone who does not receive treatment from the ghosts. People who receive treatment in the metaverse, on the other hand, will be able to conduct research, but will be monitored so closely by the ghosts that they will also be effectively useless. We must act now to try to solve this problem, or it will go unsolved."

"Amoco, if what you're saying is correct," Viola said, "I'm not sure you could have called with worse news. I'm still processing all the implications, but I think it's pretty clear that our way of life has just ended. I'll do what I can to help."

"So will I," Petra said.

~~~~~

Surely someone would be getting Amaya out of the metaverse soon. Maybe they were having trouble figuring out the shot.

Amaya panted with her hands on her knees and reminded herself that it would all be over soon.

"Amaya," Bren said, placing a hand on her shoulder. "I'm going to miss you."

Amaya straightened up as far as the pain in her stomach would allow and, with one arm still wrapped around her stomach, she hugged Bren. "I'm assuming you'll be staying in the metaverse?" she asked him.

"I have no reason to leave. I love it here."

"Ah, Bren," Nyala said, "don't tell me that we've lost you to the world of the chipped."

He shrugged. "What can I say? I thought it was difficult getting by before. Can you imagine how tough it will be without electricity?"

"At least it will be equally tough for everyone," Nyala said. "And with your aeroponic greenhouse, you're a step ahead of everyone else."

"That greenhouse was a pain in my back. Literally. It's yours now. You should send someone over to protect it so that it doesn't get taken over by scavengers."

Amaya didn't know what living without electricity would look like, but the greenhouse would clearly be an asset.

"Thank you, Bren," Nyala said. She still looked stunned by LP's announcement. "I'll head out and take care of that now."

"Nyala," Amaya said, "can you check that someone is disconnecting me? We should check with Amoco to see if he wants to be disconnected as well."

"Of course." A tearful Nyala hugged both Bren and Opali goodbye. "See you on the other side," she said to Amaya. A couple of seconds later, Nyala disappeared.

"Opali," Amaya said, "I don't know how much longer I have until I'm disconnected. I just want you to know how much I appreciate you defending us." She hugged Opali and wiped away a tear. "I'll miss you."
~~~~~

"I'll miss you too," Opali said. "Thank you for being so nice to me in the game."

"What do you mean?" She had hardly been nice to Opali. "I was cranky and short-tempered with you…"

Her arms itched. She scratched at them. It felt like a thousand mites were crawling under her skin. The mites pushed their way into her muscles and joints. Her entire body ached. Amaya reminded herself to breathe. The transition was starting.

The Rupture

Sunday, continued

As soon as Hank exited Panacea, he sprinted from the library up the stairs and down the hall to the bedroom with Amaya's pod. Hopefully, the medical staff had known to start her transition from the metaverse. Georgia wasn't far behind him as he took the steps two at a time. Outside, the sun had set, turning the windows into an inky black that reflected a ghostly appearance back to him. He was surprised to see that it was dark out, but with the game lasting for hours, he shouldn't have been.

The door to the bedroom with the pods was ajar, and it clattered into the wall when Hank pushed it open. June was hovering anxiously near Amaya's pod, her eyes red and swollen with tears. On the far side of the room, Amoco, Cooper, and Viola reclined in their pods with various tubes, IVs, and electrodes connected to them. Someone had removed Mariela's pod in the two days since she had passed away. Forlorn marks in the carpet marked where it had stood.

The medical staff had just finished removing most of the devices connected to Amaya, but nothing seemed to be happening. Every so often, a tech would give an update on her vitals, but minutes passed and Amaya didn't move and the med staff wasn't doing much.

Moments later, T-Rock and Nyala rushed into the room, both still wearing their projection suits with the headsets over their heads. Nyala skidded to a stop and threw her headset into a corner. "What's happening?" she asked.

"Nothing so far." Hank paced back and forth.

Nyala went straight to Amaya's bed and hovered as closely as she could without getting in the way of the medical staff.

T-Rock placed his headset on the table with all the monitors on it and looked at the screens showing the vitals on all the pods. He walked among the beds, feeling their pulses as he went, and undoing the clasps and buckles on his projection suit as he walked around. He stopped short of Amaya, standing back and watching the medical staff hovering over her.

"How long will it take?" Nyala asked.

"This is new for us," the doctor said. "We've never administered one of the exit shots before, so we're not sure what to expect."

"How has it gone for other people who have taken it?" Nyala asked.

"We haven't received any reports of it successfully being used." The doc seemed apologetic. "It's so new—Dr. Mason just released the formula. We have no information on how it works, including proof that it even works."

Nyala's raised voice cracked as she spoke. "Then why did you give it to her?"

"The electricity intolerance changes everything. The ghosts can only provide the treatment to people who are in pod warehouses. She won't survive living in the metaverse unless we move her pod."

Nyala rubbed her head. "I know. I'm sorry I snapped at you. It was what she wanted. I'm just scared for her."

"What will happen to the others?" T-Rock asked.

"Amoco has asked to have the exit shot as well. We'll process him out after we finish with Amaya. Cooper and Viola are being moved later this week into a Bo Place warehouse."

"They won't receive treatment until then?" Nyala asked.

"Unfortunately not. We have a spot reserved for them but aren't able to get transportation until later this week. We'll just have to hope they will be okay until then." The doctor clasped his hands in front of him. "If you'll excuse me, I'd like to get back to Amaya."

It wasn't clear what the docs and medical techs were doing while they hovered over Amaya. T-Rock hung his projection suit over a lounger and joined Georgia, Nyala, and June near Amaya's pod.

"June, are you okay?" Hank asked. Hank stood next to June, out of the way of the medical staff tending to Amaya.

June's eyes were heavy with sadness. "Oscar and I decided to enter the metaverse. Oscar needs medical care that requires electricity, and I don't want to leave Oscar again, so wherever he goes, I go."

LP's announcement about the electricity intolerance had been made less than twenty minutes ago, yet June and Oscar had already made a decision. How many other people out there were making the exact same decision? "It's going to be a madhouse scramble for space," he said. "Do you have a pod reserved?"

"Already done."

Amaya blinked and turned her head in their direction. Her unfocused eyes still seemed foggy.

"Her blood pressure is high but coming down," a tech said.

"June," T-Rock leaned over to wrap June in a bear hug, his voice somber and quiet, "being here without you or Oscar will be like a beaver trying to live without the trees it needs to create a dam."

June offered a half-smile. "T-Rock, we'll miss you too, but you'll have everything you need here. Oscar has made sure the estate is well-protected and is set up to function off grid."

"But what will happen to the estate with you and Oscar in the metaverse?" T-Rock asked.

"Let me talk to Oscar, but I think you need to be in charge. You, more than anyone else, know how to keep this place operating once it's off the grid. Oscar and I can sign a document letting you use the estate indefinitely. Feel free to use it as you best see fit."

A part of Hank was jealous that T-Rock had such a clear role and so much to offer. No doubt he would keep many people alive and healthy.

T-Rock wiped a tear from his eye and clapped June on the back. "Thank you so much, June. I'm going to turn this place into a haven for as many people as we can handle. It'll be like a beehive—everyone will have a role and everyone will be taken care of."

"There are other estates in the area that are also self-sufficient, like Amoco's. You should check in with them about setting up additional beehives."

"Good idea. Thanks, June."

T-Rock was the perfect person to run a haven, or beehive, if that's what they were going to call it. If anyone knew how to survive without electricity, and lead others in learning to live without electricity, it was T-Rock. Another pang of jealousy. There had to be something Hank could do that would give the same sense of having something to offer that T-Rock had, even if it wasn't on the same scale as running an entire haven. Or beehive. Make that multiple beehives, if Amoco and other landowners joined in.

T-Rock, or the queen bee as Hank had started to think of him, clapped his hands together. "I have information that I give out in my survival course. Stuff like how to make a solar oven, how to dig a well and latrine, where to find food. I have around twenty handouts total."

Nyala finished peeling off her projection suit, revealing the leggings and tank top she wore underneath. She draped the suit over her arm. "T-Rock, we should print those out before the power goes out. We can send people across the city to hand them out and to let them know about the havens."

"I agree. I'm going to turn the power off once Amaya and Amoco are out of the metaverse, so I'd better get started printing."

"Use Oscar's high-speed printer," June said. "He has around thirty reams of paper in the printer room."

Nyala raised an eyebrow. "Thirty?"

"I know; only Oscar would have that much paper. T-Rock, that printer is hyper fast, so if you get started now, you can probably be done by the time Amaya and Amoco are out of their pods and stabilized."

"Will do." T-Rock picked up his projection suit and helmet. "Once I get the printing started, I'll be back with some candles for you all. It's going to be dark when the electricity goes off."

"Will Cooper and Viola be okay?" Nyala asked.

June placed a hand on Cooper's pod and looked at him through the cover. It made her look even sadder.

The doc stepped away from Amaya. "They should be fine here for a while with the electricity off. We'll use backup batteries for their pods. I'll talk with staff to come up with a plan to do minimal monitoring on them."

"Blood pressure stabilizing," the tech standing by Amaya said.

Georgia crumpled into one of the loungers and closed her eyes.

Hank sat on the arm of the lounger. "What was it like playing the game with LP?" he asked her.

She grabbed his hand and squeezed it. "It was like trying to herd cats, except that it was just one really stubborn cat and the cat thought it was in charge and was supposed to be herding us. Not to mention that we were supposed to be changing the cat's personality from a killing machine into a cuddly lap kitten."

Hank laughed. He rubbed her warm, silky hand with his thumb.

"Do you know what you're going to do?" he asked. "Receive the treatment in the metaverse or live without electricity in the solid world?"

Georgia sighed. "I don't know. I haven't had time to think about it."

"I got a notice from Elliat that the pod warehouses are already filling up," Nyala said. "You had better decide quickly. People who wait will have the decision made for them when there aren't any more pods available."

Things were changing fast—so fast it was disorienting. Hank needed to decide whether to stay in the solid world or enter a pod, and he needed to do it soon before all the pods were taken. Whatever he did, he wanted to stay connected with Georgia, but did Georgia feel the same way?

An idea tugged at the corners of his mind. It was a way he could feel useful, but he needed Georgia's help to do it.

"I'm going to start working on Amoco," the tech said.

"I can't see," Amaya said. "Am I back at the estate?"

"Your vision may take a while to clear up," the tech said. He turned to all the bystanders. "Can you all leave us alone? I'll let you know when she's ready to see you."

Hank stood up but didn't let go of Georgia's hand. "Can we talk?" he asked Georgia. "Somewhere else?"

"Our old room is across the hall."

Our old room. The one that they had stayed in back when he was helping Georgia adjust after she left her pod. The room with the bed where they finally had enough space to spread out but had still slept curled up, keeping each other warm. That room.

"It'll do," he said.

~~~~~~

Two armchairs were angled toward diamond-paned windows in an alcove that Hank had almost forgotten about. In front of the chairs was an oblong table, its size perfect for a tea tray. Georgia placed the two pale pink pillar candles that T-Rock had given them on the table and lit them with matches also provided by T-Rock. Despite the occasional animosity between him and T-Rock, Hank had to admit that there wasn't anyone better to have around in a crisis.

With the flickering light from the candles, they were all ready for the electricity to be shut off. As soon as both Amaya and Amoco were out of the metaverse and medically stable, T-Rock was flipping off the master switch to the house. It wouldn't be long now.

"Would you like some tea?" Hank asked. "I could grab some from the kitchen." Tea would give him something to do with his hands. He was fidgety and nervous about what he wanted to say to Georgia.

Georgia shook her head. "My stomach is unsettled, so I'll pass for
~~~~~~

now."

It was just as well. If he went to get tea, he might lose his nerve and never say to Georgia what he needed to say. He turned his chair to directly face hers. "I have a lot I need to say to you." He kept talking before she could respond. "I know I've been a jerk lots of times. I picked fights with people. I didn't respect your space. I tried to be close to you when you weren't ready for that. And I've made stupid mistakes that I can never forgive myself for."

Georgia leaned toward him, her elbow resting on the arm of her chair. She seemed to understand that if she interrupted him, he would never be able to finish what he needed to say.

He ran his hand across his chin. The stubble had built up over the last few days. Was the nausea he felt from the electricity intolerance or was it from nerves? He took a deep breath. "I know what I'm going to do. I know the choice I need to make, and I'm hoping you'll be a part of it."

Georgia nodded. "Okay, I'm listening."

Good, she hadn't shut him down yet. She might walk out of his life at any moment, and if he didn't take the chance now to tell her what he was feeling, he might never get it.

"I was thinking during the game that I don't know who I am anymore. I used to be this guy—you knew that guy—the one who didn't really think about others, who reacted to people without thinking. I don't think I'm that guy anymore. But now I don't know who I am. It's like everything that made me who I am is gone. I don't even have my martial arts classes anymore."

"You'll find yourself," Georgia said. She took his hand. "Crisis has a way of bringing out who people truly are."

He grasped her hand. "Well, that's the thing. I think I already know. I think I've figured out who I am now, what my part is in this crisis." He paused. "But I was hoping we could do it together. I want you to be a part of it."

"Tell me what you're thinking."

"First, I need to explain something. I've started to feel sick from the electricity, but I've noticed when I use my chip, it doesn't make me sick. I think because our chips run off the electricity in our bodies, we are some of the few people in the world who can be off-grid but also stay in touch with people in the metaverse."

Georgia rubbed his hand with her thumb. "That's a big deal. I always knew we were unique." She smiled. "Is it part of your plan?"

"It is. Just a warning—the plan involves you, but if you don't want to do it, I'll figure out another way. I wouldn't want to stop you if you want something different."

"Go ahead. I'm dying of curiosity."

"The idea solidified for me when T-Rock mentioned the handouts for people on how to survive without electricity. We need a way to get that information out, and not just here locally, but all over. But more than that, once people are disconnected, we'll need a way to communicate with each other. We'll need a way to get information out and to let people know what's going on in the rest of the world."

"So what are you proposing?"

"I'll travel the world and connect with other communities."

"And how would I be involved in this?"

"Because we can still go back and forth between the metaverse and the solid world, we would meet in the metaverse. I would provide information on how things are in other communities to you, and you could share it with the people here in Glorietta Pass. You would report to me on how things are going here and let me know if there are important developments, and I would share it with people out there."

"I wouldn't be going with you?"

His heart skipped a beat. He very much wanted Georgia to go with him. "It would make me so happy to have you with me."

"But your plan is to share information using our still-working chips?" she asked.

"I just thought, if you go with me, how would T-Rock and Nyala and whoever else stays here know what's going on out in the world? If you stay, I can report back to you on how the rest of the world is doing, and update them on how things are elsewhere."

"Does it make a difference if they know what's going on out in the world? It's not like they can change things if they know."

Hank hadn't anticipated that Georgia would want to go with him. She had pushed him away in the past, and he hadn't realized that had changed. "I can change the plan. I'll find a way to make it work if we both go." His plan worked best if there was someone with a chip located in Glorietta Pass, but he would find another way to make it work. There were always alternatives.

"But your plan works better if I stay here?"

Did she want to go with him or didn't she? "You don't want to go with me?"

"I want to travel the world with you, but I don't think I'll ever be fully 100 percent again—not after spending thirty years in a pod—and I'm not sure I'm up for going cross-country on a…horse? Or a bicycle? So tell me why being able to communicate with the people here is important."

It pained him, but she was most likely right about not being up for a cross-country trek that was going to be physically grueling. Sure, she could run again, but the years of pod-living had taken their toll, and it wasn't surprising that she hesitated to head off into the wilderness. The twinge of nausea in his stomach intensified as he gave up the idea of her traveling with him.

"Here's why communication is important. You have some of the most clever minds here. The people who are most likely to come up with a solution to the intolerance, or a new energy source that doesn't cause a reaction, are located right here. If they come up with a solution, you can share it with me and I'll share it with the world."

"But it might be years, or even decades, until anything new is discovered."

"This is a lifelong commitment."

She put her other hand on top of his. "Will I see you again?"

"That's the beauty of it. With working chips, we can see each other all the time in the metaverse."

"You, of all people, should know that it's not the same. It's not like we will be able to feel each other's warmth."

"I know." He looked down. He had a chance to be with Georgia in the way he had always wanted to be with her—curled up every night in a comfortable bed in this very room instead of temperature-less virtual contact. But as much as he wanted it, it wasn't the right thing. He took a deep breath. Interactions in the metaverse would have to be enough. "It's just something I have to do. This is my contribution to the world right now, and there's only a handful of us who can do it."

"You'll need to take some people with you. You can't survive out there by yourself."

"I'm sure I'll find people."

The lights shut off and, other than the small circle illuminated by the candles, the room fell into darkness. Less than an hour after LP had informed them of the electricity intolerance, T-Rock had already shut off the power. Hank hadn't noticed the quiet hum of the air filtration system until the hum disappeared and silence settled in the room.

Georgia looked around her. "It's starting." She shivered, even though the room already felt warmer. "It's hard not to think of this as a life-changing moment."

"It's true." The bit of nausea that had been gnawing at Hank's stomach disappeared. The enormity of how the world had just changed was hard to ignore. More than anything so far, the quick disappearance of his symptoms was a sign that their lives were never going to be the same.

Like Georgia had just done, he looked around the room. He wanted to note this place, this point in time. The moment their lives changed. Every night after sunset was going to be this dark. Every convenience provided by electricity was gone. The nausea formed a pit in his stomach again, but this time it wasn't caused by the electricity intolerance. He felt even more certain that he needed to leave, needed to be on the road, not to just stay in motion but also to help others. For the first time in his life, he had something that felt like a calling.

"Are you sure this is what you want to do?" Georgia asked.

"I'm sure."

"We'll need to make sure you have lots of supplies. And a cart or something to carry tools and the supplies. Maybe you can bring a bunch of T-Rock's pamphlets with you."

"I was thinking the same thing." He didn't let go of her hand. "But what about you? We could arrange to get together in the metaverse once a week or something on a schedule. Just to chat and spend time together."

"I'd like that."

"So you're not going with me?" He was asking questions he already knew the answer to.

She pressed his hands with hers. "Hank, I'll stay here even though I would really rather be with you. You're a part of my heart. I know I've been mad at you at times, and sometimes I've wanted to walk away, but the reality is I couldn't any more walk away from you than I could walk away from myself."

His heart stumbled and then started again at a mad, galloping pace. Was he understanding her correctly?

"I love you, Hank."

He brushed a strand of hair out of her face. "I love you, too."

CHAPTER 26

Day One of The Rupture

Monday

Today would have been her execution date, but somehow it all still seemed like a dream. Amaya, dripping in sweat as she walked with Nyala to a pod warehouse, was not going to die today. Unless the heat killed her, which seemed like a definite possibility. The sun had been above the horizon for less than half an hour and the morning heat was already at sweltering levels.

Amaya had agreed, with some misgivings, to an early morning trip to see ten-year-old Trevor and his mother one last time before they entered pods. It wasn't the wisest decision Amaya had made. Despite Elliat saying on his show yesterday that they didn't disable the chips, many people still blamed them for it. As if she weren't already hot enough, the long sleeves and hood on the jackets they wore to keep from being recognized made the heat almost intolerable.

Ever since Trevor had moved in next door to Nyala five years ago, it seemed the young boy spent more time at Nyala's place than Amaya did. The family wanted to say goodbye to Nyala before entering a pod and even though she had just exited her pod the day before, Amaya didn't want to miss it.

The pod warehouse and its buildings—the greenhouses, nutrient preparation facilities, waste processing plants, and laboratories—loomed over them as they got close. The facilities used a lot of electricity. Amaya could get an idea of how much each used based on how sick she felt while passing it.

They had left their bikes chained beside the road once the crowds became too thick for riding. They threaded their way through the line of people multiple blocks long waiting to get into the pod warehouse.

"Why is it so hot?" she complained to no one in particular.

"It's the wildfires," Nyala said. "They're pretty close to here. That's why there are spaces still open in this warehouse—no one wants to be that close to the fires if they can help it."

"Based on the number of people in line, I'd say a lot of people are willing to be that close to the wildfires."

"I guess Trevor and Tasha aren't the only ones who will take whatever they can get right now."

Tasha, right. That was Trevor's mom's name. Near the front of the line, Tasha waved her hand over her head. Next to her, the ten-year-old Trevor cracked a broad smile when he saw Nyala. After years of living next door to each other, it wasn't surprising the two had developed a close bond.

Nyala enthusiastically raised a hand in greeting. "There they are now." Nyala led the way, fighting through the thick crowds between them and Trevor's mom. Sometimes the jostling of the crowds almost knocked Amaya's hoodie off. She pulled the strings tight around her chin. The last thing she wanted was for someone to recognize them. Surely by now every single person in the world must think she was guilty of disabling the chips.

When they reached Trevor and his mom, Trevor embraced Nyala and buried his head with its large afro into the nook of her shoulder. "I don't want to go into a pod."

Nyala turned to his mom. "Are you sure you want to do this?"

"What do I know about surviving without electricity?" Tasha asked. "I never thought it would come to this, but if we're going to survive, it's going to be in a pod."

Behind Amaya, a nasal voice that she knew well reached her over the sounds of the crowd. Amaya pulled her hoodie closer over her head. With her face hidden by the shadow of the hood, she peeked to see where Elliat was.

"Folks," Elliat was saying in his podcasting voice not far from them, "there's a frenzied rush on pods. You would not believe the crowds here! All the available pods are quickly filling up and there are not enough spots to go around. People are panicked they won't get in. And not without reason—an exclusive *Business Today* poll estimated that around seventy percent of humans are choosing to live in a pod. Our team also estimated that there is only capacity for around fifty percent. Unfortunately, that means about twenty percent of people will want to get into a pod but won't be able to. That's a tragedy, folks!"

Elliat's perky reporting came across as tone deaf. Sometimes Elliat sounded like he actually might care, but this was not one of those times.

In line ahead of them, a couple was screened by the pod manager and allowed to enter the gated area. The pod manager looked like he hadn't slept in ages, with his bloodshot eyes and untamed hair sticking straight out. He turned to Trevor's mom. "Next."

She stepped up to the manager.

"How many?" the jaded manager asked without looking up from his mobile.

"Just me and my son."

The manager frowned. "You can't have kids under sixteen in here. It's against the rules."

Tasha shifted nervously. "I heard that kids were being allowed to enter pods, given the…unique situation."

"Not here. Some warehouses up the road are willing to break the rules, but I doubt you'd be able to find space. Word is they're almost full up."

"I don't know…" Tasha looked around her, her anxious eyes not focusing on any spot. "I don't know what to do. The other warehouses are full? Someone told me this warehouse would take kids, that's why I got in line early."

"Hey, lady, hurry up," someone yelled from farther back in the line. "I got sweat rolling down the crack of my butt."

"Mom, I don't want to go into a pod." Trevor tugged on his mom's arm. "Let's go."

"Trevor, this isn't a discussion!" Tasha insisted.

"Mom, we can figure out how to live without electricity."

"I don't have a job anymore," his mom snapped. "We won't have any way to survive."

"Hey, what's the holdup?" someone else yelled. The voice was dry and parched—the sound of someone who got in line hours ago without any water.

The manager leaned to the side and examined the line, then glared at Trevor's mom. "Lady, either sign up or move out of line."

"Can I have some time to think?"

"I tell you what," the manager said, "I'll help the next person, and then I'll process you after her. If you still haven't made up your mind by the time I get back with you, then you'll have to go to the back of the line."

"Is that all the time you can give me?"

"Afraid so. Everybody wants in right now. I can't risk having a revolt on my hands."

"Fine." Tasha stepped to the side.

Amaya's heart broke for her. Tasha's options were limited to bad and worse.

Trevor hung on her arm. "Mom, can I stay with Nyala?"

"No," she snapped, "you belong with me."

"Then let's not go into the pod."

"I don't know. I don't know." Tasha looked at Nyala. "What will it do to his development to grow up in a pod?"

Nyala put a hand on Tasha's arm. "He's only ten. The truth is, we don't know how it will affect a ten-year-old because it's never been allowed before. It's risky."

"I just can't." Tears streamed down Tasha's face.

Nyala grabbed her hand. "Then come with us. Don't move into the pod. We'll find a way to get by."

"Okay, lady, time's up."

"Just one second." Her voice was sharp.

"Hurry it up." It was clear from his tone that he wasn't going to wait long.

"You," Nyala snapped at the manager, "need to give this poor woman a second to make up her mind."

The manager seemed to shrink behind his tablet. Amaya cheered Nyala for taking the manager down a notch. He had a tough job, no doubt, but that wasn't any reason he couldn't give Tasha a couple more minutes to make an incredibly difficult, life-altering decision.

"You can both come with us," Nyala said.

"It's just…my workplace said that I could have my job back if I go into the metaverse. I need that income."

Amaya tried to not let them see the tears that were forming in her eyes. She didn't want Tasha to have to live without electricity if she didn't want to, but what other options did she have?

"Mom, can I go with Nyala?" Trevor asked again.

Tasha turned to Nyala. "Can he go with you?"

"Of course."

The man with the tablet motioned them over. "Time's up. Make your decision."

Trevor's voice was choked with tears. "Mom, stay with us."

"Trevor, honey, I love you, but I need my job. Nyala will keep you safe."

"You can stay with us, too," Nyala said.

Her eyes filled with water. "I can't."

"Lady, I need your thumbprint here or you need to go to the back of the line."

"Trevor, I'll always love you." She embraced him in a hug that seemed to go on forever.

Amaya's heart might never be the same.

"Lady," the harried pod manager was running out of patience, "either put your thumb here or get out of line."

Trevor's mom turned to Nyala. "Thank you." A quick hug and then she turned to the pod manager and pressed her thumb into his mobile device.

The pod manager swiped to a new screen. "I just have a couple forms I need you to sign and you can go on in."

Tasha signed each one with an angry flourish of her finger.

The manager pointed her toward the door. "Welcome to pod living!"

Tasha hugged Trevor again, and then at the manager's insistence, let him go and went inside.

Amaya snuck a look at Trevor. His face was expressionless except for rivulets of tears running down the cheeks.

"Come on, Trevor, let's go." Nyala put her arm around the young boy's shoulders. He looked back over his shoulder, but let Nyala guide him away.

Amaya attempted to blend in with everyone else when they passed Elliat. Elliat may be on their side now, but he would surely call attention to them if he saw them.

Elliat's exo-cam hovered in front of him; he appeared to be wrapping up his podcast. "This is Elliat Exis, saying goodbye to the solid world for the last time."

Well, that was the last time she would have to hear his voice. She wouldn't miss all his lies and accusations and setting people against her.

Maybe now she could start to feel safe again.

"I'm surprised Elliat didn't say goodbye to you," Amaya said.

Nyala raised her eyebrows. "Oh, he did. I just didn't think you would want to hear about it."

"What? When did that happen?"

"You shouldn't be so surprised—you slept for like fourteen hours after the game ended. I'm sure lots of things happened that you didn't know about."

"What did he say?"

"He tried to convince me to go into a pod. And when I said no, we had a very heartfelt moment where we said goodbye and many tears were shed. You would have hated it."

Amaya rolled her eyes. "No doubt."

"Dad," a teenage kid standing in line pulled on his dad's arm. "I want to go with them as well."

Nyala stopped to look at him.

"Absolutely not," the dad said. "You're old enough that the warehouse will allow you in. I'm not letting you go with some stranger."

The boy scoffed. "I won't be on my own, and I don't want to live in a pod."

Everyone in the line turned to look at them. With so many people looking in their direction, someone was going to recognize them, even with their hoodies pulled low over their faces.

Amaya tugged on Nyala's arm, pulling her away from the teenager. "Nyala, we need to go." Nyala moved an inch, but kept looking at the boy.

"Wait, I recognize you." The father drew himself tall and approached Nyala. "Let me see your face," he said.

Amaya's heart pounded. "We've got to go." She looped her arm in Nyala's and pulled her away, hoping the man would let it drop.

"Stop!" the man said.

"That's her!" The man with the teenage boy pointed at her. "That's Gidada."

A thousand faces full of angry, accusing eyes that looked ready to riot swiveled to stare at her.

Amaya looked around. There was nowhere to run—the furious faces were everywhere, blocking every escape route. Nyala looked around with wild eyes. She exchanged glances with Amaya. It was clear that Nyala didn't have any better idea how to handle the angry mob. Nyala backed up close to Amaya as the crowd advanced.

A crackle that sounded like a loudspeaker being turned on ripped through the air. A voice that sounded like LP's said, "May I have your attention, please?" The voice was broken with static, like the loudspeaker hadn't been used in decades, or maybe ever. "Ahem," the voice said. "THIS IS A PUBLIC ADDRESS." LP's unmodulated voice burned Amaya's ears. "Amaya Gidada, report to the front gate immediately."

"So you're the lady who sold us out." A muscled man who was twice Amaya's size seemed to growl at her. "Because of you…" The man froze. All around them, the throng of haters froze, their irate expressions set in stone, unchanging; their bodies as unmoving as concrete blocks.

"What's happening? Why aren't they moving?" Nyala asked.

A pop of static hissed out of the loudspeaker. "Amaya Gidada, report to the front gate immediately."

A figure moved through the frozen crowd toward them. The man, even larger than the one who had first threatened Amaya, wasn't the only one still moving. Scattered throughout the crowd, some people weren't frozen. The man's hand tucked under the hem of his shirt and lifted it a few inches, revealing a sheathed knife. Amaya felt his intense stare all through her body, her knees buckling from the hatred in his eyes.

"You took everything from me." He pulled the knife out of the sheath in a deliberate motion. The knife, with its six inches of sharpened steel, pointed at her.

Out of the corner of her eye, the teenage boy inched his way toward them.

"Stay back," she said. The last thing she needed was having some boy get hurt in an effort to be heroic. If anybody was going to save her, it would have to be her. This is what Hank had taught her—that she could only rely on herself.

The man lunged at her, his arm pulling back and then thrusting forward, the dagger-like point on the knife leading the way as it plunged toward her stomach.

There was no time to think. Instinctively, she swiped her hand to the side, pushing the knife out of the way. The startled man, surprised by her counter, stumbled to the side before turning back to face her. Before he could recover, she used all her remaining energy to deliver a kick to the crotch. The man whined and dropped to the ground.

For the moment, the threat was neutralized, but with some people in the crowd not frozen, they still needed to get out of there. She considered ignoring LP's demands and running in the opposite direction, but LP wasn't above hurting others to compel Amaya to do what he wanted. She was stuck doing what he wanted.

Nyala pulled on her arm. "We've got to go. Now."

"Take me with you," the teenage boy pleaded, clearly not ready to give up.

Amaya took off running, zigging and zagging as she worked her way through the frozen crowd. Not far behind, Nyala's feet slapped the pavement. There were other footsteps also, but Amaya didn't turn around to look. If they were running after her, they were probably planning to hurt her.

~~~~~

Why had LP demanded she go to the front gate? What would she find there? Amaya's legs burned from sprinting. It had been barely twenty-four hours since she left her pod—her legs still tired easily and her motions were clumsy.

The manager—the same one who had turned Trevor away, appeared to be waiting for them. "Arrangements have been made for you to go through the gate," the manager said, "but per regulations, you are not allowed to enter a pod." He waved his clipboard at them. "Tell your chauffeur to get out of here now. No waiting."

Their chauffeur? Just inside the gate, separated from the crowd by the chain-link fence, a cruiser hovered—it was small, probably with enough room for four people max. Its low profile and graceful arching lines said it was faster than anything Amaya had ever ridden in before. Did LP mean for them to get in the vehicle? Why was he picking them up?

One of the cruiser doors shimmered and disappeared. A female robot, more advanced than any Amaya had ever seen, put one foot out and, in an effortless and fluid motion, rose out of the vehicle. Like the vehicle, the robot was clearly top-of-the-line, no expense spared. The body was forged from the highest quality flexo-steel; its movements were like velvet. A light sheen of cerulean blue provided an undercurrent of color that highlighted the curves of the steel.

"Come on, get in!" The robot gestured to the vehicle. "We need to go before the crowd catches up with you."

The robot's face, with wide, kind eyes, showed signs of being the work of a master craftsperson, but there was something familiar about it. It looked like... "Opali?"

"Yes." She said it as if it should have been obvious to Amaya who
~~~~~

she was. "Now come on, let's go."

Trevor, who had looked dazed since leaving his mother, stood with his mouth open and wide eyes. Trevor pulled on Nyala's sleeve. "Nyala, can I have a robot?"

"No."

Trevor slumped his shoulders. "Aw."

"We can't all fit in that," the teenage boy said. Another stood beside him. Where had the second one come from?

"I'll send another transport back for you," Opali said. "Amaya and Nyala will come with me."

The entire side of the cruiser shimmered and openings appeared with four seats visible inside.

"I'm not leaving Trevor," Nyala said.

"Come on, Trevor," Opali replied. "Get in the front seat."

Nyala ran around to the far side and got into the back seat, Amaya climbed in next to her, and Opali sat in the driver's seat.

The sides of the cruiser shimmered, and the doors reappeared. Outside, the crowd started to move again.

"Don't worry," Opali said, "they can't reach us in here. The cruiser has advanced security features to protect the occupants."

"Opali," Nyala's wide eyes suggested that she still hadn't gotten over the shock of seeing masses of people frozen in place, "what was that? Why weren't they moving?"

"LP overloaded their chips so they couldn't function."

"I thought their chips didn't work anymore."

"They don't. But not having a functioning chip doesn't mean that it can't be overloaded. It only works short term, though. Some people start learning how to function despite the overload, and other people develop dementia or get chip burn, so we can't do it for a long time."

Whatever was going on, LP was clearly behind it. That was never a good sign.

Opali hit some buttons, and the cruiser hovered a few feet above the ground.

"What about my chip? Why wasn't I frozen?" Nyala asked.

Opali shrugged. "LP wants you to come with me, so he made sure your chip wasn't affected."

"And the people who were still moving around…?

"Don't have chips. We can't do much to those people."

"Where are we going?" Nyala asked. "How did you get access to get inside of the pod warehouse's fence?"

Thankfully, Nyala was asking questions. Amaya had so many questions and was still so dumbstruck by the crowd freezing, not to mention disarming the guy with the knife, that she was incapable of putting her questions into words.

"LP got special permission for me to come in here and pick you up. Apparently, when humanity is dependent on you to keep them alive by treating their electricity intolerance, you can request lots of special favors."

Opali put the cruiser into gear. "Ready?" she asked.

"Ready."

The seatback pulled Amaya forward, her body sinking into it with the force of the acceleration. Amaya touched a finger to the side panel. As expected, a force field pushed it back. So that's how the doors worked—they were force fields that looked like doors. When the doors needed to be opened, the force field turned off, and the door disappeared. It was ingenious.

It was a lot of electricity, though. Probably even more than what Amaya had been exposed to in the pod, and it was quickly having an effect on her. The last thing she wanted was to throw up in this beautiful vehicle.

She closed her eyes and tried to think about anything other than the nausea. It wasn't working.

"Opali, how do I open the door?" She had to throw up. Now. "Opali, stop the vehicle!"

"Amaya, this isn't a good time."

"Stop the vehicle!" But it was too late. Before she could open the door, the vomit hit the force field and repelled around the vehicle, ricocheting from the force field wall on one side to the other and back.

"Amaya!" Nyala yelled. "You couldn't wait?"

Amaya held her stomach. "I can't control it."

Trevor, his eyes wide while watching the ricocheting vomit, smiled for the first time since his mom had left. "Coool!" he said.

Nyala rubbed Amaya's back. "I'm sorry I yelled at you. Opali, how much longer until we get where we're going? And *where* are we going?"

"About fifteen minutes," Opali said. "We're heading to Amoco's house."

Day One of The Rupture

Monday, continued

The blades of the wind turbines in front of Amoco's house pulled and tugged against thick pieces of twine knotted to hold them in place. When Amoco put in turbines to prepare for the apocalypse, he was preparing for the wrong apocalypse. His turbines were useless now—they were at best expensive yard ornaments.

Yesterday, Amoco had returned to his house as soon as his medical checks were completed after leaving his pod. He had said something about having plans to turn off his electricity immediately after he got home. Amaya hadn't heard from him since.

Amaya had found a way to open a hole in the force field when she needed to throw up, but she still felt relieved when the cruiser slowed to a stop in the circular driveway in front of the gray stone house. Opali had run the sonic cleaner to get rid of the smell, and the last couple times her empty stomach had only dry heaved, but that was a small comfort. For her worn-out body, even hitting the button to open the hole in the force field felt like too much effort. The electricity was killing her. There was no doubt about it.

The cruiser stopped and the force field doors disappeared. She rolled out of the door and onto the gravel driveway and kneeled with her elbows on the ground and her hands on her head. Standing up was too much effort. Nyala placed a hand under her arm to help her up. With help from Nyala and Trevor, she managed to get up. She bent over with her hands on her knees and panted.

"Leave me be," Amaya said. "I'll start walking as soon as I'm ready."

Behind them, the cruiser glided forward. Opali drove around the circle with the flowers and wind turbines inside of it, and pulled off on the far side. With the cruiser moving away, Amaya felt the slightest bit better. She was still weak, but at least the dry heaves stopped.

Amaya waited at the bottom of the stone steps while Nyala and Trevor walked up to Amoco's doorway. Before Nyala could knock, Amoco opened the door. Behind him, T-Rock peered over his shoulder. Amoco was wearing his usual vest and pocket watch, but T-Rock had changed into pants made out of heavy-duty khaki fabric with lots of large pockets and a brown utility vest that also had lots of pockets, many of which appeared to be full of items. If anyone was prepared to survive without electricity, it was T-Rock.

"I must confess my surprise to see you here," Amoco said. His eyes furrowed as he examined Amaya, trying to catch her breath at the bottom of the stairs. "Amaya, you appear unwell."

"Were you in that cruiser?" T-Rock asked. "Exposing yourself to that much electricity is like a moth flying into a flame."

As if Amaya didn't already know that. She stood up straight and turned to look at the car.

The force field on the driver's side of the cruiser dropped. Opali, in her glorious robot body, emerged.

"Goodness sakes alive!" Amoco exclaimed.

Amaya looked over her shoulder at Amoco. He was staring at Opali with his mouth hanging open.

"Wow." T-Rock also looked stunned. "You don't see that every day. The agility and sleekness of a dolphin, but stealthy like a feline. Incredible."

Opali approached the group but stopped about four feet from Amaya. "Amaya, I sincerely apologize for doing this. LP insisted. The good news is, he gave me this robot body so I could pick you up."

"Where did the body come from?" Amoco asked.

"LP's been having us make them. It started not long after he was created because he wanted us to keep an eye on the humans who weren't in pods."

"The ghosts have been covertly monitoring humans?" Amoco's face turned a dark red. "How many times have I insisted that was the case, and no one believed me?"

"It's okay, Amoco," Opali said. "The materials are rare, so we've only been able to make about five of them. With only five, you don't have to worry about much spying from us."

Amoco said something that sounded like "pshaw" and rolled his eyes. Amaya didn't blame him.

She felt better than she had in the vehicle, but the robot body used a lot of electricity and her skin burned as Opali got closer. "Opali, I love you, but it's difficult for me to be around you. It's making me queasy and I'm exhausted. I hope whatever you need to say you can say quickly, because I'm not sure how much longer I can continue to be near you."

"I'm so sorry, Amaya." Opali moved a few feet away. "I'm on super low energy mode, but I know it's not enough. I'm going to keep moving away; please tell me when my presence is tolerable."

"I still feel it." Would she be able to tolerate Opali if she just stood far enough away?

Opali backed up a few more feet. The burning in Amaya's skin started to subside. "If you could back up just a little more."

Opali backed up again. At about eight feet, the burning was gone. Amaya sighed. It was possible to be in the same room as Opali and not feel like she was going to die. Having the robot body nearby was tolerable, but only for a short time. The meeting would have to be short.

Opali nodded. "Very well then, if this distance will work, I will go in first and make sure that the house is secure."

Amoco's face turned red again, but this time, a vein also popped out on his forehead. "I dare say—how could you imply that my house is not secure? I have a full complement of security devices." He sniffed. "If I do not have it, then it has not been invented."

Robot Opali shrugged. "Sorry, Amoco. LP's orders. I'd say you don't have to comply, but you know what LP does to people who don't do what he wants them to." Opali looked at one of the turbines to the side of the house, seemingly lost in thought, and then refocused on Amoco. "Everyone has to pay a price for ignoring LP."

"I can scarce afford to be punished by LP again." Amoco held the door wide. "Do what you will."

"Please wait outside. I'll let you know when I've determined that the house is safe for Amaya to enter."

Amaya thought that Amoco's head might actually explode, but in the end, he nodded and walked down the stone steps, staying as far away from Opali as possible.

T-Rock joined them at the bottom of the steps.

"How long do you think it will take?"

"No clue," T-Rock said.

Amaya needed to sit down before she fell down. She sat on the bottom step. "T-Rock, how are the preparations going?"

T-Rock sighed. "We still have so much to do. Right before I headed over here, we were trying to figure out what to do with Cooper and Viola's pods so that we can keep an eye on them without making the techs sick."

"Did you figure something out?"

"We have batteries running power to the pods. We've turned the alarms on the monitoring equipment up as loud as they go, and we have one tech at all times in the next room who can respond if an alarm goes off. We rotate the techs every two hours because even in the next room, they are still getting sick from the electricity."

"Is there a long-term plan?" Amaya asked.

"We want to get them moved back to a Bo Place pod warehouse, but we're trying to figure out the transport. There's a guy who has a specialized truck, but he stopped doing transports. He said maybe later this week if he starts feeling better."

Opali stuck her head out the front door. "Okay, you can all come in."

They gathered in Amoco's library, where the floor-to-ceiling shelves overflowed with quirky knickknacks. Amaya sat on a couch with aged green leather upholstery. Except for the cracks running through it, the leather was smooth and shiny. Across from her, Nyala sat on a couch with mottled brown leather. A side table next to the couch was taken over by something that looked like a velociraptor skull.

Trevor walked around, checking out the items on the bookshelves. T-Rock paced back and forth by the window on the far side of an ornate, executive-style desk that faced the door. Amoco stood in front of the velociraptor skull. Amaya had the feeling that he was protecting it, possibly from Trevor's curious browsing.

"I'll stay out here." Opali hovered just on the other side of the doorway. Everyone in the room could see her, but she was far enough away that Amaya's skin didn't burn.

That didn't stop Amaya from developing a bad headache, probably because of everything they'd been through. "So why are we here?"

"Because this is where the only working tesseract is," Opali said.

"Why do we need the tesseract?" Nyala asked.

The robot face showed the briefest flicker of emotion. "Because LP wants to change the agreement. And…he says if you don't accept the new agreement, then the old agreement is off and your execution will be back on schedule."

Amaya was too overwhelmed to respond.

Opali took a deep breath, despite not needing to breathe. "If you try to avoid the execution, they will stop offering the treatment for the electricity intolerance to the pod dwellers."

T-Rock stopped pacing and swung toward the door. "Why should anyone enter into another agreement with LP when he doesn't keep his first agreement? And what's keeping him from changing the new agreement when it's convenient for him?"

Opali shrugged. "There's nothing that can stop him. I think we need to accept that we are all LP's lackeys at this point."

It wasn't lost on Amaya that Opali referred to herself as LP's lackey as well. "What does he want?"

"He wants you to destroy the server farm in Area 52." Opali looked at Nyala. "That's why I'm supposed to protect Amaya. She's crucial to our survival."

"Absolutely not," Nyala said. "Amaya won't do it."

Amaya might not have a choice but to do whatever LP wanted. "Why does he want me to destroy the servers?" she asked Opali.

"He wants to make sure that no one can ever delete the ghosts again. And he wants it to be irrevocable."

"Wait," Amaya said, "how am I supposed to do that? It's almost impossible to delete data from a SOUP server, because it automatically restores from one of the other servers, and deleting one of the servers doesn't stop the rest from working. That's why we had to use the Area 52 servers to delete the ghosts before."

"Exactly. He wants you to physically make the Area 52 servers nonfunctional. Burn them down. Or make them explode. Whatever you need to do to get rid of that server farm and make sure that no one ever uses it again."

"I can't do that. It would be unsafe. I wouldn't make it out alive."

"I'll put the program on a five-minute delay." Opali opened a compartment in her chest and pulled out a square cube. The cube, made up of nested cubes within nested cubes, glowed a transparent sky blue that matched the sheen of Opali's body. It was like the cube that Amoco had given her when she first went to Area 52, except with more layers of complexity. Amoco was not going to be happy that the ghosts' tech appeared more advanced than his.

"You can use this to destroy the Area 52 servers." Opali tucked the cube back into her chest compartment. "I have a shielding satchel in the vehicle that will protect the cube when it goes through the tesseract. I also have some protective clothing for Amaya."

"What do we get out of the agreement?" T-Rock asked. "You're asking Amaya to risk her life—she'll be exposed to extreme amounts of electricity and she probably won't be able to come back. What does she get out of it?"

"She gets the satisfaction of knowing that the pod-dwellers are alive and being treated for their electricity intolerance." Opali's eyes teared up. "I'm sorry, Amaya, that's just how it is. I can't change LP's mind."

"Why does Amaya have to do it?" Nyala asked. "Can't you do it?"

"Only Amaya can do it. She's the only one who knows how the servers work and how to get in."

Nyala rolled her eyes. "It's not that difficult."

"Before she came here, Petra programmed the tesseract so that it erases any electronic data that passes through it. If I go through the tesseract, I won't remember what I was supposed to do."

"What about the Area 52 people? Do they have the electricity intolerance?"

Opali nodded. "When the wildfires caught the SOUP pools on fire, the fires were so hot that the toxin that causes the electricity intolerance was released into the air globally. The handful of people who hadn't already been exposed to the toxin are now affected by it, including the unchipped and the people in Area 52. More exposure also means people are going to get sick faster."

"How long until they'll get sick?"

"Within the next couple days, everyone in the world will start to get sick, so you might want to tell the people in Area 52 to shut down their electricity as soon as you have destroyed the server."

Nyala stood up. "You can't make her do this. It's going to kill her. Did you see how sick she got today just being in a vehicle? Do you really think she can survive exposure to the tesseract and the server farm?"

"I don't know." Opali looked like she was trying not to cry. "I'm just the messenger here. I don't want her to do this. You need to understand, I'm as controlled by LP as you all are."

The idea that Opali was being controlled by LP was new to Amaya. "What do you mean you're controlled by LP?"

Opali shook her head. "I misspoke. When he controls you all, I feel like he is controlling me as well."

T-Rock ran a hand over the stubble from his crew cut. "This seems blatantly unfair. How is it that LP gets to make the decisions for everyone? Aren't there any checks and balances among the spectrals? Can't anyone stop him?"

"Everything is voted on by the Spectral Council. The problem is that they all vote the same. And those that don't," Opali glanced down, "get removed from the council."

For a moment, no one said anything.

"To be clear," Opali continued, "if you get rid of LP, someone else on the Spectral Council will take over, and they'll make the same decisions as LP." Opali avoided eye contact with Amaya. "They really don't like Amaya since she deleted them."

It wasn't a fair characterization of Amaya's role in deleting the ghosts, but there was clearly no point in objecting.

T-Rock kicked the desk. "This is bullshit."

"What happens now?" Amoco asked.

"You need to get the tesseract up and running," Opali said. "And then Amaya goes through it."

Amoco tugged on his vest. "We are unable to comply, then. As I have just recently exited my forced time in the metaverse, I have not yet had time to locate or discover how to access the tesseract."

"No need to worry about that. We identified the anomaly a long time ago. We know where it is and how to access it. You just need to turn on the electricity to your family crypt."

Amoco huffed. "Well, I never."

No one moved or spoke for a minute.

Amoco stepped forward. "I will turn on the electricity to the crypt, but with one condition. You must wait outside."

"My job is to protect Amaya. LP doesn't want anything to happen to her."

"If you are protecting her," Nyala said, "then why are you forcing her to go through the tesseract?"

"I'm only the messenger. If it wasn't me, then it would be someone else. I'm protecting her by making sure she doesn't have to deal with any of the other ghosts."

"Then you'll have to protect her outside," Nyala said.

"Very well. But I'm not leaving until she goes through the tesseract."

"Wait," Amaya said. "Opali, what if I refuse?" Amaya needed to know how bad the consequences would be.

"The spectrals will no longer offer the treatment for the electricity intolerance to the humans. They will have to exit their pods or die." Opali shook her head. "I'm so sorry, Amaya. I didn't want to have to tell you this."

Amaya felt completely drained. As long as humans were living in pods, no one was free from the reach of LP and the Spectral Council.

Opali's eyes misted. Seeing Opali become emotional had a strange effect on Amaya that she didn't entirely understand. Maybe it was just the marvel she felt at the mastery that went into making the robot body, and the attention to detail that it could actually cry.

"Opali," Amaya said, "I know you mean well. LP has us all under his thumb."

Trevor stopped inspecting things on Amoco's shelves and pulled on Nyala's sleeve. "You should go with her."

"I'm not going anywhere. I just promised to your mom that I would take care of you."

"She needs you. I'm sure there's someone else I can stay with. Like your friend Georgia."

Nyala appeared to be considering it. Nyala looked at Opali, then back at Amaya. "If this is happening," Nyala said, "then I'm going with you. We don't know how sick going through the tesseract to Area 52 will make you feel. You need someone who can protect you and who can help you out."

T-Rock let the curtains fall back into place and turned to face the others. "Okay, she's by the cruiser. Amoco, is there any way she can eavesdrop on us?"

Amoco picked up a black, puck-like device from a shelf and flipped a switch on the bottom. Amaya's skin tingled as electricity flowed from the device. Amoco held the puck out as he walked around the room, spending the most time near the spot where Opali had stood. "This device," he said, "monitors for bugs. If she placed one, it will identify it."

After a minute, Amoco flipped the switch on the puck again and set it back on the shelf. "The room is clear. Opali did not leave any bugs."

Nyala sat down on the green couch and put her hand on Amaya's. "I'm not letting you do this alone. I'll find someone else to keep an eye on Trevor."

Amaya's heart warmed. Having Nyala along made everything more bearable. She placed her hand on top of Nyala's. "Thank you."

Nyala smiled. It was a devious smile, one that she only used when she had a plan in mind. "You'll need all the help you can get, because this is the chance that we've been waiting for."

Amaya raised her eyebrows. "It is?"

"If you have to go through that tesseract, we're going to use it to make a permanent change. We're going to make sure that LP can never force you to do anything again."

Amaya felt a lump in her stomach. There was a chance she wasn't going to like where Nyala was headed. "You're being vague. Get to the point."

"Instead of destroying the server, we can use this as an opportunity to get rid of the ghosts once and for all. The last time you deleted them, we didn't know about how they were using their own tesseract to protect the code. Now the ghosts' tesseract is damaged by the wildfires, they aren't able to send a backup copy into the future. If we delete them now, they won't be able to restore themselves. It's perfect timing, because once they repair their tesseract, the opportunity will be lost. And once we permanently delete the ghosts, you'll be free."

Amoco stroked his chin. "I can create a new cube with the program in the time it will take the tesseract to recharge."

"But what about the humans in pods that the ghosts are going to take care of?" Amaya asked. "Who will take care of them?"

Nyala shifted on the couch. "No one will. I know it sounds heartless, but we've learned LP can't be trusted. Even if the ghosts are still around, those people may end up going without treatment."

"And dying." What Nyala was glossing over was that if the people didn't receive treatment, they would die.

T-Rock checked out the window again and then moved closer to where they were sitting. "They don't have to die. They can leave their pods and be like the rest of us, struggling to learn to live without electricity."

What LP wanted, LP got. At least until they deleted the ghosts. As long as the humans in pods needed the ghosts to take care of them, all humans would be held hostage. Amaya's stomach flipped and twisted into knots at the idea that a lot of people might die. "Isn't there something else that we can do? Some way we can delete the ghosts and make sure that no one dies?"

Nyala rubbed her hand. "No. Without modern healthcare, without transportation to distribute food, without water purification and septic removal, without all that, many people are going to die."

The knot in Amaya's stomach twisted tighter.

T-Rock kneeled beside her. "Amaya, we're doing everything we can. A number of the estates here on the edge of town are independent home-steads and are off-grid. Oscar has agreed to let me turn the Stafford estate into a haven, so I've been working on outfitting it to handle as many people as possible. This estate, Amoco's, is also off-grid, and Amoco has agreed to let us use it—"

"Reluctantly, I must say."

"—which is why I'm here helping Amoco get it set up as a haven. We have volunteers who will arrive later today to get things running, and then we'll do what we can to get the word out and accept as many people as possible. We already have people visiting neighborhoods in the city and handing out information. But we're talking about the entire world here—how many do you think we'll actually be able to help?"

Amoco nodded. "We have no accommodations for these people, at least not yet, and we will need to increase local food production. We have at most a few days to set everything up, and we have no precedent for this."

"I hate to say this," T-Rock grimaced, "but no matter what we do, no matter whether the people in the pods have to leave or not…a lot of people are going to die."

"So…" Amaya took a second to think about the words she wanted to use. "To get back to what you all want me to do—you want me to delete the ghosts…again…" She took a deep breath. "Even though that means a lot of pod-dwellers currently being taken care of by the ghosts will die."

She hated the idea of kicking people out of their pods, but she could see the reasoning. LP had shown that he was willing to go back on his word whenever it was convenient for him, and as long as human lives were in his hands, he would have control over all of them. And in the end, he might decide to kill them all anyway. Not just Amoco and Amaya, but everyone. The safest thing to do was to get rid of the ghosts.

But it wasn't that easy. People like June and Oscar would get kicked out of their pods. Without electricity, all the resources in the world wouldn't get Oscar the medical care he needed and he would struggle to get by. How could Amaya be the person who did that to him? And what about Bren and his wife, who were finally living without pain for the first time in a long time? Was Amaya really going to be the one responsible for ending that for them? A chill ran up her spine. Was there any other choice?

She stalled for time before making a decision. "Isn't Bren's home an independent homestead? I think they had an aeroponic greenhouse that was off-grid."

T-Rock got up from where he had been kneeling next to her, walked over to the window, pulled the curtain to the side, and peered out. "Yes, Bren's house is self-sustaining, and he has given us permission to convert it into a haven. He says there are others in his part of town, so we have Georgia going door-to-door looking for other homes that are also independent."

"Georgia but no Hank?"

"Hank is preparing for his next adventure."

Amaya hadn't expected Hank to go anywhere without Georgia. "Which is?"

"He's planning to roam the country and then use his chip to send Georgia reports of how things are going in other places. He's also going to pass along ideas for surviving. He's working on getting supplies together and recruiting some people to be on a team with him."

Nyala smiled. "T-Rock forgot to mention that Hank and Georgia are a couple now."

"They're *what*?" It was both surprising and yet not surprising at all. Amaya made a mental note to ask Georgia about it if she ever saw her again. The knot in Amaya's stomach returned. Would she ever see Georgia again? If she survived going through the tesseract in one direction, chances are she wouldn't risk it again to return. And if she didn't return…

T-Rock let the curtain fall back into place. "Opali's coming back. Amaya, you have about ten seconds until Opali is within hearing range, so you need to decide now—are you going to delete the ghosts?"

Nyala squeezed her hand. "We'll never get another opportunity like this."

Amaya didn't want to do it, but what choice did she have? She wasn't even sure if it was the right thing, but everyone else in the room seemed so sure that it was. And they made convincing arguments that Amaya couldn't refute. "I'll do it."

Amoco headed toward the door. "I'll go get the cube ready and turn on the electricity to the tesseract. Once it is ready, we will need to slip the cube into the protective satchel that Opali is going to give you."

"Opali will be paying more attention to Amaya," T-Rock said, "so get it to me and I'll make sure it gets into the bag."

"No," Amaya said, surprising even herself with the force of her words. If she left it up to T-Rock, he might take Opali's cube out. Some part of her wanted to keep both options in play. "If someone gets it to me, I'll get it into the satchel."

T-Rock nodded. "I'll get the cube to you."

Amaya's chest tightened. It was a complicated plan. Surely something was going to go wrong, and Amaya didn't have the ability to stop it.

Day One of The Rupture

Monday, continued

Amoco left the room and not one second later, Opali barged in holding what looked like a crossbody bag with a shoulder strap and multiple items made out of some glossy black material.

The sickness came back like a punch to the gut. Amaya doubled over and willed herself not to throw up again. Her cells were being broken and rearranged in ways that could never be undone.

Opali pivoted and went back through the door. "I'm so sorry, Amaya. I forgot myself."

The nausea subsided once Opali stepped away, but it was starting to feel like some of the damage would be permanent.

Nyala gave Opali a scorching look. "You're making her sick. What do you want?"

"This is for you." Opali held the fabric in front of her. "It has shielding in it and will protect your body moderately from the electricity."

"Put it on the ground and leave us," Nyala said.

Opali paused like she was thinking through her options, then she nodded. "Okay. I'll be waiting for you at the entrance to the crypt." She dropped the material on the floor. "There's no zipper, so you may need help getting into it."

"It's not digi-skin?" Nyala asked.

"Digi-skin would have made her sick."

"Okay," Nyala said. "I'll help Amaya with it."

"There's just one more thing," Opali said. "I just wanted to apologize…I'm really sorry because I know it's important…that you'll be missing Mariela's funeral."

"I'm what?" Last time she had asked, Mariela's funeral plans were still up in the air.

"I'm sorry, Amaya," T-Rock said. "I didn't realize that you hadn't gotten the notice. We were going to hold her funeral later this morning, because Hank wanted to be there before he left town."

"Can we delay the trip through the tesseract?" Nyala asked. "Or move the funeral up? Mariela was a good friend, and even though we had our differences, I think it's important for both Amaya and I to be there."

Opali dug her toe into the wood of the floor. "I already asked LP, and he said he doesn't trust Amaya, and that she absolutely has to go through the tesseract immediately. I'm so sorry."

Opali turned and disappeared down the hallway.

"I'm sorry, Amaya," T-Rock said. "I'm sure Mariela would have understood that you can't make it. She, more than anyone, had to deal with LP and all his demands."

It just didn't seem fair. Not only did she have to go to Area 52, probably never to return, but she was also going to miss the funeral of one of her best friends.

T-Rock moved to the windows and peered out through the curtain again. "She's outside," he said after a couple of seconds. "I'll go see if Amoco needs help while you get ready. Come on Trevor." On his way out the door, he picked up the fabric and handed it to Nyala.

Nyala turned the outfit over and pulled on what may have been the leg, or possibly an arm. "How does this thing even work?" she asked.

Pieces of fabric that looked like gloves fell onto the floor.

It was completely different in style from the beige shirt and dark beige pants she was wearing. Amaya picked up the shoulders and let it drape. "I see it." Once she spotted the laces, it became clear to Amaya how it worked.

No one would ever mistake the form fitting, faux leather outfit for her usual style. "It looks like a catsuit."

Nyala smiled. "I think it's perfect. About time you found something interesting to wear."

Amaya was somewhere between laughing and crying. "What is it even made out of? It kind of looks like leather but it isn't, and Opali said it isn't digi-skin."

Nyala ran the fabric between her fingers. "I'm going with high-tech material created in a lab."

"I guess it will help with shielding from the electricity. With the hood, gloves, and shoes, it looks like it will cover my entire body."

"Come on. Let's get you into this."

With lots of tugging on the stretchy fabric, Amaya managed to get into the suit. Nyala pulled the laces going up the back of the suit tight.

Amaya slipped her feet into the shoes. She left off the gloves and the hood that covered most of her head. She would wait until she needed them. The suit pressed on her in a way that restricted her movements but also made her feel protected. "How do I look?"

Nyala smiled. "Like a badass. Are you ready?"

"Let's go."

They met Opali behind the house at the entrance to Amoco's family crypt. Amoco's yard of sagebrush and scrub oak was surrounded by rocky plateaus that formed a U-shape of small cliffs around the house and grounds. It would provide nice protection when the house was turned into a haven.

Amaya moved stiffly in the tight catsuit despite the supple fabric moving easily with her. The suit highlighted every single curve of her body, even ones that she didn't know she had. Wouldn't the shielding have worked just as well if the suit hadn't been skintight? She sighed. There was no point in wondering about it—it wasn't like Opali was going to get her another outfit.

Opali waited in front of the door to the crypt holding the bag with the cube in it. The small bag with a shoulder strap appeared to be made of the same black, leather-like fabric as the catsuit, but it also had a subtle pattern of small textured squares. Amaya and Nyala stopped short of an eight-foot radius around Opali.

"Amaya," Opali said, "I admire you for what you are doing. I have so many fond memories of the time we spent in the Zazora Game. I know you didn't feel well, but you were still so kind to me." Opali glanced down, her shy eyes avoiding eye contact. "Those were some of the best times of my life."

Amaya raised her eyebrows. "Really? Because you spent a lot of it crying."

Opali smiled and nodded. "It's true. I've always wanted to play in the Zazora Games, and you...you all...were the best. The best friends and the best teammates I could have had."

Amaya smiled. "I agree. I may have been miserable, but I also have fond memories of that time. Here's to good teammates, who make the worst times better."

Opali's smile turned into a grin. She dug her toe into the sand just like she used to do when she was a little girl. "Here's to good teammates."

T-Rock, Trevor, and Amoco joined them.

"Amoco, I'll let you open the door," Opali said. She stepped back from the wall to give Amoco space to work.

Amoco inspected the rock wall and then slipped his fingers into a cranny. A section of the rock shimmered and disappeared, revealing a heavy metal door.

"Nyala," Opali said, "there's something you should know. When we sent the transport to pick up the other boy, the group had grown. A lot. The bus brought back twenty-three kids of varying ages who are waiting at the Stafford Estate."

"What?" Nyala's voice was shocked and indignant. "Did someone get their parents' permission?"

"I doubt it," Opali said. "Those are not the times we are living in."

"We can take care of ourselves," Trevor volunteered.

"Absolutely not," Nyala insisted. "T-Rock will find someone else to take care of you all."

A tear appeared in the corner of Opali's eye as she appeared to fight to contain her emotions. Did ghosts have to control their emotions? Amaya knew the answer—Opali had wanted to be human, and she was always updating her programming to act more human. Humans struggled to control their emotions, so Opali did too.

Opali sniffed. "Someone needs to take care of those kids. They need you."

"My sister needs me, so I'm going with her."

"Amaya," T-Rock said, "I need to get back to the Stafford Estate to set up for the funeral, so I'm going to say goodbye now." He rubbed Trevor's head. "You're with me, kiddo."

There were goodbyes all around. Despite Trevor's bravado, he struggled with leaving Nyala. Amaya tried to push away the fear that she might never see him and T-Rock again.

"Amaya and Nyala," T-Rock said, "we'll visit you as soon as we have everything in place to make the trip across the desert without using electricity. Unfortunately, with everything going on here, it may be a couple of years before we're ready."

"I'll be waiting," Amaya said, even though they both knew it was a promise she might not be able to keep.

T-Rock pulled Amaya into a tight embrace. She buried her head in his shoulder and returned the hug. After a minute, T-Rock pulled away.

He grasped her hand in his, and she felt the sharp corners of the cube as it slipped into her hand.

"Take care, T-Rock," she said.

"You too." T-Rock let go of her hand, leaving the cube behind, and turned toward the house with Trevor in tow.

Amaya palmed the cube. Now she just needed to get it into the bag. "Opali, do you mind if I see the cube? I want to make sure it's what I'm used to."

"Sure." Opali handed the bag to her.

Amaya opened the drawstrings and pulled out the second cube. It wasn't just one cube, it was more of a cube within a cube within a cube. The complexity far surpassed any cube that she had seen in the past. Sharp pinpricks jabbed into her hand where the cube touched it. She put the cube back into the bag and slid Amoco's cube in with it.

Nyala was chatting with Opali—hopefully that had distracted Opali enough that she didn't see the second cube. Amaya held on to the bag. She didn't need Opali taking it back and realizing it was heavier than before.

Amoco had the door to the crypt open and was heading down the narrow and rocky hallway filled with dank air. Just like they had every other time she had been there, the sparks of light activated and swirled toward them. The sparks glowed brighter than ever before, lighting their way and making up for the lack of electric lights.

"A couple things before we activate the tesseract," Opali said. "With the time warping, you'll be arriving in Area 52 three days from now. It's possible that the people in Area 52 will have started to get sick from the electricity intolerance, but they probably won't understand why and will still be using electricity."

The electricity still being on in Area 52 would make things more difficult for Amaya, but she would need the electricity to access the server.

"Let's get this done with." She was ready. Whatever happened, she wanted to get it over with. She searched the room for the tesseract, but the crypt looked exactly the same as the last time she was there. "Where's the tesseract?"

Opali reached up and opened a door on one of the individual vaults. "The reason Amoco never discovered the tesseract is that it only activates when two of the higher up vaults are open at the same time."

Amoco huffed. "I would have figured it out eventually."

"I have no doubt. You are nothing if not persistent."

Amoco crossed his arms in a pout.

Opali ignored him and turned to Amaya. "I talked to the woman who founded Area 52, Petra, and while she refused to give any details about how to activate the tesseract, she did say the other end is located behind some heavy jackets in a closet in her home. You want to go through the tesseract with enough speed to make it through the coats even if you faint after going through. Petra said her house is set on low power, so even if you faint," Opali sniffed, "you might be able to recover enough to make it to the server."

The trip was feeling more and more impossible with every second that passed. She may have gotten out of the death sentence, but there was a good chance she would end up dead anyway. She pushed the thought out of her mind. She had to believe that she could make it through this if she stayed focused.

"Time to say goodbye," Opali said.

There were lots of hugs and tears all around. Amoco wrapped Amaya in a hug and she hugged him tight. The sparks pulled in close, lighting the area around them until the two of them in their embrace glowed with the light of day.

Eventually, Amaya pulled away. The longer she waited, the more impossible it was going to be to leave.

"I'm ready," she said to Opali.

Opali opened the second vault door. On the far wall, near the corner, a hidden panel slid to the side, and a toggle emerged from the marble wall. "That will turn on the power," Opali said.

The swirling and dancing of the floating sparks continued, but the sparks seemed to push against each other and rush in agitated groups that split up and then reformed.

"Nyala," Opali said, "do you see that toggle over there?" Opali pointed to the lever. "Get ready to flip it when I say so."

Nyala walked over to the toggle and placed her hand on it.

"Amaya, don't forget to put on your hood and your gloves. It'll take the tesseract a couple of seconds to warm up." Opali paused and then looked at Nyala. "Flip the switch."

Nyala flipped the switch. Amaya stretched the hood over her head. It snapped out of her hands and gripped her head. What kind of fabric was it? It left only an opening just large enough for her face. Once the gloves were on, they molded to her body.

Based on the buzz of electricity in the air, the tesseract was warming up quickly. The nausea returned full force, but she didn't care. She faced the far wall, nervous about the run through it.

Opali put out her hand for the satchel. "Let me put that on you. You don't want to drop it," Opali said.

Amaya kept ahold of the bag without looking like she was purposefully keeping it from Opali. Yet refusing to allow Opali to take it would just have called more attention to the bag. In the end, Opali took ahold of the strap and wrested it from Amaya's grip with little effort. The bag dangled from the strap as Opali lifted it over Amaya's head and across her shoulder.

Was there an almost imperceptible pause as Opali held up the bag? Did Opali seem to consider it for a fraction of a second, maybe making calculations and noting that the weight of the bag had changed? The only noticeable change was a frown line that ever so briefly appeared above Opali's eyebrow. Or did Amaya imagine it? Whether Opali noticed or not, she lifted the strap over Amaya's head and placed the bag on her. If she had noticed, she was letting Amaya go anyway.

The etched marble wall in front of Amaya changed texture—it shimmered and developed a gelatinous structure that transitioned to hazy with what looked like swirls of smoke. Amaya couldn't see through it, but it no longer looked like the wall was solid.

"Are you ready to run?" Opali asked.

"I'm ready."

Nyala stood beside her. Amaya felt calmer knowing her sister would be going with her. She made eye contact with Nyala. "Are you ready?"

Nyala crouched, like a sprinter getting ready to run. "I'm ready."

"On three, then. One...two..." Amaya took a deep breath. "Three!" She pushed off, heading full speed toward what seconds before had been a solid wall.

Next to her, Nyala also broke into a run. Visible out of the corner of Amaya's eye, Opali's hand shot out and grabbed Nyala's arm. Nyala's momentum pulled her in a half circle around Opali and away from the tesseract.

The last thing Amaya heard as she went through the tesseract was Opali saying to Nyala, "LP wants you to stay here."

CHAPTER 29

Day Two of The Rupture

Tuesday

Business Today

"All the business news you need to know"

Tuesday, May 28, 2115

By Elliat Exis ~ *Business Today's* only Newsoogle winning reporter!

Welcome to the Rest of Your Life!
Greetings fellow pod-dwellers. If you're reading this, then you are one of the lucky ones who has secured a pod for yourself. And if you're like me, you no longer feel the nausea and prickling skin of the electricity intolerance. What a wonderful thing it is to be in a pod!

Of course, if you're like me, you're also wondering how the people who aren't in pods are doing. It's been two days since the earth-shattering announcement made at the end of the exhibition Zazora Game, and I'm still trying to wrap my head around it. What does this mean for humanity? Did enough people stay in the solid world to keep humans in existence? Will those people—soft from living surrounded by technology—be able to survive without it?

These are all important questions that we will probably never know the answer to. My new motto is going to be, "Don't worry about things that you can't control." So going forward, this podcast will focus on the metaverse only.

Tune in tomorrow as I interview people who watched

the Zazora Exhibition Game to see what their reactions were! Until then, my thoughts go out to those people still living in the solid world. Best of luck to them as they struggle to get by without any modern conveniences.

~~~~~

Hank wiped the sweat from his brow and avoided stepping on a pile of horse crap that was gently wafting fumes his way. It was already mid-day and about six hours later than Hank had hoped to get started with the trip. It was high time to get on the road.

Yet delaying his departure time to attend Mariela's funeral had been important. He had been close to Mariela at one point, and he was having a hard time accepting that she was dead. He had hoped that the funeral would help him come to terms with her death.

He had even spoken at her service, talking about how much he respected her willingness to make tough decisions that no one else wanted to make, and how she followed her inner principles even when it made other people upset with her.

Hank's roan-colored horse chomped on the grass in the center of the circular driveway. Outside the circle, the Stafford Estate house loomed over them at the top of a long row of steps. Off to the side, the three small cottages were welcoming, with gardens in front and brick paths leading up to their doors.

Away from the buildings, platforms with tents dotted the acres of field that stretched from the winding driveway to the line of trees that blocked the view of the estate from the road. People wandered among the tents, setting up new ones as newcomers arrived at the estate. Everyone who arrived was given a job—gathering firewood, setting up tents, cataloging seeds. T-Rock somehow organized them all.

Not far away, four other horses grazed as their riders got them ready for the long journey ahead. Nyala hefted a bag drooping with the weight of supplies over the roan's back. On the other side of the horse, Trevor helped get the bag settled and made sure the knots would last. It turned out that he had a knack for knots.

Food, a sleeping bag, a compass, and a printed map of roadways— the bag contained everything he and his companions would need. Well, not everything. There were also the five donkeys, one for each rider, that were loaded with packs and pulling a small cart. They had spent hours discussing what to bring with them. A wrong choice could mean ending
~~~~~

toes-up in a grassy field somewhere or face down in a muddy ditch.

"Are you sure you don't want to go with us?" he asked Nyala. "We could use your fighting skills."

Nyala rolled her eyes. "Don't be ridiculous. You know I'm needed here to take care of the kids. Plus, you're probably going to get yourself killed during your first week on the road."

Well, that stung. He would prove her wrong…hopefully.

Trevor came around the back of the horse. He made sure the horse knew he was there—just like Hank had taught him. "Come on, Nyala," Trevor said. "Let's go with them. Someone else can stay with those other kids."

"No." Nyala was firm. "Absolutely not. You're not leaving this compound. It's not safe out there."

Hank understood the pull that leaving had on Trevor. Trevor's situation was a lot like his own growing up—parents in virtual reality, surrounded by other kids who competed with him for adult attention. Would it be such a bad thing for Trevor to venture outside of the compound? "Maybe if Trevor came with me, he would grow up faster."

Nyala's response was quick and sharp. "He doesn't need to grow up faster. Trevor's not being pampered in some luxury res-home like you grew up in—he's going to be living without electricity and having to help out a lot just to keep things running." Nyala rolled her eyes. "He's not going to end up a man-child like you did."

Wow, Nyala was really cutting to the bone today. It was a good thing she didn't want to go with him. "Suit yourself," he shrugged. What was wrong with her? He was already in a bad mood—he was nervous about the trip and his heart hurt whenever he thought about leaving Georgia. Nyala could take her negativity and go jump off a cliff.

He pulled the belt tighter on the horse's girth. He wasn't taking a chance on the saddle slipping off. The horse stepped to the side and let out a brief neigh. Hank scratched her shoulder. "Sorry, girl." He let the girth out a notch.

The door to the Stafford house opened and Georgia emerged. She paused at the top of the stairs leading up to the house and looked out at them. She made eye contact with Hank and for a second, he couldn't move. They stared at each other for what felt like minutes, but was probably only seconds before Georgia started down the stairs.

The wind caught her skirt and pulled it around her legs. It reminded

Hank of that warm day when the wind had pulled her skirt in the same way. It wasn't that long ago, but so many things had changed; it felt like forever ago. How could he even consider leaving Georgia? Especially now when they had just taken things to a new level and it was going so well?

He would try one more time to convince her to go with him, but he knew what the answer would be. They both knew that for the plan to work, one of them had to stay behind. They needed Georgia here. In the two days since they had found out about the electricity intolerance, she had designed the tented platforms for people to stay in and was working with T-Rock to get hundreds of them built. She had also made plans to fully stock the seed bank so that they would be able to grow enough food to last for years.

She was even helping Nyala find volunteers to help take care of the 372 kids that had shown up that morning in the buses that Opali had sent to the pod warehouses. Surely Opali must have known that it was an unrealistic number for Nyala to take care of—Opali should have told them to stay with their parents. But according to Nyala, it sounded like Opali hadn't wanted the kids to go into the metaverse. Nyala had been too preoccupied with Amaya going through the tesseract to realize what was going on. Once Nyala understood just how many kids had shown up, it was too late to do anything about it.

In the hours since the kids had arrived, they were already helping set up tents, making pathways, digging outhouses—gone was the modern concept of childhood for those kids. They were working just like every-one else.

Georgia scratched his horse behind the ear. "I see you're just about ready to go." Even though she was smiling, her eyes were sad. It mirrored how Hank felt.

He embraced her. "Almost ready." His heart felt like someone had put a vise around it.

"T-Rock and Petra said to let them know when you're ready to leave so they can say goodbye."

"Of course. I think Petra almost likes me now. And T-Rock, too. I wouldn't dream of leaving without saying goodbye to them."

Georgia touched Nyala's arm to get her attention. "Do you think Amaya will have arrived in Area 52 yet?"

"Not yet. It's only been two days; she won't show up there until tomorrow."

Going through the time warp associated with the tesseract was one of the most unsettling experiences that had happened to Hank. It felt like seconds to him, but days had passed. Probably Amaya was going to have the same uncanny experience.

Trevor ran over and threw his arms around Georgia. "Georgia, can you take care of the other kids so that Nyala and I can go with Hank?"

Georgia's eyes opened wide. "Has Nyala agreed to this?"

Nyala snorted. "Most certainly not."

"I can take care of the kids," Georgia said. "We have many volunteers to help out. If you want to go, you should go."

Georgia was right. There were lots of other people who could help out with the kids. Nyala wasn't indispensable.

Georgia looked at the other riders preparing their horses. "It's great that Hank has four people going with him, but if there were one more, if you went as well, I would feel more at peace with the entire venture."

"What about me, Georgia?" Trevor asked. "Wouldn't it be better if I went as well?"

Georgia rubbed his head. "No, Trevor, you're much too young."

"Even if I wanted to go," Nyala said, "they're about to head out the door. It's too late for me to get supplies and everything I need."

Nyala was wrong—obviously she hadn't heard about the one guy who dropped out. "You're in luck—there was a sixth rider who changed his mind. We already have everything packed and a beautiful black horse picked out."

Trevor jumped up and down. "Nyala, now that you're going, you have to take me with you. You promised my mom that you would take care of me."

Hank chuckled. "Seems like you're out of excuses. You have volunteers to take care of the kids, you have a horse and supplies, and you have a sidekick. We can find another horse for him and he can share our supplies."

Hank hoped he wouldn't regret encouraging Nyala to bring Trevor. The kid would be a liability and Hank would never get past the guilt if something happened to him. They didn't know what they were going to be dealing with, and it would be dangerous at times. But some part of Hank knew that Nyala would never let Trevor stay behind. She felt responsible for him in a way that she didn't for the other kids. Plus…there was something about Trevor that reminded Hank of himself. Trevor should have a chance to have the adventures that Hank never got to have.

When Nyala didn't respond to his encouragement to go on the trip, Hank added, "It's decided then. We'll get horses for you and Trevor."

Nyala's mouth hung open. She closed her mouth. Then opened it. Then closed it. "Okay," she said at last.

Georgia gave Nyala a quick hug. "I'll go tell T-Rock to get the other horses."

So Nyala was going with them after all. She had been rude to him earlier, and a part of him was still mad about that, but Nyala was tough and if she was going with them, then he was happy about it. Even if she came with an attitude. Maybe Trevor's cheery optimism would offset Nyala's crankiness.

What was he thinking encouraging Trevor to come along? The kid was only ten years old. Surely it was a mistake. But he was also running around in circles, skipping and jumping with excitement, and it appeared that Nyala and Trevor were a package—no Trevor, no Nyala. Hank pushed his worries out of his mind.

"Grab whatever small things you want to take with you, but do it quickly," he said to Trevor and Nyala. "I want to take advantage of as much daylight as possible. We're already getting a late start."

Without losing a second, Trevor took off running toward the house. Nyala followed at a more moderate pace, but Hank sensed she was excited as well.

T-Rock showed up leading the two additional horses and Georgia arrived with the supply donkey just as Nyala and Trevor exited the door of the Stafford house. Petra followed behind Nyala and Trevor. They waited for her as she took each step on the long staircase, one foot at a time. Nyala offered a hand, but Petra shooed it away.

Hank ran up the stairs two at a time and met them halfway. "Are you ready?" he asked.

Nyala held up a backpack. "I've got my stuff. I told Trevor he could only take what he could fit in a backpack. Otherwise, we would have ended up with a stack of books from Oscar's library."

Trevor smiled. "I still kept two books."

"Please explain to me," Petra said in a voice that suggested she was about to ask a question that would make clear how stupid some part of their plan was. Petra could spot a weakness in any plan a mile away. "Your chip still works, as does Georgia's, due to your trip through the tesseract when all the other chips were disabled."

Hank nodded and waited for her to continue.

"Because they operate by drawing low levels of energy from your body, they don't require electricity to operate and you can still use them." She paused, apparently waiting for him to confirm what she had just said.

"That's correct." So far, she hadn't pointed out some fatal flaw in his plan. It was surely coming, though.

"Your plan is to wander around the country, find people still living, then meet up with Georgia in the metaverse, and report back on what you have found?"

Hank nodded again.

"And the reason you are doing this is because…?"

She was getting closer to when she would point out why the plan was stupid. He could feel it. It was in her voice and the way she always sounded like she was looking down her nose at him, even when she was staring at the stairs as she walked down them one foot at a time.

He matched her progress down the stairs. "I'm going to take a bunch of T-Rock's brochures. He created them on all sorts of subjects—like how to use aluminum and solar power to create a working stove, or emergency first aid tips."

"Humph. That sounds helpful, I suppose." It was a begrudging admission from Petra. "But is it worth it? How many people will you reach with these brochures? And surely it will be dangerous for you. Is it enough to risk your life for?" Petra stepped off the bottom step and picked up the pace when she hit level ground.

"It's not just that. We'll also be sharing information about discoveries. Cures, new sources of energy that don't set off the intolerance. Things like that. If people here discover them, then we'll share them with the world. If people we meet out there have made discoveries, we'll share it with people here."

Petra stopped walking for a moment and appeared to consider what he said. This was it. This was where she told him why his idea was a complete waste of time.

"I *suppose* I see the value in it."

He smiled. It wasn't much of an endorsement, but he would take it.

Petra reached his roan horse. She leaned toward Hank, and in a conspiratorial voice said, "I brought something for her." She reached into her pocket and drew out a carrot. The carrot made a crisp popping noise as she broke into small bits and fed it to the horse. The other horses, seeing the carrot, trotted up to Petra. "Don't worry, I have you all covered as well." Petra drew carrot after carrot from her pockets until she had given them all a treat. She scratched behind their ears and whispered soothing comments to them. When the food was gone, the horses wandered away and grazed on the grass.

"T-Rock," Petra said, "I have a request."

T-Rock handed the horse he was leading to Nyala and walked over to Petra. "Sure, Miss Petra. Anything I can do."

"I want to go back to Area 52."

"I'd love to help you out, but we're not prepared to cross the desert right now. It's a long walk, or a long ride if we take the horses, and right now we don't know how to take enough water."

Water was the biggest challenge. It was why Hank had chosen his route to follow streams and rivers, so they were headed in the opposite direction from Area 52.

"I know we can't travel there now." Petra sighed. "We placed Area 52 in the middle of the desert so it would be isolated, and once Dan turns off the electricity and the umbrella protecting it comes down, I think they will be glad to be isolated."

"Did you talk to Deputy Dan?" T-Rock asked. "Let him know what's happening?"

"I spoke to him this morning. He wasn't happy about permanently turning off the electricity, but he said they are starting to feel ill, so if I taught him right, he will do what he has to. We spoke only briefly before I couldn't tolerate the call anymore, so hopefully he understands."

"Did he say anything about Amaya?"

"I calculated the precise time that Amaya should arrive in my closet. He will be there waiting for her…" Petra looked at her antiquated wind-up watch, "in thirty-one hours and thirty-six minutes."

It was a relief that Dan would be there to meet Amaya. She had looked in bad shape during the game; going through the tesseract would be tougher for sure. She would need someone to pick her up and get her away from the electricity emitted by the tesseract.

T-Rock put his hands on his hips. "So you won't be going back to Area 52?"

"Silly boy." It almost sounded affectionate when Petra said it, "I've spent a lot of time thinking about it, and my place is with Area 52. It's been almost my entire life—it's an inseparable part of me. I need to be there, no matter the cost."

"No matter the cost," T-Rock repeated. "Are you sure?"

It was becoming clear where Petra was headed with this.

Petra wound her watch. "T-Rock, will you take me to Amoco's place?"

Trevor's brows bunched up. "Miss Petra, you aren't thinking of going through the tesseract, are you?"

"Trevor, that's exactly what I plan to do."

"But…won't it hurt?"

"Yes, it probably will."

"Will it kill you?" Trevor's eyes were moist.

"I don't know. There's a good chance it might, but that's a risk I'm willing to take. I'm prepared to die, but if I die, I want to do it in Area 52. As long as I'm there, I'm okay with whatever happens to me."

Trevor put his arms around Petra even though he had just barely met her. After a second, T-Rock, Nyala, and Georgia also wrapped their arms around her in a group hug. Hank and Petra had their differences at times, but they also had moments where they had connected. He shrugged and joined in on the group hug.

After a minute of being wrapped in the embrace, Petra said, "Okay, okay, you all need to get on the road." She wiped what may have been a tear from her cheek. "T-Rock, can you take me?"

"Yes, Miss Petra. I have my bicycle over here. You can ride in the cart." T-Rock pointed to a bike that he had modified with a large basket for carrying stuff around the estate.

Hank idly scratched his horse's neck while he watched T-Rock peddle off with Petra sitting stick straight in the basket. She didn't turn to look or wave at them as they headed around the corner.

"I forgot to say goodbye to T-Rock." Hank clapped a hand over his mouth. "How long will it take him to get back?"

"Based on how long it took us to get here from Amoco's place the other day, he's going to be gone for hours," Nyala said.

"You could always wait to leave until tomorrow," Georgia said.

It was tempting to spend another night with Georgia before heading out. Hank looked at the horses and donkeys, patiently grazing in the field with the packed bags hanging from their backs, only needing to have their bridles put on and they were ready to go. If he didn't leave today, he might never leave. "I've been saying goodbye to T-Rock ever since we started planning this, and we agreed that we'll see each other again someday, so it's not goodbye forever." He looked at Nyala. "What do you think? Do you want to wait to say goodbye?"

Nyala sniffed. "I hate goodbyes. Georgia, if you could tell T-Rock how much I appreciate him and will miss him, I would be really happy not having to do it myself."

Georgia looked at the ground. "Sure, but you'll still have to say goodbye to me. I'm not letting you get away without at least a hug."

"Of course, I wouldn't think of it."

Hank shifted his weight back and forth, waiting for the embrace to end. He had been dreading saying goodbye to Georgia. Of the multitude of ways he had rehearsed saying goodbye to her in his head, none seemed adequate.

His heart leapt into his throat when she let go of Nyala and turned to him.

"I'll walk you back to the house," he said. He wanted one last private moment with her.

She took his hand and he gripped it tight. They walked to the landing at the top of the steps and turned to look out. The six horses and five donkeys grazed in the center of the driveway loop. The guardhouse stood watch where the loop joined together, and at the edge of the substantial property, a gate kept out any intruders and another guard shack controlled who was allowed to enter.

In the fields stretching away from the house, hundreds more tents made out of whatever materials they could find were being worked on by throngs of people who had found them and joined their community.

Farther in the distance, new fields were being planted with seeds from the seed bank. There were already gardens on the other side of the house, but those would barely be enough. Hundreds of people had shown up, and Hank wouldn't be surprised if hundreds more managed to find them. The only reason they weren't being overrun was that most people didn't know about it yet, but that would change as the volunteers biking through the neighborhoods in town got the word out.

The estate had turned into a commune of sorts. T-Rock, in addition to everything else he was doing, was putting together a council to set the rules. Some rules were clear from the start. Everyone was welcome, but people who behaved poorly would be kicked out, and everyone would be expected to contribute if able. Hank smiled to himself. Who would have thought that he would have been intimately involved in setting up a commune?

Would T-Rock be able to make it work? Could he keep the people alive and prevent them from attacking each other? Was it enough?

He put his arm around Georgia. "Do you think we'll make it?" He shivered even though he was warm.

"Don't worry about me. I'll be fine. T-Rock's the best survivalist in the world—there's no one better to keep me alive than him. And he'll keep all these people alive as well. And you're going to stay alive because if you don't, I'll be heartbroken." She buried her head in his chest. "And you can't do that to me."

He leaned in until his head touched hers. "That wasn't what I meant."

"We're going to be good. We'll talk all the time. It will hardly feel like we're away from each other. And you'll have lots of stories to share, and I'm sure I'll have lots to tell you as well. We've been apart before and we managed to stay close. We can do it again."

He kissed the top of her head. "That's still not what I meant."

He felt her take a deep breath. "I know what you mean, and I don't know. If people knew how to live without electricity and if we already had stuff like outhouses and wells with buckets to get water and home gardens, we would be fine, but we're not prepared, and no one is used to living like this anymore. But with people in pods unable to reproduce, and who knows what the death rate will be for people not living in pods…"

She pulled back and looked him in the eye. "We're doing our part. You, I, and a whole bunch of other people are going to save humanity."

He leaned in and kissed her, savoring the feel of her lips, noting how she tasted, how she smelled, storing every moment of it to get him through the long, lonely times, and the touchless contact of the metaverse. It would be years until he saw Georgia again, and he wanted the memory of kissing her to be just as vivid years from now as it was at that moment.

CHAPTER 30

Day Three of The Rupture

Wednesday

Georgia opened the flimsy door to the makeshift hospital that volunteers had constructed from lumber scavenged from an old barn on the estate. There were gaps between the boards, but with summer approaching, it would do for now. The light from a wood-burning stove and some candles provided a dim glow that cast shadows in the corner of the room.

It had been three days since the exhibition Zazora Game, and Georgia was still trying to process how much her life had changed since then. Every day, more people arrived at the estate, and some of them were injured and in need of medical treatment. The treatment they received was rudimentary, and the effectiveness varied—people with broken bones were expected to do well, as long as they didn't have complications, while people with more serious illnesses, like cancer, could only hope for a miracle.

A hastily constructed brick stove with a wood fire burning in it heated up the room. Georgia wiped the sweat from her forehead. A volunteer with a wind-up watch kept an eye on a boiling pot of water to make sure it boiled long enough to sterilize. The volunteer looked up from the watch and nodded at Georgia. Off to the side of the stove, where it was warm but not hot, Amaya's cat Meechi was curled up in a contented ball.

In addition to the stove, the entry room had supplies piled around the edges and an ornate reception desk that was scuffed after being dragged from the estate's library. A young woman sitting at the desk had fallen asleep with her head on her arm and candles burning on either side of her.

Under her arm was a pen and some paper made out of pulp where the woman was copying instructions on how to treat infections without modern antibiotics. T-Rock had used all the paper at the estate to print pamphlets, so they resorted to creating pulp from the books in the library. It was painful watching the vintage books turned into pulp, but there weren't many other options.

Georgia blew out the woman's candles before she lit herself or the paper on fire. The woman had been working day and night to help out, and grabbed a few minutes of sleep wherever she could find it. But sleep could only be denied for so long.

In a side room lit with candelabras, T-Rock, in his utilitarian khakis with lots of pockets in them, was instructing a group of volunteers. Georgia overheard him saying, "I once survived for a month in the wilderness with nothing but the clothes on my back. I foraged for food just like the newt. I hunted for seed just like the yellow-bellied sapsucker." He must be teaching his class on how to find food in the forest.

T-Rock's classes typically started after dark, when the work of the day was winding down, and went for four or five hours or until the attendees started falling asleep. From the droopy eyes of the learners, it looked like they might be finishing up soon. Georgia had already heard many of T-Rock's classes, but she could probably use a refresher on this one. She glanced at the watch. It was almost ten. Maybe she would skip T-Rock's class in favor of getting some sleep—the woman with her head on the desk wasn't the only one who was short on sleep.

Georgia wandered into the back of the classroom to listen for a bit. She wasn't sure if she was there to visit T-Rock, or to not be alone, or just to be distracted from the pain in her soul. All day, every day, Georgia's heart hurt. It hurt for the people who had passed away, for the people who were suffering as they adjusted to a new way of living, and for the people who she no longer had contact with. Mostly, it longed for Hank's return. They checked in briefly in the metaverse every evening, but there was no doubt that the life of a nomad left little time for anything else.

During the day, Hank's group planned their travels based on where they could find water, stocked up on supplies, and tried to avoid saddle sores. In the evening, they cooked, fixed their equipment, and took turns being the lookout. In the few days since the group had left, they had arrived at one small community where they were treated with suspicion and the information they provided on survival was dismissed by many people who weren't even willing to look at it.

Georgia's heart broke when Hank told her about how many people in the community had already passed away.

T-Rock started discussing berries. One of the candles burned out and one of the learners started snoring. T-Rock would be ending his lesson soon, and then what would Georgia do? She was tired, exhausted even, but she didn't want to sleep.

T-Rock's lesson was interrupted by voices yelling outside of the hospital. Seconds later, the front door crashed open. The woman at the desk startled awake. The man boiling the water dropped his watch.

A group bustled in, all hovering around a woman with her arm clenched to her chest.

"She needs help," one of them yelled.

"She broke her arm," another called out. "Someone help her."

"Class is done," T-Rock said. "But I recommend you all stay for a real-life demonstration." T-Rock waved the newcomers into the classroom. "Come on in." He pointed to a student. "I need your chair."

The student hurried to put his chair next to T-Rock. T-Rock was as cool as ever under pressure.

T-Rock looked at the woman. "Have a seat."

She sat in the chair. All of T-Rock's students stayed in their seats, riveted by the change in instruction from theoretical to practical.

"What happened?" T-Rock asked.

"I tripped over a branch in the road and landed badly." The woman exhaled. "It's too dark without the moon out."

T-Rock nodded and palpated her arm. The woman winced. Georgia winced along with her. T-Rock had once explained to Georgia how to set a bone, but Georgia had hoped never to see it done in real life.

He paused his examination in the middle of the forearm. "I feel it. It's a closed fracture halfway up your ulna. It should be easy to set."

Georgia shivered. It made her queasy to watch, but she didn't want to leave.

"Georgia."

Why was T-Rock calling *her*? "Yes?"

"I need you to help me."

"Me?" Her voice squeaked.

"The others haven't reached that part of the training yet."

She nodded. She had a side of her that she could call on to respond to emergencies. It was the part of her that put all the queasiness to the side and did what needed to be done. As soon as she knew she was needed, that she was the only one who knew how to help, that side of her switched on. Gone was the hesitation, and with it the part of her that was waiting for someone else to deal with the problem.

She strode to the front of the classroom. "What do you need me to do?"

"I'm going to hold on to the upper part of the arm and keep it still." T-Rock wrapped one arm around the woman's torso and then used both hands to firmly grip her arm near her elbow. "You're going to pull on the lower part of the arm, just like I told you about, and push gently on the bone right here." He pointed to where he wanted her to push.

Georgia pushed any thoughts other than the steps that T-Rock had just mentioned out of her mind. She could do what was needed. She grabbed the woman's forearm with a firm hand and placed her other hand on the ulna.

"Ready?" she asked.

Both T-Rock and the woman said, "Ready."

"Slow, steady traction," T-Rock said. "This may take a few minutes."

Georgia pulled with one hand and pressed on the arm with the other. At first, nothing happened.

"Are you okay?" T-Rock asked the woman.

She nodded.

"A little more pressure should do it."

Georgia focused on the arm and adjusted the pressure. The woman appeared to be in pain but not distressed. Georgia closed her eyes and paid attention to how the bone gave slightly under the pressure of her hand. She adjusted again. The bone shifted under her hand and, with a pop, fell into place.

"Ah!" the woman called out. She jolted upright and then relaxed. "That feels better."

"Let's get this splinted," T-Rock said.

Georgia stepped back. The queasiness returned as she watched T-Rock direct the students to bring him items and showed them how to wrap the arm into place. She had done it. She had set a broken bone. Could she do it again? If she had to, she could. She could find that part of herself that responded to emergencies, that shut off all her normal reluctance and dampened her desire to flee from serious medical problems.

She had been helpful, and she wanted to do it again. There was only one conclusion—she would train to be a medic.

The moon provided at most a faint illumination of the path on Georgia's walk home. She stepped carefully—the last thing she needed was to end up with a broken bone like the woman at the clinic.

Her eyes drooped and sleepiness made her stumble. As tired as she was, there was a good chance she wouldn't be able to sleep. How had Hank described the feeling? Tired but wired. Exhausted but unable to sleep.

The brick path wound among the gardens, cottages, and open areas where the construction of sleeping platforms had stopped for the night. She reached a section of the path that ran parallel to the edge of the forest. Tucked into the forest was a small chapel.

Maybe the cool, calm air in the chapel would help her sleep. She hadn't been inside a chapel for decades. Not since before she had entered Panacea. At least a hundred lit votives in red glass holders covered the altar rails in the front of the chapel. The delicate scent of beeswax reminded her of the candles her mother used to light.

She found two spots where the previous candles had burnt out and replaced them with new votives. She lit the votives and knelt in front of the altar. The prayers came easily to her, despite being the first time in decades that she had said one. She prayed for Hank, for her friends, and for everyone who was struggling. She prayed for Mariela, even though her struggle was over.

She clasped her hands in front of her and gazed at the small stained-glass window of a dove with rays of light bursting out of it. The soft light of the candles glinted off the metal, outlining the dove.

She started to feel sleepy, like maybe she could actually fall asleep rather than just lie in bed with her eyes open as she had done on so many nights, when a wave of nausea passed over her. Still kneeling, she looked over her shoulder.

A robot made of metal that glowed a light cerulean blue stood in the back of the chapel. Based on what Nyala had told her, it had to be Opali. What could Opali want with her? She stood and faced the robot.

Opali nervously rubbed her hands together in what seemed like a very human gesture. "Hi, Auntie Georgia. I would hug you, but I know that would make you sick."

"Opali, I've looked everywhere for you in the metaverse. I was worried sick about you." Georgia had last seen Opali in the exhibition game. Three days had gone by since then with no sign of Opali. "I was starting to think that something had gone wrong."

"I'm sorry I didn't stop by sooner. I didn't want to make you sick."

"It's worth it to know that you're doing okay."

"Have you been following the news in the metaverse?"

"Not really, no. I find it doesn't have much relevance to me anymore."

"Then you don't know."

"Know what?"

"I stole my body. That's why I can't go back in the metaverse. The ghosts don't have real jail, so if I connect to the metaverse at all, they'll dissolve my code as punishment."

"You stole that body?" It was the most elegant robot body that Georgia had seen. No wonder Opali had taken it. "Why?"

"I don't know. I guess I didn't want to lose touch with people in the solid world."

"Are you completely separated from the metaverse? You can't go back into Panacea anymore?"

"Completely separated. My code only exists in this body. If something happens to the body, then my code will be lost forever." She smiled. "It makes me feel very human."

"Do you want me to check the news and let you know what's going on in Panacea?"

"Maybe just this one time? Someday I'll figure a way to get back in, but for now I just want to make sure everything's okay there."

"No problem." Georgia ignored the queasiness in her stomach. With Opali at the back of the chapel, it would be tolerable for a little longer. "I'll check if Elliat has posted anything helpful." Georgia did a quick search and found Elliat's latest broadcast.

> My fellow pod-dwellers. Thanks for joining in again. I've been settling into pod life and finding it is everything I ever wanted. Of course, I have a Tier One advertising value, so life is good for me. I've heard that some of you are only Tier Threes. I suggest that you try to up your advertising value by getting more followers, and posting more interesting content more frequently. Allowing your conversations and other interactions to be used as training data for the AI will also up your advertising tier.
>
> In other news, Opali Stafford still has not been seen.

Word on the street is that she stole a robot body worth many millions of dollars. Not to mention the equally expensive vehicle that she still hasn't returned. I spoke with Opali's grandmother today to see if I could get a comment, and she, quite rudely I must say, told me to "go away and never contact her again."

Please forgive my gossip—though I know you love it—but I heard that June Stafford's advertising value was very low because she was completely disconnected for so many years. She was rated as a Tier Three. I imagine she will want to get her tier up because the reports I've been getting say that being a Tier Three is no fun at all. In fact, I've heard that it is quite painful.

Tune in tomorrow when I will go over what we know about the newly created advertising tiers. I combed through all the info I could find so that you, loyal viewers, do not have to. There's still more unanswered questions than answered, but one thing we do know is that it's better to be a Tier One than a Tier Three. So come on people—you have the power to influence which tier you are in. Get out there and get your advertising value up!

Georgia shared what she had learned with Opali. She would have to read Elliat's post tomorrow on the advertising tiers. Hopefully it would answer what they were and where they had come from, as well as give more insight into whether she should be concerned about June being a Tier Three.

"Will you be coming around more?" she asked Opali.

"I don't want to make people sick, so I'll keep my distance."

"It was good to see you."

Opali smiled. "You too. Before I go, can you light a votive for me? I'm not sure what to expect of my new life. It's been a bit of a difficult adjustment at times."

"Of course. I'll do that now."

Georgia turned back to the candle rack and found another empty spot. As she lit the votive, she noticed that the nausea was gone. Opali had gone.

CHAPTER 31

Day Four of The Rupture

Thursday

Cooper added the smell pack to his food. He took a deep breath of the cheesy smell of mac 'n' cheese floating up from his pasta. Some people would say it was simple, basic even, but it was Cooper's favorite comfort food. And he needed comfort food after attending Mariela's digi-funeral that morning.

Not to mention, with the abrupt end two days ago of reporting from the solid world, he had no idea how everyone was doing. He knew that June and Bren were okay, but what about Amaya, Nyala, T-Rock, Hank, Georgia, and Amoco? How were they?

The last time he talked to his mom, she was staying in his cottage, taking care of his dogs, and helping get the estate set up to operate without electricity. That was two days ago, and she was doing okay then, but with the electricity off, was she still doing okay? What was life like out there?

A contact request from Viola popped up above his pasta. He waffled on declining it—surely there was nothing she had to say to him that he wanted to hear. In the end, he hit 'accept.'

Viola's hair was uncombed, with groups of strands each apparently doing their own thing. She looked frazzled, haggard even. "Cooper, I'm sorry to bother you, but there's something I haven't told you and it's kind of important."

He took a bite of his pasta. "What is it?"

"I don't have time to tell you right now, but you'll find out soon enough. I just hope you're not too angry with me."

What was the point of calling him to tell him that she couldn't tell him something? "Viola, what the hell is going on?" He felt no need to hide how annoyed he was with her.

Needles stabbed into his skin, sending bolts of pain into his body. Cooper gasped. He couldn't breathe. He heard rasping noises as he dragged air into his lungs. Had Viola poisoned him? He needed to get out of here. Get out of Bo Place. Get back to the solid world. It took all his concentration to draw air into his lungs, and it still wasn't enough. He was going to die.

His vision blurred. Was there someone beside him? Was someone calling for help? Where was he? The mist clouding his vision receded at a glacial pace.

Someone showed up beside him.

It sounded like someone was running.

"He's out," a voice yelled.

Seconds later, other voices and shadowy figures showed up.

"How did that happen? Were we expecting that?"

"We need to get his heart rate down."

"Viola's out too."

"Crap. How are they doing?"

His chest heaved as he pulled in breath after breath. The pins under his skin moved around, rearranging his molecules. In the background, the panicked voices continued.

"Both their heart rates are elevated. Viola's is coming down quickly." Someone touched his shoulder. "Cooper, you're okay. Take deep breaths."

"Whh…" The words weren't coming out of his mouth. He tried again. "Wha…"

"You've transitioned out of Bo Place. Based on what we saw with Amaya and Amoco, it's normal for you to feel some pain, but it should fade soon."

The outlines of the estate's bedroom came into focus in the background.

"What happened?" His voice was scratchy from not having been used for two weeks. "Why did…I exit?"

"We don't know," someone in a lab coat answered while looking frantically back and forth between two screens.

"I know." Everyone in the room turned to look at Viola. She was sitting up in her pod. With her head shaved, she was looking much more polished than she had in the metaverse. "I expelled everyone from the Bo Place metaverse."

There was a moment of stunned silence.

"All of them?" a tech asked.

"Every last one."

Cooper's blood pressure shot up. Viola had gone too far this time. "What the hell! Why would you do that?"

"You wanted out, didn't you?"

"Don't tell me you ejected 200 million people because I wanted to leave?"

"No, I did it to save humanity. There are now 200 million more people in the solid world, and many of them are of child-bearing age. Assuming a survival rate of one percent over the next year, that means 2,000,000 more people in the solid world."

"I thought you didn't make an exit shot for Bo Place?"

"I made one. I just didn't release it because the Bo Place board of directors told me not to. But I've had a change of heart and decided that the board can go to hell."

"But Viola," one of the techs said, "why didn't you let people choose if they wanted to take the exit shot? Why did you give it to everyone?"

"If I had let people choose, it wouldn't have been enough to save humanity. I ran the numbers, and only a few would have chosen to take the shot. We needed all 200 million to make any difference given the loss rate."

Cooper struggled to sit up.

Viola, on the other hand, somehow managed to climb out of her pod. She was shaky and used the pod for support, but she still managed to stand. "It's not much, but it's a start and it's the only thing that will keep humans from dying out—I hope you can appreciate that." She was speaking directly to Cooper.

"I'm in too much shock to appreciate anything right now." He turned to one of the people standing around them. "Is my mom around?"

"She's in your cottage."

"I'm going to see her."

"Get him a mobile chair." A man motioned to someone standing off to the side who pushed a mobile chair towards Cooper. The man dropped the side of the pod down and helped Cooper transition into the chair.

Viola placed her hand on the arm of the mobile chair. "Cooper, we'll talk."

Cooper couldn't tell if Viola was telling him or pleading with him, and he didn't care. "Sure. Whatever."

He and Viola would talk someday. But not now. Cooper was too confused, too disoriented to even consider talking anytime soon. For now,

Cooper planned to forget that Viola even existed.

~~~~~

"Amaya."

"Amaya, wake up."

"Come on, Amaya, we need to get you out of here."

A hand shook her. Where was she? Her body ached from having been stabbed with what felt like a thousand small daggers, and each attempt to move took her breath away and doubled the pain.

Looking around her, all she saw was coats. And she saw Dan, kneeling beside her and looking concerned. Someone must have warned him she was coming. His shoulders seemed broader and his hair blonder than the last time she saw him. Maybe it was a result of all the time he spent outside dealing with the cryogens. "I hope you aren't here to arrest me."

"No, Petra wanted me to help you. In case you had a hard time going through the tesseract."

"Thanks," she wheezed. Her lungs clamped in on themselves and stung with each breath. "That was surprisingly"—she stopped to catch her breath—"kind of you."

"Don't thank me. I just do what Petra tells me to do."

Where was Nyala? Oh right, Opali had stopped Nyala from coming with her. Amaya would have to face the server farm alone. For most of her life, Nyala had been there to protect her, but on some level, Amaya realized that the only person she could rely on, even as she headed off on a mission that might kill her, was herself. It was a desolate feeling to know that, fundamentally, she was alone in the world.

"Ready to get up?" Dan asked.

"Can you give me a second?" Her wheezing continued. "I'm having a hard time talking."

"Of course." He held his radio up to his mouth and pushed a button. "Power down," he said into the radio and then turned back to her. "Petra said to wait until you were through to power the tesseract off. She doesn't think it matters if the power is off, but said not to take a chance."

The only sound was the pained drawing in of her breath. Each time she was exposed to intense electricity, it felt like the molecules in her body were forcibly jumbled and would never go back to normal. With the power off, the daggers no longer stabbed her and the nausea faded. There was still some electrical current, though. She could feel it. "Did
~~~~~

you turn off electricity to the entire area?"

"Petra recommended we do the city block. Said to wait until you do whatever you have to do before we shut everything down."

Amaya pulled herself together. She managed to sit up, but needed more time to catch her breath before she could get up off the cold floor.

Dan, never a big talker, surprised her when he kept talking. "I was skeptical when Petra first told me about the power and being allergic to it, but I can feel it now. When the power is turned off, I feel better."

"Me too." She held out a hand to Dan. "Can you help me up? I'm going to lie on the couch for a bit until I get my strength back."

Dan jumped to his feet, picked up the black bag with the cube, and extended a hand to Amaya. Once she was standing, he looped her arm over his shoulder and led her to a dark, Victorian living room with couches covered in flowery fabric.

"This will do." She collapsed onto the nearest overstuffed couch. Her legs draped over the edge, but Dan picked them up and put pillows under her head and legs.

Dan sat down on the couch across from her. "Don't know how Petra is going to handle this."

She pushed back the hood on the catsuit. "Handle what?"

"She's coming through the tesseract. First, she told us to go ahead and turn off the power after you got through. She doesn't think it will make a difference if the tesseract doesn't have power on this end when she gets here later today."

"How much later did she leave after I did?"

"About five hours." Dan's words tumbled over each other. "She said the well-being of the residents is the most important thing, and that she's willing to take a chance on the tesseract not working properly with the power down, so I'm supposed to turn off all the power and destroy the solar array as soon as you're done. But I'm looking at you, and she's a lot more frail than you, and you look like crap. So how is Petra going to survive?"

"I don't know, but she's pretty tough; maybe she'll surprise you."

"I wish she had stayed there and not taken a chance on returning."

"I'm guessing she knew the risks she was taking, and she decided that it was worth it to return to her home."

"She said if she dies, she wants me to be in charge. She told everyone that."

"Oh." That was indeed surprising. Dan had grown a lot, but he wasn't exactly known for his ability to think independently. On the other hand, he had really stepped up since she had known him. Maybe he would make a good leader. "Congratulations."

There was one thing that Amaya had been wondering about. "So if you shut down the power, the tesseract will be turned off?"

"Correct."

"Does that mean the Faraday cage will also be down?"

"True."

It was one small bit of good news in a bunch of bad news. Maybe someday, then, Nyala or one of her other friends might make it to Area 52. And if they did, there wouldn't be anything to stop them from getting in.

"So what are you doing here?" Dan asked her.

Amaya felt well enough to sit up. "I've been sent on a mission by the ghosts. Can I run an idea by you?"

"Yes."

"I've been threatened by the ghosts—they say they will go back on their agreement not to kill me if I don't destroy the server farm here. Not the Area 52 part, but the part that backs up all the data from outside of here."

Dan nodded. "Okay."

"But then I agreed with Nyala and T-Rock and Amoco that I would run their program instead. Their program deletes all the advanced ghosts permanently, which would be fine except that the ghosts are treating the pod-dwellers for the electricity intolerance, so if I delete the ghosts, around three billion people will be sick again and have to leave their pods. But the advanced ghosts will be gone, and we won't have to worry that they will go back on their agreements or threaten to kill humans."

Amaya paused. Dan stayed quiet, listening but not responding. At least he was listening.

"The thing is, we have a one time opportunity to delete the ghosts because the tesseract that they use to protect themselves has been damaged. If we don't take advantage of this opportunity now, it will be lost forever." Amaya paused to take some deep breaths. When she was able to speak again, she said, "I'm really confused about what to do. I said I would delete the ghosts, but I'm not sure that I can live with the impact on the pod-dwellers. But I don't want to let Nyala, T-Rock, and Amoco down. And I want to get rid of the threat from the ghosts."

"It's a big decision," Dan said.

Dan's comment was an understatement—it was a huge decision. It was a life-changing decision for billions of people, and that was all Dan could come up with? That it was a big decision? Amaya checked herself. She didn't have any reason to be upset with Dan. She had been unrealistically hoping he would say something and it would clarify what she should do. It was unfair of her to be upset with him for not saying some wise thing that would make everything okay.

"So let me understand," Dan said. "People in pods won't die as a result of you deleting the ghosts, instead they'll have to live without electricity, just like people did in the 1800s."

"Yes."

"They won't die directly because you deleted the ghosts, but death rates were higher in the 1800s, so you think more people will die because of the lifestyle."

"Yes. But we're also not used to living that way anymore. They'll be stuck living without electricity like the rest of us, but we don't know how to live without electricity anymore."

"So your big question about whether to get rid of a dangerous group of digital beings is based on your concern that a large group of people will have to live like they are in the 1800s?"

"Yes, but…it's just…compared to how things would be if they stayed in their pods, lots of people will die. Possibly lots and lots of people."

He looked down at his hands, and it seemed like the conversation was over. After a few seconds, he continued, "It seems to me that you shouldn't worry about what other people want you to do. You're in an impossible position where there is no right answer, so I think the best you can do is figure out which option is least likely to haunt you when you put your head on the pillow at night. Once you figure that out, you'll know what to do."

Amaya nodded. It didn't solve her dilemma, but it wasn't bad advice.

"I think I'm ready now." The daggers were still there, and her stomach felt like she had eaten moldy bread, but it seemed like she was feeling as good as she was going to get for now.

"Do you want me to drive you?" Dan asked.

"How far away is it if I walk?"

"In your condition, probably two hours."

"I'd like a ride then." She'd probably throw up more in the vehicle, but she wasn't up for walking for two hours.

"No problem. It's on my way to the solar array." Dan shifted in his seat. "Some of our people are getting really sick—it'll take me about forty-five minutes to get to the array and another fifteen minutes or so to shut it down. I'll leave the power to the server room on for now so that you can do what you need to do, but then I'm turning it off in one hour no matter what."

"Okay, I can work with that." She needed time to get to the server entrance, go down the elevator shaft, set the program to run, and get back up. An hour seemed like plenty of time.

Dan held a hand out to her. "Ready?" He supported her as he guided her out to his jeep. "Have you decided which program you're going to run?"

It took fifteen minutes of her time for Dan to drive her to the server. The watch that Dan gave her to track time burned her hand. She dropped it in the bag from Opali and let the bag dangle from her hand. It was subtle, but she could tell the extra weight of the watch. If she could tell the weight of the watch, then surely Opali, with her robot senses, would have noticed the extra weight of the second cube.

There was a moment, before Amaya had gone through the tesseract, when Opali had ever so briefly paused while holding the bag with the two cubes in it. If Opali knew about the second cube, what did that mean? It wouldn't have taken much for Opali to deduce that the second cube was for deleting the ghosts—was she really willing to allow the ghosts to be deleted? She had always wanted to be human—maybe this was her way of standing up for humanity? If Opali didn't want to stop her from using the cube to delete the ghosts, then maybe that should be the one that Amaya used.

"We're here." Dan pulled his jeep up on the grass right outside the mausoleum with the server access point. "I hope you don't mind if I run. It's a long way down to the solar array."

"No problem."

Amaya opened the door and stepped out. Her legs buckled under her and she toppled to the wet grass.

"Are you okay?" Dan yelled through the open door.

"I just need a few seconds to rest." Instead of a yell, her voice was weak and breathy. "Go on to the solar array."

"I'll help you up." Dan opened his door.

She sat up. "No! Please don't bother. I'd like to rest here a bit before I go on, but I'm fine."

"Are you sure?"

"I'm sure. Get out of here."

"Good luck then."

She nodded. "Thanks. You too." She laid down on the moist grass; dappled light from the rays of the midday sun bathed her. Without her thick hair to warm her head, a cool breeze chilled her.

Next to her, the sound of the jeep door slamming shut was followed by the soft rumble of the engine as it backed up. The tires threw up dirt as Dan spun the jeep around and headed in the other direction. Every movement triggered the stabbing daggers and her arms felt weighted with lead. She closed her eyes to rest.

Amaya had fallen asleep again. Or was it passed out again? At this point, there wasn't much of a difference. She opened the black bag and pulled out the watch. Another fifteen minutes had passed. No problem. Half an hour was plenty of time. Or it would be plenty of time if she could get her body moving. She put the watch in the satchel, then pulled off her gloves and dropped them in.

In the distance, billowing smoke from the wildfires glowed shades of gold and red. Through spreading the toxin, an unintended consequence of the wildfires was that no part of humanity was untouched by the electricity intolerance. The power of humanity was, once again, unmatched by the power of nature.

Looming ahead of her, a classical mausoleum—with Greek columns and all—doubled as an entrance to the server farm. She crawled to a marble bench to the side of the oversized mausoleum door and pulled herself to standing. With one hand bracing herself against the cool marble wall, she turned the door handle and pushed. Nothing happened. She pushed again. The mausoleum door refused to budge. She hunkered down and shoved the eighty-year-old door with her shoulder. With a sharp crack, the door gave way and Amaya stumbled into the small building.

Marble bunkers filled with coffins lined the aisle leading to a door on the far end. She slid the rusty door to the elevator open. Waves of electricity rushed out and hit her full force; she doubled over as the dry heaves twisted her stomach. Unable to stand up straight, she stumbled into the elevator and used the top of her head to hit the button labeled "Server Room."

The three-minute descent to the server farm dragged, seemingly lasting forever, and she got sicker with each foot the elevator descended. The question of which program to run weighed on her. She still felt as uncertain as ever. With a grinding of gears and a solid clunk, the elevator stopped at the bottom. The opening doors scraped and groaned and stopped short with a screech.

Amaya looked at the watch. Twenty-seven minutes remaining, and she needed to leave at least five to get back up the elevator before the power turned off. But if she was too late—would she be able to get out? She pushed up the escape hatch in the ceiling of the elevator cage. There was a telescoping ladder up to the hatch.

The ladder clicked as she extended it to the floor. She grabbed the side and climbed up. Each step up the ladder was painful and took an effort that felt like the final stages of a marathon, but eventually Amaya got to where her head poked through the escape hatch.

The elevator shaft was gloomy, but off to the side a ladder extended upwards and far above her disappeared into the darkness of the shaft. Even when she had been healthy, it would have been an impossible feat for her to climb all the way to the top. She would have to take the elevator out before the power went out or not exit at all.

She headed back down the ladder. Leaving enough time to exit, she had twenty-two minutes left. Twenty-two minutes to figure out which program to run, get it started, and get out of there. Plenty of time—except that she still had no clue which program to run.

Amaya squeezed through the barely open outer elevator doors. The brightly lit, spacious room containing the Area 52 server farm was filled with white servers. Off to the side, the door to the enormous Panacea server room was wide open—apparently they had forgotten to close it the last time they were there.

Unlike the well-lit Area 52 server room, the dim emergency lighting in the Panacea server room provided barely enough light to see the rows upon rows of black server cases with their blinking red and white lights. The low ceiling over the server room made it feel small even though the rows were so long they stretched out of sight. Dying cleaner bots left trails through the dust on the floor, and the main access terminal was covered in cobwebs that still showed streaks in the dust from the last time she was there.

Her entire body buzzed. She couldn't tell the difference anymore between herself and the machines. The musty air and low ceiling made her claustrophobic. Standing took a huge effort. Amaya dropped the black bag and leaned against the wall. She needed to think. She pushed back the hood of the catsuit and slid down the wall until the cold concrete floor stopped her descent. Half of what she breathed in was dust and the other half cobwebs.

"Something bad happens every time you visit this room."

Amaya startled at the sound of the familiar voice and swung her head to the side. Could it be? Barely visible in the dim light was a face that always seemed to be smiling, bright clothing with confusing patterns, and chaotic brown hair.

"Grace?" Amaya's heart leapt and stumbled over a confusion of feelings—happiness at seeing Grace, grief over the memory of Grace's death, and relief at not being alone.

Grace sat on the stool in front of the main terminal and tucked one leg onto the crossbar. "You seem surprised to see me."

Surprised was an understatement. "Well, you're dead."

"As long as you remember me, I'll always be with you."

Grace was the only person who had been with her when the ghosts were deleted the first time, so it wasn't surprising that she would think of Grace right now. But it was disconcerting to see Grace take solid form so clearly in front of her.

"So you're not alive?" Amaya knew the answer to her question, but she needed to check just to make sure.

Grace smiled, but it didn't reach her eyes. "Sadly, I didn't perfect the art of reincarnation before I died."

Amaya stood up and brushed herself off. "I guess it was too much to hope for. How are you here then?"

"You wanted me here—you needed support, so I'm here to support you."

"I'm so happy you're here."

"Plus, you're losing touch with reality."

Well, that wasn't so great. "I'm glad you're here, even if it means I'm losing it."

Amaya hugged Grace. She felt surprisingly solid.

"You don't have much time," Grace said, "so let's get started. Are you inadvertently deleting the LP100 model ghosts again like last time?"

"No, this time I know I'm doing it. I mean, I think I'm doing it."

Grace's brow furrowed. "It upset you so much last time—it wasn't that long ago when you tried to destroy the computer just to stop the ghosts from being deleted. What's changed?"

Grace seemed older than her eighteen years of age. Maybe that's what being dead would do to a person. Or maybe it was what Amaya needed now.

Amaya told Grace how, with the tesseract being damaged, they had an opportunity that might never come up again to delete the ghosts. "It's now or never. Every time LP changes his mind, or wants us to do something for him, all he has to do is threaten to harm the humans or withhold treatment and we will have no option but to do what he wants. There is nothing to stop him from changing his agreements on a whim."

"So, it comes down to…do what the ghosts want and take a chance on them continuing to manipulate you, or delete the ghosts and stop them from manipulating you, but at a cost?"

"That's it. I can get rid of the ghosts permanently, but then the humans in the metaverse will die or be stuck living in the solid world without electricity against their will. Or I can destroy the server farm like the ghosts want and protect the humans in the metaverse, but then the ghosts will continue to control us."

"Can you find the formula for the treatment for the electricity intolerance?"

"I was just thinking the same thing." Amaya accessed the terminal and started searching through the Panacea servers. It was a lot of data to go through. The old-fashioned progress bar showed the search progressing steadily, but slowly.

"Grace, there's something I need to tell you."

"I know what happened to my mom," Grace said.

"It's just—I feel bad. I was mad at Mariela, and I hadn't talked to her for days when she died." Mariela was always on Amaya's mind. "I miss her, and I feel bad that I didn't reconcile with her before she died."

"There's one thing I learned about my mom," Grace said, "is that sometimes it's hard not to be mad at her. But that doesn't mean that I love her any less."

Amaya half-smiled. "How did you get to be so wise?"

Grace chuckled. "Well, I'm pretty sure it wasn't from my father."

Despite herself, Amaya laughed.

An alert dinged when the search reached the end. The list of search results, ordered with the best results at the top, extended down the screen.

Grace pointed at the third result. "I think that's it." Her voice was excited with anticipation.

Amaya accessed the file that appeared to be the formula for the treatment for the intolerance. A security notice popped up. She used various tricks to break the security on the formula. Every attempt was blocked.

The time was counting down and the minutes were passing by, but the file stubbornly refused to allow her to access it. She took fifteen minutes of her time trying everything she knew to access the file, but in the end she had to accept that the protection put in place by the ghosts was unbeatable.

"I don't think I can do it. Whoever put the security on this file did a good job."

"You need to decide what are you going to do," Grace said. "You don't have much time left."

Amaya looked at the watch. Eight minutes until she needed to exit. She had dithered and gone back and forth for so long and spent so much time talking to a figment of her imagination that she was stuck having to make a decision on impulse.

Nyala had made a good case for deleting the ghosts. They would never get another opportunity like this. "I'm going to delete the ghosts." There was silence. Where was Grace? Amaya turned in a circle. Grace was gone. She was on her own after all.

Amaya reached into the black bag and pulled out the cube from Amoco. It was smaller than the one from Opali—it glowed blue but without the bright central core. It was hot in her hand. She took a deep breath and placed it on the server terminal. It glowed brighter. The pain in the pit of her stomach grew worse. She doubled over and clenched her hands to her stomach. She heaved.

What had Dan said? There was some important point, something about being able to sleep at night. Her nausea was only partly from the electricity; it was also because this wasn't the right decision.

She swiped the cube off the terminal. It popped and clattered to the ground with a hiss.

Dan had said she needed to figure out which option was least likely to haunt her when she put her head on her pillow at night, and deleting the ghosts wasn't it. Grace was beside her again. Where had she been?

Amaya turned the black bag upside down and dumped Opali's cube out on the counter in front of the server. A piece of paper fluttered out.

Grace's eyes opened wide at the sight of the larger cube. It glowed with pale blue strands of light that seemed to explode from a bright central core.

"Wow," Grace said. "We don't have anything like that here in Area 52."

"It's unique…the only one in the world."

There wasn't much time left—with the five-minute delay on the cube, she needed to start it now or she would miss her window. Amaya picked up the cube—it felt solid and heavier than expected. Pinpricks of pain twisted into her hand as she placed it on the terminal. It wasn't the sort of decision that made her happy, but it was the right one.

The cube glowed deep blue with a bright white central core. Tendrils grew out of the cube and dug into the terminal. The program would take care of itself; all Amaya had to do was get back to the surface before the five-minute delay was up.

As she turned toward the door, the slip of paper caught her eye. The writing on it appeared to be a link to some online video footage. There was no way anyone other than Opali could have put the paper in the bag.

"Grace, I have to watch that footage."

"Oh no, Amaya, this is *not* a good idea." Grace shook her head. "You need to leave now."

Amaya pulled the keyboard for the terminal out of the cabinet. "It won't take me long." The light was dim, but it was enough for her to type in the location that Opali had written in her precise script.

A result popped up on the screen. Amaya pulled up the metadata. It appeared to be a meeting of the Spectral Council from the day after the exhibition game. "It won't kill me to watch a couple minutes of it," she told Grace.

"It might. You should go."

Amaya knew that Grace was right. She should leave now. But if Opali had wanted her to see it, there was probably a good reason. Plus, Opali had written down the location instead of sending it through a message, which probably meant that she didn't want LP to know. Amaya could watch one minute and still make it up the elevator before Opali's program started destroying the server.

Amaya opened the file. The footage started off with the meeting being called to order. LP entered with his usual fanfare and then droned on with boring announcements. Amaya skipped ahead a few minutes.

A ghost who looked like she never smiled was speaking. "LP, can you tell us why you entered into an agreement to provide treatment for the electricity intolerance to the humans living in pods?"

The other ghosts twittered and whispered among themselves. It hadn't occurred to Amaya that the other ghosts would question LP's decision.

"Please do explain," another ghost said. "We know that you're not given to generosity, and it's questionable that you care about humans, so why did you agree to it?"

"Silence!" LP roared. The room went quiet. "You doubt my decisions? As long as the pod-dwellers are dependent on us caring for them, the humans won't delete us."

The first ghost shook her head. "But you've committed us to at least a century of caring for them. Some of the younger humans could easily live another 100 years."

LP smiled a cagey smile. "I know. It was a brilliant decision on my part. That means that we have a hundred years before we have to worry about the humans deleting us."

"Whatever you say, LP," the serious woman said. "If you think that's the best."

"Darn it," Amaya said. "Opali's right—the Spectral Council does agree to whatever LP says."

"He really has them under his thumb," Grace said.

"I have a surprise for you all," LP was saying in the footage.

Amaya focused again on the screen.

"I have a plan for the humans," LP said. "It's a brilliant plan that is going to make us all rich."

A number of the ghosts on the Council sat up straighter. The room waited for him to continue.

LP raised his hands like a preacher addressing his flock. "We are going to harvest the advertising value of the humans."

Grace shook her head and chewed on a knuckle. "Harvest doesn't sound good."

Amaya nodded.

"We will," LP paused for dramatic effect, "provide the treatment based on the person's advertising value tier level.

Grace turned to Amaya, her face serious and concerned. "What's an advertising tier level?"

"I don't know, but I think we're about to find out."

LP had a smug smile. "We will calculate the advertising value of each pod-dweller. People with a Tier One advertising value who also agree for us to use all their data for tracking, advertising, and AI training will receive full treatment for the electricity intolerance."

Amaya anticipated where LP was heading, and she didn't like it.

"Tier Threes," LP said, "are of such low value that they will receive the treatment as promised, but only enough to keep them alive."

Grace gasped. "Does that mean what I think it means?"

"I think LP is saying that the Tier Threes will be in pain. Their basic needs will be met, but nothing more."

"Why is he doing this? Do the ghosts need the money?"

"Not at all. The pod warehouses are self-sufficient. Even the cleaning, repair, and medical bots are essentially free. When LP says he wants to earn more money, that's because he was based on Liam Price, and Price put money before everything else."

"So you're saying—" Grace's voice broke, "they are letting people live in pain to earn money they don't need?"

Amaya didn't respond. What was there to say except that it was heartbreaking?

"Can't you do something?" Grace asked.

"Do what? There's nothing I can do. The only thing is to delete the ghosts, and that would only make things worse for the people in the pods."

Grace's voice cracked as she argued, "But some of these people will live for decades…"

"I know, Grace, I know." Amaya had never felt so helpless. Not when she was tricked into deleting the ghosts the first time. Not when she was bullied in junior high. None of that compared. None of that was a match for a ghost modeled on a businessman who put earning money over everything else.

"It's time for you to go," Grace said. "You're down to the wire."

A flash of inspiration hit Amaya—there was one more thing she could do. It was last minute and would probably be inadequate, but she had to try. She grabbed the cube and yanked. She had to stop the program from running before she could put her idea into place. The tendrils withdrew with a snap and whipped into her hand, burning lash marks into the skin. The acrid smell of burning flesh mixed with the stench of her vomit and the mustiness of the server room.

"I don't think that did anything." Grace said. "The program is already on the server."

Amaya panted from the pain of the burnt flesh. Grace was right. Removing the cube was pointless at this point.

She looked at the watch. Only four minutes left until the program started. Seven minutes until Dan turned the power off. The changes she needed to make weren't complicated, but even if the destruction of the server started slowly, there was no way she could write the code and get up the elevator before the power turned off.

She had to make a decision. Get out now, or make the changes and be stuck in the server room.

She looked around her. Was it worth being stuck underground? What if the changes didn't work? Was she willing to die a quarter mile underground on the uncertain chance that it might work? She was going to try even if it didn't work out. She had to do something.

"I have an idea," she said to Grace. "But first, let me check one thing." She ran another search. The results she wanted showed up quickly, and they had only the most rudimentary security protection. It surprised Amaya the things that people didn't think to put security on. "We can use the backdoor that Amoco installed to change the treatment levels for the people in the Tier Three advertising level. They will receive the full treatment and won't be in pain."

"Amaya, I know from experience that wanting to help others can turn out badly. Are you sure you want to do this?"

"I'm sure."

"You won't make it out on time."

"I know."

"It might not work."

"I have to try."

"Okay then," Grace smiled and rubbed her hands together in anticipation, "let's save some people from spending the rest of their lives in pain."

Amaya was confused. "I thought you didn't want me to do it?"

"I just wanted to make sure that you were sure about it. But if you've made up your mind, then I support you fully."

"Okay then." Amaya nodded. "Let's get to work."

"So how will it work?" Grace asked.

"The information online is the ghosts' only source of memory. Normally, the auto-synchronization program keeps people from entering false data, but Amoco installed a backdoor in the Panacea server farm on one of our earlier expeditions. The backdoor has special properties. Using it, I can change any of the Panacea data without a trace. I'll just have to cover my tracks."

"Won't the ghosts or the humans notice that something has changed?"

"I'm sure someone will notice the change, especially when the Tier Threes are no longer in pain. So here's my plan—I'm going to create a fake video of LP announcing the change that will be released publicly. LP won't want to admit that the video could have been created without leaving any trace of the change or sign of who did it—it would ruin his credibility if word got out. I can almost guarantee that LP will find it easier to live with the consequences than admit that he didn't create the announcement."

"But couldn't LP change his mind in a couple years without losing face?"

"That's where the second part of my plan comes in. I'm going to put my own security protocols on the tiers. LP won't have access anymore to change it back. He may figure out some day how to change the Tier Three treatment levels back to where they were," Amaya smiled, "but not if I have done my job correctly."

Grace smiled. "I think my mother would be happy with this."

Grace was right. Mariela would have been thrilled to see LP taken down a notch. Amaya got down to work.

At first nothing seemed to happen with Opali's program. Then three minutes later, on the far side of the room, at the end of a row that she hadn't been able to see until now, a spark flared and spewed like a flamethrower. The other server cases at the end of the row also sparked.

Amaya sped up her pace. It took her about another minute to get through all the steps. It wasn't much, but with the way ghosts' memories worked, they would believe whatever the digital record was. And even if LP suspected something was wrong, which he surely would, he would never publicly admit it. She took another minute to erase her tracks. There would be no record that things had ever been any different. Amaya crossed her arms and smiled.

She looked at her watch. There was only one minute left until the power went off. There was no point in getting into the elevator now. Dan had been clear that he was going to cut the power when the secondhand hit the one-hour mark and not one second later. If she tried to leave now, she would be stuck in the elevator. In the choice between being stuck in the elevator versus stuck in the server room, she preferred to be stuck in the server room.

"It's done," she said. "Now we wait and see. Although we may never know."

The inferno at the end of the row picked up speed and rushed closer. It sped toward her like a fiery accident on a high-speed highway—the flames bursting out under high pressure and the cases exploding like fireworks. She had at most seconds before the flames reached her. She stumbled over the stool and tumbled to the ground. She scraped her hands and knees on the cold concrete floor. She picked herself up and bolted out of the room.

Just as the heat from the blaze reached her, she grabbed the heavy door and slammed it shut, using her body weight to pull it tight and make sure it sealed. The door looked fireproof, but it seemed unlikely anything was sufficiently fireproof to stop what was happening to the servers.

She scrambled toward the elevator, stumbling over her own feet. Amaya squeezed her way through the partially open doors and prayed the metal elevator cage would protect her. Her heart felt like it was going to explode. She half-fell, half-collapsed onto the elevator floor. The sound of hissing and exploding server cases carried through the heavy door from the other room.

A minute later, the lights on all the Area 52 servers went out, and the hum from the servers died down. Dan had turned off the power. The emergency lighting went out and she was left in complete blackness. The comforting hum of the servers was replaced by the hypnotic hisses of the flames in the next room.

"Amaya. Pull down your hood and close the elevator doors."

Amaya groaned.

"Amaya, are you listening to me?"

Her elbow hurt. Her hands hurt. Her knees hurt. What had happened to her?

"Amaya, I can't do this for you. You need to pull down your hood and close the elevator doors."

Amaya blinked. Her eyes felt like sandpaper. She must have passed out again. A diffuse glow provided enough light to see the outlines of the elevator and not much else. Grace sat in the far corner of the elevator cage, her knees tucked under her chin.

Amaya sat up and rubbed her elbow. "How long have I been out?"

"Long enough for the door to the Panacea server room to start to melt. It's going to turn into an inferno in here soon."

Amaya peered out through the opening in the elevator doors. The door to the Panacea server room sagged and drooped and looked like it might give out at any moment.

"Pull on your hood, Amaya. You need it to protect you."

Amaya pulled up the hood and tugged it around her face. "Done."

"Can you get the elevator doors closed? When the server room door gives out, the heat is going to explode out here."

Amaya shoved the doors with her feet. They remained firmly in place. Whatever damage the electricity had done to her body left her barely able to lift her legs. She shoved harder, but the doors refused to budge.

"Hide now," Grace said. "Hide in the corner. It'll protect you some from the heat. Cover your head."

Amaya rolled to the side of the elevator that was out of the direct line of sight of the Panacea server room. She curled into a ball and wrapped her arms around her head. It wasn't a second too soon. The heavy door blew off its hinges and crashed to the ground. A surge of heat rushed out of the opening and slammed into the Area 52 server room. Amaya pulled her arms tighter around her head and tried to find whatever oxygen she could in the blaze that rushed into the elevator and turned it into a furnace.

For once, she didn't pass out or throw up, but being passed out might have been preferable as she dragged oxygen-starved air into her lungs and the room around her tinged black despite being lit by a raging fire. The elevator cage swirled around her, and she worried she could fall through the floor. The inside of the catsuit itched as sweat drenched her.

"Grace," she gasped, "am I going to die?"

There was no reply. Where was Grace? She wasn't wearing

protective gear like Amaya—had the flames engulfed her? Was she dead? But hadn't Grace already died? There was another time—yes, the dust storm—something had happened to Grace then. Something that had broken Amaya's heart. Was Grace dead? Had Grace died again? Where had she gone? Amaya pulled her knees to her chest and wept.

Hours later, the light shining into the elevator from the fires had subsided. She rolled over to sit up. Her face and her hands were burned, but at least the high-tech material of the catsuit had mostly protected her skin.

Amaya squeezed out through the elevator doors—the catsuit dampened the searing heat of the metal doors. The Area 52 servers hadn't burned, but they hadn't escaped unscathed. Char marks from the heat blast had turned the normally white servers into a mix of charcoal gray and black. Embers expelled from the Panacea side littered the floor, some of them still burning. Smoke filled every breath. She gulped in air, trying to get what oxygen she could.

Back in the elevator cage, Amaya sat without moving for what felt like hours. There was nothing for her to do but obsess about her choices. She second-guessed all of them, and in the solitude of the elevator, with no clear future for her except to suffer a slow death half-a-mile underground, all of her choices felt wrong. The change to the tiers wasn't enough, and there was nothing to stop the ghosts from harming humans in the future to get what they wanted. When that happened, she would regret not deleting them, and it would hurt that they had lost their chance to get rid of the ghosts.

The still burning embers provided a flickering light. It might be impossible, but there was nothing else for her to do but to try to climb out of the elevator shaft. She grabbed onto a rung of the ladder to the escape hatch. The metal scalded her hand, and raw sores almost immediately popped up. She let go and shook her hand.

She looped her arm over the rung and locked it with the other arm, with the catsuit protecting the skin on her arm. She stepped onto the first rung, her foot shaking uncontrollably. She pulled herself up with shaking knees and ankles and grabbed onto the next rung. She made it one rung, and then the next. Only a quarter mile or so more to go.

On the fourth rung, as she attempted to push herself onto the next rung, her leg refused to push up her body. Her body felt like it was made out of iron weights. No matter how much she pushed, her fatigued leg didn't move. She lowered herself, getting ready to jumpstart her step up onto the next rung. She had to do it if she wanted to get out of there.

She pushed off, springing up to the next rung. She grappled for the rung, the bar slipping through her fingers. She crashed into the unyielding floor of the elevator. She wheezed and struggled to catch her breath. Maybe this was what she deserved. She had failed to protect the humans from the ghosts—slowly dying at the bottom of a dark elevator shaft seemed like a fitting end for her.

Her body refused to move or respond to her quiet pleas to get up.

The light from the embers disappeared, taking with it the blurry lines of the elevator. She couldn't remember if she had been lying on the floor for minutes, or hours.

A hand touched her arm. "It's going to be okay, Amaya."

The world went black.

CHAPTER 24

One Week after The Rupture

Saturday

"Amaya."

Somewhere in the darkness, a woman's voice called her name.

"Amaya, wake up."

It sounded like Grace.

"Grace? I can't see you."

"I'm right here." The voice was closer now. "You're in my old bedroom in Area 52 and I'm sitting on the bed next to you. Give your eyes a second to adjust and you'll see me."

Everything was blurry, but just like Grace had said, she was there, perched on the edge of the bed. It reminded Amaya of the day they met—how Grace had checked on Amaya in this very room. "Why do you keep showing up?"

"You've been sleeping a long time."

"I'm awake right now, aren't I?"

"No, you're not. You haven't been awake for two days." Grace's hand pressed on Amaya's arm. When she spoke, her voice was low and serious. "You can't sleep forever."

Why was Grace pressuring her? Anger swirled through Amaya's body, twisting her stomach and filling her skin with heat. "Why should I wake up? I let everyone down. I made a promise to Nyala, Amoco, and T-Rock, and I didn't keep that promise. I couldn't bring myself to delete the ghosts and now they still exist and who knows how long it'll be before they demand something else and threaten to hurt humans if they don't get their way."

"You did what you thought was right."

Amaya huffed. "The best I could come up with was to change the treatment so that the Tier Threes won't be in pain. I'm not even sure it worked, but if it did, will it really make a difference? How long until LP figures out a way to change it back? Was not deleting the ghosts the wrong decision?"

"What does your gut tell you?"

"I don't know. My gut and I aren't really in touch right now. I've lost everyone I cared about. You died, Mariela's gone, and I don't know when I'll ever see Nyala again. The only person I know here is Dan, and he's…well…Dan. What are the chances I'll ever see Georgia, June, T-Rock, and Amoco again? Cooper's stuck in Bo Place, so there's another person I'll probably never see again."

"Cooper's here."

"What do you mean?"

"He's sitting right there. Don't you see him in the rocking chair?"

Amaya squinted her eyes and a shadowy shape that might be Cooper emerged. Figures that looked like three dogs were resting at his feet. "Is it really him?"

Grace smiled and nodded. "That man over there who's drooling while sleeping and who hasn't showered in days is indeed my father."

For the first time, Amaya felt a bit of hope. Felt that maybe she wasn't all alone in the world. "Is he real?"

"Of course he's real," Grace said. "So now will you wake up?"

~~~~~

At first Cooper had worried that the squeaking of the rocking chair would wake Amaya, but it had been over forty-eight hours since he had found her sleeping in a bed at June's house in Area 52 and so far nothing seemed to make her stir. At this point, he was more worried she might never wake up.

The darkness of another night was setting in, and the sputtering candle did little to offset it. After he had found himself unexpectedly standing in the Stafford Estate house with nothing on his back—make that with nothing but his clothes tucked away in a drawer somewhere—he had fled. He wasn't even sure what he was running from. All he knew was that he was so angry with Viola that it felt like his blood was boiling, and the only thing that seemed to make it better was to run from it all. Away from Viola, away from the house where he had first met Mariela, away from all the memories.

He was suffering from the electricity intolerance, but it wasn't bad yet. The med staff said they didn't have much information to go on, but he had probably twelve hours until he would be so sick he couldn't function anymore.
~~~~~

So he picked up his dogs from the cottage and drove. He turned off the auto-pilot on the hovbus and floored the accelerator. No one cared that he took the hovbus because they couldn't tolerate driving it. He had planned to spend all of the twelve hours driving at a recklessly high speed with the AC as high as it would go. But after four hours, the asphalt bored him, and that was when he made the decision to turn left onto the dirt path heading to Area 52.

The mountains on full display in the distance made it clear that the protective umbrella surrounding Area 52 had come down. Two hours later, the dirt road ended in the foothills. He left the hovbus and started up the incline with his dogs running around his feet. With his muscles weakened by two weeks in a pod, the climb went slowly.

He took frequent breaks and considered turning around many times. But each time he had continued walking toward SkyWater, despite being unsure what he would find there. The smoke from the wildfires left the view hazy and tinged in red. On the northern horizon, in the direction of Glorietta Pass and the Panacea headquarters, the sky glowed even at night with the light from the wildfires.

Arriving in SkyWater dehydrated and with feet full of blisters many hours later, he had used Deputy Dan's phone to track down Georgia, who, after a very brief call, had agreed to contact June in the metaverse. June had happily agreed to let him take over her place and told him where to find the pillar candles she kept tucked away. He lit the candles and looked around. The big shocker was when he had found Amaya sleeping like a rock in Grace's bed. He hadn't even known that Amaya was in Area 52. Her breathing was ragged and she had some burns on her face and hands, but otherwise she appeared okay. He didn't disturb her except to put cream on the burnt skin twice a day.

Each night for the last two nights, he had settled into the rocking chair in Grace's room. The first night he had burned the candles all night while keeping an eye on Amaya. The regret set in at the end of the night when he realized that the following nights would be spent in darkness if he didn't figure out how to make the candles last. He spent the daylight hours tearing threads out of June's clothing and braiding them into wicks for the candles.

The next night he saved the melted wax, poured new candles, and cut a couple inches of wick for them. He dipped the wicks in the melted candles and then set them to harden. If he only used a couple hours of candlelight a night and then spent the rest of the evening in darkness, he might get the candles to last a couple of weeks if he was lucky. After that, all night, every night, would be dark.

He had one candle still burning tonight—a holiday candle with fake holly and a little golden bell on it. The candle sputtered and almost went out. It was time to blow it out so that there would be something for tomorrow. The flame flickered and danced as he slid it across the dresser next to the rocking chair.

It was a lonely way to spend the evenings, even with his dogs and June's dog Squeegee curled up at his feet. The only thing that made it better was knowing that Amaya was there, although with her endless sleeping it almost made him feel more alone. With the room dark, it was almost impossible to stay awake, and his eyes closed and he drifted off to sleep.

"Cooper?"

He startled awake. Amaya was stirring. She was waking up. Maybe there was hope for her after all. He wiped the drool that had escaped down his chin and got up and sat on the bed beside her. "How are you feeling?"

"Awful. My entire body aches. How long have I been asleep?"

"I'm not sure. You were already asleep when I found you, but for at least two days now."

"Are you seriously saying that I've been asleep for two days?"

"I'm seriously saying that."

"That's what Grace told me, but I didn't believe it."

The comment about Grace was odd, but maybe it was the rambling of someone who had just been dreaming.

Amaya touched her face where it had been burned. "My face hurts. And there's stuff on it."

"I've been putting burn cream on it. Luckily June had some."

"Oh right. The fire in the server room."

This was obviously a story that he would have to ask Amaya more about later.

"You also burned your hand. I've been putting cream on it as well."

Amaya fell silent. Her eyes flicked around the room, but she appeared to be turned inward, as if doing some sort of internal reflection. "Do...do you know how I got here?" Her eyes searched the room.

"I have no clue. Do you at least know what you were doing here in

Area 52?"

Amaya smiled. "That I know, but I'm not sure I'm ready to share with you yet. I'm still feeling pretty tired, and it's not a short conversation."

"Well, rest up for sure. We'll have plenty of time to talk. But first, when you asked how you got here, did you mean June's house?"

"Yes."

"So you don't know how you ended up in that bed?"

"I've no clue."

"What's the last thing you remember?"

"I was in the server room, the power was out, and I was too weak to climb up even a few rungs on the ladder, much less the quarter mile to get to the top. The last thing I remember is blacking out." Her brow furrowed. "The thing is, I can't imagine who could have gotten me out of there. Unconscious bodies are heavy, and without the elevator working, I don't think any human would be strong enough to carry me."

"I doubt this is related, but there was one odd thing when I arrived at Area 52."

"Go on."

"I had planned to turn around and head home when I arrived at the area where the portal used to be. That would have gotten me back to the estate about the time that I would have become really sick from the electricity intolerance. But as I was approaching Area 52, I saw that the tesseract was down, so I thought why not continue in the direction I had been heading?"

"Okay." It was clear from her tone that she was waiting for him to get to the point.

"The point is, when I arrived at the area where the portal used to be, there was a vehicle there. It was a very fancy cruiser, top-notch and stylish, unlike anything I've ever seen before. It seemed so unusual to see it parked in the middle of nowhere. I know it seems unlikely, but do you think whoever was driving it could have had anything to do with your rescue?"

Amaya startled upright, her eyes wide. "Wait...are you saying that Opali rescued me?"

Georgia knelt at the altar in the small chapel. It was her favorite place to relax, even though there were often many other people there. She lit her votives. It was still too early for her daily check-in with Hank, so she sent a quick message to Bren and his wife asking how they were doing. While waiting for a response, she checked out Elliat's latest post.

> Fellow pod-dwellers—I'm getting some breaking news. Apparently there is a new development in the advertising tiers. LP, the premier LP100 model ghost, has announced that the tiers will be discontinued effective immediately. That news will come as a great relief to June Stafford and all the others who were in the lowest tier.
>
> There's no explanation from the ghosts for the change of heart, so we will just have to thank the Oragle for the change and hope that one day we learn more.

Georgia received a reply from Bren. He and his wife had been classed as Tier Threes, but with the change in policy, had just started to receive the full treatment for the electricity intolerance. Bren couldn't be happier.

It seemed like there must be more to the story about why the ghosts had changed their policy about the advertising tiers, but Elliat didn't share that information. Maybe someday she would learn what happened.

~~~~~

So this was it. For the rest of Amaya's life, she was going to be spending her days doing the stuff that she needed to do to survive—walking to the well to get water, making wicks, growing vegetables. It was physically demanding but it wasn't a bad life—she had Cooper to keep her company, the location was beautiful if cold at night, and for now the days were sunnier than they were dark.

Today her plans were different than usual—she and Cooper were walking down the hill to visit Petra. Petra had survived the trip through the tesseract but had been bedridden in the days since. Petra's house was on the main road and only about a mile downhill from June's house. The narrow roads lined with pine trees were covered by a blanket of needles that hadn't been disturbed by the passing of any vehicles in days.

The few people they passed looked at them suspiciously and sometimes moved to the opposite side of the road. The guarded reception of the neighbors was offset by the joyful play of the dogs. Grace's dog
~~~~~

Squeegee had become close friends with Cooper's two dogs. The dogs chased each other into the woods and then chased each other back, checking on the humans and then running off again. Despite everything else, watching the dogs play brought Amaya joy.

It had been four days since she had destroyed the server, and she was still coming to terms with what she had done. She questioned the decision every day, but always came to the same conclusion. Yes, the ghosts were still a threat, but she had avoided harming millions of people, and that was the important thing. But no matter how many times she convinced herself that she had done the right thing, she still felt guilty about it.

She had a lot of distractions, though, to keep her mind occupied. Mostly she worried about not being prepared for all they needed to face. They were getting by for now, but they were still relying on items that had been produced before the electricity was powered down. At some point, before the matches were used up, she would need to learn to make a fire without them. She had burn cream for now, but what about when that ran out?

Not to mention all the other things that were necessary to keep them alive. Like when the summer heat hit, how would they keep their food from spoiling? The large agricultural complexes wouldn't function without electricity, so they would need to start a garden. There was so much they needed to figure out, and she had so little knowledge about living without electricity.

Amaya knocked on the heavy door to the old library that had been converted into Petra's house. The thick door with complicated patterns carved into the dark wood absorbed the knock, dampening it into a tapping noise at best. There was no doorbell, but after a few seconds, the door clicked open.

The heavy door required extra effort to push open. Amaya stuck her head in and peered into a darkened room. Amaya remembered it as a museum of the fake armageddon that Petra had used as an excuse to isolate Area 52. Not seeing anyone, she called out, "Hello! Can we come in?" Getting no response, she headed toward the room where she had rested on the couch not more than a week ago.

Petra was on one of the flowered couches with a bunch of overstuffed pillows supporting her in a reclined position. She appeared to suppress a smile when she saw them. "Well, if it isn't my two favorite thorns in my side." Her smile spread wider and reached her eyes, though the corners of her mouth appeared to be engaged in a fight, like some part of her was uncomfortable smiling. "Please have a seat." She pointed to another flowered couch across from her.

Petra had opened the blinds since the day that Amaya had recovered on the couch. Sunlight flooded the room and highlighted all the antiques and the ornate furniture that filled every corner of the room. They sat on the couch that Petra had pointed to, and Cooper's two dogs settled at his feet while Squeegee curled up on Amaya's foot.

Even though each breath she took was heavy and seemed to require effort, Petra wore her usual flowered shirt and khaki slacks. The gold bracelets that she always wore, however, were in a pile on a table next to the couch. They were the only sign that Petra might not be feeling well.

The conversation was pleasant and light-hearted. Amaya planned to keep the visit short, but after checking on how Petra was doing and some other pleasantries, she had one question that she wanted to know before she left. "Did anyone see someone unusual, or unknown around here, walking around the day the power went out?"

"Of course, I thought you knew." Petra spoke with some effort, stopping at times to catch her breath. "Although when you say unusual—I think that's an understatement."

"Who was it?"

"It was your friend, Opali Stafford. It caused a stir when people saw a robot walking through town. Not to mention that she was carrying you, so she cut quite the figure." Petra paused. She closed her eyes and took a deep breath. "She scared a lot of people though, so I'm going to have to ask you to tell her to stay away. We're dealing with so much uncertainty right now, the last thing we need is to have people scared of a robot walking through town. It reminds them too much of the cryogens."

Amaya bristled at Petra's restrictions, but it wasn't like she expected to speak to Opali again. "Don't worry about it. It's not like I'm able to spend time around her—even on low power, she emits more than enough electricity to make me sick."

"Well, if you do see her, please let her know how impressive I think her construction is. And then tell her to go home and stay there."

Amaya nodded. If she ever saw Opali again, Petra's demands were the last thing she planned to mention, but it didn't hurt to pretend to agree. Cooper looked sideways at her. He didn't appear to be convinced by her easy agreement.

Petra shifted on her pillows. "I have some other advice."

Cooper raised his eyebrows. "Go on."

"I had Dan set aside all the books in the library that deal with survival. We have a large selection covering a wide variety of topics. I'd like you to stop by the library to pick them up."

"We can do that," Cooper said. "We'll go by there on the way home."

Petra glanced at the dogs. "You can't take your dogs with you in the library."

"You know the regular rules don't apply now."

"When I created this community, I never thought that all the rules would be thrown out the window just because of a little thing like not having access to electricity." Petra rolled her eyes. "What is this world coming to? Maybe being at the end of my life isn't such a bad thing."

"Don't say that," Amaya said.

Petra seemed tired and her skin was sweaty even though the room was cool, but she didn't seem close to death.

"I can feel it," Petra said. "When I went through the tesseract to get here, it felt like every single fiber of my being was somehow damaged. I can feel my body giving out. After using a microscope to examine my cells, my doctor thinks I have a new type of cancer that's aggressive and spreading rapidly."

"I'm so sorry to hear that." Despite all their differences in the past, Amaya had grown to like Petra. "Is there anything we can do for you?"

"Get those books from the library. Cooper, use your speed-reading skills and extraordinary memory to take notes on the most useful stuff. Your teaching skills will also come in handy, because you will need to educate everyone on what to do. Don't forget that there are five communities, so you will need to travel to all of them. If you want to do something for me, don't leave any of my people without knowledge."

Cooper kneeled beside Petra and grasped her hand. "I can do that."

"What can I do?" Amaya asked.

Petra examined her closely. "Your skills aren't relevant anymore, but at least you aren't dependent on a chip like most of the people where you're from."

"Surely there must be something that I can do."

"The most useful thing you can do right now is to have children. Other than that, I can't think of anything."

Was Petra serious? It sounded like something people said to women back in the 1800s.

Petra shifted her weight and sighed heavily. "What did you do to my server room? No one has dared to go down there, but I hear that the environmental monitors registered quite the conflagration before the power shut off."

Amaya shrugged. "It might be okay. Some of the servers are probably damaged, but the others probably just suffered cosmetic damage. It's nothing compared to the Panacea server room. That place is never coming back. I'm confident that every single server box in the Panacea area has been completely incinerated."

"I'm hoping there's an explanation for why you felt the need to burn it all down." Petra stopped talking and waited for Amaya to expand on what happened.

"I had to do it. The ghosts threatened to harm humans if I didn't." It was as much as she was willing to explain at the moment. "It was a tough decision, and I made the best decision at the time that I could."

Petra nodded. "How are you feeling about it now? Do you wish you had done something different?"

"I don't know," Amaya said. "I don't know."

~~~~~

It had been two days and Petra's question still haunted Amaya. Did she wish she had done something different? Would she change things if she could do it all over again?

Amaya plunged the shovel into the ground in front of June's house. The hole she was digging was about a yard on each side and after a lot of effort, she had reached about a foot down. Unfortunately, Cooper said that latrines needed to be a lot deeper than a foot. She shoved the shovel into the ground again, loosening up as much dirt as possible and then tossing it into a pile on the side. It seemed odd to be digging an outhouse in the front yard, but Cooper had said something about the latrine needing to be downhill from the well.

Not that they had a well yet. Cooper and some neighbors were digging it in the backyard right now. Between the two of them, Cooper undoubtedly had the hardest job. The latrine only needed to be three to four feet deep; the well needed to be closer to two hundred feet. Or more.
~~~~~

No one was quite sure how deep it needed to be, but the few neighbors that had already dug theirs had gone down over two hundred. It required a complicated setup using pulleys and harnesses and ropes to remove the dirt and get the people in and out. It looked unsafe.

Whenever she had downtime, Amaya pondered Petra's question about how she was feeling about what she had done. Fortunately, her days were demanding, so she didn't have much downtime. She spent the sunshine hours going to the stream to pull water and carrying it a mile uphill to June's house, hunting for firewood in the forest, searching for food, putting cream on her burns, reading books on survival, making wicks, handwashing laundry, and doing other tasks that needed to be done just to survive. There was never enough daylight for it all.

She had learned to chop wood, make a fire that didn't burn out but also didn't use more wood than necessary, and cook over a fire. Someone had broken into the grocery store and stolen all the first aid supplies, so she was also working on creating homemade first aid items. Turns out that creating a bandage from torn clothing wasn't nearly as easy as using a commercially created stick-on bandage.

Plus, she was running out of clothing to use to make stuff. At the rate Amaya was going through Grace's and June's clothing, it would last a few months at best. She had also set aside some of Grace's clothing for herself. Grace's quirky and brightly colored clothing was fun and a change from her usual boring beige clothes.

Once it got dark, though, everything stopped, and they did nothing. The candles weren't bright enough to read by and she didn't know how to knit at all, much less in the dark, so she sat by the fire until it burned out and then fell asleep. Or more likely, she fell asleep and then the fire burned out. It was the most sleep she had gotten since she was a small child. But before the crackling of the fire lulled her to sleep, before her body gave out each night from exhaustion, was also the time when the worries and fears set in.

Amaya set her shovel down. Up the road, Snoogums was shuffling his way up the hill toward her. He didn't pick up his feet when he walked, so a small dust cloud trailed behind him. It took a minute, but when Snoogums finally reached her he was out of breath and had to rest with his hands on his knees.

Eventually, he stood up. "Miss Amaya, I have something to tell you."

"What is it?"

"Deputy Dan told me to come here."

"Go on then."

"Miss Petra died."

Amaya startled. Petra had seemed so alert when they had last talked. What had happened? Turns out Petra was right when she had said she was near the end. "What did she die from?"

"Deputy Dan said you would ask that."

"Well, then, what was it?"

"He said, and I quote," Snoogums lowered his voice and put his hands on his hips, apparently mimicking Dan, "tell Amaya that the doctors think it was an aggressive form of cancer, probably caused by the electricity intolerance compounded by advanced age." His voice returned to his regular register. "Did you understand that?"

"I did. Thank you for remembering all of it."

Snoogums sat down on the pile of dirt and threw handfuls of it back into the hole. "Miss Amaya, I'm sad about Miss Petra. She was mean to me, but in a way that I kind of liked her."

"I feel the same way."

"I'd help you dig the hole," Snoogums said, "but I don't do hard labor."

"Of course you don't." Amaya rolled her eyes. "But if you don't stop throwing the dirt back in, I'll bury you in this hole."

Snoogums stood up and wiped the dirt off his hands. "I'm going then." He shuffled up the road to his own house.

If Petra had succumbed to cancer, did that mean that Amaya would too? Amaya had been exposed to much higher levels of electricity than Petra had. She felt...no, she knew, that permanent damage had been done to her body. It was exactly like Petra had said—every fiber of her body felt like it had been damaged. Every molecule had been rearranged.

Amaya sighed and shoved the shovel into the ground so it stood upright in the latrine pit. She stepped out of the hole and sat on the soft pile of dirt. Just like Snoogums had, she threw piles of dirt back into the hole.

Snoogums' comment about Petra resonated with Amaya. Petra was difficult to deal with, but she was always consistent in putting the well-being of Area 52 first. She had a cause and she was dedicated to it. With the electricity intolerance, a new era was beginning. And that era didn't need Petra.

Did that era need Amaya? Sometimes it felt like it didn't. She still hadn't figured out what she had to contribute. She wasn't much use for physical labor because she tired easily, and obviously her computer skills were irrelevant now. Maybe Petra was right. Maybe the most useful thing she could do now would be to have kids. Who would have thought that turning off the electricity would have reduced her to nothing more than a child-bearing vessel?

Surely there had to be a role for her in this new world. Some way that she could make a contribution. Whatever it was, she would figure it out. She would learn new skills and make the best of her current situation. She didn't know how long it would take, but a year or five or ten from now, things would be different. She would move on with her life and find her place in this new world.

Epilogue

100 YEARS SINCE THE RUPTURE

100 Years Since The Rupture
May 26, 2215

It's hard to believe that today is already the one-hundred-year anniversary of The Rupture. That's one hundred years since the humans split into two groups on May 26, 2115, with one group living in the metaverse and the other group living without electricity outside of it. One hundred years since my life changed and so did everyone else's.

You know, I have one hundred years of experience watching humans, and I've learned a few things about them. I've learned that you read about our lives and wonder if the right decisions were made. Or you ponder whether things would have turned out different if different decisions had been made.

You might even wonder about me. Maybe you ponder whether I'm human, or close enough to human to deserve to be treated like one. You almost certainly wonder if I'm sentient. I get it. I've pondered these same questions for over one hundred years.

But probably more than anything, you probably wonder what happened to my friends. Of course, you already know what happened with the electricity intolerance. You wouldn't be reading this if you didn't.

But before we dive into the details, let me get one important thing out of the way. None of the people you've heard about here are still alive. Don't be sad about that. Most of them lived long lives. Even Trevor and Snoogums, the youngest people in this accounting, would have been 110 if they were still alive today. That's a long time to live nowadays. The irony is, I tell you not to be sad yet I don't take my own advice. I miss them every day, and I miss Amaya above all.

I just realized that you may now be feeling sorry for me. I'll let you make up your own mind, but to do that, you need to know what happened after The Rupture. And who better to start us off than Elliat Exis?

~~~~~
~~~~~

Twenty Days Post-Rupture

My dear followers, what a pleasure it is to present to you the first installment in my new series: Panacea Notables. Panacea Notables are in-depth profiles of people who are key players in the Panacea metaverse.

I can't think of a better person to begin this series with than the new CEO of Panacea Corp, Viola Mason. No one has been more influential than Dr. Mason in shaping our new world, so when it came to choosing my first profile, she was an easy choice.

Mason, in a shocker of an announcement, was named the new CEO of Panacea Corp one week ago. This came as a surprise to many who thought that Mason had burned all her bridges and would never find work again after she forcibly, without their consent, ejected 200 million people from the Bo Place metaverse and shut down their warehouses.

I'm sure I'm not the only one who has a long list of questions about Mason's hiring. Isn't Panacea Corp taking a big risk by giving her the top job? Should I be worried that tomorrow I'll be kicked out of Panacea just like all the Bo Place denizens were kicked out?

I spoke with Mason and she assured me that I have nothing to worry about. She described the ejection of the Bo Place denizens and the shutting down of the pod warehouses as a humanitarian action that was designed to ensure the survival of the human race. She also said that when she took the job with Panacea Corp, she signed multiple legally binding agreements that nothing similar would happen. She also agreed to have monitoring put into place to keep her from taking any similar actions.

But at least one big question remains—did Mason have this deal arranged with Panacea Corp when she ejected the Bo Place residents? She single-handedly wiped out Panacea Corp's main competitor, so maybe getting the CEO job was a reward?

When I spoke with Mason, she insisted that she did not have any arrangement with Panacea Corp, and that they didn't approach her until a week after she 'saved humanity' (in her words). Can we believe her? I guess we will never know the truth.

Tune in tomorrow for more details on Mason's background, and some thoughts about what we can expect from her in the position.

~~~~~

JULY 26, 2115

Two Months Post-Rupture

Loyal followers, sorry to keep you waiting so long for the second installment of Panacea Notables! The person we're profiling is someone who, a couple months ago, no one would have expected to be on this list. In fact, when he competed in the Zazora Exhibition Game, no one even seemed to know his last name.

If you don't know his name now, then you haven't been paying attention. Because he's the person who is leading the development of a new era for our fellow humans living without electricity. So what do we know about Bren Brentwood?

Let's start with the Foundation for Advanced Intolerance Reduction and Development of Alternative Energy Sources, or FAIR/DAES for short. As you could guess from the name, the foundation was created by June and Oscar Stafford for two main purposes—finding a cure for the electricity intolerance and developing alternative energy sources that don't trigger the intolerance.
~~~~~

I spoke with Brentwood, the unlikely choice for Executive Director of the Foundation. As surprising as his appointment was, Brentwood has made some bold moves that have drawn criticism from many directions but have also been praised by others. Here's some of the highlights from the interview (full interview available on my homesite).

Exis: Bren, you've been criticized for hiring LP, the first LP100 model ghost—the one the other advanced ghosts were modeled on. He doesn't need a job, and you didn't need to hire him—so what made you think, "I'm going to hire this guy who has threatened my friends, and humans in general, to work for me?"

Brentwood (with a mischievous smile and a gleam in his eye): At the basic level, it's a strategy of keeping your enemies close.

Exis: Is part of your strategy eventually getting him to reveal the formula for the electricity intolerance treatment?

Brentwood: LP has made it clear that he'd rather be modeled on Little Bo Peep than reveal the treatment, and Elliat, I believe him. The treatment is the only thing that is keeping the humans from deleting the spectrals. He would be signing his own end if he gave us the treatment.

Exis: Aren't you afraid that he will sabotage your work on developing a treatment, then?

Brentwood: Oh, I'm sure he would. I don't trust him any farther than I could throw him. That's why he won't go anywhere near that research.

Our assumption is that the spectrals can see everything we do. That was part of the decision to bring LP on—he knows what we're doing anyway.

Exis: Tell us about the research on the electricity intolerance. How's it going? Are you making progress?

Brentwood: I have the distinguished Amoco Cadiz leading that research effort. That's all I'm willing to say and all you need to know.

Exis: I heard that Cadiz had originally decided not to enter Panacea?

Brentwood: Wow, do you have listening devices everywhere?

Exis: I have a lot of sources. Is it true?

Brentwood: It's true. After being forced to enter Panacea by the spectrals, Amoco had had enough of virtual reality. It was clear to me, though, that he was the best person to lead the foundation's research agenda, so I recruited him.

Exis: And you went to some extreme lengths to recruit him. Is that also true?

Brentwood: Seriously, where do you hear all of this? But yes, it's true. I didn't have any way to get a hold of him from inside the metaverse, so I exited my pod and tracked him down at his place. He was reluctant at first, but then once he thought about it, he realized how essential this research is and he said yes.

Exis: That's dedication to your job! How did you find a pod for him? I thought they were all taken?

Brentwood: People don't live forever, Elliat. That's part of the drama of life. Pods are opening up all the time. There just aren't very many of them, and you have to know the pod is available and grab it before someone else takes it. That's tough for someone who's living outside the metaverse to do, but easier if they know someone, like me, inside the metaverse.

Exis: Does it bother you that some people think you're
not up to the job?

Brentwood (smiling that mischievous smile again):
Not at all. I live to prove them wrong.

~~~~~

MAY 24, 2116

One Year after Mariela Stafford's Death

*A year after my Aunt Mariela died, I saw Amaya again when she and
Cooper held a memorial service for Mariela. Years later, when I started
working on Amaya's memoir, she shared her experience of the memorial
service with me. I hope you'll forgive my creative liberty, but I've added
to what she shared with me using details that I deduced from my algorithm and from reading her vitals and non-verbals.*

~~~~~

"Are you ready for this?" Amaya asked Cooper.

It was long past time for her to mourn Mariela's death. They had been
so caught up in their own concerns, their own quest for survival and
learning about how to live without electricity, that they had little time
left for anything else. Then a few days ago, while starting to doze off in
front of the fire after dark, Cooper had suggested a memorial service.

"It's been a year since her death," he had said, "and since neither of
us were able to attend the funeral, I thought we should do our own recognition."

"Where will we hold it?" Amaya had asked. "Here on the mountain,
or down in the desert next to where Grace died?"

"I'd like to visit Grace's gravesite," he had said, "so let's hold it
there."

After two days of preparation, they had left at the first light of dawn
to complete the arduous six-hour trek from SkyWater to where the portal
to Area 52 used to be.

Amaya clambered down the steep rocky slope to the flat desert where

Grace's gravesite was. Cooper followed behind her, the gravel cascading down the short slope as he slipped down it.

"Is Deputy Dan joining us?" Amaya asked. It had been an impulsive decision to invite him, as he was the only other person in Area 52 who had known Mariela.

"He said he was doing some checks of the Area 52 perimeter, and then he would join us. We may have to wait."

"No problem." With the days getting longer, they had plenty of time before they needed to head back up the hill.

The warm, dry air of the desert contrasted with the cool, clear nights on the mountain. Amaya inhaled the smell of rain, freshly fallen not long ago. The recently emerged sun was quickly baking off the humidity. Grace's headstone, covered in dust, marked the spot where she had passed away.

Grace Barua Stafford O'Connor
A shining star who will always guide us
February 15, 2097 – April 8, 2115

Amaya wiped the dust off the headstone.

"I've brought the firedust."

Amaya turned to see Dan walking toward them in plain clothes.

"Where did you get firedust?" she asked. As far as she knew, Area 52 didn't have any.

"It was in your bags when I arrested you last year. I confiscated it back then as a potential weapon."

Amaya rolled her eyes. "You knew it wasn't a weapon. You were at Grace's funeral."

Dan huffed. "I knew nothing of the sort."

"Let's get started," Cooper said. He had black circles under his eyes. He hadn't smiled once during the entire six-hour trip that morning.

"One moment." Deputy Dan appeared to look off on the horizon. "I think one more person is going to join us."

Cooper looked as startled as Amaya felt.

"Really, who?" Cooper asked.

"See that dust cloud there?" Dan pointed at the horizon. "I think that's her now."

"You invited Opali?" Amaya's heart leapt at the realization that there was only one person who would be driving a car toward them.

Dan nodded. "I can still tolerate very small amounts of electricity, as long as my exposure is short. So I turned on the phone that you all left me and texted Opali."

Amaya had many questions—how was the device still working? How did Dan know how to get a hold of Opali? How did he know to invite her? None of the questions needed to be answered now, though, so she pushed them to the side.

Opali's car pulled up at high speed and abruptly slid to a stop not far away in a cloud of dust. The familiar nausea hit Amaya like a ton of rocks. Amaya doubled over but managed not to throw up. Opali threw the cruiser in reverse and backed up. The nausea subsided.

Opali emerged from the car and headed in their direction. She smiled and waved as she approached them. Her robot body looked a little worse for wear, but despite a couple scrapes and an occasional dent, it was still as beautiful as the first time Amaya saw it.

Opali stopped about ten feet away. "I'll stay back here," she called out. "Thank you for inviting me."

Amaya and Cooper both waved to Opali. "I wish we could chat for longer," Amaya said, "but it's difficult to talk when you can't get close."

"No need to worry about that. I'll come visit again sometime, and we can talk loudly to each other from eight feet apart then. But today is all about the memorial service."

Amaya nodded. "Let's get started. Deputy Dan, can you hand out the firedust?"

"Of course." Dan gave out handfuls of firedust. "But no need to call me deputy anymore. I've resigned my position to take over as the Regent of Area 52."

"The Regent?" Cooper asked.

"Petra gave me the title before she died. It gives me authority just like the Elders used to have. The vote to make the position of Regent official was held today, and it was approved."

"A vote?" Amaya asked. "I didn't know about a vote."

"Only Area 52 citizens can vote."

Amaya shook her head. They would probably never allow her to officially be an Area 52 citizen.

"Okay, *Regent* Dan," she emphasized 'Regent,' "why don't you get us started off?"

"Okay," Dan said. He paused before speaking. "I only knew Mariela a brief time, but she was tough, dedicated, and willing to sacrifice for others. Like the time that she got out of the truck to get in the helicopter, because she didn't want Nyala and I to get caught up in it." He threw his firedust on the ground. It erupted in flames.

"I'll go next," Opali said. "I resent that Mariela deleted me, but I understand the reasons why. She was as predictable as anyone else, but she wasn't like anyone else. She was tough, uncompromising, and never hesitated to make the difficult decisions. I didn't always agree with her choices, but I know she was always trying to do the right thing, and I respect that." Opali threw her firedust in the air.

Amaya went next. "I may have been too hard on Mariela. The things I criticized her for the most, I ended up doing things that were just as bad. I enjoyed her sense of humor and how she watched out for others, even if she didn't always do things the way that I would have. She was always a good friend who looked out for me." Amaya threw her firedust on the ground. The flames burst up, cleansing Amaya of the sadness. It wasn't gone, it just transformed into something more manageable.

Cooper spoke next. "Mariela, I never told you how much I loved you, and I'm sorry for that. You lied to me and pushed me away more times than I can count, but you were also like a warm spring day after a cold winter. I remember the first day I met you. I was five and you were nine and your parents had just died. You wore all black and your eyes were sad and red from crying and I was scared of you because I had never met someone who was grieving before.

"But I was also drawn to you and you were nice and didn't say anything when I followed you around the house. Even back then, I knew you had greatness in you. Even before you started moving up the ladder at Panacea Corp, I thought that you would be in charge someday. I've always admired how strong you can be, and was touched by how vulnerable you were at the same time. You were the love of my life, and I miss you every single day."

Amaya brushed a tear from her cheek. There was so much about Cooper and Mariela that she hadn't known.

Cooper threw a large handful of firedust on the ground. The flames created shadows that danced on Cooper's face, giving him a fierce scowl.

"May the memory of Mariela Stafford live on..." Amaya stopped herself. "May the memory of Mariela Stafford live on forever."

The firedust burst into flames with renewed vigor, twisted into a funnel with oranges and yellows that gave way to purples and dark reds before disappearing into the ground. There was a moment of silence as no one spoke.

"Before we go," Opali called out from ten feet away, "do you mind if I turn on the hologram on Grace's headstone?"

"You can do that?" Amaya asked. "I would love to see it."

Grace's image emerged from the stone and expanded to a life-size projection in front of it. She was just as Amaya remembered—smiling like she had just said something funny. They spent a while at the tombstone, chatting about Grace and Mariela. They couldn't linger too long, though. There was still the six-hour walk back home. They said goodbye to Opali and started the trudge back uphill.

~~~~~

Opali here. I'm not ashamed to admit it—I stole the hologram from Grace's grave. I have plans for it. Those plans also involved an after-dark trip to the Area 52 server room to get some data that I need. I won't tell you why yet—I want to see if it works out first before I start talking about it. There may also be more theft in my future, but don't tell LP.

~~~~~

JULY 18, 2119

Four Years Post-Rupture

MEMORANDUM
Restricted – For internal release only

To: Bren Brentwood, Executive Director of FAIR/DAES
CC: June Stafford, President of the Board of FAIR/DAES;
            FAIR/DAES Board Members;
            FAIR/DAES Research Personnel
From: Amoco Cadiz, Lead Researcher of FAIR/DAES
Date: July 18, 2119
Re: My Resignation

It is with much sadness that I am proffering my resignation from FAIR/DAES. After serious reflection, I have determined that it is time for me to leave behind my infinite supply of digital hats and move on to a new line of research in the solid world.

When I started with FAIR/DAES four years ago, I had hoped to develop a treatment for the electricity intolerance. While developing the treatment was easy and accomplished within a year, the challenge has been in accessing the materials needed for the treatment. Unfortunately, the Spectral Council controls all physical aspects of our daily lives, including anything that requires the use of machinery, extraction of natural resources, medicine production, or any activity requiring the use of electricity outside of the pod warehouses.

I have spent the last three years trying to engineer a way around this problem, and I have come to the conclusion that it is unsolvable. We consequently have the knowledge to address the electricity intolerance but not the means to do so. I will leave this problem to others to continue to work on, and I wish them success in an endeavor that, in my professional opinion, is unlikely to be successful.

I am sure that some of you are curious as to what my next steps are. My first action will be to exit Panacea and return to my home, which I miss very much. Based on satellite footage, I believe I may find it much altered, with the addition of huts and facilities for the many people who have moved there to find a safe haven. But no matter the changes and the many new residents, I will be happy to be there. The times we live in mean that we cannot expect things to be unchanged and have to accept some small deprivations.

My second step will be to begin my new research agenda forthwith. I have long suspected, but have been unable to pursue my investigations further, that there may exist another source of power that may not trigger the electricity intolerance. I plan to focus my full attention on exploring this further.

~~~~~
~~~~~

Four Years Post-Rupture

MEMORANDUM
Top Secret Level Three – Maximum Compartmented Information

To: Bren Brentwood, Executive Director of FAIR/DAES
CC: June Stafford, President of the Board of FAIR/DAES
From: Amoco Cadiz, Lead Researcher of FAIR/DAES
Date: July 19, 2119
Re: Further details on my future research agenda

I have been asked to provide more details on my future research agenda, with the understanding that once I leave the Panacea metaverse, I will no longer be able to communicate details of my investigations. While I realize that creating a new security protocol for this document may have been an unnecessary and excessive precaution—doing so will keep it from the prying eyes of the Spectral Council. I find it is easier to be overly cautious rather than to be less cautious and regret it later.

In brief, my future research is simple—in my family crypt there are 'sparks,' for lack of a better name, that provide light. I believe these sparks were created by a woman who was possibly the most superb inventor who ever existed, Petra Dmitrova (who, to my regret, I believe has passed away).

The goal of my research will be multiple—first, to determine if the power of the sparks to provide light can be enhanced; second, find methods to share them with others; and third, explore other applications (low wattage, presumably) where the 'sparks' can be used to replace functions that electricity would have provided in the past.

Bren and June, it has been an extraordinary pleasure working with you. I hope our paths cross again in the future.

~~~~~

Five Years Post-Rupture

For the last five years, Amaya had gazed in wonder at the night sky every single evening. She still remembered vividly that night when, for the first time in her life, the band of the vast Milky Way visibly stretched across the sky above her. It had brought a pleasant, warm feeling to her chest, but that warm feeling was accompanied with something that didn't have a name but could probably best be described as dread.

It was the realization that before, light pollution had obscured the delicate light from other galaxies and solar systems. But now, no electricity, no light pollution. The visible Milky Way was a symptom of changing times.

A streak of light burned across the sky. Amaya let out a wistful sigh. Another satellite gone. Once stellar technology, but now relics of the past, every day the thousands of satellites dwindled as their orbits decayed and they fell to Earth.

Amaya pulled her sweater closer around her.

"Mommmm!!" a four-year-old's voice called out. "I want you to read the bedtime story tonight."

Amaya looked through the sliding glass doors into the house. A young, pajamaed girl stood on the staircase holding a candle. Before everything changed, Amaya had never imagined she would allow a four-year-old to carry a candle around. Now she didn't blink an eye at it.

"I'll be right there!" she called out.

"Don't go anywhere!" a laughing voice called out from the darkness. Down the hill from the deck, figures were hidden behind glowing lights that hovered in the air, almost like lanterns. The lanterns cast stark and distorting shadows on the faces of what appeared to be five people. The gravel of the driveway crunched underfoot as they approached.

"Who is it?" Amaya squinted in the darkness. Her heart sped up, getting its hopes up about who the figures would be. Her mind told her heart to slow down, don't get too excited yet, it's too early to say who they are.
~~~~~

"Have you forgotten us already?" the laughing voice called out.

Her heart was convinced. That voice couldn't belong to anyone other than Nyala. She made her way to the steps from the porch.

"Mommm, where are you going??" the four-year-old demanded.

"Gracie," Amaya yelled toward the house, "come out here and meet your aunt!"

"My who?" Gracie yelled.

"Your Auntie Nyala!"

"Auntie Nyala?" Gracie hurried up her pace. "I love her!"

"Careful with the candle!" Amaya yelled.

Of course Gracie loved Nyala, even though they had never met. That was just the sort of kid she was. Gracie reached the top of the porch steps. Amaya held out her hand and helped the young girl down the steps one step at a time.

The group of five arrived at the bottom of the steps at the same time Amaya and Gracie got there.

"What did I hear about being an aunt?" Nyala asked as she wrapped Amaya in a bone-crushing hug.

Amaya smiled. "Just doing my part to contribute to the survival of the human race." She turned to the four-year-old in hand-sewn pajamas. "Gracie, this is your Auntie Nyala."

Amaya turned her attention to greeting the other four members of the party. Georgia, Hank, and T-Rock as well as a teenager that Amaya could only assume was Trevor. All looked fit, healthy, happy even. She had wondered about them so many times over the years; a huge burden lifted from her shoulders as all her fears for their welfare melted away.

"Why did you all arrive at nighttime?" she asked. "Those are cool lanterns, but surely it would have been easier to arrive during the day?"

Georgia smiled. "There was something we didn't want other people to see, so we waited on the edge of town until it got dark. It's also why our lanterns are on low."

"Okay, I'm curious. What is it?"

"Not what. Who. Opali wanted to visit as well. Plus, she helped us get across the desert."

Amaya squinted and looked toward the treeline. There, in the darkness, a bit of steel with a bluish cast glinted in the light from the lanterns. "Opali! So good to see you!" Amaya raised a hand to wave.

Amaya hadn't seen Opali in five years, and she was going to hug her.

She didn't care if it would make her sick. She strode over to Opali and wrapped her arms around her. The steel robot frame was surprisingly warm and felt softer than Amaya had imagined. The hug lasted for five seconds. It was five seconds of intense nausea, but it was worth it. There was no other way to welcome her old friend who had saved her life in the server room.

Amaya backed up until the nausea faded.

"Amaya, I'm so glad you're okay," Opali said. "I hope you don't mind if I sit on your porch."

Amaya smiled. "Not at all. I need to get these people settled in, and probably get them some tea to warm up, and then we'll talk."

Amaya turned toward the house. Nyala was holding Gracie, who leaned her head on Nyala's shoulder like they had always known each other.

"I can't believe you have a kid," Nyala said.

Amaya laughed. "Not just one. I have two kids. And another on the way."

Amaya slid the glass door to the porch closed behind her. Inside, the kids were in bed and the guests were relaxing by the fire. Opali sat on the side of the porch farthest from the living room. Amaya took a seat on the other end.

"How've you been?" she asked Opali.

Opali shrugged. "I'm isolated sometimes. LP kicked me out of the metaverse, so I can't spend time with the other spectrals. I spend time with Georgia but I can't get too close to her, so it's difficult. I also help T-Rock out with his stuff, but still, the humans have to keep their distance."

"I'm so sorry." It sounded very lonely. "Do the other spectrals ever leave the metaverse? Like you did?"

"The pod warehouses require some maintenance, but the bots pretty much take care of it. Once in a while, there's something unusual that needs to be done and they use one of the other robot bodies, but LP doesn't allow them to talk to me."

"That's too bad. I guess I had hoped LP would soften his stance over time and allow you back."

"Well, you probably haven't heard, but Bren kept up your experiment to make LP nicer…"

Bren? Amaya would have to ask about that later.

"…and it worked. LP is much nicer now than he used to be. He kept the changes to the advertising tiers that you created. The Tier Threes now get the full treatment for the intolerance."

Amaya thought about asking Opali how she knew that Amaya had changed the advertising tiers. But there was no need to—Opali had always been adept at predicting the behavior of humans. Surely it hadn't taken much effort for her to figure out that it was Amaya.

"So if LP is nicer, why hasn't he let you back in?"

"Well, I think he probably would have, that is, until I stole another robot body."

Amaya's eyebrows shot up. "You did what?"

"You heard me."

"What are you going to use it for?"

"I'm not ready to tell you yet."

"Okay." Not knowing was going to drive Amaya up the wall, but she didn't push.

"Amaya, have you been back to the server room?"

"You're asking if I've climbed a half mile in complete darkness down a ladder to see what it looks like? No, I haven't. I'm curious, but not that curious."

"I'm going down there. There's something I need to do."

"What?"

"I don't want to tell you about it right now."

Amaya sighed. Another secret.

Amaya added some more wood to the fireplace. The living room was warm from the heat of the fire, but for the first time since the electricity had been turned off, it was also well-lit with the light from the lanterns the guests brought with them. Bright enough for reading, even.

Nyala sat with one arm draped into the crib. Mari was tucked under the blankets with her tiny hand grasping Nyala's finger. T-Rock and Georgia sat on the couch, while Hank appeared to be getting more tea cups in the kitchen. Trevor, much like when he was younger, was lying on the floor playing with the three dogs. Amaya did a double-take—there weren't three dogs, there were four.

"Did you all bring a dog with you?"

"Yeah," Trevor said while being kissed by Rowdy and stepped on by

Spot. Spot's tail was wagging so hard, she looked like she might fall over. "We couldn't leave Fido behind."

Well, that explained the fourth dog.

"What about the cats?" Amaya asked. "Are Midnight and Meechi still alive?"

Georgia smiled. "They're alive and as demanding as ever. They've moved into the cottage with me. We thought about bringing them with us, but cats aren't the best travelers so my roommate is taking care of them."

"Is Cooper around?" T-Rock asked.

"He's off in FairWeather doing a training. It's a new one we just created on growing tomatoes." Last summer people had problems with leaf blight on their tomatoes so Cooper had created a training on it. "He's going to be so frustrated that he wasn't here when you all arrived."

Amaya still had lots of questions, though the visitors had answered many of them earlier. She had learned about how Hank and Nyala had just returned within the last month after spending five years traveling the country. She also learned, much to her surprise, that Nyala and Trevor had gone with him. Georgia had shared how she was enjoying being a medic, and T-Rock, not surprisingly, had been voted mayor of the community at the Stafford Estate, which had grown to include around 2,000 people.

The group also asked about Amaya's life in Area 52. She told them about the kids, and about how she had found her post-electricity calling as a historian, and that working on the history of Area 52 was challenging because so much of the history had been hidden away. Although Snoogums had helped her quite a bit with his memories of a document he had found when he was eight.

Amaya also needed to clear the air with Nyala and T-Rock. She still had moments where she questioned her decision to not delete the ghosts, but over the last five years, she had grown to accept it. It had been a tough decision without a clear best option, and she would have questioned herself no matter which option she had chosen. But it still worried her that maybe the others were upset with her.

"Are you mad at me for not deleting the ghosts like I said I would?"

"Not at all," Nyala replied. "You made the best decision you could using the information you had. And time has shown that it was the right decision."

"I agree," T-Rock said. "You made the right decision."

She would probably never have the confidence in her decisions like Nyala would have had in the same circumstances, and likely she would have to rehash the decision over and over again until she died, but each time she worked through it in her head, she came to the same conclusion. Not deleting the ghosts was the right decision.

Knowing that things had turned out for the best was gratifying, and would go a long way toward addressing the residual guilt that she felt over not deleting the ghosts.

"What is this new light source you're using?" she asked.

Hank came running out of the kitchen. "That's my job to tell you about." He picked up one of the lamps and handed it to Amaya. "Look at it closely—does it remind you of anything?"

The light appeared to be made of small specks of light. "Is it the sparks from Amoco's family crypt?"

"It is!" Hank beamed. "We're leaving a few with you, and I've written down how to create more for yourself. Amoco figured out how Petra made them. Turns out they aren't all that useful for running machinery, or at least not yet, but they make a pretty effective light source. And they don't trigger the electricity intolerance."

Amaya inspected the lantern, turning it so she could see it from all sides. "Incredible. I can finally read again!" Their work during the day didn't leave time for reading, and candlelight just wasn't a strong enough light source. "This is so amazing. Please tell Amoco thank you!"

"I'll let him know," Hank said. "We asked if he wanted to come with us, but he said something about not wanting to sweat."

Amaya smiled. That sounded like Amoco.

"How long are you staying?" she asked.

"If you'll have us," Georgia said, "we were thinking we might stay a week or so. We have people pulling extra shifts to cover during our absence, so we probably shouldn't stay much longer than that. We don't want to burn people out."

Amaya tried to hide her disappointment that they wouldn't be staying longer. It was still great to have them there, if only for a week.

"I'm staying forever," Nyala said. "Unless you kick me out." She gave a little laugh.

Amaya's spirits lifted. After five years, she would have her older sister around again. "What about Trevor?" she asked.

Trevor picked his head up from playing with the dogs. "I'm staying, too, whether you want me or not!"

Everyone laughed.

"I assume Fido is staying also?" she asked.

"Well, duh," Trevor said. "I'm not letting him go now."

The following morning, Amaya sat on one end of the porch sipping her tea and Opali sat on the other. It was cold out, but multiple thick blankets helped keep Amaya warm. After five years of having the fireplace be her only source of heat, she had gotten used to the cold, mountain air.

Opali had used the cover of darkness the night before to access the server room. She still didn't tell Amaya why she had wanted to go there, and although Amaya was dying of curiosity she didn't ask. Opali would tell her when she was ready.

"How did your mission to the server go last night?" she asked.

"I got what I wanted, and I'm ready to tell you about it now."

Finally! "Go ahead."

"I was downloading everything there related to Grace. I'm going to make a hologram with her personality, and if I can, I'm going to upload it into the robot body I stole."

"Really?" The idea of creating a Grace hologram was a wild idea, but certainly feasible. "Why Grace?"

"I always wanted a sister and Grace kind of felt like a sister to me. Plus, she died too young. I know it's not really her, but I want to give her a chance to live a little longer. Or at least the memory of her."

"As long as we're alive, Grace will live on in our memories."

Opali glanced away. "That's the thing. I'm not putting the Grace replica together for now. It's for after…"

Opali stopped talking. She didn't have to finish her sentence for Amaya to understand. She wanted the Grace replica for after the rest of them were dead.

Amaya shifted forward in her chair, leaning closer to Opali. "Opali, is it lonely for you? I mean right now?"

Opali looked away. "Sometimes."

"Why don't you stay here? We can spread the word in the community that you're here, and I know Petra was worried people would be afraid of you, but I think once people get used to you, they'll be fine with having a robot around. They might even appreciate the things you can do."

The metal of the robot body seemed to glow a brighter blue, but maybe that was just the sun rising. "I'd like that," Opali said. "I'd need to spend some time in Glorietta Pass so that I can work on my Grace replica, but more than anything, I'd like to stay here."

"It's settled then. We'll find you a place nearby to stay, and you can come visit whenever you want. Gracie is going to think that you are the coolest thing ever, even if she can't get close to you."

"There's another advantage to me staying here," Opali said.

"What's that?"

"When I was in the Area 52 server room, I downloaded anything relating to the history of the area. I can tell you what I learned, and you can write it down. It turns out that there was a lot of information about the early days of Area 52 that was hidden away in files with primitive password protection."

There was so much that had been lost about the Area 52 history, and Amaya wanted to get started writing it down right away. Or at least right after she finished her tea. "Opali, that would be amazing."

"But in return," Opali said, "I'd like to write your memoir."

"Oh no," Amaya laughed, "I don't think so. No one wants to read that."

"You've been a central part of some of the biggest moments in history. I'd like to write Cooper's as well."

Something about Opali's argument almost convinced Amaya, even though the idea of writing her life story had seemed absurd a moment ago. But Opali was right, she had seen events that had changed the course of history. "I'll consider it. That's the most I can commit to at this time."

Opali smiled. No doubt her algorithm had already figured out what Amaya's answer would be.

~~~~~

SEPTEMBER 3, 2120

Five Years Post-Rupture
~~~~~

MEMORANDUM
Top Secret Level Three – Maximum Compartmented Information

To: June Stafford, President of the Board of FAIR/DAES
From: Bren Brentwood, Executive Director of FAIR/DAES
Date: September 3, 2120
Re: Update on LP experimentation

I am writing to give you an update on the Spectral Personality Amplification and Adjustment Project (SPAAP). Five years ago, FAIR/DAES hired LP, the original LP100 model spectral that the other advanced spectrals were based on. The stated reason for LP's hiring was to work on the SOUP insufficiency. The unstated reason, which has not been shared with LP, was to determine if LP's personality could be altered. I provide updates on both projects below.

SOUP Insufficiency: With a limited presence in the physical world, the spectrals have found it challenging to expand the capacity of the SOUP. This is the project that LP thinks he was hired for. The sudden increase five years ago in the number of people living in pods has greatly expanded the demands on the SOUP, yet we have only had minimal success so far in expanding the storage capacity. It is possible that we may already be losing data due to lack of storage space. No one knows for sure.

SPAAP: The real reason we recruited LP was to see if we could alter his personality. This project is based on a theory first proposed by Amaya Gidada that LP's personality could be manipulated using exposure to kinder personalities. The theory saw limited success in the exhibition game and we concluded that it might see greater success if continued over a longer term.

The selection of LP's research partner on the **SOUP Insufficiency** was crucial to influencing LP's personality and the success of SPAAP. We chose the most thoughtful and gentle researcher we could find. This longer-term experiment has shown great promise over the five years. LP's personality has synced closely with his research partner's. More crucially, during those five years, LP has not rescinded the changes to the advertising tiers. SPAAP has tentatively been deemed a success.

~~~~~

DECEMBER 26, 2133

Eighteen Years Post-Rupture

Amaya left this world, left me, today. She was only 54 years old. The world will not be the same without her. I'd like to say more, but I can't. I just can't.

~~~~~

Her poor kids. They're still so young. Sixteen, fourteen, twelve, and nine years old. That's too young to lose a parent. I was with them when she died. Or more specifically, I was eight feet away from them when she died. They can't tolerate my presence any more than their mother could, unfortunately, but we've still grown close.

Cooper and Nyala are heartbroken. We're all heartbroken. The community in Area 52 has grown to love Amaya, and the house has been bustling with activity as people bring by food, flowers, and share how much she meant to them and how much they enjoyed reading the historical documents she wrote.

Amaya passed away from a novel cancer brought on by all the times she was exposed to electricity without treatment. It was the same type of cancer that killed Petra, and so many others who had excessive exposure to electricity without treatment.

Snoogums, who now goes by Mongoose even though he's twenty-eight and everyone thought he would have grown out of that phase by now, is arranging the memorial service. Speaking of Mongoose, I'd better make sure that he's not setting up one of his practical jokes for the memorial service. We thought he would grow out of that, too, but apparently we were wrong.

~~~~~
~~~~~

100 Years Post-Rupture

Every night I watch the satellites, and think of the time spent with Amaya, sitting on her porch after dark and counting how many fell from the sky that night. Amaya's grandkids sometimes join me now. Not many satellites are left—our tally never gets over one anymore. Amaya's grandkids tell me that people ask them what those streaks of light are. To me, they are reminders of a time long since gone.

~~~~~

I finished the Grace replica not long after Amaya passed away. I needed someone else to provide me company. From the moderate amount of information I have on Grace, she resembles her closely, but her personality doesn't have as much complexity as the real Grace's did. I quickly discovered that I could predict everything she was going to say or do.

I've included additional personalities, basically everyone that I've known and cared for over the years, and added in some randomization as well. She's no longer an exact match for Grace's personality, but she now has the capacity to surprise me sometimes and has become good company. I've taken to calling her New Grace, since she's not (and never really was) the old Grace.

One friend isn't enough, though, so I've kept up my relationships with Amaya's grandkids, great-grandkids, and now even her great-great-grandkids. They are all wonderful people who have created a large family for me, although they still have to keep their distance, which is why it's also nice to have New Grace.

~~~~~

Humanity passed a sad milestone last year. The last person in the pod warehouses passed away. The spectrals have long since let the pod warehouses fall into disrepair, but their decrepit and rusting hulks continue to dominate the landscape in some places. No one has any use for them anymore. The humans could delete the spectrals now, but no one still living really knows about them or how to delete them.

LP has relaxed his position toward me over time. I'm still not allowed in the metaverse, but he has allowed me to communicate with some of the other spectrals.

That's how I found out that LP's research on expanding the capacity of the SOUP made minor progress, but it wasn't enough. After so many people moved into the metaverse with The Rupture, as well as all the stuff that the spectrals were creating over the 100 years since, there just wasn't enough room for everything.

LP started purging spectrals, especially the poorly designed ones and the ones that wandered the metaverse randomly and never did anything. He also purged a lot of other stuff, but it wasn't enough and I heard that some data disappeared. Of course, no one knows what disappeared or how much of it was lost.

The designers of the SOUP never anticipated this problem. What we thought was infinite turned out not to be. I guess there are limits to everything.

One of Amaya's great-grandkids works on the spark energy source, and he keeps me updated on their progress. From what he tells me, I anticipate at most five to ten years until they figure out how to harness the sparks to power devices. They'll also need to create devices that run on spark energy, because the old electric appliances won't do.

This fascinates me. Humans will once again be able to use devices to access the trove of digital information that has amassed over centuries. They will be able to enter the vast, complex metaverse that is teeming with spectrals but not a single human.

There are so many questions—what will people who have never used an electric device think of the metaverse? What will they do with all that accumulated information—some of it valuable, some of it plain insipid? How will they sort through all of it to get to what is useful? What data is missing, and how important was it?

But the biggest question for me is, will they learn from the past or will they repeat it?

THE END

A MOMENT OF GRATITUDE

I want to take a moment to send a
heartfelt thank you to my beta readers—
Brian, Kate, Grace, Karen, Melissa, and Brooke. You
made it through early versions full of typos, plot holes,
and more nonsensical sentences than I care to admit.

You all have my everlasting gratitude—your insights
and suggestions made the books immeasurably better!
You've also encouraged me and picked me up when my
spirits flagged. Thank you for sharing this journey with
me and reminding me why I started writing!

In addition to my beta readers, I'm also sending a
special thanks to Nicky, Midi, Pax, and Yarpy for
keeping me company during long days and late nights.

And perhaps most important, thank you to the readers.
You made it through over 1,000 pages and a couple
main character deaths to get to this point in the trilogy.
You are troopers! Your positive reviews and
encouraging comments made writing a joy.

PANACEA TRILOGY

In ***Panacea Genesis***, Mariela Stafford's life has hit rock bottom. Her boss, the CEO of Panacea Corp, created a digital clone of himself, demoted Mariela, and gave the clone her job. Now the clone wants her to help it kill the CEO. It's 2115, and embedded chips and extreme weather have led to a market for habitation pods that keep a person's body alive while they spend all their time in the metaverse. As a VP of the world's largest metaverse company, Mariela must figure out a way to stop the clone.

In ***Panacea Exodus***, the world is still dealing with the aftermath of the Panacea outage. A new person is in charge of research at Panacea Corp, and she's planning to create a disposable army through controlling the embedded chips of cryogens—people who have had their bodies frozen after passing away. The team must find a way to stop her while dealing with nonstop downpour, jail time, and a horde of curious gawkers descending on a remote area to watch the cryogen invasion.

In ***Panacea Omega***, after the chips are disabled, a Panacea Corp competitor rushes to market their new shot that allows people to enter the metaverse again. Unconcerned that the shot alters their DNA and they'll never be able to leave, people return to the metaverse in droves and many enter for the first time. But there are side effects that have consequences for everyone. At the same time, members of the team are put on trial by the digital ghosts.

Stay Informed

Sign up for our mailing list to be updated on future book releases at:
fireforgedbooks.com

Reviews

Whether you loved it or hated it, reviews are always helpful to authors.

Please consider leaving a review and know that it will be appreciated.

ABOUT THE AUTHOR

L. Ana Ellis, a sleep-deprived government worker by day, lets her imagination roam free while writing science fiction late into the night. After spending her days toiling over spreadsheets in a windowless cubicle with fluorescent lighting, and unbeknownst to her coworkers who think she spends her evenings watching cat videos, at night she creates worlds that are more of a commentary on the present than an accurate prediction of the future.

Speculating about how societies will change in the future fascinates her; she is undeterred that so far she has been wrong 100% of the time. When she's not pondering how societies operate or writing about alternate realities, she enjoys Ren Faires, Cons, and, as her coworkers suspect, watching cat videos.

She lives in the Washington, DC area with her husband, two cats, and the occasional foster kitty. When procrastinating, she occasionally posts on Instagram as @lanaellisbooks. She publishes under the indie press Fire-Forged Books.

www.fireforgedbooks.com

www.ingramcontent.com/pod-product-compliance
Lightning Source LLC
Chambersburg PA
CBHW030626310726
48979CB00003B/909